FIRST KISSES

"Come, Rianne," Pagan said from behind her. "I'll take you to your room."

Outside her door, he pulled her to a halt. He placed one large, tanned hand on the door beside her head and looked down at her. "I like having you around," he said softly.

Rianne looked up at him. He was so close, his lean, sculpted face only inches from hers. Then he put his other hand on the door, enclosing her between his arms. He was going to kiss her. His mouth moved closer, slowly, oh so slowly. His eyes drifted closed, his eyelashes a black fringe against his cheeks. Rianne felt his lips against hers, butterfly soft. Then he retreated an inch, smiling down at her. "You're supposed to close your eyes," he murmured.

"Was I?" she asked.

"That was your first kiss."

"Yes, it was the first."

"And did you like it?"

She was caught by the heat in his eyes, the passion that tightened his jaw. "Yes."

"Shall I kiss you again?" he asked.

"Yes," she whispered.

He gathered her in. It was like stepping into a fire, his body coming against hers hard, demanding, and possessive.

Rianne gasped, █████████████████████████ pleasure of it. . . .

D1044278

WENDY GARRETT
WESTERN ENCHANTRESS

ZEBRA BOOKS
KENSINGTON PUBLISHING CORP.

To Elizabeth and Christopher,
my joy.

ZEBRA BOOKS

are published by

Kensington Publishing Corp.
475 Park Avenue South
New York, NY 10016

First Printing: May, 1993

Printed in the United States of America

Chapter One

"Good heavens!" Rianne exclaimed under her breath when she got her first glimpse of Henderson City.

'City' was an overly optimistic name for the little town, she reflected a bit grimly. There were a number of log structures and a few frame buildings, most of which looked hastily constructed even at this distance. All seemed to be floating in a sea of mud. The wagon lurched, forcing her to clutch the swaying seat with one hand and her hat with the other.

"Is it always like this?" she asked the driver.

He glanced at her briefly from beneath the brim of his hat, then turned his attention back to the road in front of him. "Like what?"

"Mud. Mud everywhere." Risking disaster, she let go of the seat to indicate the rivers of muck that served as streets.

"Nah." Leaning to spit over the side of the wagon, he added, "In winter it's froze."

"Oh." She folded her gloved hands in her lap, wondering what she'd gotten herself into.

"Where do you want me to let you off?" the driver asked.

Reaching into her reticule, she took out a yellowed and much-creased piece of paper and carefully unfolded it. "I need to go to the Golden Bear."

5

"The Golden Bear?" He turned to stare at her incredulously. "You don't want to go there. Take my word for it."

"I *do* want to go there," she said firmly. "I've come all the way from Wickersham, England, to see my father. He lives at the Golden Bear."

He grunted. "Who's your father?"

"Alastair Kierney. Do you know him?"

"I know Kierney."

"That's marvelous! This was the last address I had for him, and I was so afraid he'd moved. But I had to give it a try, didn't I?" She knew she was babbling, but excitement was coursing through her in a wild rush. After all these years, she was going to see Father at last! "Tell me about him, won't you? Have you known him long? Is he well?"

Her answer was another grunt. The hat didn't move, didn't even twitch. She'd been rebuffed, and most thoroughly. Well, it didn't matter. After all these years, she was going to see her father again! Even though she hadn't been able to be with him, his letters had opened a window for her, giving her a glimpse of the great, wide world that lay beyond Wickersham. And although she had missed him terribly, those letters had let her share some of the danger and daring of his exciting life.

Clasping her hands in her lap again, she contented herself in scanning the countryside. The land was folded in and over on itself, ranks upon ranks of hills that were hoary with trees. Although it was late May, patches of snow still lay upon the slopes.

"It's a hard land, isn't it?" she asked.

"Yep. Hard land, hard men, and hard living," the driver replied. "I don't 'spect you'll like it."

A thrill went through her, part anticipation and part dread. Her father's last letter had been full of the Klondike and his hopes for making the big strike. It had sounded so grand, so terribly exciting. 'It's the greatest adventure of our time', he'd written. 'I wish you could be here to live it with me.'

Well, now she was here. Would he be pleased, she wondered, or would he not want her around?

"Silly," she murmured under her breath. "Silly to be so nervous. After all, I'm twenty-two years old, a woman grown. If he doesn't want me, I'll just have to go on with my life." But what a terrible disappointment it would be after all these years of loving him, of treasuring his love in her heart like a warm winter fire.

The wagon made another series of bumps, bounces, and lurches as it turned onto Henderson City's main street — a sagging street sign proclaimed 'Main Street'. She found Henderson City even less prepossessing close-up — weathered buildings, weathered people, men whose eyes were as cold and hard as granite. And everywhere, the mud. 'Hard men, hard living', her companion had said. Now she truly understood.

The wagon squelched along slowly, drawing her anticipation out to a fever pitch. When the vehicle finally pulled to a halt in front of a weathered, two-story frame building, she was trembling with nervousness.

"Is this the Golden Bear?" she asked.

Silently, the driver thrust his thumb overhead. Rianne tipped her head back and saw a wooden sign hanging from a bracket on the building's facade. The sign bore a rather lurid painting of a bear that looked more yellow than gold. A strange sign for a hotel, she thought.

She turned back to the driver. "What does that — " she began, but broke off when a babble of men's voices sounded inside the building. The babble rose to a shout, then a roar, and a moment later was punctuated by the sound of breaking glass.

"What — " she asked in bewilderment.

"Fight," the driver said.

The door opened suddenly. A tall, dark-haired man strode out of the Golden Bear onto the narrow boardwalk that separated the building from the street, propelling another, smaller, man before him. The smaller man was rather frail and elderly, with a creased face and a mane of white hair. He was also very drunk; even as she watched, he stumbled, nearly pulling his companion off balance.

"Don' push," the older fellow slurred. "Can't . . . seem t'get my feet under me."

"Then you shouldn't be getting into fights with men twice your size," the tall man said.

His voice was deep, with a husky timbre to it that sent a shiver down Rianne's spine. She looked, really looked, at him for the first time. He was a head taller than his companion, his shoulders correspondingly broad. Her pulse quickened as she took in the rugged, sharp-planed handsomeness of his face. Black hair and eyelashes, and a bold slash of dark brows accented his ice-blue eyes. His black suit emphasized the breadth of his shoulders and the paleness of his eyes.

"Le' go!" the older man cried, trying to pull free of the other's hold.

"All right," the tall man growled. "But don't come back in until you can behave yourself, Alastair."

"Alastair!" Rianne gasped in utter shock. *"Father?"*

The tall man swung around to look at her, his eyes wide with surprise, and abruptly let go of Alastair's collar. The old man staggered, his arms windmilling frantically, then plunged into the mud below. To Rianne's horrified gaze, it seemed as though the stranger had pushed him deliberately.

"You barbarian!" she cried, swinging one leg over the side of the wagon, then the other. "I'm coming, Father!" Her long skirt billowed out around her as she jumped down into the muck beside him.

He lay on his back, his white hair spread out on the surface of the mud. He didn't seem to be conscious. Knee-deep in the thick ooze, Rianne struggled vainly to lift him. Her long skirt soaked the liquid up and became a heavy weight that hampered her movements. She pulled at her father's arm, but he merely flopped and floundered like a beached fish, hindering her more than her sodden clothing.

Her feet went out from under her, and she sprawled on her back in the mud. Her wide hat plopped into the mud beside her, a mass of wadded veil and mud-soaked ribbon.

Startled, she stared up at the sky, where tiny puffs of cloud floated, serene and uncaring. And then a dark, broad-shouldered form blocked her view. The man clamped his hands on her wrists and, as she gasped in shock, easily lifted her up and out of the mud. The buildings flashed by in a blur as she was spun onto the boardwalk.

She turned in time to see the tall stranger grasp her father by the scruff of the neck and seat of the pants and heave him bodily out of the muck.

"You, sir! What do you think you're doing?" she demanded.

Grinning, the man gently deposited a sputtering Alastair on the boardwalk.

That grin made Rianne furious. "So, you think this is amusing?" she demanded.

The creases on either side of his mouth deepened. "Actually, yes."

"How dare you! A poor old man, who happens to be a bit . . . a bit—"

"Drunk," he said, crossing his arms over his broad chest. "More than a bit, if you ask me."

"I didn't ask you! And then you pushed him—"

His eyes narrowed. "I did *not* push him."

"You did!" she cried. "I saw you."

"Didn't," Alastair said, sliding to a sitting position against the wall. "I fell. He tried t'catch me."

"Oh." Outrage drained out of Rianne like water from a sieve. "Oh. I-I appear to have misinterpreted what happened. I'm sorry, Mr., ah—"

"Roark. Pagan Roark."

"Rianne Kierney." She started to hold out her hand, then remembered that her gloves were as muddy as the rest of

9

her and dropped it back to her side. Odd, that she was so flustered; all her friends in Wickersham had always admired her unshakeable self-possession.

Pagan studied her, noting the slim curves beneath the fawn tweed traveling suit, her oval face, creamy skin and eyes the color of pure, warm honey. Her hair, what he could see of it beneath the mud, was light brown, smooth and lustrous as silk. It beckoned him, and he had a sudden urge to run his hands through it. He would never have expected Alastair's daughter to be a beauty. A surprise, but a most pleasant one.

"Will you forgive me for my hasty accusation, Mr. Roark?" Rianne asked again.

He smiled. "Miss Kierney, I believe I'd forgive you anything."

Gazing into his eyes, Rianne felt her heart begin to race. Bold—that was the perfect description of Pagan Roark. His eyes, his manner, the firm sweep of his jaw all told of a man who went after what he wanted, and got it. Disturbed by her reaction to him, she turned away hurriedly and knelt beside Alastair.

"Hello, Father," she said, for lack of a better greeting. What *could* she say to the man whose love had brightened her childhood, and whose absence had changed the direction of her life? Hello was a start, at least.

He peered at her, but his eyes didn't seem to want to focus. "Who . . . Wha'?"

"It's Rianne, Father. I've come to visit."

"Visit? Here?" Alastair scrubbed the back of his hand across his face, smearing the mud even more. "Wha' for?"

Rianne was stunned. "Don't you want to see me?"

" 'Course I do." His head bobbed up and down in a bleary nod. Then he seemed to collect himself enough to truly look at her. "All grown up, aren' you, sweet?"

"Yes, Father. Are you all right?"

"Jus' fine, sweet. Happens all the . . . well, never mind."

So, Rianne thought, he'd almost said 'it happens all the

time'. She glanced at Pagan, seeking information, but his face was impassive, his eyes hooded and impenetrable.

"Well, Rianne," Alastair said. "D'you come all the way from England jus' to wallow in the mud with your errant father?"

"No, Father. I came . . ." Rianne smoothed her skirt with hands that were suddenly trembling. "I came to see you."

Alastair tried to get up, but couldn't. A moment later his head lolled back and he began to snore. Rianne looked up at Pagan Roark helplessly.

"Here, let's get him off the street," Pagan said. Heaving the old man's inert weight over his shoulder, he turned toward the door.

"Hold on," the wagon driver said. "What am I supposed to do with her bags?"

"Take them inside, of course," Rianne said.

Pagan swung around to stare at her. "You can't stay here."

"Of course I can. This is a hotel, isn't it?"

The driver gave a snort.

Pagan, his mouth twitching with suppressed humor, said, "No, not really."

"Well then, he can take my things to the nearest hotel that is *really* a hotel," Rianne said.

"There isn't one." Pagan shifted Alastair slightly. "I'll see what I can do about making arrangements for you to stay with one of the families here in town."

"Thank you, Mr. Roark. But please don't trouble yourself. No matter how crowded you are, surely I can make up some sort of bed in my father's room."

"Space isn't the problem," Pagan said.

Rianne sighed. She had just received a terrible shock, and the last thing she wanted just now was to play word games with this man. All she needed was a bath and something soft and warm on which to sleep, and she just couldn't believe there wasn't *some* sort of hospitality Mr.

Roark could offer. Setting her jaw stubbornly, she walked past him and opened the door.

"Don't say I didn't warn you," Pagan called after her.

"Consider me duly warned, Mr. Roark," she said, stepping over the threshold. But a moment later she faltered to a halt in shocked astonishment as she realized that The Golden Bear was a saloon. She'd heard tales of American saloons, but never in her wildest imaginings would she have expected to step foot in one.

The central room was low-ceilinged and dark even at midday. A sheet-iron stove made an attempt to warm the area, but put more smoke than heat into the room. Men lounged against the polished wood counter that ran the length of the room.

And among the men were women whose manner and shockingly skimpy attire advertised their profession. Rianne took a deep breath in an attempt to calm herself as she realized just what kind of situation she'd gotten herself into. This wasn't at all the sort of adventure she'd dreamed about. But then, her whole experience today had been a brutal surprise.

Suddenly she noticed that everyone was staring at her, the men with open lechery, the women with ill-concealed hostility. Pagan, still bearing Alastair on his shoulder, moved to stand beside her.

"This lady," he said, emphasizing the last word, "is our good friend Alastair's daughter. Miss Kierney will be staying with us for a short time, and I expect you to show our guest every courtesy."

"What'd he say?" one man asked.

"Hands off the lady," the bartender growled.

"Exactly," Pagan said. His ice-blue gaze moved around the room. "Are there any objections?" It was an open invitation to any man who cared to challenge his authority.

There were no takers. "Good. I'm glad we all understand one another," Pagan said, nodding in satisfaction. He

12

glanced at the bartender. "We'll be needing three baths, John."

"Yes, sir."

After one last look around the room, Pagan took Rianne's arm and ushered her toward the stairs at the back of the room.

"Hell, he always grabs the best ones for himself," someone muttered.

It was softly spoken, but Rianne heard nonetheless. Her cheeks burned. How dare these people assume . . . ! She thrust the thought aside, squaring her shoulders with stubborn pride. This didn't matter. She wasn't going to *let* it matter. Good heavens, she had traveled halfway around the world, endured storms and seasickness and horrible food. Compared to that, a little embarrassment was nothing. Someday, she would look back on this and laugh. It wasn't amusing now, however, not amusing at all.

Pagan was very much aware of Rianne's disapproval as he led her down the hall toward the rear of the house. She *should* be shocked; a woman like her was as out of place here as a robin in a flock of vultures. There's going to be hell to pay for lovely Miss Kierney's sake, he thought, scowling.

"I ought to take you downstairs and put you back on that wagon," he growled. "You don't belong here."

"Perhaps not." Reaching deep, she found the courage to lift her chin in defiance. "But I'm not leaving until my *father* tells me to."

Pagan studied her face in mingled amusement and admiration. If he was any judge of females—and he was— Rianne Kierney was a most determined woman. It was useless to try to talk sense into her, so he didn't try.

As they moved down the hall, she ran her fingertips along the white-painted walls. In contrast to the dim smokiness of the room downstairs, the upstairs was clean and well-lit. It might almost have been a hotel—almost.

And what of its owner? she wondered. He strode along

beside her, seemingly unaware of her father's weight upon his shoulder. An educated man by his speech and manner, there was yet something untamed about him. Downstairs, he had faced that group of hard-bitten men coldly and with supreme confidence, and she'd known he would have fought had anyone challenged him. *They* had known it, too, and not one of them had dared. There had been respect in their eyes when they looked at him, and she didn't think respect was something they gave easily. It told her much about the man who had earned it.

"You're very quiet, Miss Kierney," he said, breaking into her reverie.

"I was just wondering . . . Never mind. Does my father live here?"

"Yes."

As they passed one of the doors that were spaced at intervals along the hall, Rianne heard laughter from within— a man's and a woman's voices mingled. Horribly embarrassed, she put her hands over her hot cheeks.

"I warned you," Pagan reminded her.

She couldn't look at him. "Yes, you did, and I didn't listen. But I had no idea . . . I mean, I thought perhaps you were overcrowded. I never imagined that the Golden Bear was a, a—"

"Saloon?" he prompted.

"That isn't precisely the word I would have used, Mr. Roark."

"Let's use it, for lack of another." He reached the end of the hall, where two adjoining rooms were located. "Would you open that door, please? No, the one on the right."

Following her into the room, Pagan heaved Alastair's unconscious body down on the bed.

Rianne bent over the old man and began unbuttoning his shirt. "Now, Mr. Roark, tell me about my father."

"What exactly do you want to know?" he countered, reluctant to be the one to tell her just how low Alastair had fallen.

"Does he do this often?"

Pagan raked his hand through his hair. "Rather often."

"I see." She looked up, directly into Pagan's crystalline eyes. "He's a drunk, then."

"What do you know about drunks?"

"We have them even in England, Mr. Roark," she said. "My neighbor, Mr. Jenks, frequently fell asleep in the road on his way home from the pub. We children used to laugh at Mr. Jenks, thinking him rather droll all sprawled out in the dirt with his mouth open." She took her handkerchief, which by some miracle had escaped a mud-bath, and began wiping at the crusted dirt on Alastair's face. The white stubble on his chin seemed somehow pitiful, a stark reminder of how he had aged. "But somehow I don't think it quite so amusing any longer."

"What do you plan to do about him?" Pagan asked.

"I couldn't say now." Rianne paused in her ministrations to look up at him. "For all I know, he may not even like me."

Admiration shot through Pagan. Rianne Kierney seemed to be a woman who faced life squarely, without self-deceit. He liked that in a woman. He liked *her.* "He talks about you all the time, you know."

"No," she whispered, a tentative happiness blossoming in her heart. "I didn't."

When Pagan saw the joy light her face, he was glad he'd said it. He'd never seen a woman look so genuinely, innocently happy. I wonder how she'd look after being loved by a man, he thought. No, not just *any* man — by me.

Rianne saw admiration in his eyes, and something else. Something that sent a tendril of warmth coiling through her body. Hastily, she looked down at her father again. "Will he sleep long?" she asked.

"Several hours, I would think. You've got plenty of time to bathe and rest."

She sighed. "I'd love a bath."

Pagan smiled lazily, his mind conjuring a delightful picture of her in the tub. That sweet, creamy skin, slick with soap . . . Bubbles? No, he decided, not bubbles. Nothing to interfere with his view of her.

Alastair rolled over with a groan, dispelling Pagan's pleasant daydream. "Whazza . . . som'body . . ." the old man mumbled, flailing his arms.

Concerned that he might fling himself off the bed, Rianne tried to roll him over onto his back. Pagan took her by the shoulders and moved her aside. His hands left her, but the memory of his touch seemed to remain in her flesh. Absently, she rubbed her shoulders while she watched him tend her father.

"You've done this before," she said.

"Once or twice."

Rianne cocked her head to one side. "Indeed? How long has my father lived here?"

"A couple of years."

"Then you've done this more than once or twice, Mr. Roark."

He shrugged. "A good scrubbing and a gallon or so of coffee ought to perk him up. Why don't you go scrape some of that mud off?"

Abruptly she became conscious of how awful she must look. Good heavens, she even had mud in her hair! "I'd forgotten. I must look a sight!"

"A most lovely one."

She tried to smooth her matted hair. "Nonsense. You either have a very glib tongue, Mr. Roark, or you're sadly in need of some spectacles."

He grinned. "There's nothing wrong with my sight."

Rianne's cheeks burned. She wasn't used to compliments from men; her mother had been much too vigilant a chaperone for any young fellow to get to the compliment stage. Leonora Kierney had been respected, even a bit feared in their little community, both for her acerbic tongue and her unswerving decisions. Once judgement was passed, there could be no changing her opinion.

16

But Rianne didn't think Pagan Roark would have been the least bit intimidated. If he'd wanted to court her, he would have. If he'd wanted to kiss her, she had no doubt that she would have been kissed. The thought of kissing Pagan Roark brought an even hotter blush to her face.

"You're even prettier when you blush," he said.

She turned away hurriedly, grasping for what few shreds of self-possession still remained to her. "Thank you for taking care of my father all this time, Mr. Roark. I only hope I can repay your kindness some day."

He reached out and gently forced her to face him again. There was a whirlpool of heat in his eyes that drew her irresistibly—drew her in and surrounded her, tapped a well of feelings she hadn't known she possessed. She felt warm and cold and warm again, and it was all she could do not to sway toward him.

"Alastair is my friend," he said. "I don't need payment for helping him out."

"There's nothing wrong with accepting gratitude, Mr. Roark."

"Gratitude is an insipid emotion, Miss Kierney. There are others that are far more interesting."

Rianne looked away, avoiding his words and his gaze. Gently, she stroked a wisp of white hair away from her father's forehead. It had been a shock finding him like this. He'd sounded so vital, so daring in his letters. His Klondike had glittered, so vividly had he painted it. She had found a city of mud, and a man who was a shadow of his former self.

"So sad," she murmured. "So very sad."

Pagan knew she hadn't been talking to him. But her obvious misery struck something in him, something he hadn't known was there. A rush of tenderness swept through him. Barely, he resisted the urge to stroke her shoulders. Slim shoulders, but straight and proud, and he knew her skin would feel like silk. Yes, she was out of place here, a vulnerable innocent who needed protection from nearly every-

17

thing and everyone. She'd never last, never fit in. Still, the temptation to kiss that full, sensuous mouth was almost too strong to resist.

Rianne stared up at him, her eyes wide. He wanted to kiss her. She saw it in his eyes, felt it like heat lightning through his hands that still held her shoulders. Her heart pounded with what might have been excitement, or perhaps fear.

Pagan sensed her confusion. Abruptly, he let her go and stepped back. "Your bath should be ready by now. Leave your father to me. I'll take care of him."

"Yes. Thank you." It took an effort of will for Rianne to look away from him, and even more to turn and walk into the other room. Once there, she bolted the door and leaned her back against it. A long sigh escaped her, but she didn't know if it was relief or disappointment.

Chapter Two

"Get hold of yourself, Rianne Kierney!" she muttered, shaking her head to chase the spell cast by Pagan Roark's ice-blue eyes.

Slowly, her surroundings came into focus. The room was clean but Spartan, furnished with a bed, one chair, one obviously handmade table and a battered bureau that held a badly silvered mirror. There was a much-used fireplace on the far wall, and the bed had been placed close beside it to take advantage of its heat. Rianne shuddered, trying to imagine what winter was like here in the northern wilderness.

Then her gaze settled on a temporary, but most welcome visitor to her room: a tin tub full of steaming water. She hastily began shedding her muddy clothes.

"Ahhhh, Heaven!" she sighed, sliding into the welcome luxury of clean, hot water.

The soap smelled of roses, and brought a sweet-sharp longing for England. Strange, she hadn't thought to miss Wickersham. But then her adventure hadn't turned out precisely as she'd thought it would, either.

She sank as far down into the tub as she could, her long hair floating around her. Disappointment rode her hard. Her mother had been strict and repressive, a woman unable to show love even to her own daughter. But Rianne had warmed herself with the memories of her fun-loving father, whose love was as generous and easily expressed as his laughter.

She had been devastated when he left, and equally determined to find him again one day. But finding him in what seemed to be one of the most godforsaken places on the face of the earth . . . perhaps *the* most godforsaken spot, she amended. And not only that, to find him residing in the local bawdy house.

Sudden tears stung her eyes, and she wiped them away hastily. She had missed her father terribly. 'He didn't care about us', her mother had said, over and over. 'All he cares about is himself and his precious good times. Forget him, child. You'll never see him again'.

Rianne, watching the cold look of hate on her mother's face, refused to believe it. She held to the memories of being swung into the air by her handsome father, the sound of his laugh, the feel of his arms around her, warm and comforting. And although she missed him terribly, she understood why he had left. After all, she prided herself in being like him. She, too, chafed under the restrictions of life in Wickersham; she, too, wanted to roam the great, wide world.

But he'd left her for *this?* She had clung to the memory of his love and his warmth, using it to compensate, just a little, for what her mother had been unable to give. Had she deluded herself? Had she needed love so badly that she had created it where none existed?

"Oh, Father," she murmured. "I don't understand any more. All I can hope is that you have some answers to some very hard questions."

Added to this new, frightening reality was her confusion about Pagan Roark. His bold gaze was much too disturbing, her own reaction to it even more so. She had never met a man who had affected her so. She was intrigued by the untamed, masculine force she'd glimpsed beneath his urbane exterior.

She tried to banish all thoughts of Pagan Roark from her mind, but he seemed to have taken up residence there, a most unwelcome feeling. "Don't be an idiot," she chided herself. "The mystery of Mr. Roark's baser nature will just have to remain unsolved. Your adventure, my girl, lies somewhere other than this awful place."

She began washing her hair, soaping it twice to make sure she got every bit of mud out. After squeezing most of the soap out, she groped blindly for the pail of rinse water that was sitting beside the tub. Finding it at last, she poured its contents over her head. The water was cold. Ice cold, like melted snow.

"Oh!" she cried as the frigid liquid poured down over her.

Someone rattled the knob of the hall door. "Rianne! Are you all right?"

Pagan Roark! The sound of his deep voice snapped her out of her shock. "Yes, yes, I'm fine," she called hastily. "It was the water. The rinse water . . . they didn't heat the rinse water."

"Ah." He coughed, but it sounded suspiciously like a laugh. "Are you finished with your bath now?"

"Not quite." She felt her cheeks redden. Good heavens! What was wrong with her? She'd all but told the man she was undressed! She found herself trying to cover her breasts as though he could see through the door. What was it about the man, she wondered, that made her so aware of her nakedness? "Mr. Roark, could we continue this conversation later?"

"We could, except for the fact that I've got your bags here with me."

"With you?" She echoed, glancing around the room a little wildly. No, there were no bags. She'd been so involved with her own thoughts that she hadn't noticed they weren't here. "But I assumed—"

"So did I," he finished for her. "But instead of bringing

them up, the driver dumped them downstairs; no one noticed until now."

The husky timbre of his voice sent a chill running down her spine. "Oh. I see. Well . . . just a moment." Stepping out of the tub, she picked up the towel and shook it out. It was much too small to cover her sufficiently, so she tucked it around her head to contain her wet hair. Her gaze lit on the thick woolen blanket on the bed. Snatching it up, she wrapped it around herself.

She padded to the door. Pressing the fingertips of her one free hand against the wood, she tried to imagine what he was thinking. Was he merely impatient, or was he imagining what she looked like without her clothes? "Mr. Roark, would you leave the bags outside the door, please?"

"They're very heavy. You'll never get them inside."

She sighed. The bags *were* heavy, for they contained everything she possessed in the world. She might be able to drag them inside, but not while holding the blanket around herself. On the other hand, opening the door and facing Pagan Roark clad only in a blanket was terribly disconcerting.

For a moment she hesitated, then her chin went up in defiance. Pagan Roark was *not* going to bother her. Taking a secure hold on the blanket, she swung the door open.

And there he was, lounging against the opposite wall like some great, half-tamed wolf. Rianne froze, caught by the admiration and blatant male hunger in his eyes. Predator's eyes. God help the woman he decides to stalk, a small corner of her mind said, for she is surely lost.

With an effort, she tore her gaze from his and shifted it to the two large traveling bags that sat on the floor at his feet. "Would you mind bringing them in?" she asked, retreating into dignity to cover her confusion.

"At your command, Miss Kierney." Pagan bent and

picked the bags up easily, then moved past her into the room. He stopped, the bags forgotten in his hands, when he caught sight of the tub. His gaze returned to her, taking in the fresh-scrubbed pinkness of her skin, the drops of water that still clung to the tops of her bare feet.

She walked past and his gaze followed, drawn to her back where the blanket had sagged to reveal the sweet curve of her spine. Smooth skin the color of warm ivory made a stunningly sensual contrast to the coarse blue fabric of the blanket. The sight of her rocked him to his toes.

When Rianne turned to thank him, she saw desire, hot and raw, blazing in his eyes. No man had ever looked at her like that, with emotion so primal, so compelling. It should be frightening, but it wasn't. An answering heat blossomed to life within her, a coiling of sweet sensation that made her blood run like fire through her veins.

Pagan saw the answering spark of desire come into her eyes. Beautiful eyes, he thought, flecks of pure gold running through warm honey. He could also see her back in the mirror behind her, and noted that the blanket had slipped another inch or so. The sight was irresistible. *She* was irresistible. "Rianne," he said, taking a step toward her.

His voice snapped Rianne back into reality. She shook her head, alarm rushing through her like a cold tide. What had happened to her that a total stranger could affect her so quickly, so profoundly?

"Stay away from me," she said.

Pagan stopped. Plenty of women said 'no' when they meant 'yes', but their eyes always spoke the truth. And hers showed genuine fear. Fear of him or fear of herself, he didn't know, but this was not the time to find out. It took a surprising amount of self-control however. If only that blanket wouldn't keep slipping. . . .

"Fix the damned blanket, will you?" he growled.

Rianne glanced behind her and gasped when she saw

the amount of skin that was showing. Snatching the blanket higher, she only managed to reveal an expanse of slim, shapely leg. Quickly realizing what she had done, she shifted the blanket yet again.

Pagan watched the proceedings, torn between irritation and amusement. He saw half-naked women downstairs every night, and none affected him like one fleeting glimpse of Rianne's skin.

Finally getting the blanket arranged to her satisfaction, Rianne turned to him, fairly seething with embarrassed outrage. "Thank you for bringing the bags, Mr. Roark," she said as coldly as she could. "Now if you don't mind, I'd like some privacy."

He grinned, amusement winning out. "You managed that rather well, you know. Very few women could act so dignified while wearing nothing but a blanket. Which, by the way, is beginning to unwind again."

"Liar." Rianne knew the blanket was in place; her hands were beginning to ache they were holding it so tightly.

"All right, Miss Kierney, you win." Pagan threw his head back and laughed. He swept her a half-mocking, half-admiring bow, then strode out of the room.

Rianne ran to the door and slammed it. After locking it, she leaned against the wood and heaved a sigh of relief. Surely Pagan Roark was the most infuriating man on earth. She remembered the way he had looked at her – as though he could see right through the blanket – and her flesh seemed to retain the heat of his gaze.

"Forget him!" she muttered. "What does he matter? A few days from now Pagan Roark will be nothing but a memory."

A thunderous snore from the next room reminded her that the biggest challenge was yet to be faced; her father. There were so many things to be said, so many questions to be answered. His love may have been an illusion, but it was one she was terrified of losing. For then she would be truly alone.

She felt exhausted. The anticipation that had sustained her throughout the long journey had drained away, leaving only reality. She looked at the bed longingly. A few minutes' sleep would surely buoy her spirits. Besides, from the sound of things, it would be a while before her father was in any condition to talk.

Pulling her warmest woolen dressing gown from one of the bags, she slipped it on and curled up on the bed. She briefly savored the smell of clean sheets and the softness of the feather pillow beneath her cheek, then all awareness faded as sleep claimed her.

A man's shout woke her a short time later, bringing her upright with a gasp. Then she heard another bellow and a moment afterward, a splash. This time she was able to place the sounds as coming from the room next door. She smiled; evidently it was time for Father's bath.

There was a great deal more bellowing during the next few minutes. Alastair berated Pagan soundly and with great inventiveness, then went on to curse the saloon owner's father, grandfather and great-grandfather.

Rianne listened with some trepidation, not because of the language, which *was* truly horrible, but because she was afraid Pagan would knock the old man across the room for what he was saying.

But Pagan only laughed and said, "Your daughter is in the room next door, Alastair. She's probably swooned by now, felled by your black tongue."

There was a loud sputtering, as though Alastair had swallowed water, then silence. Rianne wished she could see the expression on his face. Was it hopeful? Or was it merely resigned?

With a sigh, she pulled a russet-brown dress out of her

bag and shook the wrinkles out of it. It was a simple garment, its only ornamentation a few narrow bands of lace upon the leg-o-mutton sleeves and high-necked bodice. Then she pulled out clean undergarments — chemise, drawers, stockings, corset, petticoats — and began to dress.

It was only then that she became nervous. She peered at her reflection in the mirror, wishing she didn't look so pale. What was she going to say? What should she do with her hands? Should she smile, or should she try to look cool and composed? It wouldn't do to rush in and say, 'Hello, Father. I've come halfway around the world to see you. Do you still love me?'

She pinned her mother's cameo brooch to her bodice, then touched the outline of the locket that hung around her neck. He had given it to her on her tenth birthday, and she'd worn it over her heart ever since. Would he remember it? She hoped so, more than she cared to admit.

"All right, Father," she murmured. "It's time." She walked slowly to the door that separated her room from her father's. Just as she raised her hand to knock, the door opened.

Pagan stood there, his wide shoulders seeming to fill the doorway. For a long, heart-stopping moment he just looked at her, then reached out to take her hand and draw her farther into the room. His palm was warm and strangely comforting.

Alastair was standing in front of the fireplace, bleary-eyed but obviously more coherent than he'd been earlier. "Hello, Rianne," he said. He held out his hand to her, and she noticed how badly it trembled.

"Hello, Father." It took great effort to keep her voice from quivering.

Pagan put his hand on Rianne's shoulder briefly. "I'll leave you two alone," he said.

A moment later the door closed behind him. Left alone

26

with her father with no idea of what to say or do, Rianne nearly panicked. She clasped her hands in front of her to hide their trembling.

"Father—"

"Rianne—"

They spoke at the same time, their voices a jumble. Rianne smiled and said, "You first."

"How did you find me?" he asked.

"In your last letter, you said the Golden Bear was your home. I took the chance that you would still be here."

"But I sent that letter a year ago!"

She shrugged, feigning casualness. "More than a year, actually. But it was all I had." *You're* all I had, she added silently.

"Ah." He rubbed at his chin. "Now. *Why* did you come?"

He might have been talking to a stranger. Dread rose in her, fueled by the uncertainties of their time apart. She had refused to believe her mother's damnation of this man. Had she been wrong? Had she been wrong all these years, and had he not loved her after all? Please, Lord, she prayed silently, don't let it be so!

She pulled the locket up over her head and offered it to him. "Do you remember this?"

"Ahhh, yes, I remember." He took it from her, his fingers caressing the smooth gold oval gently.

Rianne closed her eyes. If her next words were unwelcome, she didn't want to see it on his face. "Do you remember why you gave it to me?"

"I remember," he said emotionlessly. "I told you to keep it with you always, to remind you how much I love you."

"You left the next day. I've worn it ever since."

"Ahh. Yes, I remember." He moved away from her, and a moment later she heard the bedsprings creak.

Rianne opened her eyes. He was sitting on the edge of the bed, both hands pressing the locket to his forehead.

To her astonishment, she saw tears on his cheeks. She was even more surprised to feel moisture on her own.

"I never stopped loving you," Alastair said. "You might have had this locket, but I carried you in my heart, and your memory was clearer than any bauble could ever be."

"Why did you leave?" she asked softly.

He's old, Rianne thought, thin and sick and old. His trousers and shirt must have fit at one time, but now they hung on him loosely. There were holes in his stockings.

"Did Leonora speak of me?" he asked.

"Yes," Rianne said. "But not well. She hated you until the day she died." A harsh truth, but one that needed to be brought into the open or it would forever haunt them.

"She's dead? I . . . I never got to say I was sorry. I wanted to." He rubbed the back of his neck.

"Father, I have to know why you left me. And why didn't you ever come back? I needed . . ." She broke off, fighting the tightness in her throat.

He gave a nervous cough. "I know there can be no excuse good enough for what I did. All these years I've tried to justify it to myself, and . . . and I couldn't."

"Father." Her voice was gentle. "Just tell me."

"I'll try." Alastair smoothed his white hair back from his face. "I'm a wandering sort of man, always have been. But Leonora . . . Leonora . . . well, sweetheart, you're a woman grown now, so I can tell you this. She caught me, plain and simple. We were lovers. When she got with child, her Papa came after me. He was a rich, powerful man. I ended up marrying her and working for him in his law office, writing letters and toadying up to his customers. Hell, I even bought a house—me, who had never settled anywhere long enough to unpack my bags. And then you came, and I thought myself the luckiest man on this earth. You were my joy, all those years."

He got up from the bed and began pacing the room. "But Leonora hated me for having to be forced to marry

28

her, and she grew more sour and disapproving with every passing year. Finally I'd had enough. I went back to America, to Texas, bought land and started running cattle on it."

"And you never set foot in England again," Rianne whispered, "even to see me."

He hunched his shoulders as though she'd struck him. "I meant to come back for you, even if I had to take Leonora, and that's saying a lot. But then the ranch folded. I didn't have enough money to buy food let alone passage to England. I drifted around after that — Arizona, Kansas, Oklahoma, places I don't even remember — trying to get up another stake. Loneliness gets to a man, Rianne darling, and so does guilt, and I had plenty of both. I started drinking to dull the edge. The years went by and I just . . ." He spread his hands helplessly. "Never got the stake, never got back to England, to you."

It was brutal honesty, and judging by the pain in his eyes, more brutal for him than for her. Rianne blinked tears away.

He continued, speaking quickly as though to get it over with. "I used to tell myself that you were better off with your mother, Rianne. Many's the time I didn't have a roof over my head, times I had to ride with men who'd as soon slit your throat as look at you. That was no kind of life for a child."

He hung his head, guilt and despair etching his face. He was a weak man, she realized, unable to determine his own direction. He had let the wind blow him where it would and, as a result, had embittered Leonora and hurt his child.

Rianne searched within herself for anger, but there was none. She was at a crossroads; she could hate him or forgive and go on. Her mother had chosen hate, and it had blighted her life, embittering her so deeply that she couldn't even put her arms around her own child.

Taking a deep breath, Rianne chose forgiveness. For her father's sake, and for her own, she would put the past aside and create a better future for them both. Looking at the misery in every line of his body, she realized he had punished himself far more than anyone else ever could.

She went to him and, putting her hand beneath his chin, she lifted his face to hers. "Mother never forgave you. She remembered only the bad times and died a bitter woman. But I remember a father who loved me, and whom I loved."

Hope came into his eyes. "Then it wasn't all lost. I left something with you."

"Yes, Father. You left me your love. It drew me halfway around the world in the hope of finding it again."

"Can you forgive me?" he asked.

She closed her eyes. "Yes. From this moment onward we have only the future."

He looked at her. "You're all grown up now, and I don't even know you. What have you become, Rianne Kierney?"

"I'm nothing special," she said. "If I hadn't come here, I would have been a governess or teacher somewhere, I suppose."

"Nothing special?" he echoed. "You came halfway around the world by yourself, and you say you're nothing special? Your mother must be spinning in her grave!"

"I was good to Mother," Rianne said. "But this is *my* life now, and I plan to do as I please with it." Suddenly she noticed that Alastair was looking at her with a very strange expression on his face. "Whatever is the matter, Father?" she asked.

"Why . . . Ah . . ." Then he started to laugh. He laughed until the tears ran down his face. "You sound just like me," he gasped. "You *are* just like me. By all that's holy, it must have driven your mother crazy."

Her mouth dropped open. Was that why her mother

had watched her so closely? Was that why there had never been much physical contact between them, why Leonora had always avoided her embraces? Rianne sighed, remembering how she had craved the comfort of her mother's touch, and how bewildered she had been when it hadn't come. Yes, the memories of her father's love had been bright and warm, but they hadn't the power to comfort a frightened child during those nights when the thunder rolled and the lightning crackled, when imagined ghosts lurked in the shadowy corners of her room. Those were the times she'd cried for the lack of her mother's embrace.

Resolutely, Rianne pushed those memories away. The past was gone. She'd found her father again, and that was a gift beyond measure. She reached out and he responded instantly, taking her hands in his. This is what I came for, she thought, sighing contentedly. This is what I needed.

"How about some coffee?" Alastair asked, turning her toward the table, where a big tin coffeepot and a cloth-covered basket sat. "There's our dinner. Pagan brought it up for us."

"How thoughtful." Rianne was grateful to have the chance to discuss Pagan Roark without seeming overly interested in the man. Keeping her voice carefully casual, she asked, "Have you known Mr. Roark long?"

"Oh, nearly four years now. He's pulled me out of some scrapes, lent me money when things were desperate. A good friend, a damned good friend."

Rianne felt a rush of gratitude toward Pagan; no matter how enigmatic and disturbing the man might be, he had helped her father in time of need. She wouldn't forget his kindness. It made her even more curious about him, for she wouldn't have guessed him to be a kind man. What else, she wondered, was yet to be discovered?

"What brought him here to Henderson City?" she asked. "He doesn't seem to be the sort of man to be running a, er, hotel in a remote spot like this."

Alastair shrugged. "Actually, Pagan won the Golden Bear in a poker game a few years back. He came here with gold fever just like everyone else, and he says the Bear gives him a base to work from. He's got a claim near Black Cloud Creek and another up near Mansion Rock. If he hits gold in either of them, I expect he'll shake the dust of Henderson City off his boots fast enough."

Rianne lifted the lid of the tin pot and peered inside, hoping that it might contain tea.

Her thoughts must have been written on her face, for Alastair chuckled and said, "I'm afraid not, my girl. We only have coffee around here."

"I've gotten used to coffee—somewhat," she said. "I'll pour while you get your boots on."

There were two earthenware cups on the table, one of which had been used. She tipped the coffeepot and began to pour. "Good heavens, Father!" she said, a bit alarmed by the syrupy thickness of the liquid. "Is this coffee, or mud from the street?"

"Coffee, darling." Alastair wriggled his right foot into a boot. "I think."

"Mud or no, we'll make do." Humming under her breath, she took the cloth off the basket and peered inside. There were biscuits, some sort of leathery-looking meat, a wedge of rather disreputable-looking cheese and a bowl of tinned peaches. She was so happy that even the unappetizing food didn't daunt her in the least.

Alastair claimed his cup of coffee and he sat on the edge of the bed. "That's very pretty," he said.

She looked up in surprise. "What?"

"Your voice. It's lovely."

"Thank you." Her cheeks warmed. "I love to sing. I was a soloist in the Wickersham Church choir. It was the only sort of singing—" She broke off, not wanting to sound disloyal to her mother.

Alastair, however, had no such qualms. "It was the only

singing Leonora allowed you to do," he finished for her.

"Yes." Rianne sighed. "I wanted so much to go to London to see *Carmen,* but Mother thought opera was immoral."

She nearly added 'Mother thought nearly everything was immoral', but managed not to. Glancing at her father, she realized he'd had precisely the same thought. At the same instant, they began to laugh. It was this joy Rianne had missed since her father had gone; somewhere, somehow, her mother had forgotten the simple, carefree freedom of laughter.

Rianne was the first to gain control of her mirth. "Oh, Father, I feel terrible laughing about Mother this way. Poor thing, she was a desperately unhappy woman and made her own life miserable."

"And yours?"

"She could have, if I'd let her." She smiled at him. "But you see, I was sustained by a wonderful memory of a man who was warm and loving, and who knew how to laugh."

"Ahhh, Rianne, darling, you make me glad to be alive."

Rianne lifted her cup in a toast. "To life, then."

"To life." Grinning, he added, "To the future. May it be an interesting one."

She echoed his smile. Truly, the whole world had opened up and now, for the first time, she felt able to conquer it.

Chapter Three

"Father, would you like another biscuit?" Rianne asked.

"Yes, and another bit of cheese, if you don't mind." Alastair patted his lips with his napkin. "I suppose this isn't the best meal you've ever eaten."

"No, but it isn't the worst, either." She delved into the basket and, after serving her father, sat back in her chair. "Do you like it here in Henderson City?"

He chuckled. "No one *likes* living in Henderson City. They just do."

"Then you won't mind leaving?"

"Leaving?" His eyebrows went up. "Why . . . Ah . . . I hadn't thought about leaving. Why do you ask?"

She looked deeply into his eyes, wanting to see how he felt about this issue that meant so very much to her. "I want you to come live with me. I don't have much money, but it's enough to buy a small place somewhere, perhaps Oregon."

"Oregon." His gaze drifted away from her. "Well, now. That's a real interesting idea, sweet. But right now my head is pounding like a drum. Can't we talk about this tomorrow when I'm feeling a little better?"

"All right, Father." Disappointment shafted through her, but she repressed it sternly. At least he hadn't said no. "Do you think—"

"Vilain! Roue! Menteur!" The high-pitched shriek came from the hallway outside.

"Father, what's going on?" Rianne asked in alarm.

"It's just Felice on one of her rampages," he said, nibbling on his cheese.

"Well, shouldn't we do something?"

"No, sweetheart. This happens all the time. She'll scream and stomp her feet, perhaps smash a few vases and such. Then she'll be fine."

The woman continued to shriek in French, her voice growing louder and more shrill by the moment. Then another voice drifted through the door. Recognizing the familiar husky quality of Pagan's voice, Rianne's attention sharpened. He wasn't arguing with the Frenchwoman; if anything, his low tones showed he was trying to calm her down. Rianne felt a twinge of guilt at her eavesdropping, but truly, she couldn't help but listen; the woman was screaming at the top of her lungs right outside the door.

"Non, non, non! Don' try to sweet-talk me, Pagan Roark! I'm not going to sing, I tell you!" the woman cried. "You think I'm stupid, that I don't see how you look at the *Anglaise* downstairs when you challenged all those men?"

Rianne put her hand over her mouth, unsure whether to laugh or gasp in horror. Here she was, listening to an argument between a man and his jealous mistress — over her! Nothing like this *ever* happened in Wickersham. Her short stay at the Golden Bear was truly proving to be an education. Then Pagan began to speak, and she lowered her hand and listened intently.

"The young *lady* is none of your business," he said, sounding more bored than angry. "You and I never were, and never will be, lovers."

The Frenchwoman's voice became wheedling. "Ah, *cher,* you don' mean that. Do you think I would stay in

35

this pigsty of a place if I thought there was no chance for us?"

Pagan chuckled. "You're wasting your time, Felice. I've known too many women like you."

"Pah!" the Frenchwoman spat. "I lay my heart at your feet and get nothing! No man treats Felice Cardonne like that!"

"I didn't invite you to come, and I didn't ask you to stay," Pagan said. "But I *do* pay you to sing."

There was a quiet grimness to his voice that alerted Rianne to danger. He had reached the limit of his patience. Felice, however, didn't seem to understand the chance she was taking.

"I don't want your money," the Frenchwoman said petulantly.

"No? Does that mean you won't sing tonight?"

"*Oui.* And what will you do about it, eh?"

"I'll ask you to pack your bags."

"Ahh, *mon cher,*" Felice said, her voice becoming as sultry and caressing as a kiss. "You can't mean that."

"No?"

"*Non.* I know men, and I know *you.* You protest, you say you are not interested, but I don't believe it. If you will just relax and let Felice take care of you, I will show you how wonderful *l'amour* can be."

"Love?" He laughed. "Is that what you call it?"

"It does not matter what you call it," she said. "Kiss me, and you will understand."

Rianne's back stiffened. She felt a sense of violation that was as powerful as it was surprising. How dare the woman try to seduce Pagan right outside this room?

Without thinking about what she was doing, Rianne stalked to the door and opened it. Pagan was leaning against the opposite wall, his arms folded over his chest. Despite the languid pose, Rianne knew by the coldness

36

of his eyes that he was angry. Then his gaze swung to her, and his eyes warmed.

"Hello, Rianne," he said.

The Frenchwoman put her hands on her hips and surveyed Rianne from head to foot. "So this is the little *Anglaise*," she purred. "She seems a bit skinny for your tastes, *cher.*"

Rianne studied the other woman from beneath half-closed lids. Felice was lushly pretty, with generous features and an even more generous figure. She was wearing a red velvet dressing gown that contrasted sharply with her black hair and eyes, and the bodice was cut so low as to be almost nonexistent.

With mingled anger and embarrassment, Rianne turned away from that overabundant display of flesh to look at Pagan. "Mr. Roark, I—"

"Mr. Roark, indeed!" Felice gave a trill of laughter. "So young, so innocent-looking! *Mon Dieu!* She is even blushing. Is that what you like, Pagan?"

Lifting her chin defiantly, Rianne said, "I'm not here for what you think, Mademoiselle. I came here to see my father, nothing more."

"Hah!" Felice took a deep breath, straining the front of the dressing gown. "You lie badly, *Anglaise*. Why don't you admit the truth?"

Rianne drew herself up in furious dignity. "It seems to me that it is *you* who has difficulty recognizing the truth. Mr. Roark has told you often enough that he isn't interested in you, and you still refuse to believe him."

"That is because I know men," the Frenchwoman said, smiling like a cat that has just caught the mouse.

"Perhaps it isn't you who knows men, Mademoiselle, but they who know *you*—all too well," Rianne said.

Felice gave a shriek of rage. "How dare you! You little fool, I shall rip you to ribbons!" She advanced on Rianne, her fingers curled into claws.

37

Pagan pushed off from the wall with a lithe heave of his shoulders. When he spoke, his voice was deadly calm, deadly quiet. But even Felice didn't make the mistake of challenging him this time. "That's enough, Felice. Pack your bags and get out."

"You . . . you . . . Pah!" The Frenchwoman spun around and flounced down the hall. Just before turning the corner, however, she whirled and pointed at Rianne. "You think you're going to hold him because you're a *lady?* Well, let me tell you something, *Anglaise.* Your fine Pagan Roark has said many times that there is no such thing as a lady, just women, and they're all the same under the skin. Remember that, *Anglaise.*"

Rianne marched back into her father's room, very conscious of Pagan striding behind her. She was overflowing with a jumble of emotions: embarrassment and anger, triumph and confusion. Why on earth had she gone out there to confront that woman? It certainly couldn't be because Pagan Roark needed her help; he seemed capable enough of handling Felice on his own.

Not daring to look at either Pagan or her father, Rianne busied herself collecting the cups and dishes and putting them back in the basket. Her hands, however, were shaking so badly that the crockery rattled, betraying her agitation.

"Your daughter seems to have quite a temper, Alastair," Pagan said, his voice full of amusement.

"Indeed she does. Got it from her mother, I'm afraid; Leonora was a Tartar."

Pagan laughed, his voice rolling through the room like rich velvet. He studied Rianne, noting the stubborn set to her jaw, the outraged line of her shoulders. She certainly had spirit, facing Felice down like that. The rabbit confronting the leopard. Come to think of it, the rabbit had come off rather well in that exchange. Miss Rianne Kierney was turning out to be a fascinating woman, full of surprises. He was beginning to look forward to finding out what came next.

He was distracted by a roar of voices from the saloon downstairs, a vast male shout demanding entertainment. Pagan grimaced. It was Saturday night, and men had come in from even the most remote camps to hear Felice sing. They weren't going to be happy when they heard she was gone.

As though reading his thoughts, Alastair said, "They're going to be very disappointed to have Alastair Kierney playing the piano when they'd been expecting to see Felice Cardonne's legs . . . I mean, hear Felice Cardonne's lilting soprano."

Rianne chose to ignore the issue of legs, focusing instead on the other part of her father's statement. "Did I hear correctly, Father? Are you saying that you play the piano in Mr. Roark's . . . saloon?"

"I do. I even get a percentage of each night's take . . . er, proceeds." He smiled at her happily. "I've always had an ear for music. *That* you inherited from me."

Rianne put her hands on her hips, looking from Pagan to her father and back again. Alastair looked as grateful and eager as a wizened puppy. Pagan's face showed nothing at all, but she guessed he'd hired the old man in kindness, giving him food and shelter and allowing him his dignity as well.

Kindness begets kindness, she thought. One of the most vivid memories she had of her father was him telling her that a Kierney always paid his debts. Well, it seemed as though her father owed Pagan Roark, and she had the means to pay. Sudden recklessness surged through her. Forget convention, she thought. Remember how bland and uninteresting life had been when there was nothing but propriety. This is your chance to break those bonds. I *will* help them, saloon or no! And Mother can just spin in her grave.

"I can't allow you to go down there alone and face a horde of angry, drunken men, Father," she said.

Alastair waved his hand negligently. "It won't be so bad, truly. They're more bark than bite."

"I'm glad to hear that." Rianne crossed her arms over her chest. "Because I'm going to be singing with you."

Both men stared at her, their eyes wide with surprise. Then Alastair burst out, "Are you mad, Rianne?"

"Probably."

"I forbid it!" the old man cried.

"I'm sorry, Father, but my mind is made up. It will only be for tonight, after all."

Alastair's mouth opened and closed soundlessly for a moment, and then he turned and appealed to Pagan. "Do something!"

"Do be quiet, Father," Rianne said calmly. "Mr. Roark, what do you think of my offer?"

"Can you sing?" Pagan asked.

"I sang in the Wickersham Church choir." Rianne met his gaze levelly.

Pagan's brows went up. "Church choir?"

"Is something wrong with that?" She squared her shoulders, ready to do battle.

Pagan thrust his hands in his trouser pockets and stared at the floor, trying to sort through his emotions. Part of him wanted to laugh, part to accept her offer out of sheer curiosity, and yet another part of him instinctively rejected the idea of her facing that drunk and rowdy crowd.

Rianne took silence for acquiescence. "Now, I'm not familiar with, er, your patrons' sort of music. I realize that hymns are not the usual fare in these places—"

"No," Pagan said, keeping his face straight with an effort, "they're not."

She clasped her hands in front of her. "Well, I *do* know 'The Blue Bell of Scotland—' "

"Good God!" Alastair burst out.

"Don't be profane, Father," she said, then continued as though she hadn't been interrupted, "And I do follow music well. Surely I might be of some help to you."

Pagan's desire to protect her won out over curiosity. "It's kind of you to offer," he said. "But no."

"No?" she asked in surprise. Refusal was the last thing she had expected.

"No," Pagan said. "It will never work."

"Are you saying I won't do?" she asked, searching his face for some clue as to what he was thinking.

The question, so humbly and innocently put, affected Pagan profoundly. He'd thought himself a man who could no longer be surprised by women and their ways, but Rianne was proving him wrong at every turn. "You can't imagine what it's like down there. Men's tempers rise as the level of whiskey goes down, and that's a very rough lot, even sober. You haven't been brought up to—"

"But I *was* brought up to help a friend in need." She went to him and put her hand on his arm, adding softly so that only he could hear, "It's the only thing I can give you in return for all you've done for my father."

He turned away, raking his hand through his hair. The noise downstairs rose and ebbed, a veritable tide of sound. If she went down there and they *didn't* like her, they'd shout her out of the room. He didn't want to see that happen, or to feel responsible for the hurt she was bound to feel.

"No," he said. "I can't let you do it."

Rianne put her hand on his arm, bringing him back around to face her. "Please, Mr. Roark. Let me try."

He looked into her eyes. Warm, honey-brown eyes full of sincerity. She truly wanted to help. And there was also a hint of the stubborn Kierney pride he so admired in her father. All protest drained out of Pagan. He knew

41

she was feeling beholden to him. Being a man who disliked owing others, he had no choice but to respect her need to help him.

"Mr. Roark, I . . ." Rianne's voice trailed off as her gaze was ensnared by his. There was such warmth in his eyes that her breath caught in her throat. She looked at the firm curve of his mouth, wondering what it would be like to be kissed by him. The prospect of it was exciting and heady, but dangerous.

"Are you sure you want to do this?" he asked.

"I'm sure."

"All right." Suddenly he smiled, a quick flash of white teeth. "They'll behave themselves, if I have to knock a few heads together to convince them."

Alastair cleared his throat loudly. Rianne looked away from Pagan, the spell broken.

"You're both out of your minds," the old man said. "They'll break everything in the place."

Rianne laughed. "Have you so little faith in my singing, then?"

"Faith!" Alastair snorted. "I won't need faith, I'll need a shotgun. Hymns!"

"Father, surely a little culture won't hurt them. Besides, if you'd write down the words to some songs, I can practice a bit before coming downstairs."

He threw his hands up in the air, signaling defeat. "I have some sheet music around here somewhere. I never use it any more. Felice usually sings the same few songs over and over—"

"I'll be sure to pick something different, then," Rianne said. *I'm sure that if Felice Cardonne showed enough bosom and leg, the men didn't care if she could sing at all.* Glancing up at Pagan Roark, she saw amusement on his face. It was almost as if the man had read her mind.

"You're as stubborn as your mother," Alastair said.

Rianne smiled. "No, Father. I'm as stubborn as *you.*"

"God help you, child, for it's brought me nothing but trouble." He turned away and began going through the bureau drawers, muttering, "I know I left them in here somewhere . . . or was it downstairs . . ."

While her father was occupied with his search, Rianne turned back to Pagan. "Mr. Roark, there is one thing I must ask of you."

"I'm yours to command."

"You'll make certain that no one . . . accosts me?"

"You have my word." He took her hand and raised it to his lips. "No one will come near you."

Rianne looked into his eyes. There was reassurance there, and a warm promise that made her knees feel strangely weak. After the way he had stared down that roomful of men this afternoon, she didn't doubt his ability to protect her. Smiling a bit shakily, she nodded.

Slowly, he raised her hand to his mouth again. His lips were slightly parted, his breath hot against her skin. A tiny, leaping flame of passion flickered in his eyes. For one seemingly endless moment she was caught, mesmerized by that heat.

Yes, he would protect her from any other man. But who would protect her from him?

Pagan sat alone at the table nearest the piano, absently listening to Alastair banging away at the instrument. Rianne hadn't come down yet, but the men, assured that there would be a singer tonight, had settled down to their usual Saturday night drinking and gambling.

He sensed rather than saw Rianne come into the room. She was wearing a primrose yellow dress, high-necked and prim, with wide sleeves that made her look very fragile. Her hair was drawn back into a simple chignon in the back, with none of the front curls so fash-

43

ionable now. Simple, pure, innocent. She looked as delicate and out of place as a lace veil in a briar patch. God, what had possessed him to let her come down here?

He watched her face closely as she looked around at the crowd of bearded, roughly-dressed men. Her face was composed, but pale, and she didn't seem to be aware that her hand had crept up to her throat. Then her gaze met Pagan's, and the uncertainty in her tawny eyes drew him irresistibly. He rose to his feet and went to her, striding through the jostling, noisy men as though they didn't exist.

"Miss Kierney," he said, taking her hand and raising it to his lips.

"Mr. Roark." She dipped into a curtsey, a dimple appearing at the corner of her mouth.

Pagan tucked her hand into the crook of his arm and led her into the room. The men turned to look at her curiously as she passed, and a questioning murmur flowed beneath the hum of conversation. Pagan ignored it, concentrating instead on the faint floral scent Rianne was wearing. Delicate and musky, it was perfect for her . . . perfect for him. He had the feeling he'd remember that scent for a long, long time.

He glanced at her from the corner of his eye. Her profile was graceful, her nose straight, her chin firm. There was a hint of a blush on her high cheekbones, and her downcast eyes were shaded by feathery lashes that looked like they'd been dusted with gold.

"You can still change your mind," he said.

She looked up at him, her full lips pressed into a stubborn line. "No, I can't. A Kierney always keeps his word."

"And pays his debts."

"Yes, Mr. Roark."

They reached the piano, and Alastair rose to take his

daughter's other hand. Pagan disengaged himself, giving Rianne's elbow a reassuring squeeze before returning to his table.

Alastair placed Rianne beside him, where she could see the sheet music he was using. The din abated somewhat as the miners realized that the entertainment was about to begin. With a flourish, Alastair played the opening chords of the "Blue Belle of Scotland".

"What the hell is this, a Sunday picnic?" one man bellowed.

"Don't the little gal dance?" shouted another. "C'mon, honey, show us them long legs!"

Alastair stopped playing. Pagan took his pistol out and laid it on the table beside his whiskey. Casually, he rested his hand on it while he surveyed the room. "The lady is here to sing, nothing more. Is that clear?"

No one spoke. Satisfied, Pagan turned and nodded at Alastair to begin again.

Clasping her hands in front of her, Rianne started to sing. Pagan sat forward, astounded by what he heard. He'd expected her voice to be a light soprano, as fragile as the woman herself. But Rianne's voice was rich and deep, with a faintly smoky quality to it like fine brandy. No girl's voice, this, but a woman's, full of life and passion. It drew him in, flowing over and around and through him, smooth as silk, sultry as an embrace. God, he'd never heard anything like it!

To hell with the "Blue Bell of Scotland". He didn't care *what* she sang, as long as that marvelous voice kept on. And, glancing around at the rapt faces of the men around him, he saw that she'd caught them, too. Rianne Kierney was a natural entertainer, one of those rare people who could reach out and take an audience into her hands and make them hers.

The song ended, but instead of waiting for applause, she swung right into another. "Where Did You Get That

45

Hat?" soon had the men clapping and stomping their feet. Despite the noise they made, her voice soared above it, rich and sensual, seeming to gain strength from their response. Then she quieted them with "Beautiful Dreamer". Hearing a sound nearby, Pagan turned to see Francois Gruillot openly weeping. Hulking Francois Gruillot, who could break an axe handle between his hands, was crying.

"Ah, très belle, très belle," the huge man said, pulling a bandanna out of his pocket and wiping his streaming eyes.

When the beautiful old song ended, the echoes of her voice seemed to hang upon the air. Pagan sighed, only then realizing that he'd been holding his breath. A moment of silence reigned. Then the men began to clap, cheering and whistling. One fellow went so far as to fire his pistol into the air, an act Pagan forgave, considering the circumstances.

Pagan's awareness of the noise faded as his gaze focused on Rianne's face. She looked around the room, shyly pleased, yet obviously a bit overwhelmed by the strength of the men's reaction. Then she smiled. Putting her hand to her lips, she blew the audience a kiss.

It was then, in that brief, stunning moment when she responded so naturally and generously to the miners' outpouring of approval, that Pagan's simmering desire for her flared to white-hot. That stunning, sensual voice had revealed the true Rianne Kierney—a woman of passion so deep a man might drown in it.

Pagan had known many women in his thirty-two years. Many were like Felice Cardonne, shallow and spoiled, seekers of sensation or money—anything that would briefly fill the emptiness of their souls. But Rianne was real. He wanted her. He wanted her with an intensity he'd never felt for any other woman.

Pagan knew he couldn't let her go until he'd tasted the

passion she didn't seem to be aware of herself. Taste it, then plumb the depths of it. It was as though Destiny had brought her across the world to him. His whole being yearned to possess her—all of her, the woman and the voice.

She thought she was going to leave Henderson City soon. Oregon, Alastair had said. Smiling, Pagan stroked his thumbnail along the line of his jaw.

"You can make all the plans you want, my lovely Miss Kierney," he murmured under his breath. "But you're not leaving until *I* decide it's time."

Chapter Four

Rianne was stunned by the miners' enthusiastic applause. They liked her! She'd been so nervous about singing tonight, afraid of being hooted out of the room. Being accepted like this was wonderful.

Her gaze was drawn to Pagan Roark. He was sitting at his table, seemingly relaxed, but he was staring at her with such intensity that she wondered why she didn't feel his gaze like a flame on her skin. She was shaken by it, and by the knowledge that it was *she* who had created it in him.

He rose from his chair and strode toward her, never taking his gaze from her face. Her world narrowed to those crystalline eyes of his, glowing with emotion. As he stopped in front of her, she tipped her head back to look at him, wondering if the quivery feeling she felt was dread or desire; perhaps it was both.

He extended his arm. Her fingers shook slightly as she laid her hand on his forearm and let him lead her to his table.

"Just for a short while," he said, holding a chair out for her. "The men tend to get wild once they get loaded up with whiskey."

"Do they always get wild?" she asked.

He sat down across from her. "Yes. These men spend weeks at isolated claims. Many of them do not see another human being in all that time and, when they come to town, they let loose. I don't want you here when things get rough."

Rianne propped her elbows on the table and leaned her chin upon her hands. *He* didn't want her here. There was something both disquieting and exciting about that notion. It should have been a casual statement, the sort of thing any man would have said to his friend's daughter. But somehow it wasn't.

"Mr. Roark—"

"Pagan."

"Such short acquaintance—"

"That doesn't mean we can't be friends."

He smiled at her, a roguish grin that Rianne couldn't help but return.

"Very well," she agreed. "Pagan. What are you doing here?"

That charming little dimple was back, he noted, wishing he could kiss it. He liked hearing her say his given name. "Do you mean here in the Golden Bear, or here in Henderson City?"

"Both."

He chuckled. "Perhaps I just like running a hotel."

"Hotel?" She raised her brows. "Really, Pagan."

There it was again. His name. It sounded like music when she spoke it. What would it sound like if she sighed it in passion? He had every intention of finding out. "What were we talking about?" he asked.

"Have you forgotten so soon?" she asked.

"I'm afraid I became lost in your eyes," he said. "Did you know they've got flecks of green amid the brown?"

She glanced away, wanting to escape his scrutiny. A change of subject was in order, too. "You were about to tell me how you came to live in Henderson City, and how you came to be the proprietor of the Golden Bear."

49

He shrugged. "An accident. I happened to have a better poker hand than the owner, and won the place, lock, stock and barrel. I should have sold it or perhaps played another hand so he could win it back. But I'd spent most of my life moving from place to place, and the idea of having a permanent home appealed to me. Not that I'd mind finding a nice, fat vein of gold, either." He smiled crookedly. "Like every other man in this room."

Rianne looked past him at the faces of the prospectors. They were drinking with a sort of desperation that brought pity into her heart. "It's a lonely life, isn't it?" she asked.

"Yes," Pagan said. "But tonight you made it a little less lonely—you were a sensation, Rianne."

"Oh . . . I'm so glad they liked me. I was terribly frightened at first, but it turned out to be a marvelous experience. Singing in the church choir was nothing like this!"

"They loved you," he said, "and so did I. It was as though you were singing to me, and only to me."

Rianne looked away, unable to meet his gaze. It sounded so sincere, so very . . . intimate. Had her singing truly touched him like *that?*

His words cut through her reverie. "A voice like yours wasn't meant to be drowned in a choir." As she opened her mouth to protest, he raised his hand to stop her. "I don't mean there's anything wrong with religion. But God has angels aplenty to sing to Him. There's little enough beauty in *this* world without reserving the best for the next."

She flushed in pleased embarrassment and put her hands up to her hot cheeks. "Oh, dear, not again. I seem to be blushing a great deal lately."

"It's enchanting," he said. His voice was a caress.

The note of desire in his voice made Rianne blush

50

even more, and the heat of her skin was echoed by a coiling flame deep inside her.

She couldn't understand what it was about him that made her feel so strangely. At another time, she would have been reluctant to stay in the company of a man who had such a disturbing effect on her, but just now she was riding a wave of confidence born of her success. So, recklessly, she stayed.

One of the saloon girls came up to the table. Her hair hung loose in a wild mass of curls around her shoulders, and she was obviously not wearing a corset beneath her low-cut blouse. Rianne managed to keep from blushing this time, but she didn't know what to say. Her strictly religious upbringing certainly hadn't prepared her for *this* situation.

"Miss Kierney, this is Marie," Pagan said.

Marie didn't smile, and the expression on her rather broad, pleasant face was cautiously friendly. "Pleased to meet you. I just wanted to tell you that I liked your singing, Miss Kierney. It was real nice of you to help us out tonight."

Rianne opened her mouth to reply, but the other woman continued with dogged determination, as though this was a planned speech she had to get through before she forgot it. "Now, Miss Kierney, your pa told us you were brought up real strict, so I know it was hard for you to come down here and sing. All us girls want you to know we appreciate it."

Rianne's discomfort melted away. Marie had come here to be nice, and to thank her; who was she to judge her because of her profession? 'Judge not, sayeth the Lord, lest ye be judged.' "I was glad to help, Marie," she said, impulsively adding, "and call me Rianne."

Marie smiled for the first time, revealing a gold front tooth. "Rianne, then. Well, I'd best be back at work."

51

Before Rianne could say anything else, Marie had melted back into the crowd of men.

Pagan watched the play of emotions on Rianne's face, glad that she'd been kind to Marie. Another woman might have snubbed a 'soiled dove' no matter what she'd come to say. He noticed that the yellow light of the lanterns warmed Rianne's light brown hair, frosting it with gold. A few tendrils had strayed from her severe chignon to frame the sweet oval of her face with curls. His hand twitched with the desire to touch her, to run his fingers down the silken curve of her cheek.

Seeing a dangerous warmth come into his eyes again, Rianne looked away hastily. Her gaze fell on her father, who was standing at the bar with his back to her, a half-full bottle of whiskey beside him.

Even as she watched, he drained the contents of a tumbler and filled it again. It was plain to see that he had settled in to finish the bottle. Disappointment dulled her triumph; she'd thought her father would stay sober tonight of all nights. They still had so much to talk about, their whole future to plan.

"Does this happen every night?" she asked without looking away from Alastair.

Pagan stared at her, confused, then realized she was talking about her father. "Nearly so."

"I'm going to stop him." She started to rise from her chair, but Pagan grasped her wrist, holding her back.

"He won't listen. I've tried." When she was settled in her chair again, he let her go. "He's a grown man, Rianne. Neither you nor I can tell him where to spend his money or how to live his life."

"But that isn't any kind of life," she protested.

"It's what he's chosen."

"I can't believe that. The bottle chose it for him." Then she sighed, smoothing her hair back with her hands. "Oh, I'm not so naive to think that I can change him overnight, but I *do* intend to help him. It's just that I'd hoped . . . Oh, never mind."

Pagan saw her pain. He ached to take her into his arms and comfort her. Alastair had told him something about her mother's cold, unforgiving nature. Because of Leonora Kierney's suspicions, her harping tongue and inflexible judgments, Rianne had grown up virtually friendless, with only the memories of her father to show her a parent's affection and laughter. A very lonely life. And now she'd come to Henderson City to find her father at last, and he was more interested in the bottle than in her.

"I'm sorry, Rianne," he said simply.

"So am I." Unshed tears stung her eyelids.

Pagan was so intent on Rianne that he didn't see Francois Gruillot approaching until the man was standing beside the table.

"Mademoiselle," the huge prospector rumbled.

Pagan got to his feet, ready for trouble. Francois was normally a mild man, but once he got some liquor in him, he could be trouble. If he decided to claim Rianne—which was entirely possible—he could be stopped only by shooting him or knocking him unconscious.

To his relief, however, the man took Rianne's hand in his enormous paw with gentle reverence. "You touched my heart, Mademoiselle Kierney. If you need anything, you call on Francois Gruillot, eh?"

"Why, thank you, Monsieur Gruillot," Rianne said, touched by his obvious sincerity. "You are most kind."

"I have a great favor to ask," the big man said.

"Favor?"

"Do you know the 'Marseillaise'? I would be very happy if you would sing it for me."

Rianne glanced at her father. "I don't know it,

but I'll be happy to try if my father has the music."

"He does," Pagan said. "He used to play it quite often."

"Well, if he'll play, I'll sing," Rianne said.

"He will play." Francois Gruillot strode to the bar and picked Alastair up by the back of his shirt and the seat of his pants. Carrying the struggling, protesting old man to the piano, the prospector sat him on the stool and said, "Play, Alastair. The 'Marseillaise'."

Rianne covered her mouth with her hand so that her father wouldn't see her smile. Oh, this was amusing! More than amusing, it was enlightening. If she could keep singing, perhaps she could keep her father from drinking. It didn't matter if the crowd got wild; just now she'd brave it for her father's sake. She rose to her feet, but Pagan caught hold of her hand.

"It won't work, Rianne," he said, as though he'd read her thoughts. "You can't stop him from drinking."

She turned and looked deeply into his eyes, willing him to understand. "He's my father."

He held her hand for a moment, his palm warm and firm against hers. She took comfort from that contact, and from the sympathy on his face. He *did* understand. Although she'd only known him a few short hours, this man was somehow able to look beneath the surface and see her hopes and fears, understand her dreams. That knowledge stirred her immeasurably.

Then he released her slowly, almost reluctantly, and she went to join her father at the piano.

Alastair bent over a stack of sheet music, sifting through it in search of the "Marseillaise". Rianne stood behind him, looking over his shoulder as he worked. Many of the titles were unfamiliar to her. Not for the first time she regretted the tightly confined life to which her mother had bound her; she had stood still in

54

her safe little Wickersham nest while the rest of the world was moving forward in leaps and bounds.

Then her gaze focused on her father's hands, and she forgot about everything else. They were an old man's hands, spotted with age and painfully thin, hardly more than wires strung on bones. His fingers trembled as he paged through the sheet music. The sight stretched her heart nearly to breaking with love and pity and the need to help him. Impulsively, she reached around him and put her hand over his.

He smiled at her over his shoulder. "We're quite a team, aren't we?"

"Yes, Father." She returned his smile with a rather shaky one of her own.

"Ah, here it is!" He straightened, holding a piece of sheet music. "Let's get this song over with while Mad Francois is still in a pleasant disposition."

"I think he's a very nice man."

Alastair stared at her wide-eyed. "Francois? Rianne, the man bites trees in half with his teeth. Bears and wolves run from him screaming in terror. Hell, he chews two-penny nails instead of tobacco!"

"Oh, Father, really." She glanced at the polished brass spittoons that sat on the floor on each end of the long bar. "And even if he does, I'm sure it's much neater than chewing tobacco."

" 'Marseillaise!' " Francois boomed.

Alastair slid into his chair hastily. Rianne stood where she could see the music and the audience. Her gaze automatically went to Pagan. He smiled, lifting his glass in a toast. She felt warm all over.

The first lively chords of the "Marseillaise" began. As Rianne began to sing, Francois joined her enthusiastically, his rumbling bass vibrating through the room. When the song ended, other men requested their favorites. Rianne sang, and sang some more. If Pagan didn't have the music for a song, the prospectors themselves taught it to her.

One tune in particular caught her fancy. It was a love-ballad, the melody hauntingly familiar as though graven on her heart without her knowing. Remembering what Pagan had said earlier, she closed her eyes and sang it to *him*. She didn't know why, and didn't stop to think about it; it just felt right. For some strange reason, she wanted her music to touch his soul.

When the last, long-held note ended, she opened her eyes and looked at him.

He was watching her, a strangely tender look on his face. Tender, and incredibly possessive. She *had* touched him! Her heartbeat thundered in her ears, louder than the applause. She was filled with a mixture of elation and triumph and awe of what she had done. That she could have such power over a man was a profound revelation for her. Profound, and heady.

"That's all for tonight. I can't play any more, and I'm damned parched," Alastair said, bringing her back to earth with a jolt.

"I'll get you some water," she said.

"Water!" he repeated in horror. "No, sweet. You go on upstairs now. You've done enough singing for one night."

She was desperate to keep him with her and away from the whiskey. "Why don't you come with me, Father? We have so much to talk about, so many plans—"

"I'll talk to you tomorrow, darling girl." He fairly bolted away from her. A moment later, he filled a tumbler with whiskey and drank it avidly, as though he'd just come from a week in the desert.

"Come, Rianne," Pagan said from behind her. "I'll take you to your room."

The triumph drained out of her, leaving her exhausted. Without protest, she put her hand on Pagan's proffered arm and let him lead her from the room. Several men called out farewells, and she forced herself to smile as she turned and waved.

Disappointment rode her heavily as Pagan led her up the stairs. She should have known. She should have expected that her father wouldn't change overnight merely because she had come to Henderson City. The future suddenly seemed daunting, shadowed by Alastair's need for whiskey.

Pagan watched her profile as they walked, thinking how lovely she was, and how sad. It was a damned shame that Alastair was too selfish to put his whiskey aside for one night. He wanted to see her laugh. He wanted to kiss her, to see what she looked like in the depths of passion. *You will,* he told himself. *There will be time for all those things.* But he didn't want to wait. He wanted her now. And claiming her would keep her here with him. She'd belong to him. *For as long as it lasts,* a small, cynical corner of his mind corrected.

They reached Rianne's room, and Pagan pulled her to a halt outside the door. Rianne put her hand on the knob and turned to face him, ready to say good night. But he placed one large, tanned hand on the panel beside her head and looked down at her with a very serious expression on his face.

"Are you sorry you came?" he asked.

"Oh, no." She looked down at her clasped hands. "I expected that it would take time for Father to . . . adjust to having me around."

"I've adjusted already."

His voice was as smooth and caressing as a summer breeze. Rianne looked up, startled. "I beg your pardon?"

"I like having you around," he said softly.

Rianne looked up at him. He was so close, his lean,

sculpted face only inches from hers. Her heartbeat quickened as her gaze traveled his features, settling finally on his mouth. It was firm and masculine, his lips strongly molded.

Then he put his other hand on the door, enclosing her between his arms. He was going to kiss her. She knew she could get away from him by merely opening the door and slipping inside, but something held her rooted to the spot. His mouth moved closer slowly, oh, so slowly. She watched it, and him, waiting to learn what he would feel like, what he would taste like.

His eyes drifted closed, his eyelashes a black fringe against his cheeks. Rianne felt his lips against hers, butterfly soft. Then he retreated an inch, smiling down at her.

"You're supposed to close your eyes," he murmured.

"Was I?" she asked, still bemused.

"That was your first kiss." It wasn't a question; he knew it was. *I was the first, the very first.* It was a heady thought, and made him burn to teach her more. Much more.

"Yes, it was the first."

"And did you like it?"

She was caught by the heat in his eyes, the passion that tautened his jaw. "Yes."

"Shall I kiss you again?" he asked, although he had every intention of doing so.

"Yes," she whispered.

Again, he brushed his lips over hers. And again. Rianne found it exquisite, lovely, but yet not enough. She closed her eyes and waited, not knowing how to ask for more. She felt his hand cup her chin and turn her face upward. His thumb traveled the curve of her jaw, then moved to stroke slowly over her full lower lip. Such a seemingly innocent touch, but it sent a wave of heat washing through her.

And then he kissed her again, that same soft touch. Too soft. Wanting something else, something more, she moved closer.

With a harsh sigh, he gathered her in. It was like stepping into a fire, his body coming hard against hers, demanding and possessive all at once. His mouth captured hers, and there was nothing teasing about it now. His tongue stroked over her upper lip, then the lower, then traced the line between. Rianne gasped, her senses reeling from the sheer pleasure of it.

His mouth closed over hers, catching her exhalation. He cupped her head in one large hand as he explored the sweet depths of her mouth, then nibbled and sucked at her lips until she was trembling from the feelings he was evoking in her.

Pagan felt her tremble and rejoiced in it. He, too, was shaken by what was happening. She might be an innocent, but her response was deep and true. Too many women were practiced in the art of making love, but lacked real sensuality. Money, not the man, raised their desire. But Rianne was a rare gem, intelligence and beauty and true, sweet passion. If it was in his power, he was going to possess her, body and soul.

Rianne went up on her tiptoes, wanting to get closer still. It was as though some kind of madness had come over her, changing her from her old self to a woman of wanton desire. She didn't object—couldn't object—as Pagan's hands began to stroke restlessly over her back. Nothing mattered just now except his kiss and the sweeping, liquid passion coursing through her body.

He tore his mouth from hers and began exploring the smooth flesh of her throat. "You're beautiful, beautiful," he muttered against her skin.

Rianne could only sigh. Then a sudden burst of laughter from the stairway jolted her back to earth, and the realization of where she was and what she was doing crashed in on her.

"Stop!" she whispered urgently, pushing at him with frantic hands. "Someone's coming!"

"You're right," he agreed, raising his head as he reached for the doorknob. "Let's go in your room. No one will bother us there."

"No!"

"No?" He pulled her against him, his pale eyes glittering with annoyance. "That wasn't the message you were giving a moment ago."

Shame reddened her cheeks. It would be easier to lay the blame at his feet rather then admit that she had simply been carried away by her emotions. But she was no liar, and no coward, either. Lifting her chin, she met his gaze directly. "I . . . I . . . didn't know . . . didn't expect . . ." She took a deep breath. It needed to be said, so she made herself say it. "If I led you on, I'm sorry. I didn't mean to."

Pagan was tempted to kiss her again. As a man of experience, he knew he could overcome her reluctance. But something stopped him. He didn't want to take her by guile, or with the slightest bit of reluctance on her part. When they made love, it would be wholeheartedly, with no reservations, no holding back. So he controlled the raging need of his body.

Cupping her face between his hands, he gazed deeply into her eyes. Pools of warm honey, uncertain now, but yet retaining some of the passion he'd raised in her.

"Do you realize how special that was?" he asked.

"W-What do you mean?"

"Your response to me. Our response to one another."

She closed her eyes, for she wanted to hide the warmth his words engendered in her. For a moment she'd been swept into a world where nothing mattered

60

but sensation, the wonderful feel and taste and smell of Pagan Roark. She didn't have the resources or experience to chart her way safely through that world.

One of the saloon girls and a miner appeared at the end of the hallway, tearing Rianne out of her reverie. The man was very drunk, leaning on his giggling companion. They went into one of the far rooms and closed the door with a crash.

Rianne pulled away from Pagan, hideously embarrassed by what she'd witnessed — and appalled by her own behavior. Truly, she must have been possessed by some sort of madness to stand in a public place *kissing* him. She knew how weak she'd been at that moment; she'd been too lost in him and in her own desire to deny him.

"Rianne —"

"Don't. Don't say anything." Sure that her tumultuous emotions were written upon her face, she turned away hastily. "I-I've got to go."

He put his hands on her shoulders and turned her around to face him. She looked bewildered and bemused and uncertain all at once. And yet, beneath the surface, there was a heady sensuality that nothing could conceal. Grasping her chin in one hand, he tilted her face up.

"Please, don't," she whispered.

Her eyes shone with suspicious moisture. With sudden, swift surprise, he realized just how momentous that kiss had been for her. Her very first. The very thought that no man had touched her before sent a wave of triumph coursing through him. It was special to be so privileged. But it was also special because Rianne herself was special. He'd never thought of himself as a compassionate man, but she seemed to have the ability to touch something deep inside him he'd never known existed.

It was an interesting revelation, and only made him more determined to have her for his own.

"Good night, Rianne," he murmured, then let her go.

She stood and watched him stride away in that cat-footed silent way of his. He'd let her go. Relief and a strange, treacherous disappointment warred in her.

"Good night," she whispered to the empty hallway.

Chapter Five

Rianne shifted restlessly under the blankets, wishing she could stop thinking about Pagan Roark. But the memory of his smooth, velvet voice and the feel of his mouth on hers was much too vivid. Why did she find him so compelling? Certainly he was handsome. No, more than handsome; he was completely, blatantly masculine, with a streak of fierceness that made men walk clear of him and attracted women like bees to honey.

"And how do you know that, idiot?" she asked herself. "Because Felice Cardonne spent a year in this terrible place in the hope of becoming his mistress. And because *you* are so attracted to him that you fall at his feet the moment he kisses you."

Ah, but such kisses! a traitorous corner of her mind whispered. She'd wanted to be kissed; she was surely the only unkissed twenty-two year old woman on two continents. Wasn't it worth a little embarrassment to have had that wish fulfilled so thoroughly? Perhaps. But she had a feeling she'd set something in motion she didn't quite know how to control, and it made her uncomfortable.

She sat up, plumped her pillow savagely, then lay down again. A moment later she turned onto her right side, then her left, then tried lying on her stomach. But with the din downstairs and her own discomfiture, it was obvious that sleep was going to elude her. Her skin felt over-sensitive, even the thin cotton nightgown an irritant. It was as though a storm were imminent, the very air charged with anticipation. But the night was clear. The storm was inside her, roused by Pagan Roark, and she had no idea what to do to stop it.

"Good heavens, don't carry on so. It was only a kiss!" she muttered into the pillow.

Only a kiss . . . Only a kiss . . . Only a kiss. It was a refrain in her mind, insistent, annoying because it was untrue. There would be nothing simple about a kiss that had changed her so profoundly. Or a man. In the few short hours since she'd met Pagan Roark, she'd become aware of herself as a woman. Did it happen like this to everyone—one huge, disturbing revelation?

Then she heard her father's voice, and her attention snapped to him. He was singing the "Marseillaise" in a very off-key voice. The awful singing came closer, along with a series of bumps, as though he were bouncing from wall to wall.

Flinging the covers aside, Rianne reached for the dressing gown she'd laid at the foot of the bed. As she slipped it on, she heard the outer door of her father's room open. The singing grew louder and even more awful. A small corner of her mind took note of the fact that Francois Gruillot must have left the Golden Bear, for he'd surely take exception to such a ghastly rendering of his favorite song.

She opened the adjoining door and rushed into the other room. "Father . . ." she began, stopping short when she saw Pagan Roark standing there with her father over his shoulder.

The old man's arms were waving in time to the music, and his white hair hung down over his face.

Alastair finished the song. For a moment Rianne feared he was about to begin another, but he only laughed and said, "That Ben Jacoby thin's he can push Alash . . . Alashair Kierney aroun', but I showed 'im. Din' I show 'im, Pagan?"

"Sure, you showed him," Pagan agreed with an equanimity born of long practice.

"Pu' me down," the old man ordered.

Pagan obeyed, steadying him with a hand on his shoulder. Alastair blinked at him, then turned to peer at Rianne. "Who're you, girl?"

"I'm Rianne, Father," she said, feeling as though a knife were twisting in her heart. He didn't remember her!

"Nope. Don' know you. Rianne's in bloody old England," he slurred. "Wi' her bloody mother. My baby . . . Wait, I got a picture of her aroun' here somewhere." He patted his pockets, the movement making him sway. "Mus' have left it somewhere. Texas, maybe, with my goddam ranch. What the hell. Don' matter anyway." He laughed again.

Rianne put her hands up to her cheeks and found that her skin had turned ice-cold. She was unable to speak, unable to move, unable to do anything to release herself from the horrible shock.

"Your daughter is right here, Alastair," Pagan said.

His voice released Rianne from her paralysis. "Why don't you try to get some sleep, Father? It's been a very long day for all of us. And night."

"Night's jus' begun," the old man protested.

"It's over for you," Pagan said. "Go to bed, Alastair."

The old man looked from Pagan to Rianne and back again. "You think I'm drunk. Well . . ." He listed to one side, then corrected himself and continued, "I'm not drunk. I'm jus' a little . . . I'm jus' . . ." With a huge yawn, he turned to the bed, fell down on top of the blanket, and was immediately asleep.

"Shall we undress him?" Rianne asked faintly.

Pagan shook his head. "He won't care. He's dead to the world."

"Yes. I suppose I'd better go back to . . ." Rianne swallowed convulsively. To her surprise, the room started to tilt around her.

Pagan saw the color drain from her face. He was at her side instantly, his arm going around her waist in support. "Here, lean on me, honey," he said.

Feeling numb, as if she'd received a mortal blow, she let him lead her back into her room. She disengaged herself from his grasp and sat on the bed, her hands clasped in her lap. He moved away from her, and a moment later she heard the rasp of a match. Light flared in the room. She didn't want the light, didn't want him to see her face, so she bent her head and fixed her gaze on her tightly interlaced fingers.

Unshed tears stung her eyes. Not now, not when my heart is bared before him! she thought as she tried to force them back. But it was no use. One big drop splashed onto her wrist, then another.

A moment later the bed creaked as Pagan sat down beside her. His arm came around her shoulders, strong and comforting.

"It's all right," he murmured. "It was the drink talking, not Alastair. He loves you, always has."

The tears rushed out in a flood. Ashamed of her uncontrollable outburst, she put her hands over her face. Pagan's arms came around her tightly, pulling her against the solid warmth of his chest. His kindness was her undoing. She hadn't been able to cry when her mother died; not even the terrible, final sound of earth thumping down onto the coffin had broken her reserve then.

But now, in Pagan's arms, she sobbed out her grief for her mother, her father, for the love she had craved so desperately and couldn't have. Even on her death-

66

bed, her mother hadn't been able to embrace her. She had staked so much on finding her father and reclaiming the closeness they had shared during those few, precious years of her childhood. And now he didn't even remember she was alive!

Her deep, wrenching sobs tore at Pagan's heart. He rocked her slowly, wishing he might take the hurt from her into himself. And that too was strange, for he usually found women's tears tiresome. Gently, he slid one hand beneath her knees and lifted her onto his lap. It gratified him that she didn't withdraw from him. She seemed to take comfort from the contact, pressing her palms flat against the damp linen of his shirtfront. His own hands spread out across her back possessively.

He held her, stroking the hair that tumbled over her back in loose curls. It felt like the finest silk beneath his hands, her body fragile yet all woman. Her bare feet peeped out from beneath the voluminous dressing gown that would have been more appropriate on an elderly maiden aunt. There was nothing ridiculous about the garment, however; on her, it looked like something one of Raphael's angels might have worn. He was shaken by the depth of his desire for her. Whatever she might be—angel, woman, Siren whose voice could pull a man's very soul from him—he wanted her more than any woman he'd ever known.

Rianne's storm of tears lessened, then stopped. Abruptly she became aware of the deep, steady beat of Pagan's heart beneath her cheek. Realizing that she was sitting on his lap, she moved away to the bed—much safer ground. "I-I'm sorry," she said, unable to meet his gaze. "It's just that my mother's death, the voyage here from England, and now learning about Father's drinking—everything just crashed in on me at once."

"I don't mind." His deep voice seemed to sink into her body, touching every last fibre of her being.

67

She felt terribly exposed, as though all her doubts and insecurities lay bare for him to see. And yet it was not the exposure of her feelings that disturbed her so, but rather that she was completely vulnerable to him now. "I think I ruined your shirt," she said hastily, anxious to focus his attention on something else.

"To hell with the shirt."

Her gaze snapped to his. There was a raging storm in his eyes, as powerful as the one that had gripped her a few moments ago. This one, however, was passion, not sorrow, and struck an answering chord within her. She was caught, helpless in the tornado winds of desire. Buffeted by the power of them, she swayed toward him.

With a groan, he pulled her back onto his lap. He kissed her temples, her brows, her tear-wet lashes, tasting salt and passion and need. Then his mouth fastened on hers, a starving man finally allowed into the feast. He explored the sensitive inside of her lips, ran his tongue along the edges of her teeth, delved deep to savor the honeyed warmth of her mouth.

Rianne clung to him fiercely, reveling in his strength, his compassion, his desire. His thighs were tense beneath her, the stark brand of his manhood hard against her buttocks. She should be shocked. She should stop this, push him away, make some sort of protest. But her arms only pulled him closer, her tongue moving against his in a dance as old as time. She needed his warmth, his tenderness, this wonderful new feeling of being cherished.

His mouth left hers, leaving her bereft. *Speak now,* a small, sane corner of her mind cried. *Stop him before it's too late!* She opened her mouth, but the only sound that emerged was a sigh of pleasure as his lips moved in a moist, searing path along her throat. It was already too late.

She arched her back as his hands caressed her thighs, the curve of her hip, her ribs. He untied the belt of her dressing gown, and a moment later the garment drifted down her arms, leaving her clad only in her thin cotton nightgown.

Pagan lifted her and placed her on the bed. He stretched out beside her, laying one muscular leg across her thighs in masculine possession as he looked at her. Her hair was spread across the blanket in a silken fall, the lanternlight gilding it. Her nightgown might be simple and girlish, but her eyes were a woman's, heavy-lidded with desire. Her nipples were erect, clearly visible through her gown, revealing that she needed him as much as he did her.

Triumph and tenderness surged through him. With reverent hands, he untied the ribbons that closed the bodice of her gown. Instead of removing the garment, however, he pulled the cotton taut across her breasts so that he could see the rosy outlines of her nipples.

"Beautiful," he murmured.

Rianne gazed up into his crystalline eyes, glorying in the raging passion she found there. No man had ever looked at her this way, as though he wanted to consume her utterly. No man had ever called her beautiful before. It stirred her unbearably, made her reach out and pull him down so that he could kiss her again.

But it was not her mouth he kissed. His tongue ran over her nipple in a delving motion that felt like fire even through the fabric. First one breast, then the other, over and over until she was gasping from the pleasure of it.

She moaned in protest when Pagan gently disengaged himself, then moaned again in passion when he rose to straddle her thighs. He spread his hands out over her ribs and looked at her, his face tight with leashed passion. She wanted something she sensed only he could give. She arched her back, silently pleading for whatever it was.

With a hiss of indrawn breath, he spread her bodice open, baring her breasts. Rianne felt cool air on her overheated skin, then the heat of his hands as he claimed her fullness. She gasped as his thumbs stroked slowly over her pouting nipples, circling the areolas, then gently rubbing the center nubs to even tighter erectness.

His mouth closed over her nipple, suckling her, and the world dissolved in fire. She was held in sensation's thrall, and a swirling liquid heat settled in her core like molten gold. Her skin was over-sensitive, every inch of her body aching for his touch. Of their own volition, her hips moved upward, seeking greater contact with his hard-flexed thighs.

A groan came from deep within his chest. He shifted so that he was lying fully on her, his arousal thick and hard against her belly as he claimed her mouth with gentle savagery. The contact sent a rush of sensation coursing through her body, a wild surge of feeling that was exciting and frightening all at once. Tearing her mouth from his, she buried her face in the curve between his neck and shoulder.

"It's too much," she moaned.

He raised his head and looked at her with eyes that blazed with an all-consuming desire. "Oh, no, darling. This is only the beginning. There's much, much more. Making love is beautiful, the most beautiful thing a man and woman can share. Trust me."

She did trust him. She had to; she was too far lost in the mists of passion to do anything else. With a soft sigh, she raised her lips to his. He took what she offered so tenderly that her breath caught in her throat.

"Pagan!" a man shouted from the hallway outside.

"Where are you, man? We've got all hell breaking loose downstairs!"

Pagan groaned, burying his face against the smooth, scented flesh of her shoulder. He realized now that he'd been hearing crashes from downstairs, but his mind had been occupied elsewhere. For a moment he considered leaving, but the urgings of his body were too powerful. "Let them tear the damned place down," he rasped, gazing at Rianne. "I want you too badly."

But Rianne's sensual world had shattered around her, leaving her only cold reality. She stared up at Pagan, horror rushing in on her as she realized what had nearly happened between them. With a flurry of limbs, she squirmed away from him and fled the bed.

"What the hell?" he growled.

She held the edges of her bodice together with shaking hands. "Please, leave!"

"Leave?" he echoed, his voice becoming dangerously gentle.

"I'm not sure how this happened," she said, perilously close to tears. "I'm sorry. I expect it's my fault. But I do know it can't go any farther. I . . . I'm not a loose woman, Mr. Roark—"

"Call me Mr. Roark again and I'll turn you over my knee."

She clutched her bodice tighter. "My inexperience—"

"Only because of my damned bad luck."

"What?" she asked, truly bewildered.

He laughed, partly in amusement at his predicament, partly in bitterness at what had been snatched from his hands. "I was trying to say that if my luck had been better, you wouldn't be quite so inexperienced now."

"Oh!" Her cheeks flamed hotly.

Someone fired a pistol downstairs. With a sigh, Pagan swung his legs over the side of the bed and got up. He stood before Rianne for a long breathless moment, then smoothed a tumbled lock of hair back from her face.

"You're not a loose woman, Rianne," he said. "But you're a passionate one."

"Passion should be between husband and wife."

He laughed, genuinely this time. "You *are* innocent."

Grasping her by the shoulders, he pulled her against him and claimed her lips in a kiss of pure possession. She tried to shake her head, to deny him, but he caught her jaw and held her still while he plundered her mouth. And even though she knew he was forcing a response from her, she had no power to withhold it from him; the now-familiar heat coursed through her veins, making her weak, making her wanton. With an effort of will, she forced it back long enough to tear herself free of him.

"Do you still refuse to admit your own passion?" he said, his smile triumphant and very self-satisfied.

Her temper flared at the sight of that smile. He thought it funny? She was devastated by her loss of control, her abandonment of upbringing, convention and common sense, and he thought it *amusing?* "I retract my apology," she said as haughtily as she could. "I'm sure I'm not the first . . . maiden you've seduced."

"No, you're not," he agreed, his voice silky. "But you're the most beautiful—and responsive—of the lot."

"You . . . you . . ." She couldn't think of anything bad enough to say.

"I wouldn't try a game of insults if I were you," he said. "That is another matter in which I have far more experience than you."

"Get out!"

"And something I'd rather not teach you." His smile broadened. "Whereas for the other—"

"Get out!" Truly furious now, she stamped her bare foot as hard as she could.

Pagan would have liked to continue this conversation, for she was nearly as luscious in anger as she'd been in passion. But a loud crash from downstairs moved him toward the door. Opening it, he paused in the doorway to look back at her. "We *will* talk of this further, Rianne."

Before she could answer, he was gone. For a moment she stood, hands clenched at her sides, then went to stand in front of the mirror. Now that he was gone, her anger cooled, leaving her tired and appalled at her own behavior. She stared at her reflection. It was as though another woman were looking out at her, a woman whose mouth was swollen from a man's kisses, whose eyes knew passion. She leaned forward to become better acquainted with the new Rianne Kierney. The one who had sought adventure so eagerly.

"Well, you got a bit more than you bargained for, didn't you?" she asked her reflection.

She turned away, absently tying the ribbons on her gown. This had truly been a day for revelations, not the least of which was her tempestuous response to Pagan's touch. How was she going to face the man tomorrow, knowing the liberties he'd taken? No, the liberties she'd *encouraged* him to take. Even here, alone as she was, her cheeks burned at the memory. Was she so desperate that she would grasp at physical desire as a substitute for true, honest love?

Then she straightened, her chin going up stubbornly. It was obvious that the Golden Bear was not an appropriate home either for herself or her father. There was too much temptation for them both. For Alastair, it was whiskey; for herself, it was Pagan Roark. Both were equally dangerous, both bore a price that was much too high to pay.

She began to pace the room, her nightgown swirling out around her swiftly moving feet. Her father needed her. He was old and sick, and Providence had sent her here just in time to help him. The decision-making was up to her; as Pagan had so succinctly put it, the whiskey did the talking—and thinking—for her father. First thing in the morning, they were leaving Henderson City to make a new life in a new home.

For his sake, and for hers.

Chapter Six

Rianne woke at dawn feeling fuzzy-headed and depressed. The Golden Bear was mercifully quiet. Perhaps she could get herself and her father packed, hire a wagon, and be out of Henderson City before Pagan woke. After the horrible day she'd had yesterday, surely luck owed her *something*.

She dressed in a brown wool traveling suit and white shirtwaist then pulled her hair back in a severe bun. A glance in the mirror reassured her that she was sufficiently prim and proper-looking. How different this Rianne was from the one who had looked back at her last night! With a sharp sigh of irritation, she turned her back on the mirror and the memory, and began packing her belongings.

A few minutes later she opened the door into the adjoining room, dropping her heavy suitcases just within the opening. Her father was lying on the bed, snoring. The blanket was pulled up to his chin. Just now, with his mouth laxly open and his hair sticking up around his head in thin wisps, he looked terribly frail and old. The sight only reinforced her decision to take him away from here.

"Good morning, Father," she said briskly.

"Mmmmmph. Go 'way."

"Not just now, Father. It's very important that I talk to you."

He rolled onto his side, putting his back to her, but Rianne wasn't about to be dissuaded. Marching around the bed so that he was facing her again, she said, "It's no use. You might as well wake up, for I'm going to plague you until you do."

"Have pity, Rianne."

She felt a rush of satisfaction; at least he recognized her this morning. "Father, we're leaving Henderson City this morning. I want you to get dressed while I pack your things."

His eyes opened. "Leaving?"

"Leaving," she affirmed. "Now."

"Ahhh, my head feels like it's going to explode." He pressed his fingertips against his temples. "Look, darling girl, couldn't we talk about this later?"

"No, Father."

"Please, Rianne. I'm a sick man."

His words triggered a memory from Wickersham. Countless times she'd watched drunken Mr. Jenks play this same game with his family. He had a headache, he was ill, or he had to see someone—the needs of his wife and children could be attended to later. But later he was drunk. And so the cycle continued day after day until his family stopped asking him for anything.

"Father, do get up and get dressed," she said. "I'll pack your things while you're doing that."

"Rianne, I can't leave."

"Of course you can, Father." Rianne began putting his few pitiful belongings into an even more pitiful carpet-bag. So little to show for a lifetime, she thought sadly. A few clothes, a tattered copy of Shelley's poetry, a pocket watch with a broken crystal was all her father possessed in the world. Her mouth thinned. Well, he had *her* now. She was going to see him well again, and happy.

76

She glanced over her shoulder at Alastair and was surprised to find that he hadn't moved. "Father, what's the matter? If you're worried about how we're going to live, don't worry about a thing. I've money enough to get us started somewhere."

He slid up to a sitting position, clutching the blankets to his chest. "Well, ahhh, there's a bit of a problem, sweetheart. You see, I owe Pagan some money. I couldn't possibly leave until I repay him."

"That's a problem that is easily fixed, Father. I'll just pay him what you owe, and—"

The outer door opened. Rianne whirled, the carpetbag still dangling from her right hand. Pagan stood in the opening. He was wearing dark blue trousers and a shirt that was open at the neck, revealing a triangle of dark chest hair. He looked devastatingly handsome and a bit dangerous. Her breath caught in her throat, and her heart felt as though it were going to beat its way right out of her chest.

God help her, the very sight of him set her to spinning, body, heart, and mind. She didn't want to feel like this! But he was staring at her as though he wanted to eat her alive, and every treacherous bone in her body responded in kind.

Then his gaze shifted to the carpetbag. A door seemed to shut down over his face. His ice-blue eyes took on that feral gleam she'd seen last night when he'd faced down a roomful of armed, drunken men. Now she could see why no one had challenged him; it was all she could do to keep her knees from quaking. Then his eyes changed again, becoming merely cynical, and she let out her breath in a sigh of relief.

"Going somewhere?" he asked.

"Yes." She was overly aware of the carpetbag in her hand, but didn't quite know what to do with it. Finally, she put it on the floor.

His voice was deceptively gentle. "Would you mind telling me where?"

"Ah . . . San Francisco." Truly, she hadn't thought where she was running *to,* only what—and who—she was running *from.*

"I see." He leaned his shoulder against the doorjamb and studied her, hiding his shock beneath a poker player's impassive face. And it had been a shock. He'd expected to have more time to convince her to stay—and last night had shown him just how pleasurable that convincing was going to be. His dreams had been full of Rianne Kierney, her beautiful, sultry voice, the smell of her skin, the feel of her in his arms, welcoming him, loving him. If he didn't have the reality, he'd be haunted the rest of his life. He didn't like what he was about to do, but she'd forced his hand. Whatever the cost, he had to keep her.

The long silence unnerved Rianne. Glancing at her father for reassurance, she saw that he'd fallen asleep again. He was snoring peacefully, oblivious to the tense scene. She wished she could escape so easily.

She squared her shoulders, determined to deal with the situation as gracefully as possible. There was no reason for her to feel guilty about leaving, or any reason why she should have to justify herself to Pagan Roark. He had no right to care whether or not she stayed. Perhaps he didn't; he lounged against the doorway, seeming as relaxed as a great, sleepy cat. But a glance at the taut line of his jaw made her realize that he was very displeased at finding her ready to leave. Very.

Deciding that it would be best to pretend that everything was normal, she placed the carpetbag beside her suitcase. It took an effort of will to keep her face serene as she turned back to Pagan. "I'd be most grateful if you would hire a wagon for me," she said as casually as she could manage.

78

"No," Pagan said, even more casually than she had.

"I see." She took a deep breath. "Well, I'll have to do it myself, then. Can you at least recommend someone trustworthy?"

"No, I will not."

Rianne didn't miss the fact that he said 'will not' instead of 'can not'. He wasn't even giving the pretense of being polite. Her eyes narrowed with annoyance. "Really, Pagan. There's no need to be discourteous."

"I'm the soul of courtesy," he said. "I'm just not going to hire a wagon. And neither are you." He strode into the room, closing the door behind him.

"You can't stop us from leaving." Despite her bold words, a thrill of fear shivered through her. He had closed that door with an air of forbidding finality.

Pagan smiled. "Yes, I can."

"This is ridiculous," she snapped, defiance flooding in with a rush.

"Your father owes me money. I'm afraid I can't just let him walk away from that debt."

Oh, the money! Rianne thought, feeling like a complete fool. She'd mistakenly supposed he wanted to keep her here because he desired her. What an idiot! She should have known better. He'd made it obvious last night that their . . . encounter hadn't been the great revelation for him that it had been for her.

"Well, if money is what you want, I'll pay you," she said, pique putting venom into her voice. Snatching up her reticule, she reached inside. "How much does he owe you?"

"Thirty thousand dollars."

She stared at him blankly, sure she hadn't heard correctly. "What did you say?"

"I said your father owes me thirty thousand dollars. I doubt you carry quite so much with you."

She swallowed convulsively. "He can pay you back a little at a time."

"Come now, Rianne. I know Alastair Kierney as well as anyone. He wants to pay me back — when he's sober. But the moment he sees a bottle of whiskey, all those good intentions are forgotten. If he walks out that door, so does my thirty thousand dollars."

"*I* will see to it that you get paid," she snapped.

His eyebrows went up. "Oh? How are you going to go about it?"

"I'll find work."

"What sort of work?" he asked.

"A governess—"

"A governess makes barely enough to live on, as does a seamstress. I expect to get paid before I reach my dotage, you know. Are you expecting an inheritance, perhaps?"

"No," she whispered. She found that she was crushing the reticule between her hands. With forced gentleness, she set it aside. "Just how did my father come to owe you thirty thousand dollars?"

"He made a wager and lost," Pagan said.

She shook her head. "I can't believe you would accept a bet that size from a penniless man."

"He wasn't penniless," Pagan said. "There were three other men at the table, sons of rich men from the East. Your father had phenomenal luck that night; he'd won just over thirty thousand dollars from those three. When it came down that last hand, he bet his cash and I bet the Golden Bear."

"But—"

"Let me finish," he said, holding his hand up. "I won that hand, of course. But he wasn't willing to accept it. 'Cut the deck', he said. 'Double or nothing'."

Rianne sighed. "So you did, and he lost."

"He lost." Actually, Pagan had taken the old man's

80

IOU without expecting to collect the money. Alastair's luck that night was the sort that only touches a man once in a lifetime. Alastair had insisted that Pagan take a half-share in his claim as security against the debt. Truly, he didn't expect to be repaid even now; the debt was only the means by which he would keep Rianne here.

"There has to be a way," she said fiercely. "I refuse to leave here without my father!"

"I'm sure we can come to some compromise," he said.

Her head came up in shocked horror. Surely he wasn't going to demand that she . . . Then he started laughing, and her horror turned to puzzled outrage. "Would you care to explain what you find so amusing?" she demanded.

"You should have seen your face," he gasped between chuckles. "Ahh, Rianne, you never cease to surprise me. That's what I find so refreshing about you." His mirth faded. "No, I am not going to demand your body, delectable as it is. When we make love, it will be because you *want* to."

Rianne clenched her hands into fists. 'When' the rogue had said! How arrogant to assume . . . Truly, he was despicable! "That will happen, Mr. Roark, when snakes learn to waltz."

"I thought we'd progressed to Pagan," he murmured.

"You were wrong."

Pagan's amusement went up a notch. What a delightful woman she was! So innocent and prim-looking, but possessing Lucifer's own temper and passion hot enough to sear a man's soul. Damn it to hell, he had to have her for his own. Rianne Kierney was too precious a prize to let slip away.

"What do you suggest we do about my father's debt?" Rianne asked.

Pagan sat down on the bed and stretched his long legs

81

out in front of him. "If you agree to stay here for a year and sing at the Golden Bear, I'll consider the debt paid."

Rianne felt the blood drain from her face. "You must be mad!"

"Where else could you make thirty thousand dollars in one year?"

"But . . . but *live* here in this . . . this . . ."

"Saloon?" he supplied.

"You can't be serious."

He smiled. "I am. Very."

Rianne whirled and stalked to the window. She stared out at the street below, seeing the mud, the shabby buildings, the rough-hewn men. A year, Pagan had said. A year of her life spent in this godforsaken place. A year living under the same roof with a man who, with a single look or touch, could tear her serenity to shreds. She wished she were more worldly; she was swimming in waters far too deep for her, and she had the feeling she was going to drown.

Without turning to look at Pagan, she asked, "And why, pray tell, are *my* services so valuable?"

"You can't be that naive, surely," Pagan replied. There was a hint of laughter in his voice that stiffened her back even more. "You're special, Rianne. You know it, I know it, and every one of those men who heard you sing last night knows it. Believe me, you're worth every cent of the thirty thousand dollars."

"And that is your sole motive for keeping me here?"

"Yes." *Liar!* he thought. But it was the only answer he could give lest he reveal just how strong and confusing his feelings were. To say 'I'm keeping you here because I don't know how to let you go' would make him vulnerable to her, and that he wouldn't do. He'd learned the hard way to keep his feelings to himself.

Rianne was glad her face was hidden from him. So, he'd made himself quite clear: she was a commodity to him, nothing more. He didn't care a whit for her feelings; she was just something to be used to make money for him. Astonishingly, she felt like crying. *You fool, you hardly know the man!* But she still felt as though something precious had been taken from her. Perhaps it had; her innocent trust in people's goodness was forever gone, blighted by his betrayal. If she were wise, she'd leave this sordid place, today, and put Pagan Roark out of her mind for good.

She turned to look at her father. He had slumped down in the bed, his chin resting on his chest. White hairs stubbled his lower face, making him look ill and disreputable. If she left, he would surely drink himself to death. Yes, he was weak. Yes, he had run away from his family and responsibilities. But he was her father, and she loved him. She was the only person who cared enough to try to save him from the bottle—and from himself. With a sinking feeling in the pit of her stomach, she realized that this was not a decision she could make based on wisdom. There was only her father, and her love for him.

Arms akimbo, she met Pagan's gaze levelly. "You have proof of this debt, I suppose?"

He nodded. "A note written in his own hand. Or you can ask him when he wakes up."

"He told me about it already. Just not the fact that it was thirty thousand dollars." She turned back to the window again. But she saw nothing; her gaze was turned inward. Last night Pagan had seemed so kind, so generous and understanding, so . . . loving. 'Trust me', he'd whispered to her in the heated pleasure of their desire. Fool that she was, she *had* trusted him. She'd believed his pretty compliments, allowed her good sense to be drowned in his beguiling kisses and roaming hands.

Now he sat there, the cold, hard businessman, and casually demanded a year of her life. For money. He knew she wouldn't leave her father. He *knew* her honor would compel her to take that enormous debt as her own. Tears stung her eyes, brought by the enormity of Pagan's betrayal. During those magical, fevered moments last night, she had been willing—no, God help her, she'd been eager—to give herself to him. She had let him see her softness and vulnerability, and he had taken it as weakness, using it to further his own ends.

God forgive me for what I'm about to do, she thought. Singing in a brothel! If her mother weren't already in her grave, this would have killed her.

"Very well, Mr. Roark. I accept your offer. I'll sing for you for a year."

Pagan smiled, watching the slim, straight line of her back. She was furious just now, but he'd find a way to change that. She belonged to him now. For a year, he amended silently. Surely that would be enough time to purge himself of this uncharacteristic obsession. "Good, we're agreed, then. It won't be too bad a burden, Rianne. A few hours' singing on Saturday nights, and the rest of your time free. There are many people who would envy you."

She glanced at him over her shoulder. There was a triumphant light in his eyes that infuriated her. He'd won, and he was gloating. Well, he may have won, but he wasn't going to get away unscathed. Turning to face him, she looked at him from beneath her lashes. "We should have our agreement in writing."

"That won't be necessary," he said. "Your word is good."

His voice was caressing, evoking memories and feelings she didn't want to admit existed. Using her fury as a lash, she drove them away. "I know. But yours is not," she said, lifting her chin disdainfully.

Pagan's good humor vanished. "Are you calling me a cheat?"

84

It was a challenge, and Rianne accepted it. "Yes, I'm calling you a cheat!"

"I see." Cold anger shafted through him. No one spoke to him like that, no one! He surged to his feet and strode toward her.

Rianne realized she'd gone too far. His eyes were slits of icy rage, and a muscle jumped in his tight-clenched jaw. But her own anger was burning high, and instead of retreating, she folded her arms over her chest and watched him come. "If you *dare* hit me—"

"I don't hit women," he growled, grasping her by the shoulders.

"No, you have other ways of dealing with them, don't you?" She tipped her head back and stared down her nose at him. "Now I understand what Felice meant when she told me you think all women are alike: they are things to be used—their feelings, their bodies, their honor, all manipulated for your own gain."

"Perhaps. But they've all enjoyed it."

"You . . . you cad!" With an inarticulate cry of fury, Rianne slapped him across the face.

Pagan's fingers flexed convulsively, and he pulled her up onto her tiptoes, unsure exactly what he wanted to do with her. But he realized that at this moment she was consumed by pure, unadulterated rage, and didn't give a damn about the consequences. His anger cooled, tempered by admiration at her audacity. He'd dealt with angry women, weeping women, manipulative women, but never one who affected him so strongly. Such fire and courage was rare, more precious than gold.

Rianne was appalled at what she'd done. She had never struck another person in her life, and had never expected to. But truly, he had pushed her beyond the bounds of control. She tried to pull away, but his grip was like iron. Then, slowly but deliberately, he pulled her against him, pressing her tightly against his body.

85

He was blatantly aroused, the thick line of his manhood branding her even through the layers of petticoats she wore.

She should have been disgusted. She should have screamed or pushed him away, or both. But she stood frozen, completely, utterly aware of the potent male promise of him. And it was not disgust she felt, but desire. That he could wring that response from her, even after what he'd done, was the most humiliating thing of all.

Stubborn pride gave her the strength to control her teetering emotions. "Take your hands from me," she snapped.

For a moment Pagan was tempted to force the issue; there was a flaring response in her honey-brown eyes that proved how deeply she'd been affected. But then common sense prevailed. She needed time to get used to the idea of staying here.

Reluctantly, he let her go. "I'm not interested in fighting with you, Rianne."

"Of course not," she said bitterly. *"You've* gotten what you wanted."

"Not yet," he said softly. "But I will."

Abruptly, he turned on his heel and walked out of the room. Rianne glared at the closed door, wishing there was something to throw at it. He'd gotten the last word, after all.

She went to retrieve the carpetbag. With shaking hands, she began unpacking her father's things and putting them back into the bureau, muttering a steady monologue under her breath.

"Arrogant, hateful man . . . how dare he speak to me . . . no respect for my feelings at all . . . Drat!" That as one of the bureau drawers stuck. She wrenched at it savagely. It came clear out of the bureau, landing on her foot with an impact that made her cry out in pain.

Alastair roused with a snort. "Whazza . . . Mmm, I seem to have drifted off there." Propping himself up on his elbow, he asked, "Is something wrong, Rianne? Are you hurt?"

"No, nothing's wrong. I just dropped the silly drawer on my foot," she said, knowing that she couldn't—mustn't—confide in him. She simply could not let him know that she'd pledged herself to a year's servitude because of him. Oh, no. She knew Kierney pride too well for that. It would destroy him, take every bit of self-respect he still had. Whatever the cost, he must not know the price she'd paid to stay with him.

He sat up to get a better look at what she was doing. "I thought you were leaving."

"I-I've changed my mind."

"Good."

Rianne went to sit on the edge of the bed. "It's more than just your debt to Pagan, isn't it? You really want to stay in Henderson City. Why?"

"Hand me that book," he said. When she obeyed, he slid a piece of paper out from between the pages. "This is my claim. There's gold there, I can smell it. If I could only work it properly, I know I'd strike big."

"But that's the answer!" she said excitedly. "You can give it to Mr. Roark in payment of your debt."

"No!" He clutched the deed to his chest protectively. After a moment he sighed and slipped it back into its hiding place. "Pagan already owns half of it. And right now, that's half of nothing. If I could only find the gold!"

There was a glitter in his eyes, almost as though he had a fever. Then Rianne realized he did: gold fever. He was chasing a will-o-the-wisp, mortgaging his future for a phantom.

Her thoughts must have shown on her face, for Alastair reached out to take her hands in his. "Rianne, darling, this is the only dream I have left. The gold is there, I can feel it in my bones. All I ask is a little time."

"Oh, Father," Rianne murmured, despair clenching her heart. Then she straightened. This dream might just be the way to pry her father away from the bottle. And time was something she *could* give him. "All right, we'll make a bargain. You say you need time; I'll give you a year. But during that year you must work the claim. If you don't strike gold, you'll give it up and come with me."

"To Oregon?"

"Not necessarily." *Oregon isn't nearly far enough from Pagan Roark,* she thought sourly. "Perhaps we ought to try Australia."

"Eh?" Alastair stared at her blankly.

"I was teasing, Father. Truly, the whole world is open to us. A great, new adventure. Why don't we wait until the year is up before deciding?"

He beamed at her. "Done! And maybe Australia wasn't such a bad idea at that—opals, you know."

"Opals!" She couldn't help but laugh. "Father, you're incorrigible!"

"I know."

They shook hands to seal the bargain. Rianne was pleased to see color come into his cheeks at last; perhaps some good would come of this situation after all.

Rising from her perch on the edge of the bed, she smoothed the creases from her dress. "I'd better go unpack my own things," she said.

"Rianne?"

"Yes, Father?"

"You were a sensation last night. All the men were begging for you to sing again. I hope you'll consider it."

"I . . ." She froze in the act of picking up her suitcase. "I'll be glad to."

"Good girl." He rubbed his hands together, like a small boy about to have something delightful. "I can't wait to tell Pagan. He'll be very pleased."

Rianne bent over the suitcase to hide her face from her father. *Damn* Pagan Roark, she thought. It was the first time in her life she'd said that word. It seemed to be a time for firsts. Her first kiss, her first profanity, her first journey into the world of betrayal.

Well, she was a quick learner, and this had been a very enlightening lesson. It was time that Pagan Roark experienced a first of his own: his first comeuppance.

Chapter Seven

Rianne finished unpacking, then sat on the edge of her bed to try to decide what to do next. She was accustomed to being busy; her mother believed strongly that work built a person's character. So Rianne learned to dust and cook and sew. Those skills had stood her in good stead when Grandfather Woodward died, leaving more debts than legacy, and the servants had been let go.

But here she was, committed to this benighted corner of the world, with nothing to do but twiddle her thumbs until next Saturday night.

"This isn't going to do," she said to herself. "Not at all. Let's just go downstairs, Rianne my girl, and see what's for breakfast."

She went to the doorway of the adjoining room to see if her father had awakened yet. He had pulled the blanket over his head to avoid the sunlight streaming into the room, and was snoring loudly and happily in his dark cocoon.

With a sigh, she went downstairs alone. She found the bartender and another man cleaning the night's mess from the saloon, righting overturned tables, picking up pieces of shattered chairs, and sweeping the broken glass that lay everywhere.

"Hello, Miss Kierney," the bartender said, leaning on his broom handle for a moment. He was short and stout, with dark brown eyes and a sheeps-coat of blond curls covering his scalp. "I'm the barkeep, John Ferguson. This is Stu Colher. He helps me out sometimes."

The other man was ferret-slim, ferret-quick, with brown hair and a thick red beard. He appraised Rianne from the corners of his eyes.

Rianne acknowledged the introductions with a nod. "Pleased to meet you both."

"Pagan said I was to get you anything you needed," John said.

Don't you dare ask! she told herself. But her mouth opened, unbidden. "Isn't he here?"

John shook his head. "Went to Ogilvie for a couple of days."

Rianne felt oddly deflated. She didn't understand why; the last person she wanted to see was Pagan Roark. But then, so much had been happening so fast that there wasn't much she understood any more, least of all her feelings for Pagan Roark.

"What can I do for you?" John asked, breaking into her thoughts.

"I'd like something to eat. I don't mind fixing it myself, if you would just direct me to the kitchen."

"Right through that door," he said, thrusting his thumb at a curtained doorway behind the bar. "It ain't much; we all usually eat whatever comes to hand."

"I'll do fine," she said, turning away. "Thank you."

Suddenly she glimpsed a man's motionless form huddled on the floor at the far end of the bar. He looked completely limp, almost as though he were . . . "Mr. Ferguson!" she called in a harsh whisper. "That man! Is he—"

"Oh, yeah. That's Scut Waller. Don't worry about him; he's just drunk, Miss Kierney."

"Scut?" she repeated. "I'm unfamiliar with that name. Is it a common one here?"

"Well, ah, not really. It's a sort of nickname," the bartender said.

Alerted by a strange note in his voice, Rianne glanced from one man to the other. Stu Colher turned away hurriedly. Rianne fixed her gaze on John Ferguson. "And this nickname—does it have a particular meaning?" she asked.

"Well, ah, I don't rightly know. Why don't you ask Pagan when he gets back?"

"Very well, I will." She headed toward the kitchen, her shoes crunching on broken glass.

Parting the draperies, she stepped into the dark room beyond. Truly, Mr. Ferguson hadn't exaggerated when he'd said it wasn't much. Light came from a tiny cobweb-shrouded window and a single oil lantern that hung from the center of the ceiling. A water pump sat in one corner, a battered bucket beneath it, and beside it was a very dirty cast iron stove. On the opposite wall were a table and benches that needed a good scrubbing.

"Ahh, I see I won't have to twiddle my thumbs after all," she said, pushing her sleeves up as high as they would go. "And once it's clean, I'll see about cooking something decent. I don't intend to be eating rock-hard tinned biscuits and moldy cheese for the next year."

She set to work with a will, scrubbing everything with strong lye soap until it shone. Upon checking the provisions, she found the kitchen overstocked with flour, beans, and tinned peaches, and out of almost everything else. She did find the makings for biscuits, and soon had a large batch cooking.

As the delicious aroma of baking biscuits began to permeate the room, she went out to the front to find Mr. Ferguson. He had finished sweeping, and was in the process of wiping off the tabletops.

"Mr. Ferguson, is there somewhere in town where I might purchase some supplies?"

"There's Pearey's General Store, down the street," he said. "You want something, you tell me and I'll get it. Pagan said you was to have anything you wanted."

"Very well." She took a deep breath. "We need potatoes and rice, carrots or whatever fresh vegetables are available—"

"Nothing fresh."

"Tinned, then. I'll want apples and lard, corn meal and baking powder and eggs. Some lamb perhaps—"

"Salt beef, more likely. Or ham."

"Both, please." She pushed a stray lock of hair back from her face. "What about chicken?"

"For chicken and dumplings, maybe?"

"I make excellent dumplings. Mr. Ferguson."

He grinned. "I'll see what I can find."

"Buttermilk . . ." Seeing his mouth open, she raised her finger and said, "Tinned milk will be fine."

"Yes, ma'am."

A door opened and closed upstairs, and a female voice called, "Are those fresh *biscuits* I smell? Oh, Lord, I'm starving! . . . and somebody's cooking biscuits."

John looked at Rianne beseechingly. "Couldn't I wait until after the biscuits are done afore going? Them girls are going to come down here like a flock of Harpies, and there'll be nothing left but crumbs."

Rianne smiled. "Of course."

In a few minutes, all five of the Golden Bear's resident 'ladies' had gathered in the kitchen. Rianne already knew Marie, and John Ferguson introduced the others: Willa Garvey, dark and stolid and slow-moving; Alva Drewett, a tiny woman with a sharp, delicate face; blonde, blue-eyed Jewell Sampson, whose nasal twang revealed her Kansas origin; and Kate Aguelard, square and plain, but who possessed beautiful green eyes.

"Well, now that you all know each other, I'll get on to

93

the store," John said, scooping four biscuits into his hands. "You ladies have fun now."

A moment later he was gone. Rianne and the others stood a bit awkwardly, unsure of what to say. Finally Rianne smiled and said, "Why don't I play hostess, although I know I have far less right than any of you."

Marie laughed, her gold tooth glinting in the light. "You go right ahead, Miss Kierney. None of us can tell hostessing from the back end of a mule."

It wasn't as shocking as Rianne would have expected; in fact, she didn't blush at all. Gracefully, she indicated the table with her outstretched arm. "Please, won't you sit down, ladies?"

"Thankee kindly," replied Jewell, taking a place at the table. The rest followed suit.

Rianne put a bowl of biscuits on the table, then sat in the empty place beside Marie. "There isn't any butter, but I did find some molasses."

"Sounds jest fine," Marie said, reaching for a biscuit. "It was real nice of you to fix these for us."

Her action was a cue for the others; in what seemed to be mere moments to Rianne's startled eyes, all but three of the biscuits were gone. Then she realized that everyone was looking at her expectantly. They'd saved these for her.

"Well, go on, Miz Kierney," Jewell prompted, thumping the jug of molasses down in front of Rianne. "You cooked 'em. Might as well eat a few."

"Why, thank you," Rianne said. "And please, just call me Rianne. After all, we're going to be working to-gether—"

"Not quite, honey," Alva broke in.

"Oh!" This time Rianne did blush.

"Now ain't that Pagan something, getting a real lady to sing in a place like this?" Marie asked. "Now, don't you worry about stayin' here, Rianne honey. You take it from me, there ain't a nicer man to work for."

Rianne looked around the table, seeing agreement on every woman's face. They truly seemed to like Pagan. Such an enigmatic man, she thought. One moment kind and compassionate, the next sardonic and demanding. And definitely not the sort of man who would go around recruiting girls for his brothel.

"May I ask you ladies a few questions?" she asked.

Willa laughed. "After those biscuits, you can ask anything you like."

Rianne hesitated, unsure how to phrase her next question. Finally she decided to be blunt. "How did you come to work for Mr. Roark?"

"We didn't, not exactly," Jewell said. "Pagan kind of inherited us."

"You see," Alva put in, "this place was built by old Sam Fournier. He bought us from Madam Vougeot's in San Francisco and brought us here."

"He bought you?" Rianne cried in horror. "Surely that isn't legal!"

"Maybe not legal, but it happens all the time. Nobody cares about wh . . . girls like us," Marie said. "Old Sam weren't a nice man. Not nice at all. He made us work all the time and kept most of the money for hisself. We was real happy when Pagan won the Golden Bear and decided to make a go of it. He said he didn't want to run girls, that wasn't his kind of business. But when we asked to stay, he said all right as long as we run ourselves. So, you see, we get to keep everythin' we make except for what we pay in room and board."

"Hell, none of us had anywhere to go, even if'n we wanted to," Alva said. "Whoring's the only thing I know how to do, and if'n I din't work here, I'd have to go down the street to the Nugget Saloon. And I ain't sure Lowell Mason is any better than old Sam."

"Worse," Kate interjected. "Remember Lou?"

The other women nodded. Kate turned to look at Rianne and continued, "Lou Orwell was a pretty red-haired gal from Texas who worked for Lowell. She got 'caught'—that means she got with child, Miss Kierney. It were January when she couldn't work no more, but Lowell kicked her out in the snow like a dog."

"Worse'n a dog," Jewell said. "Folks keep their dogs inside when it's cold enough to freeze a body's lungs by breathin'."

"Good heavens!" Rianne gasped. "What happened to her?"

"Pagan took her in," Kate said. "When spring thaw set in, he sent her back to her people in Texas."

Rianne blinked back tears. These poor women! "What about the rest of you? Don't you have family, homes somewhere else?"

Alva shrugged. "No'm. I'm jest grateful that Pagan lets me stay here for next to nothin'. *He* says I should save my money so I kin make a new start somewhere, but I don't think that'll work, not fer me. As soon as people find out what I've been, and they always do, I'm finished. No, I'll jest keep workin' for Pagan as long as he'll have me."

Rianne was confused by this new aspect of Pagan Roark. He'd helped these women, given them a haven and hope when everyone else had turned against them. Her own experience with him had been very different. But then, money had been involved, and one thing was certain: Pagan was a man who knew about money.

"And what I like best about Pagan is he don't . . ." Alva hesitated, evidently searching for the right words, "Well, he don't make no demands on us. If you know what I mean."

Rianne blushed again; she knew what Alva meant. To her surprise and discomfort, that news sent a wave of relief washing through her. There was no reason she should care what Pagan did, or with whom. After all, she was only here to discharge her obligation.

"Not that I'd *mind*," Marie said. "He's a fine man, so handsome and all. And ever'body knows he's a man who's goin' to make it big someday. Hoo-ee, I'd be as happy as a 'coon in a cornfield if he'd take a look at me."

The conversation was quickly getting out of hand, but Rianne was at a loss as to how to redirect it. Perhaps she should blurt out something about the weather . . .

Willa Garvey spoke for the first time. "Well, you can jest cool off them drawers, Marie Bell. You ain't his kind a-tall. Pagan's got book-larnin' and everything, and he likes his women fancy." Having delivered that startling announcement, she lapsed back into silence.

Marie laughed and poked Kate in the ribs with her elbow. "I could try real hard to be fancy."

Rianne wavered between curiosity and good manners. After a moment, curiosity won. "What, exactly, do you mean by 'fancy'?"

"Showy-like," Alva said. "Why, I seed a picture of his wife—"

"Wife?" Rianne echoed, completely dumfounded.

"Former wife," Alva corrected. "She was somethin' beautiful, yellow hair and a figure you'd kill for, and a smile you could cut yourself on."

Rianne's curiosity was flaring white-hot. "Former wife, you said. Did she die?"

Alva shook her head. "Heard tell she lit out about five years ago. Just took off. He got a paper a couple of years ago from a lawyer tellin' him she divorced him. But I tell you, he's one hard man; after readin' that letter, he laid it aside as though it didn't bother him a-tall."

Rianne sat back in her chair, astounded by what she

97

had learned. A wife—Mrs. Pagan Roark. Rianne tried to imagine a beautiful blonde with a smile you could cut yourself on, and failed completely. The thought of Pagan married to another woman was most distasteful to her, and the fact that it bothered her so much was even more disturbing. She shouldn't care about him at all. And yet the feeling was there, nagging like a sore tooth.

Pushing those treacherous feelings aside sternly, she held her chin high. She'd learn to control these unfortunate feelings. She had to. For the next year she had to remember one thing: it was money, not a woman—any woman—that was most important to him.

That resolve was easier to make than to keep, however, as two, then three days passed without a sign of Pagan. Rianne couldn't repress the troublesome thought that he must certainly be having a good time in Ogilvie. Perhaps he had a mistress there. Strangely, the thought of a mistress bothered her less than the thought of a wife. Whatever the blonde woman's faults had been, at one time Pagan had loved her enough to marry her. Could a man, any man, completely forget feelings that strong? It was the wife who had severed the marriage, not Pagan. Perhaps he still loved the woman, whether he admitted it or not.

This can't be jealousy, she told herself sternly. If only she could believe it. Somehow, Pagan Roark had managed to take over her thoughts, even her dreams.

Thursday dawned grey and dripping, a good match for her spirits. Rianne pulled her covers up over her head and tried to go back to sleep, but the rain beat a steady tattoo on her window that seemed to whisper Pagan's name to her.

"Idiot," she chided herself. "It's time you made yourself useful instead of lying abed like some wilting flower."

She tied a kerchief over her hair and went downstairs.

Yesterday she'd discovered the saloon's storeroom, stacked high with kegs and crates—enough liquor to float the entire Territory, in her opinion. Everything was dusty and full of cobwebs, and nagged at her terribly. So she gathered a bucket of water, lye soap and an armload of rags, and began setting things to rights.

John Ferguson appeared in the doorway. "What the . . . Oh, it's you, Miss Kierney. What are you doing?"

"Exactly what it looks like I'm doing," she retorted. "This is a disgrace! When was the last time someone cleaned in here? Years?"

"Uh . . . I don't rightly remember."

"Well, it's about time. Past time. I'm surprised you haven't poisoned one of your patrons by now."

He shifted from foot to foot, then said, "Miss Kierney, I don't think Pagan would want you to be doing this."

"Nonsense. Mr. Roark doesn't care what I do as long as I sing when I'm supposed to. And if I want to clean this room, I will."

"But—"

"Mr. Ferguson." Pushing a stray lock of hair back from her face with the back of her hand, she dipped her rag into the soapy water and wrung it out. "If you've nothing to do, I'll be happy to find something—"

"No, ma'am!" he said hastily. "I've got plenty of things to do." He backed up as he spoke, then turned and scuttled away.

Rianne let her breath out in a sigh of exasperation. Judging from the bewildered look on John's face, it was obvious he'd never noticed the dirt. *Men!* she thought as she went to her knees and began scrubbing the floor.

Actually, this wasn't really work. She enjoyed cleaning, and even found it relaxing. It had been one of the few ways she'd had of pleasing her mother. 'Cleanliness is next to Godliness' had been one of Leonora's favorite maxims. Rianne, ever eager to win her mother's approval, had come to enjoy this task. Now, the familiar tasks served to keep her from dwelling overmuch on Pagan Roark.

So, hidden away in the dusty little storeroom, she scrubbed and sang until the dreary day didn't seem quite so grey, and her own mood brightened with it.

It was afternoon when Pagan stopped the laden wagon in front of the Golden Bear. John Ferguson came out to meet him, and Pagan tossed the reins to him before jumping down to the ground.

"Is everything all right, John?" he asked.

"Just fine."

Pagan was distracted by the faint sound of singing. "Go ahead and start unloading, John. I'll be out in a few minutes to help with the heavy things."

He turned on his heel and went inside, irresistibly drawn by the sound of that glorious voice. *Siren's song,* he thought wryly, pulling him away from his duties. Following the thread of music, he made his way to the storeroom.

So, he'd found her at last. Rianne was on her hands and knees scrubbing the floor. She was singing "Onward Christian Soldiers," moving her brush in time to the music. Her back was to him, and he had a most delightful view of her derriere.

Then she stopped singing in mid-word. Sitting back on her heels, she put her hands on the small of her back and arched into a stretch. The sight brought Pagan's brows down in a black frown. As a child, he'd seen his mother make the same gesture many, many times. It brought back memories he'd rather leave untapped: a widow working as a common charwoman to feed her family, her early death from overwork and finally, the placing of her four sons in an orphanage. He rejected the memory savagely. He'd learned the pain in remembering such things, and the futility of it. What was past was past, and the only peace lay in living in the present.

Which brought him back to the unpleasant notion of Rianne scrubbing floors. It shouldn't bother him. But it did. It rode him like razor spurs, and he wasn't about to tolerate it. She should be wearing silks and satin and the finest lace, not kneeling on rough boards with dirty water soaking into her skirt. Unable to stand and watch any longer, he strode into the room to grasp her by the shoulders and lift her to her feet.

"What do you think you're doing?" he growled.

"Oh!" Rianne gasped in surprise, then stiffened as she realized that it was Pagan who had grabbed her so forcefully. He was in a strange, almost savage mood; his eyes glittered with anger, and his broad chest was rising and falling swiftly with his breathing.

For a moment she quailed before the intensity of his gaze, then squared her shoulders in defiance. She'd done nothing wrong, and she wasn't about to justify herself to Pagan Roark of all people. "Is this the way you greet all your employees?" she asked.

"Who told you to do this?" he demanded, ignoring her comment.

"No one. I just like to keep busy, if you must know," she said, irritated at his proprietary manner. Who did he think he was—traipsing in here like this, acting as though he owned her, when he'd been away all week doing God knows what with God knows who? Truly, he was an infuriating man.

"Find another way," he said.

She tilted her head back to look at him, her gaze unwavering. Although she would have preferred that he let go of her arms, she knew better than to try to shake

101

him off. "My obligation to you extends only to Saturday nights. Apart from those times, I'll do as I please."

"I think you were put on earth to bedevil me."

"Don't be ridiculous. Need I remind you that you're the one who burst in here giving orders and making accusations? If I'm bedeviling you, it's your own fault!"

It was the truth, but knowing it only fed the fire of his growing temper. All during the tedious journey from Ogilvie he'd imagined seeing joy on her face, warmth in those lovely honey-brown eyes of hers. But damn it, seeing her scrubbing the floor like that had jarred him badly. He was off-balance, his emotions sliding out from under his control.

"I pay you to sing, not scrub like a charwoman," he said. "If I catch you doing it again, I'll turn you over my knee."

Rianne's eyes narrowed. "The lord and master has spoken, and everyone must obey?"

"Yes."

"Shall I cower now?" she asked, her voice dripping with icy disdain.

Pagan's eyebrows went up. The thought of Rianne cowering—to him or to anyone—was so farfetched as to be amusing. His bad humor evaporated as quickly as it had come. What a completely unique and refreshing woman she was! "You wouldn't bend for the Queen herself, would you?"

"Not if she demanded it as rudely as you did."

"Touché." The corners of his mouth turned up slightly. "And what if I asked nicely?"

Rianne forced herself to resist the beguiling note in his voice and the bold laughter in his eyes. "I'm not the kind of woman who can drape herself over a sofa and eat bonbons all day."

At that moment, Pagan could think of many things for her to do, and all of them in his arms. But, since he knew she'd slap his face if he voiced his thoughts, he merely said, "I'll try to think of something besides scrubbing to keep you occupied."

"I think I'm capable of finding my own occupation, Mr. Roark."

A bit prickly for a Siren, Pagan thought. Still, he was inordinately glad to be back in her company again. "Are you happy to see me?"

"Certainly not." Rianne was disturbed by the unexpected turn the conversation had taken. It was a dangerous turn, made even more so by the isolation of the secluded little room. Even the drumming sound of the rain on the roof was somehow intimate, drawing privacy around the storeroom like a thick, warm cloak. It was obvious that Pagan felt it, too, for the clean-edged planes of his face tightened, and warmth rose in his eyes.

"I'm . . . I'm a mess," she said. "I'd better run upstairs and change."

"Don't go," Pagan murmured, tightening his grip on her arms. She stood stiffly between his hands, her arms held tightly against her sides. It was his nearness that was making her nervous, he realized. Interesting. Very interesting. He slid his hands down her arms, then shifted his grip to her waist.

To his surprise, he discovered that she wasn't wearing a corset; his fingers encountered only sweet, soft curves beneath her dress. It was like plucking a rose, expecting thorns but finding the scented blossom completely unprotected. He wasn't quite sure what *her* reaction was, but his was instantaneous and powerful.

"Did you miss me?" he asked again.

"No."

"No?" He put subtle pressure on her waist, making her come forward a step. "Are you sure?"

He's doing it again! Rianne thought. *He's wrapping*

103

me up with that smile, those eyes that could shatter a heart of stone. And you're a fool for letting him get away with it! "Let go of me," she hissed, letting the intensity of her voice take the place of volume.

"When you've answered my question," he said.

She took a deep breath, thoroughly annoyed both with him and with herself for allowing him to affect her so deeply. Pinning him with her most forbidding stare, she said, "I am absolutely, positively, completely and utterly certain that I did not miss you in any way, Mr. Roark. Now . . ." she broke off as he started laughing. "What's so amusing?" she demanded.

"You're the picture of offended dignity, my lovely Rianne. Such a look could freeze the blood in a man's veins."

"Dare I hope it had that effect on you?"

"I said *could.*" His voice dropped, becoming velvet-smooth. "If the man were less determined—and less interested."

"You're only interested in your thirty thousand dollars," she said.

"Ah, there's where you've misjudged me."

"I don't think so."

"Ah, Rianne, you're a stubborn, stubborn woman." He let go of her waist, but instead of turning her loose, he turned her around and tucked her left hand into the crook of his arm. "Let's go find something to eat."

She resisted his subtle pull. "There's a pot of chicken and dumplings cooking right now—"

"You've been cooking, too?" he groaned.

"—which will be ready about the time I finish cleaning this floor."

"If you push me one inch farther, I'll pick you up and carry you out of this room," he said in a pleasant tone that didn't quite mask his annoyance.

Rianne knew it was no idle threat; his eyes looked

frosty, and his jaw was set in hard, aggressive lines. Although she silently called herself a coward, she didn't dare force the issue.

"Very well," she said. "I'll leave the dratted floor. Now let go of me and let me go upstairs!"

To her surprise, he allowed her to pull her hand from his arm. She glanced up at him, then stiffened as she realized just how pleased he was with himself. Although she'd planned to walk away with her dignity intact, she had to puncture that smug self-satisfaction.

"The only reason I concede this point," she said through clenched teeth, "is because you're bigger and stronger than I am and completely without scruples. *Not* because you've gained any sway over me at all."

Without giving him a chance to answer, she turned her back on him and marched upstairs.

Chapter Eight

Saturday night came all too soon. Rianne didn't want to sing, especially for Pagan Roark. She dressed with great care, encasing herself in her stoutest corset and a stiff, taffeta-lined petticoat. Her dress was ivory slipper satin, starkly unadorned except for a thin band of blue ribbon at the hem and on the wide sleeves. The neckline was uncomfortably high, the thin lace border actually touching her chin.

Her mother had made this dress, and Rianne had always hated it. Tonight, though, it was perfect; she had the feeling Pagan would hate it, too.

She pulled her hair back tightly, controlling the thick, wavy mass in an iron-hard bun, then donned white, wrist-length gloves. Stepping back from the mirror, she regarded her reflection critically. She felt—and looked—as though she were encased in a suit of armor. Good. During the past few days, she had managed to avoid being alone with Pagan. So far, he had let her get away with it. But she knew his patience would come to an end.

A muffled shout from downstairs pulled her thoughts to the coming performance. She was as nervous about singing as she'd been that first time, perhaps even more so because tonight she had no choice. With a sigh of exasperation, she threw her brush down onto the bureau.

If only she could go back in time and start over.

She'd give much to be able to correct the mistakes she'd made since she'd been here, the first of which was offering to sing. The second, and most disastrous, was kissing Pagan Roark.

But she *had* sung. She *had* kissed him. And in doing so, she had ended up here, bound to a place she liked far too little, and to a man who threatened her serenity far too much.

Someone knocked softly at the outer door. *That must be Father, come to take me downstairs,* she thought. She had made him promise to escort her downstairs.

After taking one last look at herself in the mirror, she opened the door. But instead of her father, she found Pagan standing in the hall. Her back stiffened.

"Hello, Rianne," he said.

She hadn't seen him since yesterday, when she'd left him standing in the storeroom. But he still hadn't let her alone; somehow; even absent, he managed to dominate her thoughts, invade her dreams, and shatter her peace of mind. Her heartbeat accelerated as his gaze traveled over her boldly, leisurely.

Raising her chin defiantly, she told herself that it was anger that made her heart race so.

"Aren't you going to invite me in?" he asked.

"I wasn't planning to."

"I'm glad you changed your mind." He strode forward, stopping a scant foot in front of her.

Rianne took a step backward to put some distance between them. To make certain he realized that she had moved because of antipathy and not fear, she folded her arms over her chest and glared at him challengingly.

He grinned disarmingly, evidently not getting the message. "You're especially lovely tonight, Rianne."

"You *like* my dress?" she asked, surprise pulling the words out of her unbidden.

"The dress is an abomination." He walked slowly

107

around her, studying her from every angle. "As you very well know. But then I'm talking about the woman, not the clothes."

Seeing the heated appreciation in his eyes, Rianne knew he was telling the truth. When he looked at her, it was as though the layers of clothes were being stripped away, leaving her naked before him. She could almost feel his gaze against her skin like a physical touch. Even now, when she should hate him—did hate him—she couldn't control her own treacherous responses to him.

Irritated by her own weakness, she turned on her heel and stalked back to the bureau. "What do you want?"

Pagan's smile broadened. There were several possible answers to her questions, most of which she wouldn't want to hear. So he merely said, "I've come to escort you downstairs."

"Don't bother."

"It's no bother," he said, a faintly sardonic smile curving his mouth upward.

"I've promised Father I'd go down with him."

"Yes, I know," Pagan agreed. "But I happened to have a job for him to do. Since he was occupied, I decided to come for you myself."

He'd done it deliberately, she knew. Oh, he was an arrogant man! Fuming, she smoothed her hair with trembling hands.

"If you pull your hair back any tighter, it's going to fall out," he said, moving behind her so that he could look at her reflection over her shoulder. "And that would be a shame."

Their gazes met in the mirror, hers wary and defiant, his appreciative. Despite her annoyance, Rianne couldn't stop looking at him; his bold, rugged handsomeness, the straight nose and strong jaw, the thick black hair that made his eyes look like crystal-ice would haunt her memory forever. Even after she left Henderson City, she had the feeling that every man she met would be held up to this ideal—and found wanting.

Afraid of the feelings he roused in her, she tried to look away. But her gaze was held inexorably, like a bird trapped in a silken net. Caught. Captive. Bound by a code of honor he understood only enough to use against her. And still her body reacted to his nearness, all her senses seeming to come alive in his presence. She didn't want to feel this way.

"You're standing too close," she said.

"Am I?"

"Yes."

He took another step forward. She swallowed convulsively; he was so close now that if she leaned back, she would come into contact with his chest. In the mirror, his broad, black-clad shoulders loomed behind her, a sensual, hard-edged shadow in contrast to her white dress.

"Are you frightened of me?" he asked softly, his voice as intimate as a kiss.

She shook her head, rejecting both the idea and the intimacy. "Of course not." It wasn't true; he *did* frighten her, or at least her instinctive reactions to him did.

"Then you shouldn't mind if I stand here," he said. "I'm just looking at you, after all."

"Inspecting the merchandise?"

He cocked his head to one side. "Do you think of yourself as such?"

"Shouldn't I?"

"No." He lifted his hands, intending to grasp her by the shoulders, but changed his mind. He needed to go slowly, to give her time to forgive him for what he'd done. "I've learned that there are things in this world that a man can cherish for a time, but never keep."

"Love?" she asked without thinking, then closed her eyes, horrified that she'd said such a thing. And to *him,* of all people!

"Love is the most elusive of all," he said. "But also the most precious."

His answer astonished her; she'd expected some light, teasing reply or pretty compliment, but never that. Her heart began beating rapidly, a wild fluttering that made her feel warm all over. At least she hoped it was her heart, and not the man standing so close behind her. "Perhaps it isn't love that is elusive, but you."

He smiled. "Now that, lovely Rianne, is definitely a matter of opinion. Perhaps I haven't been elusive, just lucky."

His sardonic words dispelled her short-lived illusion like smoke. Strangely, it was disappointment, not anger, that made a hard knot in her stomach. This conversation might have been very different. If she could only establish some sort of communication with him, she might be able to understand this confusing man's nature, some idea of how to deal with him, and with her feelings toward him. They might even have talked about his wife and his marriage. But he had slipped away from her, and the moment had passed.

And the most confusing thing of all was why she'd brought up the subject of love in the first place. The word had slipped from her without the bidding of her mind. Love!

"I bought you something in Ogilvie," he said, pulling a velvet box from his pocket.

She kept her hands at her sides. "Thank you, but I don't think—"

"Don't say anything until you've seen it," he said.

He opened the box and held it so she could see its contents. Inside was a lovely garnet brooch in the shape of a flower. It was beautiful, completely inappropriate, and roused her temper all over again.

"I can't accept this," she said, her voice tight.

"Why not?"

110

"It's not proper."

"The conventions don't matter here."

She frowned. "Of course they do."

"Why do you care what anyone thinks? If you like the brooch, take it, and damn what they say."

"No, thank you." To her horror, she heard herself say, "I'm sure you know *someone* who will be delighted to have it."

"Ah, I think tongues have been wagging," he said, a smile curving his mouth upward. "You shouldn't listen to gossip, Rianne."

"Well, you shouldn't offer a lady a gift like that brooch, and it didn't stop you."

Pagan's scowl disappeared, and amusement began to light his eyes. "Does the idea of me having a mistress bother you?" he murmured.

"Certainly not." Folding her arms over her chest, she added, "I don't know why I let you get me into such a ridiculous conversation in the first place."

"It's my charm," he said, his grin widening.

"Charm is not precisely the word I would use."

"What, then?"

"Gall, Mr. Roark. Sheer gall."

"You wound me." Pagan noticed that a single curl had come loose from her tightly wound bun. It was a striking touch, both innocent and sensual, revealing the passionate woman that was hidden beneath the stiff, unbecoming dress. He wanted to release that woman, to wrap himself in her fire once again.

Watching her in the mirror, he reached up with one finger to tease the tendril of fine hair. When she didn't react, he ran his fingertip along the side of her neck and up to her ear, where he lightly traced the delicate seashell shape. *Ah, there it is!* he thought triumphantly as her face tautened. Her eyelids lowered slightly, and awakening desire sparked in the honey-warm depths of

111

her eyes. Response, sweet and pure. The sight of it made his heart contract with tenderness for her.

"In this light, your hair looks like it's been dusted with gold," he murmured.

Rianne forced herself to ignore the seductive spell he was weaving around her. She'd already learned how dangerous these feelings were. And so had he.

"You needn't spin your pretty tales on my account, Mr. Roark. I know my hair is plain brown, and so are my eyes."

"Nothing about you is plain," he said, bending closer.

She slid away from him, needing space to regain her emotional balance. How had he managed to twist her feelings so easily? In the space of a few minutes she'd gone from anger—anger she had every right to feel—to desire. He was like some elemental force, calling up the most powerful, primal emotions within her. She couldn't allow it. Somehow, she had to find a way to control her reactions. Until then, she would just have to learn to avoid the situations that put her in danger. Like this one.

"Shall we go?" she asked.

"I'm yours to command," he said, willing to leave things as they were for the moment. As long as he knew he could evoke that response from her, he could wait. With a half-mocking bow, he offered his arm.

Rianne knew that refusing to touch him would be an admission of how profoundly he affected her. Petty though it be, she was not about to give him that satisfaction. So she laid her hand on his proffered arm and let him lead her downstairs, hoping that her face was not revealing how aware she was of the lean muscles beneath her palm.

The saloon was packed with men, several deep at the long bar. The liquor was flowing freely and, from the look of the miners, had been for quite a while. Money flowed as freely as the whiskey.

"Is it always like this?" she asked, pulling Pagan to a halt just outside the door.

He shook his head. "They're here to see you."

For the first time, Rianne realized just how desperate these men were for a touch of softness, a breath of the civilization they'd left behind. Even a faded memory of love and family was an irresistible lure to a lonely person. She knew the power of that loneliness well, for it had brought her halfway around the world to try to recapture that remembered warmth.

And what was the best way to evoke such memories, even in these hard adventurers? Why, music. A song, and a Songbird. No wonder Pagan had fought so hard to keep her here; good businessman that he was, he'd known what a valuable commodity she was.

A bellow rose out of the din. Rianne recognized Francois Gruillot's bull-tones.

"Did I not tell you she would sing again?" he roared, pointing one thick finger in her direction. "The *belle oiseau-chanteuse*. Our Songbird is back!"

"What did he call me?" Rianne asked.

"He's been telling everyone about the beautiful Songbird. Every mining camp within a fifty mile radius has been buzzing with the news."

"Good heavens!" she whispered in dismay.

Pagan chuckled. "Heaven has nothing to do with it. But it *is* good for business."

He led her into the room as though she were royalty, the pride evident in his face. As they reached the piano, Alastair squeezed through the throng at the bar and came to take her hands in his.

"Hello, darling girl," the old man said. "I hope you're ready to sing your heart out; they're rarin' to go tonight."

"I'll do my best, Father," she said.

Pagan left her there beside the piano and went to

113

stand across the room, where he could watch her and the crowd at the same time. With so many men crammed cheek-by-jowl, the saloon was like a powder keg. One spark, and the whole place would go up. The air was thick with the smell of the oil lanterns and sweat and whiskey. Pagan grimaced. This was no place for Rianne. But damn it, he'd used the only thing he could to hold her, and now he was stuck.

He scanned the crowd for potential troublemakers, hoping to head off a fight before it got full-blown. Then Rianne began to sing. Silence, the most precious applause of all, fell over the crowd as the men were submerged beneath the wonder of her voice. Pagan shook his head admiringly. These were some of the roughest, toughest, most unruly men on the face of the earth, but for this one magical moment Rianne held them in the palm of her hand.

Truly, she had an astonishing voice, a true lyrical contralto, possessing range and power enough to sweep an audience along like a tempest, while retaining the purity of each note.

"And you belong to me," he murmured under his breath. His chest swelled with sheer masculine possession.

Rianne had been trying as hard as she could not to look at Pagan. But as she finished her song, her gaze was irresistibly drawn to him. He was staring at her intently, hungrily, as though he wanted to take her very soul from her. What would it be like, she wondered, to be loved—truly loved—by such a man?

Good heavens! You're truly losing your mind if the man can have this effect on you without so much as touching you! And what he wants isn't love, but a pale substitute.

His gaze holding hers, he blew her a kiss. Rianne's brows contracted in a frown. Why, the man seemed to

114

know exactly what she was thinking! Rianne forced herself to look away. Why couldn't she control her feelings? Or at the very least, why couldn't she keep from revealing them to him? Truly, this situation had become absurd, infuriating, and humiliating all at once.

She wanted to shriek at him, run from the room—anything but stand here with her emotions stripped naked. Glancing over her shoulder at Alastair, she said, "Play 'Rock of Ages', Father."

"Are you out of your mind?" he demanded.

"Not at all." *I'm lashing out at Pagan Roark the only way I know how.* "Will you play it?"

He shook his head. "It's a bad idea, sweetheart."

"Play it, please."

"No," he said.

"Very well, Father." Taking a deep breath, she began to sing without accompaniment.

"Rock of Ages" was a fine old hymn, one of her favorites. But this audience liked lively entertainment, mostly consisting of almost-bare female flesh. She hoped the saloon would empty as though the plague had been announced. It was only a small revenge after what Pagan had done to her, but satisfying nonetheless. If this hymn didn't work, she'd sing another and another. She knew many, many hymns.

A tall, buckskin-clad man slapped his cards down on the table and shouted, "What the goddamn hell is this? I didn't come all the way from Deer Creek to hear this religious shit!"

Rianne continued singing, ignoring the interruption. The buckskin-clad man and his three friends began talking as loudly as possible, guffawing and shouting jokes so crude that she didn't understand half of them. The half she did, however, made the blood rush to her cheeks. Then she saw Pagan making his way toward the troublemakers through the close-packed tables.

115

She faltered to a halt. This had gone too far. There was going to be trouble, and it was her fault. She hadn't meant this to happen; all she'd wanted was to show Pagan that she wasn't *his* to command, that in this one thing she was in complete control. But now things were going all skewed; her simple defiance was turning out to be much more trouble than she'd bargained for.

Just as Pagan reached the miner, Rianne saw a flicker of steel in the man's left hand. "Pagan!" she shrieked, "He's got a knife!"

The man lashed out then, a wicked slash that should have reached his opponent. But Pagan slipped under the knife, moving as quickly and deadly as a striking rattlesnake, and hit the man squarely on the chin. The miner staggered backward, but recovered himself quickly. Dropping into a knife-fighter's crouch, he advanced on Pagan.

"Pagan!" Rianne gasped. "Oh, dear God, no!"

Francois Gruillot loomed suddenly behind the troublemaker. The man whirled, but too late; Francois grabbed him by the wrist and the back of his jacket and hoisted him into the air.

"Let me go, you bastard!" the buckskin-clad man howled. "Ow! You're breakin' my arm!"

His friends started to rise but, suddenly faced with the business end of Pagan's big Colt, sank back down into their seats. With a smile that chilled Rianne's blood, Pagan said, "What will it be, gentlemen? Drinks or the Pearly Gates?"

They didn't meet his gaze. One of them mumbled, "We'll just have a quiet drink, Pagan."

Francois was still holding the buckskin-clad miner. The huge Frenchman matched Pagan's smile, then, seemingly oblivious to his captive man's struggles, carried him to the front door. With a tremendous heave, Francois tossed the man outside. *Through* the door.

Folding his massive arms over his chest, Francois turned to look out over the crowd. "Is there anyone else who wants to interrupt Mademoiselle Rianne's performance?"

A vast, echoing silence claimed the room.

"*Bien*." Francois nodded, his beard fairly bristling with satisfaction. "Will you continue, Mademoiselle?"

"Yes . . . I . . ." Rianne clasped her hands tightly to stop them from trembling at the enormity of what she'd done. In her childish desire to punish Pagan, she had recklessly put him in danger. Francois Gruillot had just saved her from being the cause of a terrible fight, and had most likely saved several lives. Perhaps even Pagan's. The thought of Pagan dying brought black terror into her heart like the beating of bat-wings, and she swayed with the power of it.

"She's going to faint!" someone cried.

"I am not going to faint." Rianne stiffened her spine, pushing the weakness aside. She owed Francois Gruillot. There was only one coin in which to repay this man who had saved her—and Pagan—from her folly. Unclasping her hands, she spoke in a voice that could be heard throughout the room. "The 'Marseillaise', Father, for my friend Mr. Gruillot."

After the "Marseillaise", Alastair swung into one of the lively tunes that had been such a success the week before. Rianne, responding to the audience's enthusiastic reception, began to enjoy herself. When her high collar became confining, she undid the top few buttons; when tendrils of her hair began to escape her bun, she didn't even notice.

Pagan watched the change come over her. At the beginning of the performance, she'd been stiff and formal, the forbidding dress a warning to keep away. And then something magical had happened: the shy, uncertain young woman had blossomed, becoming a vibrant, spar-

117

kling-eyed beauty. She'd become the Songbird. And in doing so, she had captivated her audience, and she'd captivated *him*.

So intently was Pagan watching her that he barely registered that Jack Hoffsteader, the proprietor of the general store, was standing beside him. Jack was short, wiry, and strong, with grey hair and eyes that shifted a bit too much for Pagan's taste.

"She's something special, isn't she?" Jack asked.

"Yes," Pagan said without looking away from Rianne.

"That woman is going to make you rich. A voice like that is almost as good as a gold mine; you're a very lucky fellow."

Pagan nodded absently.

"Ahh . . . Rumor has it you've got her for a year."

That got Pagan's full attention. He scowled, surprised by the sudden surge of anger that shot through him. His relationship with Rianne was *his* business, not fodder for gossip. And that was surprising, too, for he usually didn't give a damn what anyone said or thought of his actions. "What rumor?" he growled.

"Nothing much," Jack said, alarm sparking in his eyes. "Alastair just told me that she's going to stay here for a year so he can work his claim, and that she'd agreed to sing at the Golden Bear while she's here."

"That's not a rumor," Pagan said. "It's the truth, and I want to see that it stays that way. If I hear any embellishments, I'll know where they came from."

"Sure, Pagan," Jack said hastily.

Pagan's attention returned to Rianne. Almost as good as a gold mine, Jack had said. Well, he was wrong.

"Only a fool would fail to see that you're worth much, much more, Rianne Kierney," he said under his breath.

Chapter Nine

"Rianne, darling, wake up!" her father cried from the doorway of the adjoining room, jolting Rianne out of a deep sleep.

She sat up in bed, her startled gaze darting to the clock. It was eight o'clock on Sunday morning. Alastair was *never* up this early, even during the week. "Father, what on earth—"

"Come on, get up, time's a-wasting," he said.

"But—"

"Wear something practical; we're going to take a ride."

"Ride?" Rianne stared at him in astonishment. "Where are we going?"

"Out to my claim, sweetheart. Don't you want to see where your old father is going to be spending his days?"

"Yes!" Delight sparked through her, warm as a sunbeam. With his eyes gleaming with enthusiasm, he looked years younger, almost the man she remembered.

"That's my girl," he said. "Meet me out front."

A moment later he was gone. Rianne flung the covers aside and jumped out of bed, her heart beating with excitement at the prospect of spending the day with her father. After washing quickly in the basin, she donned her grey tweed riding habit, boots and gloves. She braided her hair, tucked it into a neat bun, then tied the ribbons of her black traveling hat beneath her chin. She studied her appearance in the mirror, wishing there had been room in her suitcases for the smart veil-trimmed top hat she'd bought to go with the habit. She didn't know why she'd bought it; she hadn't the money to keep a horse. But the day she came into her inheritance, she saw the hat sitting in the window of the milliner's shop and impulsively, she'd walked in and bought it on the spot.

She'd never regretted it; impulsiveness had been as sternly repressed in Leonora Woodward Kierney's house as had laughter.

She gave herself a wry smile in the mirror. "Just like the thief who is only sorry that he got caught, you're only sorry you couldn't wear the hat more."

"And," she told her reflection, "if you don't get yourself downstairs soon, Father may find something better to do."

Lifting the train of her skirt, she ran lightly down the stairs and through the quiet saloon. As she passed the bar, she saw the same man lying on the floor, dead drunk. Now, what was that odd name again . . . Oh, yes, Scut Waller. She was going to have to ask her father about that.

Outdoors, the world was full of golden sunlight. She took a deep breath, reveling in the beauty of the morning. Then she caught sight of her father standing a few yards away. She started towards him, then noticed that he was holding the reins of three horses and a pack-laden mule.

Three horses. "Who else is coming, Father?" she asked.

"I am," Pagan said from behind her.

Rianne froze in mid-step and slowly turned to face him. He was wearing fawn-colored corduroy trousers, crisp white shirt, and a dark brown jacket that made his broad shoulders seem even broader. He was bareheaded, his thick black hair stirring in the morning breeze, and looked so rugged and handsome that he took her breath away.

"Good morning," she said, striving to keep her voice calm.

He smiled. "It is a very good morning, indeed."

"The claim is half Pagan's," Alastair said. "I thought it only fitting that he come along."

"I see." Rianne knew she ought to resent this intrusion on her outing with her father, but somehow, she didn't. But there was still a shadow between her and Pagan, and she wanted to dispel it. "I'm sorry about last night," she said softly.

"The hymn?"

"Yes. I didn't realize the consequences would be so great. You see, I only wanted to make a point—"

"You made more of a point than you expected," he said.

She nodded. The memory of the terror she'd felt last night was vivid and strong. Yes, she had been angry, and determined to show him that he didn't control her. But the simple fact that he'd been in danger had washed that all away. It didn't mean that she was not going to continue to resist his domineering ways, however. It just meant that next time she'd find a better way.

"I was wrong to involve others in our personal differences," she said, keeping her voice low so her father wouldn't hear. "I'm sorry for that."

"Ah, Rianne, how can I not accept such a sincere apology?" Taking her hand, he raised it to his lips. "I see in your eyes that you haven't changed your opinion, just your methods. You'll find another way to make me suffer for my sins."

His words were so unerringly, outrageously accurate that she nearly laughed. She ought to be angry. But how could she when he had so accurately read her mind? It gave her a most uncomfortable feeling to know that she

121

was so transparent. A change of subject was definitely in order.

"Is the mine very far away?" she asked.

"Two hours' ride," Pagan said, taking her by the hand and leading her to the horses. "Don't worry, we've packed a lunch."

Her father handed her the reins of one of the mounts. She looked at the saddle, then at those worn by the other two horses. "But there's no sidesaddle," she said in dismay.

"There's a scarcity of *women* around here, let alone saddles to accommodate them." Pagan didn't quite smile, but the creases on either side of his mouth deepened suspiciously.

"But how am I supposed to ride?" she asked, adding, "and don't either of you suggest I ride astride."

"Wouldn't think of it," Alastair said with such an absolutely straight face that she knew he'd been about to say just that.

"Isn't there a buggy or wagon we could hire?" she asked.

"Rianne, darling, we can't," the old man said. "There's no road where we're going. Even my prospecting gear has to be packed in by mule."

"Perhaps we should reconsider this—" she began, then broke off, gasping, when Pagan swept her into his arms.

"If you two stand here arguing much longer, the day will be gone," he said.

Rianne's hands had automatically gone up to clasp his neck. Then she realized how closely he was holding her to his chest—so closely that she could feel the steady, strong rhythm of his heart. A clean male cologne piqued her nose, a scent of musk and pine that she knew she would always associate with this man.

He smiled down at her, a slow, lazy smile that made her pulse trip and stutter. Then he swung her sideways into her saddle, then grasped her ankle and guided her leg around the saddle horn. Then he stood there for a long, heart-clenching moment, his hand clasping her ankle in a gesture that was blatantly possessive. Every nerve in Rianne's body reacted to his touch. She stilled, her eyes wide, her breath suspended in her chest like a rabbit huddled between the predator's paws.

"We'd better go, or we'll be spending the night there," Alastair said, breaking the taut spell.

Pagan nodded. Rianne let her breath out in relief when he moved toward his own mount. Soon the three of them were headed north.

Once they passed the last house on the outskirts of Henderson City, they left civilization behind. Pagan led them single file along a faint track that led through the hills. The trees arched far overhead, dappling the ground with shade. The quiet was broken only by bird calls and the occasional sound of a shod hoof hitting rock. Every clearing was carpeted with delicate spring flowers, white, yellow and lavender, and the air was scented with their perfume.

Once Rianne spotted a dark, hulking shape upon the hillside above them. "What is that?" she asked in a piercing whisper.

"Bear," Pagan said. Standing in his stirrups, he clapped his hands together sharply. The bear went galloping off, its fur rolling smoothly over its massive frame.

"It's beautiful here," Rianne breathed. "Simply beautiful."

"And all frozen solid in winter," Alastair said. "It gets so cold that a man's spit will freeze before it hits the ground."

"Really, Father!"

"He's telling the truth," Pagan said. "And the wind can flay flesh from bones."

They moved forward again. Rianne stayed silent for a long time, thinking about what they'd said. For all its beauty this was a harsh, even brutal, land. And yet men had come to live here, men like her father and Pagan. Why? Was it gold alone, or did something else draw them here? She watched Pagan, noting how easily he rode, as though he'd been born to it. Perhaps he had been. She realized just how little she knew about him. How strange that this man had waltzed into her life and had taken it over so completely. For the next year, her world would be the Golden Bear Saloon and Henderson City. *His* world.

Suddenly consumed with the need to know him, she urged her horse up beside his. "How did you come to be in Henderson City?"

"I was looking for gold, like everyone else."

"But you didn't find it."

He glanced at her from the corner of his eye, wondering what had prompted this conversation. "Not yet."

"I heard that you won the Golden Bear from another man."

"I did."

Rianne cocked her head to one side, alerted by his sudden reticence. "Do you dislike talking about your past?"

"Some of it," he said honestly. "Why do you want to know about my past, anyway?"

"I don't really know," she said with equal honesty. "It's just that, well, you confuse me. You say you came looking for gold. I can understand that. But if it was gold you wanted, why did you keep the saloon instead of prospecting?"

Pagan studied her, plumbing the depths of her tawny eyes. He'd been asked that question many times before. He'd always avoided answering, for it was far too revealing. He'd learned the hard way not to let anyone see that much of him. Until Rianne. Somehow, in just a few days, she'd managed to shatter all the rules he'd made to protect himself.

"Pagan?" she prompted, sensing a conflict within him.

He let his breath out in a long sigh, realizing only then that he'd been holding it. "I never intended to keep the Golden Bear," he said. "But it was the only home I'd had since . . . I was very young. And I had the feeling that if I gave it up, I'd never find another."

Rianne knew it was only part of the story. And that was all she was going to get now, for a shutter had drawn down over his face, leaving it impenetrable. But that small bit of information had given her a glimpse of the forces that had made him the man he was today. A hard man, she thought, looking at his ice-blue eyes and determined chin. A man who'd had to fight to survive. A man who had experienced pain and privation and great loneliness. She had a sudden, strong urge to reach out and stroke his hair to comfort him. Hastily, she repressed it, knowing that he was not the kind of man who would tolerate sympathy. Some day, perhaps, he would learn to accept it, but not today.

Suddenly Pagan's gaze shifted to a point behind her, and his brows went down into a scowl. Startled, she turned to look at Alastair. He stared back at them, a bottle of whiskey poised at his mouth. With a muttered curse, Pagan turned his mount and cantered back to Alastair.

Snatching the bottle out of the old man's hands, Pagan hurled it away with all his strength. It sailed far up into the air in a graceful arc, the glass reflecting the light like a small, brilliant sun. It disappeared behind the trees, then came the sound of breaking glass.

"Why did you do that?" Alastair wailed.

"You said you wouldn't drink on this trip." Pagan got down from his horse and began going through the packs on the mule's back.

"It was just a little bit of a drink, Pagan. I wasn't going to get *drunk.*"

Grim-faced, Pagan turned around, holding another bottle. The whiskey glowed amber in the sunlight, damning evidence of the old man's weakness. Alastair seemed to crumple, his shoulders drawing in, his arms coming up in front of him as though to shield his shame.

"Oh, Father," Rianne said. Disappointment brought tears to sting her eyes. She loved her father, and held his love for her as precious, but the whiskey would be a shadow between them as long as her father allowed it to rule his life.

Pagan flung the second bottle after the first, then turned to pin the old man with a fierce stare. "Two years ago, I agreed to pay for all your equipment to mine your claim. You worked for three weeks, then found every excuse in the world to drink instead of going out there. Now you've made a bargain with your daughter, and by God, you're going to keep it. During the week, you're going to stay sober, and you're going to work this claim. I want your word on that. Kierney honor."

Alastair looked pleadingly at Rianne. She folded her arms over her chest, silently demanding his promise. If forcing this issue would bring out whatever was left of the old Alastair Kierney, then so be it.

The old man held out his trembling hands. "Look at me. I've got the shakes just thinking about it. It's going to be damned hard."

"Not as hard as it is for us to watch you drink yourself to death," Rianne said. "Swear it, Father. On your honor."

"Maybe I lost my honor along with everything else."

She looked deeply into his eyes, putting every bit of love and hope and pride she possessed into her gaze. "I don't believe that."

"Ahhh." Slowly, Alastair straightened. It was as though he'd drawn strength from her somehow; even his face seemed to fill out. "Very well," he said. "You have my word of honor."

Rianne felt the tenseness flow out of her. "Thank you, Father." Glancing at Pagan, she silently added, *And thank you for standing behind me.* They had worked toward a common goal and despite their differences, had made a very good team. She felt warm all over, and it wasn't from the sun.

"Let's go," Pagan said, checking the lashing on the packs one last time before climbing back into his saddle.

The trail ended a few miles later. Pagan continued to lead them north, evidently quite at home in the wilderness. Rianne couldn't stop watching him. As they passed through a section of dense forest, she noticed that his pale eyes almost seemed to glow in the muted light. With his black hair and sharply chiseled features, he could almost be some sort of primeval warrior.

Suddenly he stopped, motioning her and Alastair to come up beside him. When she was near enough, Pagan grasped her by the arm and pointed to a tiny dot far up in the sky. The dot grew larger and larger, until finally she made out the graceful shape of an eagle. The great bird wheeled high over their heads, then suddenly plummeted, a dark, incredibly swift streak, toward the ground. A moment later it rose above the trees again, the limp form of a small animal dangling from its claws.

"Beautiful," Rianne breathed. "Beautiful and cruel."

Pagan looked at her, echoes of the eagle's fierceness in his eyes. "Nature is never cruel, Rianne. Implacable in

127

the quest for survival, yes, but never cruel. Only humans are cruel."

"Perhaps you're right," she said. "But humans have the capacity to be otherwise."

"A philosopher," he replied with a smile.

Alastair chuckled. "No, an optimist. She just hasn't lived in Henderson City long enough."

"Isn't that the pot calling the kettle black, Father?" she said. "We are, after all, visiting a spot where you claimed to smell gold."

"You can't fault her logic," Pagan said. He enjoyed her intelligence; with all his experience with women, he'd never met one like Rianne, who could challenge his mind even as she raised his passion to fever heat. He curved his hand more firmly around her arm, waiting for her response. It came, warming her eyes and softening the generous curves of her mouth. He held her there a moment, savoring the look of her, the feel of her, then let her go.

"We're almost there," he said, urging his horse forward again. "The claim is just over that hill."

They stopped on the crest of the hill to look out over the scene below. A stream looped indolently among the narrow valleys, the clear blue water looking as though a piece of sky had melted and flowed to earth here.

"There it is," Alastair said, pointing toward the opposite hillside.

"Where?" Rianne asked. "I don't see anything."

Taking her chin in his hand, Pagan turned her face a few inches to the right. "There," he said, pointing. "Just below that tall lightning-struck pine."

She saw a dark rectangle in the shade beneath the trees. "Oh, I see it now. Is it very deep?"

"About four feet," Pagan said.

"Four feet! Is that all?"

"Mining here isn't like it was back in England, my

girl," Alastair said. "Here, even in summer, only a few inches of ground thaw. Only dynamite can dig through frozen earth. Then you've got to haul away the loose dirt and gravel, build sluices and use the water to wash the gold out."

"I must admit I don't know a great deal about gold mining," Rianne said, "but I read somewhere that people find it in the streams and rivers."

"That's the easiest way," Pagan said. "But that stream has been panned many times by many different men. No gold was ever found. Finally some frustrated miner named it Barren."

"There are men who laugh at me for putting in a claim on that piece over there," Alastair said.

Rianne didn't know whether he'd chosen a good spot or not, and didn't care; working this mine would keep him from drinking, and because of that its value to her was far greater than any amount of money. "I want to get closer," she said.

They descended the hillside and splashed through the crystal water of the stream. After tethering the horses where they could reach both grass and water, Rianne and the two men clambered up the slope toward the mine. A ledge, perhaps four feet wide, had been cut in the hillside in front of the opening.

The entrance was high enough for her and Alastair to stand upright, but Pagan had to stoop to keep from hitting his head on the ceiling. Rianne put her hand on the nearest wall and found it intensely cold, intensely hard. For the first time she realized the enormity of this task. The earth didn't give up its gold readily; a man had to wrench it out with brute force.

Perhaps this work was too hard for her father, old and frail that he was. *But the drinking will kill him for certain.* This is the only alternative. She felt Pagan's presence just behind her and was comforted by it.

"I think we've seen all there is to see," Pagan said. "Why don't we eat that lunch we brought?"

"That sounds wonderful," Rianne said. "My stomach is making an all too familiar acquaintance with my backbone."

"I'll get a fire started," Alastair said. "A cup of coffee is just what I need just now."

A short time later the fire was blazing merrily. Alastair rinsed out the coffeepot and filled it with fresh water from the stream. When he dug into the pack in search of coffee, however, Pagan stopped him.

"Why don't we try this?" Pagan asked, pulling a small blue tin out of his pocket.

"Tea!" Rianne cried. "Wherever did you get it?"

"In Dawson." Smiling, he added, "Tea over a campfire won't be as good as—"

"Tea anywhere will be heavenly," she said, taking the tin from him and waving Alastair away from the coffeepot.

Later, as they relaxed around the fire with tin mugs of tea in their hands, Pagan looked over at Alastair and asked, "Have you told her yet?"

"No, I wanted it to be a surprise," Alastair said.

"What are you talking about?" she demanded. "I don't like surprises."

Alastair snorted. "Of course you do. It was your mother who didn't like surprises."

"Why . . . ah . . . Do you know, Father, you're right!" Smiling ruefully, she poked at the fire with a half-burned stick. "Things like that just seem to pop out of my mouth unbidden."

"After hearing them so much, I don't blame you," he said.

Rianne's curiosity was too demanding to ignore. "Now, tell me about this surprise."

Pagan pulled his saddlebags closer. Reaching in, he

took a bottle of champagne from one of the leather pouches. Rianne's eyebrows went up. Surely he didn't mean to propose a toast after extracting that promise from her father! But he made no move to open the bottle, just nodded for Alastair to speak.

The old man took Rianne's hands in his. "We brought you here today not only to show you the mine, but for you to christen it."

"I thought only ships are christened with champagne," she said, both pleased and surprised at the gesture.

"This *is* our ship," Alastair said. "And we're going to ride her all the way to the Promised Land. We've even registered her name officially: from now on, this won't be claim number .60933, but the Songbird Mine."

"For luck," Pagan said. "And for a beautiful woman."

Rianne looked from one man to the other. She hadn't paid much attention to the name Francois Gruillot had given her, thinking it a frivolous thing born of too much liquor. But she realized now that to everyone else, she *was* the Songbird. As long as she lived here, she would be called that. And when she was gone, she would still be remembered by the name of this mine. She liked the idea. Not many women could claim a gold mine as their namesake.

"It's not quite ready for christening," she said.

Alastair gaped at her in bewilderment. "What?"

Instead of answering, she picked up the half-burned stick she'd been using earlier and climbed to her feet. With the charred end of the stick, she wrote a single word upon the weathered timber that formed the lintel of the entryway. Then she stood back to look at her handiwork. It said 'Songbird'.

"Now it's ready." Smiling, she held her hand out for the champagne.

Pagan brought it to her. He stayed beside her as she

grasped the neck of the bottle with both hands and swung it against the timbers with all her strength.

"I christen thee Songbird!" she cried as the bottle shattered, sending a spray of foaming champagne spurting over them.

Laughing, Pagan grasped her by the waist and twirled her around. She gasped, shocked by his sudden action, and put her palms on his chest in an attempt to support herself. Then, slowly, he let her down to the ground.

"You're wet," he said, catching a trickle of champagne that was sliding along her cheek.

His touch was hot and tender at the same time, and brought every nerve in her body to life. Disconcerted by the intensity of her emotions, she turned away. Her gaze fell on her father, and to her surprise she saw a very sour look upon his face.

"Is something wrong, Father?" she asked in concern.

"Damn waste of good liquor, that's what's wrong," he said, shaking his head sadly.

For a moment she was outraged, then realized that he was teasing her. "Oh, you!"

"I had you going there, didn't I?" He held up the teapot. "A toast, anyone?"

Rianne and Pagan picked up their mugs and held them out. Alastair poured tea all around, then held his own mug up. "To the Songbird and to the woman for whom it was named."

"To life," Rianne added, happiness rushing like wine through her veins. "And to luck."

"Hear, hear!" Pagan said, touching his mug to hers, then to Alastair's.

And so the Songbird was born.

Chapter Ten

"Now that is a sight to warm a man's heart," Alastair said in a low voice to Pagan as Rianne made another pot of tea. "A lovely girl, isn't she?"

Pagan smiled, watching the graceful sway of her hips as she moved around the fire. "I never heard a truer statement, my friend."

"She's got her mother's looks, thank God," the old man said. "And my disposition, even greater thanks to God."

"She's got one hell of a temper," Pagan murmured.

"That's spirit, not temper."

"She's stubborn."

Alastair nodded, laughter dancing in his eyes. "That she is. But she's got a voice that would make the Devil himself weep."

"That she does." Pagan's attention returned to Rianne. She had insulted him, reviled him, even slapped his face. And last night, when she'd nearly started a riot with her damned hymn, she had almost gotten him gutted like a fish. And still he wanted her.

"Another cup?" Rianne asked.

Alastair held out his mug, but Pagan shook his head. "I'm floating as it is."

"You can never have too much tea," she said as she set the pot near the fire to keep warm. "I have a ques-

133

tion to ask you two gentlemen, something that's been puzzling me for days."

"Ask away," Alastair said.

"There's a man named Scut Waller who frequents the Golden Bear."

Pagan stiffened. "Has he been bothering you?"

"Oh, no. As a matter of fact, he's never been conscious when I've seen him. But I don't understand this nickname of his. And when I asked John Ferguson what it means, he told me to ask you."

To her surprise, she saw her father blush like a girl. And Pagan seemed to be having some trouble keeping his expression neutral.

"Is it something horrible?" she asked.

"Well, ah . . ." Alastair waved his hands helplessly. "It's not . . . Oh, hell! Pagan, you tell her."

After a moment's hesitation—whether from reluctance or from stifling his laughter Rianne couldn't tell—Pagan said, "The word means a stubby protuberance like . . . a rabbit's tail."

"But what has that to do with Mr. Waller?" she asked in bewilderment.

Pagan made a noise that was half cough, half chuckle. "He . . . ah . . . I can't talk now, Alastair," he gasped, doubling over with laughter.

"Ah, hell!" Alastair raked his hand through his hair. "Marie Bell gave him the nick-name, sweetheart." His mouth was pursed, as prim as a maiden aunt's. "After he ah, visited her the first time."

"But I don't . . . Good heavens!" she gasped as she realized at last what he was trying to tell her. Her cheeks were fiery hot; surely they were as red as they felt. Pagan's laughter didn't help at all. Utterly embarrassed, she turned her back on the two men. "Poor Mr. Waller, to be branded with such a humiliating nickname!" she said.

"But he doesn't mind a-tall, Rianne," Alastair said. "His given name is Edgar, and he's always hated it."

It took Pagan several minutes to regain control of himself. Truly, she was a treasure! Not only was her naivete delightful, he'd remember the horrified look on her face until the day he died.

Rianne swung around to glare at him. "You needn't enjoy this so much."

"I couldn't help myself." With an effort, he repressed a chuckle.

His expression was so much like a mischievous small boy's that her discomfort evaporated like mist on a sunny morning. "I am certainly learning many interesting things during my stay in the Yukon. They'll make wonderful tales to tell my grandchildren on cold winter nights."

"They'll never believe you," Pagan said. "Come sit down, Rianne. This is supposed to be a day of rest."

"You're right. Even though there isn't a church within fifty miles—"

"Seventy," he corrected.

"—there's no reason not to observe the Lord's day." She sat down with her back against one of the mine's framing timbers. This might not be a church, she thought, but the tall trees arching overhead were surely as magnificent a creation as anything man might have built in God's honor. Feeling very content, she half-closed her eyes and let the essence of the forest seep into her. Surely, she thought, this was Heaven itself, with the birds singing all around, the golden sunlight slanting down through the trees, the breeze laden with the sharp scent of pine and the sweet aroma of spring flowers.

"You like it here, don't you?" Pagan asked.

Too lazy to lift her eyelids, she looked at him from beneath her lashes. "Yes, I do."

Pagan's jaw tightened. God, she was desirable! With

135

her slumbrous eyes, she looked like a woman sated by love. He was suddenly, irrationally jealous of whatever thought had made her look like that. *He* wanted to be the one to put that look on her face. Too agitated to sit still any longer, he got to his feet and stretched.

"We have two hours or so before we have to leave," Pagan said. "Why don't we ride up to the top of that ridge over there?"

"Why?" Rianne asked.

"To see what's on the other side." He grinned at her, his eyes alight with mischief.

She cocked her head to one side. The ridge was steep, the ride bound to be a rough one, and there was no good reason to make the trip at all. But that smile got her. He was daring her. And the inborn trait of recklessness that had plagued her all her life rose to the challenge. "Is this a dare, Mr. Roark?" she asked.

"It is."

"Then I accept."

Alastair snorted. "And I was going to offer you a blanket for a nice nap. Ah, the energy of youth!"

"You aren't going?" she asked in surprise.

"Do you see that spot?" He pointed to a patch of sunlight near the mine entrance. "That's where I'm going to spread my pallet and spend the next two hours in peaceful oblivion."

Rianne hadn't expected this. She'd be alone with Pagan. Two hours, just the two of them. Did she dare it? Then she looked up at Pagan and saw that the challenge was still in his eyes. If she backed away now, he would know it was because she was afraid to be alone with him. He would know that she didn't trust *herself.*

Her chin came up in instinctive defiance; she was *not* going to let him think she was a coward. "Shall we go?"

"Indeed we shall," he said, holding his hand out to her.

They went down to the stream to their horses, and a few minutes later were ascending the side of the ridge. The ground was littered with rock, and the horses lurched and jolted as they made their way slowly upward. Just staying in the saddle took every bit of riding skill Rianne possessed. But she found herself enjoying the challenge of it and reveling in the sheer wild beauty around her. And as rough as the trip seemed, she knew that Pagan wouldn't have brought her if it were truly dangerous.

Pagan stopped at the top of the ridge. Leaping down from the saddle with lithe grace, he lifted Rianne down to the ground.

"Come with me," he said. "I want to show you something."

She followed him through the trees that crested the hill. Then the forest ended as though cleft with a knife, and she found herself standing at the edge of a sheer cliff. Beyond was the wilderness. Ridge after ridge of mountains, each darker and less distinct as distance blurred it. It was wild and primeval, exactly as God had created it. Here Man was a stranger, and a weak one, made insignificant by the vast panorama of Creation.

"It's like standing on the edge of a completely different world," she breathed.

"It *is* a different world," he said. "Do you realize that there are thousands of square miles of land out there that have never been crossed by human feet? We're living the last great adventure on this continent, Rianne."

She turned to look at him. His profile was to her, rugged and sharp-planed, as clean and untamed as the wilderness. His hair stirred in the wind with the iridescent sheen of a raven's wing. And in that moment something came over her, as powerful as the tide, as sudden and devastating as a hurricane: she loved him.

It had happened without her knowing, without her

137

willing or even understanding it. But it had happened. This wasn't the fond, gentle emotion of her girlhood dreams, but a need so deep her heart felt as though it would shatter from it. A desire so powerful that caution was swept aside before it. A wish to have, to hold, to possess. It was stronger than anger, stronger than pride, stronger even than betrayal.

Perhaps the betrayal was double-edged, she thought. *Perhaps he'll admit it to himself and to me, and turn it into something very different.* "Why did you bind me in Henderson City for a year?" she asked.

He didn't look at her, but she sensed his attention focusing on her as sharply as though he'd pointed a rifle at her. "Your father owed me thirty thousand dollars. My claim was on him, not on you."

"But you knew I would pay his debt."

Pagan didn't answer at first, and for a moment she was afraid he wouldn't. Then he nodded and said, "Yes, I knew."

"At first I thought you were mad to pay me thirty thousand dollars for a year's work." Her hands were trembling, so she thrust them into the pockets of her skirt. "But after this weekend, I realized just how much money I can make for you."

"I never doubted you were worth it," he said.

Rianne struggled to read emotion in his voice, but it was colorless, telling her nothing about what was going on in his head. At another time, she would have dropped the subject. But just now, with the revelation of her love riding hard upon her, she couldn't. She had to know.

"Pagan . . . Is it the money you want?" she asked. "Is that why you bound me here?"

At that moment, he turned toward her. Their gazes locked, and Pagan's face tightened as he read the need in her eyes. Need—and love. He was shaken by it. She

138

was baring her soul to him, and it was a gift that was astonishing in its power. It demanded something from him, something he didn't expect to have to give her: the ability to touch his heart. It was a shock to discover that he couldn't withhold it at all; with her vulnerability, the open, unashamed surrender in her eyes, Rianne had taken it from him without a struggle.

He closed the distance between them. Taking her by the shoulders, he pulled her close so that she had to tilt her head back to look at him.

"I don't give a damn about the money," he rasped. "I kept you here because I couldn't let you go. Is that enough? Is that what you wanted to hear?"

"Yes," she whispered. There was a storm raging in his eyes, desire and confusion and anger all at once, and she understood what it had cost him to say that. "That is what I wanted to hear."

With a harsh groan, he crushed her against him. She was sweet and warm and infinitely desirable, and he was stunned by the force of the passion she roused in him. He forced himself to gentleness. Framing her face with his hands, he gazed down into her eyes. "Do you know what is happening here?" he asked.

She nodded. *We're falling in love.* Reaching up, she traced the firm curves of his mouth with her fingertips. He captured her wrist, pulling her hand closer so that he could kiss her cupped palm. Then his tongue darted out to rasp excitingly over her sensitive fingertips, and she shivered.

"Are you cold?" he murmured.

"No," she said with a shaky laugh. "If anything, I'm too warm."

His mouth closed over hers, gently at first, then with growing passion. Rianne met his probing tongue eagerly with her own as his hands moved down her back and over her buttocks, pressing her closer to his rigid heat.

She wasn't shocked; this was the man she loved, and she loved all of him.

She felt a slight tug at the back of her head, then a moment later the weight of her hair fell down around her shoulders. He ran his hands through it, muttering, "It's like silk, pure silk," against her mouth before deepening the kiss once again.

He nibbled his way along her lower lip, then traced the line of her jaw to her ear with his tongue, where he explored the delicate curves. She hardly noticed when he slid her jacket down her arms and tossed it to one side. When he unbuttoned her blouse and spread it open, she merely closed her eyes and swayed toward him.

"You're beautiful," he said. "I've never wanted a woman as much as I want you."

"Never?"

"Never."

He bent to kiss her again, but she held him away with braced arms. "Do you mean that? It's not just a pretty compliment?"

"Rianne, since the moment I met you, I haven't been able to think of anything else. You possess my waking moments and my dreams."

"I see." Joy swelled in her heart. For the first time since she'd learned about his former wife, Rianne was able to banish all thought of the other woman. The past was over, dead and gone. There was only the future, hers and Pagan's. Slowly, she slid her hands up and around his neck. "Kiss me again."

His mouth came down on hers, hard and possessive. She gave herself up to it, and to him. He kissed her until she was breathless with desire, until her legs turned to jelly and she sagged against him. Then, supporting her with iron-hard arms, he smiled down into her eyes.

He removed her blouse and chemise, then loosened her skirt and slid it down, leaving her clad only in her undergarments, and she didn't care. Her breath was coming in shallow pants as she ran her hands along his shoulders and down his arms, reveling in the hard, flexing muscles beneath her palms.

She straightened, pushing away from him so that she could pull his coat off his shoulders and down his arms. Triumph shafted through her when she saw his face tighten with upsurging passion, for now she knew she affected him as deeply as he did her. This was true surrender because it was shared. It gave her the freedom to be bold, as wanton as she desired. Holding her breath with anticipation, she unbuttoned his shirt and spread her hands out over the hot flesh of his chest.

"Oh, God, Rianne!" Taking her hands, he moved them down over the ridged muscles of his abdomen, then back up to his chest. He felt as though he'd been caught up in a whirlwind, caught up in a desire more powerful than any he'd known before.

He put her hands from him then, but only to spread his coat down on the thick layer of leaves that cushioned the ground beneath the trees. Then he swung her into his arms and laid her on the makeshift bed.

"Rianne," he said, propping himself over her with braced arms. For some strange reason, he was compelled to know she came to him eagerly, without reservations. "I'm going to make love to you. Is that what you want?"

"Yes," she murmured, putting her hand on his chest to feel the racing beat of his heart. "Be gentle. I've never . . ."

"I know." Taking her hand from his chest, he kissed it. "I'll be as gentle as a man could be. Trust me."

"I trust you." And she did.

He kissed her then, and it was a kiss fraught with passion and tenderness and long-withheld need. Rianne wound her hand into the thick hair at the nape of his neck and held him close. He left her mouth to explore

141

the sensitive skin behind her ear, then moved in a smooth, heated glide down the sweet curve of her throat to the scented hollow at its base.

"Oh, Pagan!" she whispered, loving his heat, his tenderness, the way he made her feel loved and cherished and consumed all at once. "You make me feel so . . . so . . . I don't know the right words for it."

"There are no words for it," he said. "Only feelings. And these are just the beginning, darling."

He sat up, pulling her with him, and removed her boots and stockings. With excruciating slowness, he began unlacing her corset, kissing her all the while. Rianne expected him to take the garment from her, but he didn't. Instead, he merely loosened it, then ran his fingertips across the oversensitive skin of her chest. She leaned toward him, wanting more. Smiling, he slid his thumbs beneath the upper edge of the corset. She gasped as he dipped deeply into the warm crevice between, then smoothed over the upper swell of her breasts. Her nipples pouted of their own accord, begging for his touch. She arched her back, trying to urge him closer. Still he teased her, coming oh so close, but never actually touching them.

"Please," she moaned. "Please touch me."

He drew in a deep, ragged breath, staggered by the power of what she made him feel. It was not only passion, although that was there in abundance. It was Rianne, the woman herself. He was possessed of a fierce, powerful tenderness for her, then need to please her, to hold her, to make her his. With a wordless growl, he stripped the corset from her.

Rianne cried out in relief as his hot mouth closed over her nipple at last. Then she cried out again, this time in heightened passion, as he moved from one breast to the other and back again, suckling, kissing, stroking her overheated flesh with his tongue and hands.

He sat up, imprisoning her with his hands on her ribs. Her nipples were stiffly erect, flushed with arousal. Watching her face closely, he ran the tips of his thumbs over the hard peaks. Her swift, sharp sigh of pleasure sent a jolt of heat rushing through him to his groin. He was close to the edge, his need for her so great that he thought he'd die from it.

Slowly, reverently, he removed the rest of her clothes, baring her to his gaze. She was beautiful, all sleek skin and slim curves. And all his. With a hiss of indrawn breath, he slid his hands upward along her thighs.

"Pagan," Rianne murmured, struggling to a sitting position. "I want to touch you. Show me what to do."

"Do whatever pleases you," he said, lying down beside her.

She wanted to touch him everywhere, all at once. Shy at first, she stroked his face, his brows, his closed eyes. But this was love, pure and vast and unrestrained, and she wanted to experience it all with him. With Pagan, for Pagan, she would dare anything. So she explored further, running her hands along his broad shoulders, the taut muscles of his arms and chest.

Her hands strayed lower, sliding with exquisite slowness over the board hardness of his belly. The territory beyond daunted her for a moment; the hard line of his arousal pressed blatantly against his pants, and all that heated strength was intimidating. Glancing at his face again, she saw that he was watching her.

"Go on," he murmured. "I know you want to."

She did want to. Her hand moved down to his belt, but still she hesitated. His chest heaved, and the big muscles in his arm quivered.

"Please," he said.

Boldly now, she moved her palm downward, stroking over the long, thick line of his erection. She didn't know much about men, hadn't seen one naked let alone

143

touched one, but she rather thought he was as much a man as any woman could hope. The potent promise of him was incredibly exciting.

She looked up at him, wanting to see if he was as recklessly aroused as she was. She wasn't disappointed; he was staring at her from slitted eyes, his jaw taut with barely leashed desire. Beneath her hand, his manhood pulsed with the beat of his heart. And hers. She smiled, flushed with the awareness of her own feminine power.

That smile was Pagan's undoing. "Enough games," he rasped, rising to his feet with a lithe heave of his body. As Rianne knelt beside him, he stripped off his boots, then unbuttoned his trousers and stepped out of them.

She stared at him, the clean, powerful lines of his chest, the long, muscular legs, lean waist and narrow hips—and most of all, his eager, upthrusting manhood, and felt a sudden thrill of uncertainty at this force she had unleashed. He knelt beside her then, reaching out to stroke the curve of her cheek with his fingertips.

"Trust me, Rianne."

Closing her eyes, she nodded. Only he could take her through this maze of passion. Only he could show her the way.

His breath went out in a long sigh. Gathering her against him, he brought her down to the coat with him. They lay side by side, so close that her nipples grazed his chest. Rianne gazed at him wide-eyed, not knowing what came next.

Cupping her head in his hand, he kissed her as tenderly as though it were the first time. She felt every inch of him against her, skin against skin. They seemed to fit perfectly, hardness against softness, all the swells and hollows a perfect match. She sighed into his mouth as his hands moved over her body, stroking her breasts, spanning her waist, sliding with smooth heat over her belly and hips, then moving to her buttocks to bring her more tightly against his hardness.

He slid one hand along her thigh to her knee, then lifted her leg and placed it over his hip. Rianne cried out in shock when his hand closed over her woman's flesh for the first time. But all protest faded as he explored her, bringing a rush of heat to match the heat of his hand. An unbearable tension built in her, love and desire clamoring for fulfillment. She began to move in counterpoint to his fingers, needing something, seeking something she didn't understand.

"Please," she moaned, burying her face against his neck. "Pagan, I need . . . Help me."

With a low groan, Pagan shifted her onto her back. Spreading her legs with his, he eased himself up to the very threshold. He held himself there, savoring, anticipating the moment of possession. He was about to claim her at last, to take her from girl to woman. His woman. He had a sudden, powerful feeling that his life would be forever changed by it.

"Look at me," he whispered hoarsely. "I want to see it happen to you."

Rianne obeyed, and was undone by the wild tenderness in the crystalline eyes so close above her. The feel of him, so close, so very promising, made her frantic. Then he thrust into her with a smooth, deft movement. Rianne stilled, startled by the sudden swift pain as he breached the barrier of her innocence.

"It will never hurt again, I promise you," he said, kissing her hot temples.

His hands moved over her, gentle and warm and urgent. Rianne began to enjoy the feel of him in her, long and hard, filling her. She was a woman now. His woman, possessed, loved, cherished. Then he began to move, slowly and gently, and her eyes flew open in surprise at the sheer pleasure of the sensation.

"Do you like that?" he murmured.

"Yes," she said. "Oh, yes."

His thrusts became deeper and harder, and the tautness within her was increasing. Gasping, she lifted her hips to meet him, and discovered that she could take even more of him that way.

"Oh, God!" he rasped against her neck. "That's perfect, love. Perfect!"

Rianne clung to him, her only anchor in a storm of sensation. He slid his hands beneath her buttocks, lifting her closer. His breath was rasping now, hers matching it. He drove deeper, and deeper still, pushing them both to the edge. And then she felt a tiny ripple deep within her, a ripple that swiftly grew and spread until it was a tidal wave of ecstasy crashing through her. She cried out, feeling Pagan's hands tighten on her, hearing his own throaty cry of fulfillment.

When she could breathe again, she whispered, "I didn't know it could be this way."

"Neither did I," he said. She had brought him to a height he'd never known, never thought existed. It had been special, as unique as this lovely, generous woman he held in his arms. He rolled over onto his back, pulling her with him and tucking her close against his side.

Almost purring with contentment, Rianne laid her head against the smooth, strong swell of his shoulder. She felt sated, secure, and very, very sleepy. But the sound of a gunshot rolling through the hills jolted her into alertness.

Pagan rolled to his feet instantly and reached for his clothes.

"Is it Father?" Rianne asked breathlessly.

"The shot came from the direction of the mine," Pagan said, tossing her clothes to her. "Forget the corset. It takes too much time."

She dressed frantically, stuffing her stockings and garters into her pocket. Pagan helped her put her boots on, then tossed her astride her horse. Rianne had never ridden astride before, but it gave her balance and control she'd never had before.

Pagan leaped into his saddle without touching the stirrups. "Don't try to stay with me. Take it slowly, and let your horse find his own way down." He dug his heels into his mount's flanks, and the animal lunged into a gallop. The pair hurtled downhill in a spray of dirt and small stones.

Without hesitation, Rianne followed.

Chapter Eleven

As Pagan plunged down the slope, he could hear nothing but the wind rushing along his head and the clatter of his mount's hooves upon the rocks. He knew he was pushing the pace more than was safe, but concern for Alastair made him risk it; there were many things that could go wrong in the wilderness.

As he reached level ground, he saw the old man appear on the mine ledge, waving his arms to indicate he was all right. Pagan sighed with relief. Then Alastair pointed to something behind him, his gestures becoming frantic.

Pagan turned and looked over his shoulder. To his horror, he saw Rianne urging her mount down the side of the ridge at reckless speed. She lay along the horse's neck, her hair flowing out behind her in a ripple of golden brown. At that pace, and with the trees before her, he knew she hadn't seen that her father was unhurt.

His heart clenched with fear for her. One misstep, one mistake, and she'd break her neck. He hauled his mount around, intending to go back up the hill to stop her, but horse and rider were coming down at him like a runaway train, and there was nothing he could do that wouldn't endanger her more.

"Slow down!" he shouted. "Rianne, slow down!"

He might as well have been shouting into a hurricane,

for all the good it did. She and her mount came plunging downhill, the horse actually sliding on its haunches amid an avalanche of dirt and debris.

By some miracle, they made it. As the pair slithered down the last few feet to level ground, Pagan began to breathe again. "What the hell do you think you're doing?" he shouted furiously, drawing his mount up beside her. "Are you trying to kill yourself?"

Without answering, she urged her horse into a gallop and headed for the mine. Pagan wheeled his mount to follow her. Despite his anger, he couldn't help but admire her. She lay low against her mount's neck, her hair streaming back like a banner, her skirt hiked up to show her shapely calves and thighs. *That is one hell of a woman!* he thought.

Now that they were on level ground, he began to overtake her. Drawing up beside her, he leaned far out of his saddle and grabbed her horse's bridle. As both horses jolted to a halt, Rianne struck at his outstretched arm.

"What are you doing?" she cried. "Father—"

"He's fine, you idiot!" Pagan shouted. "Look!"

Startled, she looked up at the ledge. There stood her father, unbloody and apparently unhurt. She took a deep, calming breath. That awful, terrifying ride had been for nothing?

She glanced at Pagan, then turned around to study him more closely. His chest was heaving as though *he'd* been the one galloping, and he had the look of a man who'd had a very bad scare.

He wasn't the only one. She'd been frightened half out of her skin—she would have jumped from the horse if she hadn't been even more afraid of falling. And yet now that she was safe, her father was safe, and everything was all right, it *had* been rather exhilarating.

"Don't you *ever* do anything like that again!" he hissed. "You could have broken your neck!"

Rianne intended to explain that she hadn't done it at

149

all; she'd merely set the horse in motion, then hung on until the end. But the furious outrage on his face sparked a chord of mirth within her that was too strong to repress. She threw back her head and laughed until the tears came.

"What's so goddamn funny?" he demanded.

"What a ride!" she gasped. "I came looking for adventure, and by Heaven I found it!"

"Adventure!" he repeated, stunned by her reaction. Again, Rianne had managed to astonish him. Most women—and some men—would have swooned at the mere thought of that wild ride. He knew she'd been frightened. But now that it was over, she didn't cry about it, or even dwell on the danger. No, her face glowed with the sheer joy of being alive. His heart turned over with tenderness for this unique woman.

"I lost all my hairpins," she said, absently reaching up to pull a leaf from her hair. "I must look a sight."

"You look fierce and beautiful, like a warrior princess," he said. "Although I would pull my skirt down, if I were you, or your father's going to wonder what happened to your stockings."

She hastily rearranged her skirt. In all the excitement, she hadn't thought about the consequences of what had happened up there on the ridge. She ought to be embarrassed. She ought to feel branded, as though her father might see her sin blazed upon her forehead. But she felt no sense of sin in giving herself to the man she loved.

"It's a shame," Pagan said softly.

"What?"

"That I can't look at your legs any more."

"Lecher."

"Lover," he corrected. "I want to touch you again."

Heat ran like brandy through her veins. She wanted him to touch her again, too. If there had been privacy . . . she sighed. She wanted to be alone with him, to love him, and to talk. Now that their love had been proven, the future stretched like a bright, shining ribbon. Not *the* future, she amended. But *their* future, hers and Pagan's.

Pagan's passion-heated gaze held her a moment longer, promising much, demanding even more. Then Alastair came striding down from the ledge, releasing her from the lovely spell. She turned to her father, noting that he had a very sheepish look on his face.

"I suppose you're wondering what I was shooting at," he said.

"Yes." Pagan and Rianne spoke in unison.

"Well," Alastair looked down, up, everywhere but at the two younger people. "A snake decided to come sleep in the sun with me," he said. "Damn near scared me to death."

"Did it bite you?" Rianne asked, instantly concerned.

"No, I, ah, think I scared it as much as it scared me."

A smile twitched the corners of Pagan's mouth. "You missed it, then."

"Hell, yes, I missed it," the old man said disgustedly. "Go ahead, smile if you want, but this is damned embarrassing for me. First I all but shoot myself in the leg, and then I see you two come tearing down the hill to rescue me, whooping like a pair of wild Comanches. It's a wonder I've got any pride left a-tall." Alastair looked Rianne up and down. "Sweetheart, you look as though you've been rolling in the bushes."

"If you'd ridden down a hill whooping like a Comanche, you'd look like this too," she said, keeping her voice calm with an effort. *Surely he doesn't know! Oh, please, God, don't let him know!*

But he turned away, apparently satisfied, and began untying the ropes that held the packs together. "Pagan, give me a hand carrying this gear up, will you? I'll store it in the mine for the time being. I'll buy the rest of the equipment tomorrow, and start work Tuesday."

"Good enough," Pagan said. "And after we get these

151

packs stowed, I suggest we head out so we don't get caught out here after sunset."

While the men were gone, Rianne retreated behind a nearby boulder and put her stockings on. There, she thought, all outward traces were gone. Inside, however, she was irrevocably changed. By making love to Pagan, she had passed a threshold of life that could never be crossed again. She had grown up, come to know a man's touch, a man's love—and her own.

"Rianne!" Pagan called. "We're ready to go."

She hurried back to the horses and found her father already mounted. Pagan stood beside her mount, waiting to help her into the saddle. As he lifted her, he brushed his lips along the curve of her cheek.

"Until later," he whispered in her ear, warmed by the uncorseted feel of her against his chest. It was strange that he wanted her more now than before he'd made love to her, but he was beginning to get used to the fact that everything about Rianne was different.

They headed back to Henderson City at a brisk pace, Pagan in the lead, Rianne next, and Alastair behind her, leading the now unburdened mule. Rianne was sitting astride; now that she'd discovered how much easier it was to ride this way, she wasn't about to return to a sidesaddle. Her father had nodded in approval, and it was then that she realized that the conventions meant nothing here in the wilderness. *Good,* she thought, *for I've certainly flouted all of them today.*

As the time passed, the rhythmic movement of the horse soothed her. The sunlight had never seemed more golden, the breeze quite so soothing. All in all, it had been quite a day. Without being quite aware of it, she fell into a doze.

Some time later, the cessation of movement roused her. She straightened, staring around her sleepily. They were back. The Golden Bear's sign creaked in the wind, and the setting sun laid blood-red rays along the street.

"Good heavens! How long did I sleep?" she asked.

"By the look of your eyes, not nearly long enough," Alastair said.

He was right; instead of feeling rested as she ought, she felt as though a heavy weight was resting on her shoulders. She nodded, but couldn't quite make herself move. Pagan swung down from his mount and came over to lift her down from hers. She swayed, partly from fatigue and partly from being on a horse for so long, and he put his arm around her waist to steady her.

"Go on upstairs and get some sleep," he said. "You've had a hard day."

She nodded again, numb with exhaustion, and went inside. There were several patrons in the saloon already, and all turned to look at her as she came in. John Ferguson was standing behind the bar, polishing the already shining top.

"Is that her?" one man asked. "Is that the Songbird everyone's talking about?"

"Hey, gal!" another man called. "How about a song?"

Rianne could hardly put one foot in front of the other let alone sing, and was very grateful when John said, "Sorry, boys. She only sings on Saturday nights."

"Hell, Lowell Mason's got somebody to sing *every* night," the first man said.

John was unperturbed. "But there's only one Songbird. And she sings for the Golden Bear. Go on upstairs, Miss Kierney. You look done in."

"Thank you, Mr. Ferguson." Delving deep inside to find a tiny reserve of strength, she turned to the watching miners. "I'm sorry, but I really am exhausted. I do hope you will all come back Saturday, however. Is there a particular song you would like to hear?"

Their sour looks brightened. One man said, "Do you know 'When You and I Were Young, Maggie?' "

"I will by Saturday."

"How about 'Beautiful Dreamer?' " another asked.

Rianne smiled. "If you come, I'll sing it."

"I'll be here," he said.

"Saturday night then, gentlemen." With a regal nod, she took her leave. Once she was out of sight however, all the starch went out of her. As she trudged up the stairs, she thought she might fall asleep right there. She'd never been so tired.

Once in her room, she headed straight for the bed, undressing as she went. "Adventuring is very hard work," she said as she pulled the covers up over her nakedness. A moment later, all awareness faded.

Her dreams were of Pagan, and they were not vague, virginal dreams. In them, she made love to him again, felt his hands on her skin, felt him inside her, filling her, loving her, making her his all over again. Fevered dreams, flesh calling to flesh, hearts twining even as their bodies joined. Love was no longer a mystery to her, but a powerful primal force that seized her even in her slumber.

She dozed, dreamed, changed positions restlessly, then repeated the process again and again. The linens were cool against her hot skin, unsatisfying. It was Pagan she needed, Pagan who could ease this ache deep in her body.

A knock sounded at her door, bringing her to a sitting position with a rush. She hoped, oh, how she hoped it was Pagan. "Yes?" she asked breathlessly.

"It's me, John," came a voice from the hallway. "Pagan said you'd be wanting a bath."

Her disappointment was sharp, but a bath was a wonderful idea. "Just a moment."

She donned her dressing gown over her nakedness, then went to open the door. John and Stu Colher came in, carrying the tin bathtub between them. She waited patiently while they made several trips downstairs to bring enough hot water to fill it. When they were finished, John laid a towel and a bar of soap on the floor beside the tub.

"Why, thank you," she said.

He nodded and ushered Stu out of the room ahead of him. Rianne locked both doors, then shed her dressing gown and climbed into the steaming water.

"Oh, Heaven!" she breathed, picking the soap up and smelling it. It was fine, French-milled soap, rose-scented and as smooth as silk.

She sank down into the water as far as the confines of the tub allowed. A good, lazy soaking first, she thought, then she'd get down to the business of washing. The sound of the piano drifted up from the saloon below, and she recognized her father's playing. A burst of loud singing nearly drowned out the instrument, Alastair's off-key bellow the loudest of all. She sighed, knowing that her father was going to take full advantage of this night of fun before facing a week's enforced sobriety at the mine. And every weekend was going to be the same.

Then she shrugged, sending wavelets rippling through the water. Two nights of drunkenness was better than seven. "One step at a time, Father. I'll be patient."

Rubbing the soap between her hands, she worked up a wonderful, scented lather and washed her face, neck and arms. Then, her eyes still squeezed shut against stray soap bubbles, she felt along the floor for the towel.

"Try a little to the left," Pagan said in his deep, honey-smooth voice.

"Oh!" Rianne's eyes popped open. He was leaning against the opposite wall, his arms folded over his chest. Her startled gaze traveled the long length of his body, noting his dark trousers and crisp white shirt and the wet hair that was combed back from his face. And although his pose was languid, she couldn't help but notice the rigid line of his arousal beneath the fabric of his pants.

155

"How did you get in here?" she asked.

"I own this place, remember?" he said. "I've got a key to every lock in the building. Besides, I would have come through solid rock to see you like this."

She almost laughed, but a glance at his face told her he was completely serious. It was incredibly stirring to be wanted so badly.

"Don't let me stop you from bathing," he said.

She met his gaze and was caught by the molten desire swirling in those pale azure depths. It sparked an answering chord within her, a sweeping tide of passion that went through her with sweet, hot power. She felt not the slightest bit of embarrassment to be watched by him; this was her love, her lover, and there was no shame between them.

With a smile, she retrieved the soap and began moving it slowly over her shoulders and upper chest. A line of bubbles trickled downward over her breasts, and her over-sensitive nipples peaked immediately.

She looked at Pagan to make sure he was properly interested. He was; his chest was rising and falling with deep, rapid breathing, and his eyes were slitted nearly closed. He looked very predatory at the moment — a wolf about to spring. Her wolf. She lowered the soap to her breasts. With tantalizing slowness, she ran the bar over her skin. Over and across, between and beneath, until she saw his hands clench into fists. She smiled, a sly, triumphant smile.

That smile got Pagan's shoulder away from the wall. *The little tease!* he thought. *She's trying to make me lose control, and by God, she's doing it!* Well, two could play that game. He strode toward her purposefully, reaching out to pluck the soap from her hands.

"I think you missed a spot," he said.

She sighed as his hands moved over her slick skin. He smoothed the fragrant lather over her breasts, lifting

156

them, moving with erotic gentleness until her flesh swelled with need.

"Put your hands behind your head," he rasped.

Lost in a fevered haze of sensation, she obeyed, giving him unrestricted access to her torso. His big hands moved over her, incredibly possessive, intensely erotic. She arched her back, a tiny moan coming from deep in her throat. Her nipples were achingly hard, and she was dying for his touch. It came at last, his thumb circling the taut peak, then stroking over the erect center.

He moved down to the other end of the tub and knelt down. Rianne shivered as he lifted her right leg out of the tub and began washing it, his hands moving firmly over the slim swell of her calf, the sensitive spot just behind her knee, and finally the smooth curve of her thigh. Just as she began to quiver with anticipation, he propped her ankle on the rim of the tub, then raised her other leg and began washing it.

Rianne thought she'd go mad with frustration. Her legs were wide apart, the water moving like hot silk against her oversensitive flesh, rousing her to even greater heights of desire. It was all she could do not to wriggle as his soap-slick hands smoothed up her leg—calf, knee, thigh. She cried out in protest as the movement of his hand stopped.

"Don't worry," he whispered, his passion-hot gaze burning into hers. "I'm not nearly finished."

He propped her left ankle on the edge of the tub, leaving her open to his touch. His heartbeat thundered in his ears, and he was so hard inside his pants it was actually painful. Rianne was more woman than any he'd met in his life, and he'd never wanted anyone—or anything—as much as he wanted her. He needed to claim her again, for he felt complete when he was with her. She satisfied something in him that he hadn't known was lacking, but which he could no longer do without.

It was an obsession, yes, but a searingly sweet one.

"Do you want me to touch you?" he asked.

Rianne was aching, ready, shaking with the need to feel the pleasure only he could give her. "Yes. Oh, God, yes!"

She closed her eyes as his hands slid along her thighs to her hips. He caressed her narrow waist, delving excitingly into her navel for a moment, then cupped his hand over the soft curls of her mound. She arched against his palm, wanting more. He slid his hand lower, parting her flesh, exploring every fold, every crevice, every reaction. And then he slid his finger into her slick, hot depths.

"Pagan!" she sighed.

She writhed as his thumb slid up to the tiny nub that was the center of her desire and began to rub. Lightning-hot flashes of ecstasy pulsed through her. And then the first tiny tremors of her climax began, growing until she was lost in a shuddering maelstrom of sensation. It was wonderful, incredible, powerful—and yet it was not enough. She wanted *him,* the man she loved. She wanted him to possess her utterly, for that was the only way to truly quench this all-consuming fire.

She opened her eyes and gazed at him. "I wish this tub were big enough for us both."

"God, Rianne!" Pagan pulled her against him, heedless of the soapy water that soaked his clothes. Watching her climax had been almost too much for his hard-held control. The time for games was over.

He lifted her to her feet and made her stand in the tub. Quickly, he rinsed the soap from her. Then he swung her into his arms and carried her to the bed. Rianne rose up on her knees to help him unbutton his shirt, but her hands were shaky, and he gently pushed them away to finish the task himself. When he stood naked, his manhood full and throbbing before him, she smiled.

"You're a beautiful man," she murmured.

He caught her against him, his mouth coming down

on hers with tender aggression. It was a hard, hot kiss from a man whose passion was raging fever-high, and she reveled in it, straining against him with equal violence.

The world tilted around her as he lifted her and bore her down to the mattress. Boldly, he fitted himself between her thighs, his erection tantalizing close to her core. Gasping with mingled pleasure and frustration, she lifted herself toward him.

Still he held back, kissing her, caressing her breasts and smooth hips, murmuring things in her ear that would have made her blush a scant day ago. But now she reveled in his touch, the sound of his voice and the caring that made him put her pleasure above his own. How very lucky she was to find a man with such gentleness and strength.

But the time for gentleness was over. Now she wanted to drown herself in the urgency of his lips and hands and the swollen manhood that pressed so tantalizingly close. She ran her hands down his back and over his hard male buttocks, trying to force him closer still.

He growled low in his throat, a throaty male sound that excited her further. Grasping her wrists, he pinned her hands over her head. Rianne looked up into his eyes, becoming lost in the wildfire of passion blazing in his eyes. *So this is love,* she thought, astonished by the power of what she felt for him. It was primal and intense, as vast and untamed as the northern wilderness. There was no resisting it, nor did she want to; she only wanted to surrender, to let it sweep her up until it touched her very soul.

He held her there for a long, heart-shuddering moment, then released her hands and brought them up around his neck. "I adore you, Rianne," he said hoarsely. "I've never wanted a woman as much as I want you."

Gazing deeply into her eyes, he slid into her, slowly

159

and deliciously, until he was fully sheathed in her hot, throbbing depths. He withdrew as slowly, then again thrust deep. And again. And again, sweet, exquisite torment. Rianne let out her breath in a long sigh, her fingernails unconsciously digging into the flexing muscles of his back. The now-familiar coiling tightness of release hovered close. She needed it, craved it, wanted to share it with him.

"Please," she whispered in his ear. "Please."

Her plea broke the last of Pagan's restraint. With a low groan, he cupped her buttocks in his hands, lifting her close, and drove into her with smooth power. She met him equally, crying out, her arms and legs clasping him in a cocoon of sweet, soft flesh even as her woman's body accepted his thrusts. Then she cried out, and he felt her convulse around him. Swept along with her on the irresistible tide of fulfillment, he poured himself into her depths.

Rianne felt him shudder, heard him call out her name over and over before collapsing on her. She held him close, her hands smoothing down his heaving back. Her man. And quite a man he was, she thought with a smile.

He withdrew from her, rolling onto his back and pulling her close against his side. She rested her cheek against the hard swell of his pectoral muscle, hearing the steady beat of his heart.

"We're very good together," he murmured. "Better than good. Much, much better."

She smiled. "I'm afraid I have nothing by which to judge."

"You can take my word for it."

Her smile faded. Oh, yes, he had plenty of experience in such matters. Despite her naivete, she knew he was a very skilled lover. And that skill could only have come from practice—a great deal of practice. She levered herself up so that she could look at him. He lounged on the bed like a powerful male animal, his eyes half closed but brimming with gratification. The thought of him lying like this with other women was not a comfortable one at all.

Wanting to jolt him out of that smug self-satisfaction, she said, "I think I'll reserve judgement for a while. After a bit more experience—"

He moved so fast she didn't even have time to gasp. One moment she was propped above him, the next she was flat on her back with a very annoyed male staring down at her with narrowed eyes.

"Are you saying you'd like to gain experience elsewhere?" he asked in that soft voice that she was learning to respect.

"No," she whispered. *Only you. You are the only man I want, the only one I can ever want.* "I didn't mean that at all."

"That's good. Because you belong to me, Rianne. No other man is going to touch you. If I could manage it, no other man would even *look* at you."

"Are you jealous?"

"Yes, I'm jealous," he growled. It was yet another astonishing revelation in a day full of them. He'd never been the jealous sort. But the thought of Rianne with another man made his blood hammer in his ears. Call it obsession, jealousy or sheer male possessiveness, she was *his.* And he would hold her. "You're mine, and don't you forget it."

"You're arrogant," she said, half-teasing, yet half-seriously. "And pompous."

"I'm just stating a fact."

"Women don't *belong* to men any longer," she said, her spirit rising to meet his challenge. "It's almost the twentieth century."

He smiled. "Shall I prove my point?"

"How, by shackling me hand and foot?"

"Oh, nothing so . . . primitive." He parted her thighs

161

with his, claiming the warm nest he'd left so short a time before. "We modern males have other methods of convincing stubborn, beautiful, passionate English ladies."

She caught her breath sharply at the feel of his hair-roughened thighs against hers, and the intimate awareness that he was aroused again. And so was she. Instantly, completely, powerfully.

"And what methods are you talking about, sir?" she asked, putting as much hauteur into her voice as she could manage.

"I'd rather show you than tell you," he said as he moved forward another inch, testing her. To his intense satisfaction, he found her warm and wet and welcoming. With a smooth, strong movement, he claimed her in the most timeless of ways.

They clung together, moved together, kissed and gasped and drove each other toward the hovering pinnacle. And just then, just when Rianne was nearing the ultimate pleasure, Pagan looked deeply into her eyes and asked, "Do you belong to me?"

Lost in the extremity of desire, she answered, "Yes, Pagan. I belong to you."

And as she dissolved in shuddering ecstasy, she knew it was true.

Chapter Twelve

The first pale light of dawn stained the sky when Rianne felt Pagan leave the bed. She sat up, holding the blanket up around her shoulders against the chill, and watched him dress. It was almost a shame to hide that sleek, powerful body in clothes, she thought, and then smiled at her own forwardness. But last night every lingering trace of reticence had been burned out of her by the raging fires of passion.

"Where are you going?" she asked.

"Back to my own room. You don't want me walking out of here when everyone else is up and about, do you?"

She smiled. "Are you protecting my reputation?"

"Yes." He shrugged into his coat, then strode to the bed and put one knee on the edge so that he could kiss her.

Rianne sighed as the kiss deepened and warmed. "Aren't you sated yet?" she murmured against his mouth.

"I thought so a moment ago." He kissed her again. "But I was wrong." Smiling lazily, he slid one hand beneath the blanket to caress the smooth curve of her waist and hip. "You're tempting, much too tempting, my lovely Siren," he murmured. "But I doubt you'd care to have the whole territory know I spent the night here."

Joy filled her at the thought that he cared so much

for her feelings. "They'll have no reason for gossip," she said. "As soon as we're married—"

"Marriage!" He let out his breath sharply, then stood up and raked his hand through his hair. "I'm sorry, Rianne. I'm just not a marrying man."

Not a marrying man? She stared at him, mortally wounded, but unable to comprehend the blow yet. "W-What did you say?"

"I'll cherish you and protect you. I'll buy you anything your heart desires. I'll do everything in my power to make you happy—"

"But you won't marry me."

"No," he said.

Rianne's bewilderment was submerged in a flood of pain and humiliation. *This can't be happening! I gave him my heart, my body, my trust, everything! He can't be throwing it away!* But he was. He met her gaze squarely, his eyes shuttered and unreadable. No, not unreadable—emotionless. Fool that she was, she had read hidden feelings where there had been only emptiness. She took a deep shuddering breath, but it didn't ease her pain.

Drawing the blanket tightly around her naked shoulders, she said, "You took my virginity."

"You *gave* me your virginity, Rianne. Our lovemaking was shared from beginning to end."

"Don't call it love!" she hissed, made even more furious by the fact that he was right. Bitterness welled up in her, as sharp and biting as gall. "I was a fool. I should have known. I *did* know. But I let my own feelings blind me to what you really are."

His eyes narrowed. "And what am I?"

"You use women. For a month, two months, however long they amuse you. And then when it becomes inconvenient, you simply walk away. Dear God in Heaven!" she whispered fiercely, even in her anger conscious of her father sleeping in the next room. "Has there ever been as great a fool as I am? How long will *I* last, do you think?"

"As long as I want," he growled, grasping her by the shoulders and pulling her up against him. "I never pretended to be anything other than what I am. And I have never lied to you."

"No?" She took a deep breath, fighting for control. She was *not* going to cry. "I know about your former wife, Pagan. Tell me now that you're not a marrying man."

He drew in his breath sharply. "My marriage is no concern of yours."

"Except that it shows you have no objection to marriage, only to marrying *me*."

"No, Rianne. It only means that I learned my lesson well, and I'm not about to make the same mistake again."

Rianne closed her eyes. Last night he'd said so many lovely things. 'I adore you, Rianne', he had whispered to her. 'I've never wanted anyone as much as I want you'. Those words had meant so much to her last night, but she realized now that they had completely different meanings to him. To him, 'adore' and 'want' meant only that he wanted to bed her. Well, he'd done it. The fact that he'd torn her heart to shreds in the process wasn't important to him.

"So it's over," she said, trying to turn away.

He forced her to look at him. "Over? Darling, you've got it all wrong. I want you more than ever."

"As your mistress."

"Yes. We're good together, Rianne. As good as two people can hope to be." Warmth rose in his eyes and tautened his jaw. His hold on her shoulders gentled, and he pulled her closer.

Rianne felt his arousal against her stomach. *He* may have been warmed by passion, but it was fury that heated her blood. Fury, and shame. She'd never known true shame before. This was no subtle embarrassment, but a feeling so intense, so painful, that she felt as though it had been graven on her heart with acid.

"Let go of me," she said with frigid dignity. "I don't want you to touch me."

"You don't mean that. Not after last night. Play the ice-maiden with someone else, but not with me. I know how hot your fire burns."

Curling her hands into fists, she punctuated each word with a blow on his chest. "Take . . . your . . . hands . . . from . . . me!"

"All right, damn it."

He was scowling now. *Good,* she thought, flushed with triumph at having shaken his arrogant self-confidence. She snatched her dressing gown up off the chair and donned it hastily.

"Last night was a mistake," she said. "The biggest mistake I've ever made in my life. The only reason I won't tell my father about this is that I'm afraid he'll call you out, and I don't think you've got any compunction at all about killing him. Perhaps I'm wrong. Perhaps a *friend's* respect is more important to you than a mere *woman's*." She tossed her hair back from her face with a sweep of her hand. "It doesn't matter. Either way, you'll do what is expedient, won't you?"

"Rianne—"

"I don't know what sort of women you're accustomed to, but I assure you I will *never* bow to your wishes. If you treated your wife like this, no wonder she divorced you!"

"That's enough!"

He didn't raise his voice, but the sheer intensity of his tone stopped her. His brows were bunched in a black scowl, and his eyes were points of glacial ice. When he spoke again, there was barely leashed anger in his voice. "Good, bad or otherwise, I will not discuss my marriage with you."

166

"Then I just have to assume I was right," she said.

"Assume anything you damn well please!"

She turned her back on him and stalked to the window. The rising sun had painted the sky in a riot of colors—pink, lemon yellow, pale, pale turquoise. She hated its beauty. How could it be so lovely when her dreams were being crushed so ruthlessly? And how could she have been so incredibly stupid! She had yearned for love while dwelling in the mist of her mother's coldness, and she had been so happy, so desperately happy to have found it at last. First, with her father, and second, with Pagan Roark. But in her need for closeness and warmth, she had mistaken passion for love. Now, in the cold, harsh light of reality, it was a poor substitute.

Whirling, she faced Pagan again. "How dare you do this to me!" she whispered fiercely, pressing her fist to her chest in an attempt to ease the terrible agony in her heart. "You knew I was innocent to the ways of men. You knew how your touch affected me, and you *knew* making love would not be a casual thing for me! Why did you seduce me when I had no way of protecting myself? Why didn't you just leave me alone?"

"I couldn't leave you alone, damn it to hell! You haunted me day and night, and I didn't have any more choice in this than you did." His scowl deepening, Pagan folded his arms over his chest. "Do you think I go around seducing virgins for the fun of it? No, Rianne."

"I think you're despicable."

"And you've got a tongue like an adder." He took a step toward her. "I've been patient, but I've taken more insults from you than from anyone else I've ever known. I'm not going to take any more."

"Oh, really?" She clenched her fists, her chest heaving with the force of her anger. "Are you going to beat me now? Is that how you deal with a woman who doesn't jump to your every command?"

"It's a tempting thought."

"Well, do it then!" she hissed. "Do it and get it over with!"

He smiled grimly. "I don't hit women, sweet. But I can make you pay in other ways."

You couldn't hurt me any more than you already have! she thought. But she would have died rather than say it aloud, for it would have given him far too much satisfaction. "You won't have the chance. I'm taking my father and leaving, and as God is my witness, I'm never coming back."

"Oh? Where will you go?"

"Anywhere. As long as I never see you again, I'll be happy."

His jaw tightened. "And what if you have a child?"

She stared at him dumfounded. A child? She hadn't considered that. Surely her sin wasn't so terrible that she should be punished so. Then a small, treacherous corner of her mind created a picture of a child with black hair and beautiful, ice-blue eyes, and a strange sense of longing tugged at her heart.

She pushed it away resolutely, for it was born of weakness. "If I should be carrying a child, it will be my concern, not yours."

"You're mistaken," he said, his voice going dangerously soft. "If you have a child, it will be *ours*. I will support you both, and I will take a hand in the upbringing."

"You have no right!"

"But I have every right, sweet."

His eyes were as pale and hard as glacier-ice, and Rianne shivered at the threat in them. It was then that she realized that if she dared take his child away, he would follow her to the ends of the earth if necessary to bring them back.

"You'll want for nothing, you or the child," he continued. "Anything that you want that is in my power to give, all you'll have to do is ask."

Rianne's hands were shaking so badly that she hid them in the folds of her dressing gown. He thought he was being generous, but he was offering nothing but money, broken dreams, ashes of her love. And in return, he would expect her to be his mistress. She was supposed to accept it gratefully, give him her heart, her body, and her future, then stand back and let him go on to the next woman when he grew bored.

Looking him straight in the eye, she said, "You can go straight to the devil, Pagan Roark."

She grabbed her suitcase and flung it on the bed, then rushed to the bureau. Snatching up an armload of clothes from the top drawer, she tossed them into the open bag, then went back to the bureau for another load. When she turned around again, however, she found Pagan blocking her path.

"Get out of my way," she snapped.

"No." He braced his hands on the top of the bureau, trapping her between his arms. The edges of his teeth showed in a smile that had nothing of humor in it, and sheer male aggressiveness seethed in every line of his body. His gaze held hers with angry challenge, and he took another step toward her.

She retreated, putting her back against the bureau. There was nowhere to go. No place to run, no one to call to for help. Trembling with impotent anger, Rianne could only hold the clothes between her chest and his. He looked determined and very intimidating. And, God help her, that primitive fierceness stirred her. She had to get away from him, today, now, or lose what little self-respect she still had.

"Get out of my way," she said again.

"You're not going anywhere," he growled, knowing he should let her go, but unable to force himself to do it. He *had* to hold her.

She stamped her foot, riding the soaring wings of pure, unadulterated fury. "I will not stay here!"

He moved forward again, squashing the bundle of clothes between them. "You don't have a choice, Rianne darling. Do you remember that piece of paper you insisted we sign?"

She stared at him wide-eyed, seeing the jaws of the trap closing in around her, but helpless to do anything to stop it.

"Well, my tempestuous little hothead, that is a legal document, drawn up, as you said, to protect us both. By your own words, you owe me the next year of your life."

"You would use even that to hold me?" she whispered.

"Even that."

His voice was harsh and strained; if she didn't know better, she would have thought he was in pain. But she did know better. Never again would she let herself be fooled by him.

"You're right, I owe you a year," she said, lifting her chin in defiant disdain. "I'm not a welsher, Mr. Roark. I will see the agreement through."

"And?" he prompted softly.

"And . . ." Tilting her head back to look at him, she spoke her next words slowly and very distinctly. "I want to make it clear that this is a business arrangement."

A muscle jumped spasmodically in his cheek, and his jaw looked as though it had been carved from granite. *So, that one had stung,* she thought. Good. It was about time she managed to strike a blow. Bitter satisfaction filled her. It was only the beginning.

"Now, Mr. Roark," she continued, "I intend to sing for you, as agreed. But sing is all I will do."

"You don't expect me to believe that, do you?" He spoke calmly enough, but that telltale muscle throbbed in his cheek, revealing his anger.

"Ah, but I do," she said. "I would rather sell my favors downstairs in that saloon than give myself to a man who betrayed my trust."

"Then keep your goddamned favors," he growled. "Sing your heart out, Rianne Kierney, for I won't be bothering you any more."

"That makes me very happy!"

"Good!" He flung himself away from her, moving to the door with long, angry strides. Jerking it open, he stalked out into the hallway. A moment later Rianne heard another door open, then close with a slam that reverberated through the house.

She stood still, frozen by a pain that numbed her very soul. She'd gotten what she wanted: his agreement to leave her alone. The victory ought to make her happy. But she didn't think she'd ever feel happy again. She'd had one day of love, one glorious day when the world had seemed fresh and new and inviting. And then that world had crumbled around her in great, crashing shards, and she knew it had been only an illusion. Her love had been a bright, shining mirror that had blinded her to reality. Instead of seeing what Pagan truly wanted—a brief interlude of passion uncomplicated by commitment—she had seen only the reflection of her own feelings.

Turning slowly, she laid the clothes back in the bureau drawer. For a moment she stared at the pile of crumpled fabric, thinking how accurately it represented her heart just now. Then she lifted her gaze to the tarnished mirror. Her face was pale, her lips trembling, her eyes pools of disillusionment, shattered hope and crushed dreams.

"You were stupid, and now you're paying the price," she told her reflection.

Noticing a small mark at the juncture of her neck and shoulder, she leaned forward to inspect it more closely. Memory flooded through her, as vivid as a caress, of last night. He had been inside her then, driving her to the height of passion with his hands, mouth, and stroking hardness. And then he, too, had lost control, his mouth sucking heat to the surface there as he poured himself into her eager depths.

Her fingertips stroked the red spot lightly. It was such a small, seemingly insignificant thing. It shouldn't matter. She could cover it with her collar, and in a few days it would be gone. But it felt like a brand, enduring and irreversible. The mark of her shame. She had offered him her love freely and with joy. He had taken her body and spurned her love. And now she had to work for him for a year, knowing that he didn't want the most precious thing she possessed.

With a hiss of indrawn breath, she began scrubbing at the tiny mark savagely, bruising her own flesh. She felt nothing, however, for her heart hurt too much for her to feel a lesser pain. Then she sank slowly to her knees. Her breath coming in great, gasping sobs, she pressed her face against the cool, uncaring wood of the bureau and let the tears flow.

"Oh, God," she moaned. "Oh, God, it hurts!"

She cried harder than she'd ever cried in her life, but no amount of tears could wash her hurt away. There had been so much love in her, so much joy and willingness to give, and now there was only anger left. It was a slow, simmering anger that seeped deep into her bones and settled like a smoldering coal in her heart. Would the fire consume her, sucking her dry until there was nothing left but a dry husk?

"Is this what happened to you, Mother?" she whispered. "Is this why your laughter shriveled and died, why you became bitter and joyless?"

For the first time she understood something of the forces that had made Leonora what she was. Perhaps she hadn't been as cold a person as she had seemed, merely one who had been disillusioned so badly there was nothing left to give.

Then Rianne's stubborn Kierney pride pulled her head

up. She was not her mother. Some day, somehow, this pain would fade. Pagan Roark might have taken her heart and her innocence, but there was more to her than that, much more. Yes, she had been used. Yes, she had been manipulated into a year of servitude to pay her father's debt. But she had her wits and her pride, and no one could take her self-respect.

She got to her feet and looked at herself in the mirror again. "You wanted to experience life, Rianne Kierney. Well, there's bad mixed with the good, and you're going through the bad just now. The good will come. It may take time, but it will come."

Time. That was the key. That, and thirty thousand dollars. The only way she could get away from Pagan before the year was up was to get her hands on the money. Her eyes narrowed. Oh, what a joy it would be to cast that money in his face before turning her back on him forever!

There was only one thing that could put thirty thousand dollars in her hands: the Songbird mine. The chances of success were slim, but any hope was better than none.

"Well, Father," she muttered. "You said you smelled gold there. Let's pray your nose is as good as you think it is."

She washed her face, erasing the traces of crying as best she could. After dressing in a blouse and the old blue skirt she wore for cleaning or working in the garden, she opened the door leading to her father's room.

Alastair lay across the bed, fully clothed and snorting like a steam engine. She hoped he'd had a very good time last night, for it was going to have to last him all week.

"Father, wake up," she called, shaking him.

"Ah, mmmph, what time is it?" he asked without opening his eyes.

"It's time to leave for the mine," she said.

173

"Tomorrow."

"Today," she said firmly. "You promised."

Groaning, he sat up and scratched the white hairs stubbling his chin. His hands shook uncontrollably. "I shouldn't have let you talk me into it. Five days all alone in the hind end of nowhere, working like a dog . . . I don't know why I let you talk me into it."

"It won't be so bad, you'll see." Rianne poured water into the washbasin. "Come here, Father."

He slid off the bed and tottered toward her. Hesitantly, he dipped his fingertips into the water. "Ah, it's too cold."

"Nonsense," she said. "It's merely invigorating. Here, let me help you. We'll have you awake and kicking in no time." Grasping the back of his neck, she held him still while she washed his face with a wet towel.

"You're taking skin off!" he howled.

She ignored him and continued working. When she finished, he was pink-faced and gasping, but alert.

"Scrubbed like a puppy, by God," he complained, reaching up to test his cheeks with his fingertips.

"Now we're going to get some coffee into you, and then we'll pick up enough supplies to last us the week."

His eyes widened. "We? Us?"

"We," she echoed. "Us. I'm going with you. With two of us working, the job will go much faster."

"What? Have you gone daft, girl?"

"Yes, Father, I have." She smiled a bit grimly. "You see, I've caught gold fever."

Chapter Thirteen

"Rianne, you can't come with me," Alastair said. "You have no idea what kind of conditions you'll have to endure. There's no shelter there, only a tent, and the work is terribly hard."

"Good heavens, Father, don't be so melodramatic. Hard work doesn't frighten me, nor does living in a tent." *But living under Pagan Roark's roof does.*

"But what about singing—"

"I sing on Saturday nights. That leaves the entire week free to do whatever I like. Now, let's get out to the general store or trading post or whatever it is. The sooner we get started, the sooner we'll be finding gold."

He folded his arms over his chest. "And why are you so interested in finding gold all of a sudden?"

"Yesterday, you called the Songbird Mine our ship to the Promised land. I didn't understand then. All I could see is what the search for gold has cost you. But now I realize what finding gold truly means, and why you've given up so much for it." She spread her hands wide. "It means freedom. The freedom to live in a place because you *want* to, not because you have to, the freedom to tell anyone in the world to go—"

"Straight to hell," he finished for her. "You do understand. If you've got enough money, no one can tell you what to do."

"Exactly." And Pagan Roark could no longer keep her here, where she had to face her humiliation every day, every time she looked at him.

"Why do *you* want this?" he asked. "Your mother's side of the family was wealthy enough."

She shook her head. "Grandfather Woodward was heavily in debt. When he died, Mother and I were lucky to keep the house in Wickersham. I sold that to raise enough money to come here. I've got four hundred and twenty-two dollars to my name."

"I didn't know," he said. "I'm sorry."

"So am I." *Sorry I ever laid eyes on Pagan Roark.* But her own stupidity had put her in this position, and now she had to do her best to get herself out of it. Like any trapped animal, she had tested the bars of her cage, and the Songbird was the only way out.

Alastair tapped her on the shoulder, distracting her from her grim thoughts. "Do you regret that you spent your inheritance and got so little from it?"

"So little?" she repeated in surprise. "But I found my father again. That makes me a rich woman, doesn't it?"

He put his arms around her. "It is *I* who is rich in that way, Rianne darling. But I'm poor in every other."

"But you have the Songbird. If your hunch is right, there's gold in that hill. Enough so that we can start over in style."

"Perhaps." He turned away, raking his hand through his thin white hair. "Perhaps."

Rianne watched him closely, noting the slump in his shoulders and the way his hand trembled slightly. With a sudden dart of surprise, she realized that he didn't want to go out to the Songbird. A very disturbing thought occurred to her: if she hadn't insisted on going with him, would he have gone out there at all? "What's the matter, Father? Why don't you want to work the mine?"

"Ahhh, you see too much, sweetheart," he said. He

176

closed his eyes for a moment, then opened them again and met her gaze squarely. "Ever since I filed that claim, I thought I wanted to work it. But somehow I never quite got around to doing it. I never admitted it to myself, but if you hadn't come, I never *would* have gotten around to it."

"Father—"

"No, let me finish. I would have stayed on here, unable to leave the mine, yet unable to make myself work it." He sighed. "You see, I came from nothing and nowhere—the ninth child in a common laborer's family. I was eight years old when I started working, and eleven when I left home for good. Except for three years when I had that ranch, I've sweated for other men's profit my entire life. Those three years gave me a taste of the dream, and I never forgot it."

"But that should make you want to find the gold even more!"

He shook his head. "No. I'm scared of it."

"Scared, Father? I don't understand."

"I know." He sighed, then turned away so that she couldn't see his face. "I'm fifty-eight years old, Rianne. I've spent my life chasing will-o-the-wisps, with nothing to show for it. The Songbird is my last chance. If I fail here like I've failed at everything else, then I won't even have the dream. *That's* what frightens me. I'll be a dried-out husk of a man, full of nothing but big talk and bad liquor."

He sat down on the bed, his shoulders hunched in dejection. Needing time to think, Rianne turned away from him and walked to the window. A column of smoke was rising lazily from the chimney of a house across the street, and she watched the grey billows thin and fade, and finally merge with the blue of the sky.

She had a decision to make, and it wasn't an easy one. The best thing for her would be to work the mine;

it got her away from the Golden Bear and Pagan all week, and also gave her hope of ending her servitude sooner. But what if there was no gold? Her father might lose all hope, all strength to fight any longer. And what then? A steady decline, aided by the bottle? How could she live with herself, knowing she'd talked him into it?

There was no decision, really. It was her shame as opposed to her father's recovery. Shame could be endured and in time, forgotten. It would be hard, but somehow she'd manage. She leaned her forehead against the cool glass of the window for a moment, then turned to face Alastair.

"If you don't want to work the mine, I shan't force you," she said. "And I won't blame you. The decision is yours."

"It is?" he asked, his eyes widening in surprise.

"Of course. I'll support you in whatever you want to do."

"But what about starting over?"

She shrugged. "We'll manage. It will take a little longer, that's all."

"Ahh, darling, you make me proud. If I had some of that strength and optimism, I think I might conquer the world. But I don't. I'm old and tired, and I just don't have the heart for the struggle any longer."

Rianne's heart sank, but she made sure her expression didn't echo her feelings. Forcing a smile, she went to him and took his hands in hers. "Don't worry, Father. Everything will work out just fine. We'll have our start soon enough."

"And with a bit less style?" he asked.

She tossed her head disdainfully. "Who cares about style?" Tucking her arm in his, she urged him toward the door. "Come downstairs with me and I'll make you some breakfast."

"Wait!" he cried, pulling her to a halt.

Startled by his vehemence, she studied his face closely. Something had happened, something important; his jaw was tighter, his shoulders squared, even the skin of his face was less slack. "What is it, Father?" she asked breathlessly.

"Pack your things, love. We're going prospecting!"

She drew her breath in sharply. "Are you sure?"

"I'm sure." He smiled, and for a moment she saw the man her mother had fallen in love with. "What a team we'll make! Oh, I'll probably start whining again when things get rough, but I want you to promise that you'll whip me back to the path."

"I promise." Joy came into her heart, making a place for itself amid the pain Pagan had left. It was surprising and very welcome. Her father had given her this. Somehow, he had found a forgotten well of determination in himself. He was going to take the risk and reach for the dream.

Feeling something on her cheek, she raised her hand to touch it. Her fingertips came away wet. *Why, I'm crying,* she thought wonderingly. Tears. Tears for the bittersweet joy, tears for the loss of innocence and the gaining of a new strength. She smiled — a bit shakily, but she smiled. "We're going to show them, Father. All those people who laughed at you, all those who didn't believe. We're going to *show* them!"

"That's my girl." Alastair threw back his head and laughed. "You're Kierney to the core, Rianne. We'll work together. And if we strike gold, we stand together and tell the rest of the world to go to hell."

"Yes!" *And Pagan Roark.* The prospect of telling him to go to hell was a very attractive one, indeed.

"Now, Rianne darling, I want you to pack your things. Bring your stoutest boots and oldest clothes. No feminine frippery; there's only going to be you and me and the squirrels out there."

179

"Yes, Father."

An hour later, Rianne was standing on the boardwalk in front of the Golden Bear, waiting for her father to come with their mounts. Two mules, their backs piled high with packs, stood tied to the hitching post in front of the saloon.

Impatient to be off, she looked up and down the street for Alastair. Instead of her father, however, she saw Pagan coming toward her. Her breath caught in her throat at the sight of him. He was obviously on his way back to the Golden Bear. It was just as obvious that he'd seen her. What was she going to do now? How was she supposed to greet a man who had taken her virginity and then spurned her love? None of the rules of etiquette covered this situation.

The sun touched his hair, casting fire-sparks off the rich blackness of it. There was a feral grace to his movements, and even in his elegant clothes he looked primitive and powerful, as untamed as an eagle, as potentially dangerous as a hunting wolf. A surge of possessiveness swept through her. Even now she wanted him. Her anger was deep, her hurt profound, but even that was not enough to blunt her desire.

She wanted to be the one, the special one, who could tame the untamed and hold what could not be held. But logic told her that he had already proved to her that she *wasn't* that one. Another woman had already taken that position. Whatever else had happened between Pagan and his wife, he had married her. Rianne sighed; it stung to know that she was merely the latest in a long string of conquests. Not the first, or even the last. A month after she was gone, he probably wouldn't even remember her name.

And yet, as she watched him walk toward her with that feral, determined stride that was so uniquely his, her legs trembled with the force of her desire for him.

180

Why did he have to be so completely, devastatingly handsome? Why did she have to be so weak? And where in God's name was her father?

As he neared, she fastened her gaze on the building across the street. Perhaps if she pretended he didn't exist, he would leave her alone. Fate was not so kind, however; he stopped beside her, so close that his chest was nearly touching her shoulder. Pride made her stand in place. She would *not* give him the satisfaction of knowing that his nearness disturbed her.

"You're out early," he said.

"Yes, I am."

Pagan leaned against the nearest pole and studied her profile, trying to gauge her mood. There was nothing, however. No anger, no recrimination, no trace of weeping. Of all the reactions he expected, this was the most disturbing.

"I see your father is packed and ready to go," he said.

"He's anxious to get started." *And so am I.*

A heavily laden wagon squelched by, spattering mud in every direction. Pagan grasped Rianne by the upper arm and pulled her away from the edge of the boardwalk. His touch was hot, even through her clothing, and evoked memories she didn't want to think about. Jerking her arm out of his grasp, she snapped, "Don't touch me!"

"Damn it," he muttered under his breath, raking his hand through his hair in exasperation. "Look, Rianne—"

"Leave me alone."

"I'm not going to leave you alone," he growled. "I claimed you, and I intend to keep you."

Although Rianne lifted her chin defiantly, inwardly she quailed. She didn't want to be near him. It hurt too much, and was far too dangerous. And so was the determination she read on his face, and the desire that heated his gaze. He still wanted her for his mistress.

And Pagan was a man who was accustomed to getting what he wanted.

She folded her arms over her chest and once again fixed her gaze on the building across the street. She couldn't look at him; the more she did, and the more she saw the hot possessiveness in his eyes, the more frightened she became. If she let her guard down for a moment, she would remember the passion and pleasure they had shared, and that would be disastrous. Anger was her only hope. She had to fan the flames high, forge it into a shield she could use to protect herself against him.

Pagan fretted under the long, uncomfortable silence. If she wanted to ignore him, why should he care? But he did. This chill emotionlessness nagged at him like an aching tooth. He would rather have endured tears and recriminations, or even open hatred. That at least would give him something to work with. Damning himself for a fool, he said, "Come inside, Rianne. We need to talk."

"We have nothing to talk about," she said.

"Yes, we do."

She glanced at him from the corner of her eye. His jaw was thrust forward stubbornly, and she knew he wasn't going to let her walk away from him. At least not yet.

"Hello, you two," Alastair said from behind her, startling them both. "Beautiful morning, isn't it?"

"Yes," Pagan growled.

Rianne turned to look at her father, relief making her legs tremble. He was holding the reins of two horses, and his boots were muddy from the street. But he was the most welcome sight she'd ever beheld in her life. Just a few more minutes, and then she'd have all week to regain a measure of emotional balance. Yes, she would have to deal with Pagan again this weekend, but perhaps then she'd have the resources for it.

"Shall we go, Father?" she asked.

"Indeed we shall, sweetheart," he said, handing her one set of reins. It was, she noticed, the same horse she'd ridden on the previous trip.

"What," Pagan said, "is going on here?"

Alastair beamed happily. "Rianne's coming out to the mine with me. We're going to work it together. But don't worry, I'll have her back here in plenty of time to sing for you."

Not wanting to miss Pagan's reaction to the news, Rianne turned to look at him. His face was a study in emotion: astonishment, chagrin, disapproval and anger were all mingled in his expression. Truly, it was most gratifying. Rianne smiled, triumph shooting through her.

That smile triggered Pagan's temper. He took a long stride toward her and clamped his hand on her wrist. As he pulled her toward the saloon, he glanced over his shoulder at Alastair and said, "I want to have a word with your daughter. Privately."

"Go ahead," Alastair said. "But you won't change her mind."

Once inside, Pagan closed the door and leaned his back against it. Rianne folded her arms over her chest and glared at him, wishing someone would come downstairs and interrupt. But the saloon was empty; even John Ferguson was asleep at this hour.

"You can't be serious about this," Pagan said.

"Oh, I am, very."

He gritted his teeth. She'd done this to get away from him, knowing Alastair didn't have the heart to refuse her. "Mining is backbreaking, dangerous work. You've got no business going out there, and you know it."

"As I told my father, hard work doesn't frighten me."

"I forbid it," he growled.

She tilted her head back to look at him and smiled. "Forbid away." she said. "I'm going."

"Damn it, Rianne . . ." Pagan broke off in mid-sentence. He'd been about to say more, a great deal more. But she had the bit in her teeth, and he was learning that to oppose her would only make her more determined. But the fact that she wanted to get away from him so badly made him want to keep her even more.

"You won't last a week," he said.

"We'll see."

"Alastair must be out of his mind to agree to this!"

"Well, we Kierneys are a mad lot," she said. "Now stand aside."

Pagan smiled one of those sharp-edged predator's smiles of his, but didn't move. "Hiding out in the wilderness won't do you any good. You belong to me, and you know it."

"Oh!" Her smoldering anger flared. Surely a more arrogant man had never been born! "I will belong to my husband, whoever he may be."

The thought of her with another man flashed through his mind, leaving outrage in its wake. Damn her for saying it. Damn her for even thinking it! Driven by a black wave of jealousy, he pushed off from the door and walked toward her. Dropping his hands heavily on her shoulders, he looked down into her face. "That was the wrong thing to say, Rianne."

She glared right back at him, unwilling to give an inch in this contest of wills. "So?"

"Why do you insist on pushing me like this?" he demanded in exasperation. "Anyone else would know better."

"Perhaps I just know *you* better," she retorted.

Pagan sighed. "Talk is wasted between us, as is anger. There is only one thing that matters." Slowly, he pulled her toward him.

"Don't," she said, panic racing through her. She put her palms flat against his chest and braced her arms.

184

He could have forced her closer very easily, but chose not to. Superior strength was not the issue here. Of their own volition, his hands roamed over her back restlessly as though remembering the feel of her skin, the wonder of her response. "You can run as far and as fast as you want," he murmured, "but you can't hide from yourself. Or your feelings."

"You've killed every bit of feeling I had for you," she said. If only it were true! If only she could feel nothing when he touched her, when she heard his voice or looked into his eyes.

"Then why do you shiver when I do this?" he asked, brushing the tips of his fingers along the line of her jaw to her ear.

"It was distaste."

Pagan knew better. "Was it?" He stroked her again, and again the reaction of her body betrayed her.

"Yes." She felt as though the room was closing in on her, pressing close, stealing her breath. "Take your hands off me."

With a hiss of indrawn breath, he let her go. "You don't give an inch, do you?"

"I've already 'given' much too much," she said as coolly as she could manage. "But that was naivete, not stupidity. I've learned my lesson, Mr. Roark. I know better than to put my heart where you can step on it again."

Pagan reached for her again, but she spun away from his hands. Frustration made a hard knot in his chest. He was quickly losing control of this conversation, and with it, his temper. "Rianne, I'm warning you . . ."

"Save your threats for someone else," she hissed. "I am neither intimidated nor interested. And one more thing: when I come back here to sing on Saturday nights, I expect to be treated like a lady."

"I'll treat you like a woman." There was a steely light of battle in his eyes.

So, she thought, he hadn't gotten his way and now he was spoiling for a fight. Oh, she knew what he'd expected. He thought she'd sulk for a while, perhaps throw a few vases like Felice Cardonne, but in the end she'd come around to his way of thinking. It must have worked for him many times for him to be so sure of himself. A little sweet-talk, a few kisses, and the women just jumped to do his bidding. Well, this was his first Kierney woman, and she wasn't about to dance to his tune.

Meeting his gaze steadily, she said, "You own my Saturday nights, Mr. Roark. But this is *my* time, and you're wasting it."

"Very well, your royal Highness." Pagan gave her a mocking bow before moving out of her way. "I give you two days out there, Rianne. You're soft. You can't imagine how heavy dirt and rocks are after an hour of hauling. You'll have to put your food in a tree to keep the bears from stealing it. The mosquitoes are beginning to fly, and ours are nearly as big as your thumb."

"Nothing," she said through clenched teeth, "could be worse than staying here with you."

Turning on her heel, she left the saloon.

"Two days!" Pagan called after her.

Alastair was already mounted. As Rianne stormed out of the Golden Bear, he raised his eyebrows. "I gather from the look on your face that your discussion didn't go well."

"If only I were a man," she said, untying her horse's reins from the post. "I'd . . . I'd . . ." She couldn't think of anything bad enough, so she didn't finish the sentence. But there was so much frustration in her that it simply had to come out. "Damn it!" she snarled. "Damn everything!"

"Where did you learn to curse?" her father asked.

"Here." Throwing convention to the wind, she mounted astride. "Before I met Pagan Roark, I'd never even *thought* of cursing."

Alastair chuckled. "Pagan does that to people sometimes."

"I don't want to talk about him any more," she said. Pagan had said and done a great many things, most of which she was paying the price for now. "Let's go, Father. There's a piece of the Promised Land waiting for us."

The Songbird was her way out. Out and away from Henderson City, and most especially, from Pagan Roark.

Chapter Fourteen

Pagan pulled his mount to a halt at the top of the hill overlooking the mine. At first he saw only the animals and the white square of the tent, which had been pitched on a small level area a few hundred yards from the mine entrance.

"Where are you, Rianne Kierney?" he asked, his gaze raking the opposite hillside.

Three days had passed since he and Rianne had parted on such bad terms. He'd told her she'd quit after two days, and she'd proven him wrong. Damn her for being so stubborn! And damn himself for coming out here to make sure she was all right.

Since she left, he'd spent every night pacing the floor of his room, unable to sleep. Fool that he was, he actually missed her! It was as though some important part of him had gone with her, and he wouldn't be whole until she came back. He'd never felt like this before, even for his former wife. When Sylvia had left him, taking everything he owned with her, he'd only felt relief.

But there had been no relief for him this time. Every moment had been spent remembering the feel of Rianne's skin beneath his hands, her marvelous voice flowing over him like a caress. He'd thought to purge his obsession by taking her to his bed, but their lovemaking had only increased his desire for her. It would be better for them both if it had not, but there it was.

He was caught, snared, drawn into her Siren's net. And there he'd stay—at least until he found a way to rid himself of this strange, driving need for her.

Something white moved on the opposite hillside, and Pagan stood in his stirrups to get a better view. His breath went out in a sigh when he realized that the scrap of white was Rianne's chemise, and then in again with a harsh gasp when he saw that she was pushing a heavily laden wheelbarrow in front of her. Even as he watched, her foot slipped, sending her to her knees. She struggled back to her feet and continued pushing.

"Damn it to hell!" he muttered, urging his mount into a canter.

By the time he reached the stream below, he saw that Rianne had gone back to the mine. He leaped down from his horse and strode up the hill. Rianne emerged from the dark shaft with another load on her wheelbarrow. Pagan grasped the end of the vehicle and took it away from her.

Rianne gasped in surprise when she felt the wheelbarrow being jerked out of her hands. The visitor was between her and the sun, so she could see nothing but the silhouette of a tall man. Still, she knew who it was. By the breadth of his shoulders, his stance, and the sudden swift tattoo of her heart, she knew him.

"Pagan!" she gasped.

Somehow, Pagan resisted the urge to take her in his arms. His gaze traveled over her, noting the simple braid falling over her shoulder, the dust that smudged her face and arms, the damp chemise that clung to the sweet curves of her breasts. There was a touch of sunburn on her shoulders despite her broad-brimmed hat. "I like your mining attire," he said.

Rianne crossed her arms over her chest. She'd forgotten the state of her dress—or undress, to be more accurate. The sun was hot, the work strenuous, and she'd abandoned her corset almost immediately. One day more had seen the disposal of her jacket, and today, her blouse. Upon seeing her with only a chemise, her father had said 'I'm glad to see you have good sense', and Rianne hadn't given it another thought. But the appreciative heat in Pagan's eyes made her feel naked and exposed.

"What are you doing here?" she asked, her tone sharp as she tried to hide her discomfiture.

"I just wanted to see how my investment is doing."

"Me, or the mine?" she demanded.

"Both."

Rianne was not about to allow herself to be drawn into one of the tense, pointed conversations Pagan seemed to like so much. "One is none of your business. As for the other . . . Father!" she called over her shoulder. "Mr. Roark is here to find out how we're doing."

"Hoy, Pagan!" Alastair's voice drifted, phantom-like, out of the mine. "I'll be up in a minute."

Rianne reached for the wheelbarrow, but Pagan put out his hand to stop her.

"You've got no business lifting a load like that," he growled. "Leave it."

"I've been hauling this wheelbarrow around for three days," she said. "I didn't have a bit of trouble before you showed up." Pushing his hand out of the way, she hefted the handles of the wheelbarrow and headed it toward a pile of mine detritus a short distance away.

Pagan cursed under his breath. Why should he care if she wanted to do a man's labor? What should it matter? But it did. Rianne should have fine clothes, jewelry — anything but living out here in the wilderness and working herself like a draft horse. As she leaned forward to force the vehicle over a bump, he lost all hope of restraint.

He went after her, his long strides covering the ground swiftly. Curling his arm around her waist, he lifted her clear of the wheelbarrow. She struggled and kicked, so he tucked her under his arm and carried her back up to the mine.

Setting her on her feet, he said, "I'm not going to watch you push ·that load, Rianne. As many times as you try, I'll stop you."

"I'll do it when you're gone, then," she hissed, furious at his casual handling of her. She had been powerless in his grasp, and it was the final, physical demonstration of her inability to stop him from taking over her feelings and her life.

Alastair appeared in the mine entrance, preventing her from saying anything else. His shirt was soaked with sweat, and fine dust had settled in every crease in his face. But he looked years younger, and he walked forward with a firm, buoyant stride to shake hands with Pagan.

"We're about ready to stop for the day," the old man said. "Supper won't be fancy—I won't let Rianne cook after she's spent the day hauling that wheelbarrow—but you're welcome to join us."

"We're having toadstools," Rianne said *sotto voce.*

Pagan grinned at her. "I came intending to share your meal. But I brought supper with me—ham and redeye gravy and bread baked fresh this morning. It's a good thing, as I see now."

"Who made the bread?" Rianne asked.

"A woman by the name of Julia Nathan arrived in town the day before yesterday. She set herself up in a tent on the edge of town, put up a hand-lettered sign that says 'Miss Julia's Restaurant', and started cooking. Lord, does it smell good! The men have been swarming around that tent like bees to honey, and I think she's going to be a rich woman some day."

"Ah, it sounds like heaven!" Alastair said, wiping a trickle of sweat from his face with his sleeve. "I'm going to sluice off some of this dirt before sampling Miss Julia's delicacies. Redeye gravy, indeed!"

Rianne didn't have the vaguest idea what redeye gravy was, but there was another, more important issue on her mind. What did Julia Nathan look like? she wondered. Was she young and pretty? Perhaps just being young and unmarried was enough in this female-starved community. Certainly Pagan seemed to be pleased at Miss Nathan's arrival in town. The question hovered at the tip of Rianne's tongue, but she controlled herself sternly. She would *not* give Pagan the satisfaction of asking about Julia Nathan.

Realizing suddenly that she'd been standing silent far too long, and that Pagan was looking at her with mingled amusement and speculation on his face, she turned away hurriedly. "I'll get the fire started," she said.

Pagan grasped her arm. "You've done enough for today," he said. "Go wash up. I'll take care of supper."

She wanted to refuse. She wanted to tell him she didn't want anything from him, not his help, not his food or drink, and certainly not his attention. But doing so would alert her father to trouble, and she didn't want that at all. So she merely nodded curtly and waited for him to let her go.

Pagan held her arm a moment longer, savoring the feel of her sun-warmed skin beneath his palm. He thought of all the women he'd known in his life—lovely women, expensive and perfectly groomed, willing and expert partners in bed. And not one of them affected him like this stubborn, sharp-tongued lady with the dirt-smudged face. He found that silk and lace, rouged smiles and artful lovemaking couldn't compare to Rianne's honey-brown eyes and smooth, velvet voice, the sheer intensity of her love and hate and smoldering passion.

There was a most intriguing emotion in those expressive eyes of hers, one he recognized because she'd brought out the very same emotion in him. Smiling, he

192

said, "Julia Nathan is fifty-two years old, stout and grey-haired."

"What makes you think I care what she looks like?" Rianne demanded, trying to ignore the rush of relief that went through her.

"You were jealous."

"I was not."

He laughed. "Ah, Rianne, don't you know you can't hide your feelings? Your eyes reveal everything that's going on in that lovely head of yours."

"Are you quite finished?" she asked.

"For now," he said softly.

Promise darkened his eyes, as well as burgeoning desire. Rianne's pulse quickened. She pulled out of his grasp, rejecting both him and her own weakness. Forcing herself not to glance back, she climbed down the slope to the stream, then walked along the water toward the spot where the hillside would block Pagan's view of her.

Feeling a trickle of perspiration running down her cheek, she reached up to wipe it off. Her fingertips came away dirty. She grimaced. Blasting seemed to send a fine powder of soil into the air, coating everything with a thin layer of grit. Sometimes she felt as though she'd never get clean no matter how many times she washed. Her imagination conjured up a vision of the woman he had married—blonde, perfumed, beautiful and beautifully dressed. *How awful I must be in comparison!*

In sudden distaste, Rianne pulled off her dirt-stained chemise and began scrubbing it in the cold water of the stream. She'd thought a few days' separation from Pagan would let her get her feelings under control. It was obvious that it hadn't worked, however, for here she was, jealous of a woman she'd never met, a woman who had come and gone from Pagan's life years ago. But the fact that this unknown woman had claimed his love and his name was a burning pain in Rianne's heart.

"You're an idiot, Rianne Kierney," she muttered savagely. "A complete, utter idiot."

With a sigh, she rose to her feet and spread the chemise out on a nearby rock to dry. Then she removed the rest of her clothes and stepped out into the stream, gasping as the cold water rose to her knees, her thighs and finally, her hips.

"You forgot the soap," Pagan said from behind her.

"Oh!" Rianne managed to keep enough presence of mind to crouch down so that the water covered her to her neck. "You cad!" she raged, turning to face him. "You scoundrel, you . . . you wolf in sheeps' clothing, you—"

"Such language," he chided. "Do you want the soap, or don't you?"

"Just leave it on the bank there and go away."

"I brought this all the way out here just to please you, and all you can do is call me names." Raising the bar to his nose, he inhaled deeply. "Ah, violets. It seems to me you're fond of violet."

Violet was her favorite scent, but she would have cut off her arm rather than admit it.

Pagan's smile broadened. "If you want the soap, come get it."

She met his gaze, ready to tell him to take the dratted soap straight to the devil. But then she realized just now much he was enjoying her discomfiture. He was playing with her, using her modesty to amuse himself. It was time for Pagan Roark to learn that she could play on *his* emotions as much as he could hers.

"Very well," she said.

Slowly and deliberately, she straightened. It took every bit of self-discipline she possessed not to try to cover her nakedness, but she managed it.

Pagan's eyebrows went up in surprised disbelief. Surely the memory of her rising up out of the water like Venus from the sea would stay with him the rest of his life. Ahh, his Rianne—always doing the unexpected, always taking his world and twisting it halfway around. The sight of her smooth, water-slick skin reminded him of the time he'd washed her, how she had responded so deeply, and how she had driven him mindless with desire.

It was all he could do not to wade into the water and crush her against him. But her face didn't mirror the soft seductiveness of her body; there was a steely challenge in her eyes that boded ill for lovemaking.

As she walked toward him with all the outward casualness of a lady taking a Sunday stroll in the park, he realized that the challenge was very real. He knew he could seduce her—the fiery passion between them was always seething just beneath the surface, ready to flare to life at the slightest provocation. But today . . . He sighed. Today, to seduce her was to lose her. And that he couldn't abide. He, who had gambled, gained, and then lost more than many men would ever possess, was unwilling to take the chance of letting this woman walk out of his life.

"You win this battle, my prickly little Siren," he murmured under his breath. "But I intend to win the war."

He watched her walk, fascinated by the way the water lapped her thighs, caressing the smooth white skin. There was a dusting of goosebumps across her shoulders, and the cold stream had caused her nipples to tighten into hard peaks. Droplets glistened like diamonds in the light brown curls that adorned her woman's mound. He wanted to lick each droplet from her, then taste the sweet silk of her flesh. He wanted to claim her, to make her his all over again, to hear her admit his possession. But he couldn't. He closed his eyes once, struggling for control of his churning emotions, but opened them immediately, not wanting to miss a minute of this real-life fantasy.

She stopped in front of him, the challenge still in her eyes, and held out her hand for the soap. Pushing his raging desire back into abeyance, Pagan dropped the bar into her outstretched palm.

"Thank you," she said.

"You're welcome."

His eyes were hooded, expressionless, and she realized that he was completely unaffected by her nakedness. *He doesn't want me!* she thought. She hadn't realized until now that she'd presumed on a desire that wasn't there any longer.

God give me strength! he thought, savagely restraining the need to touch her. If he wanted a second chance with this lovely, willful woman, he couldn't go leaping upon her like some wild animal.

Rianne wanted to cover herself with her hands and slink away, but pride forbade it. She'd started this, and win or not, she had to see it through. With twenty generations of Scottish pride to stiffen her back, she turned and walked back to the center of the stream. When she glanced over her shoulder to see if Pagan was still watching her, she found only the empty riverbank.

"Oh, God!" she moaned, pressing the soap against her breasts. "Oh, God!"

But even misery couldn't long withstand cold rushing water. She washed quickly, shivering all the while. The smell of violets was strong upon the air, and she thought she'd never truly like that scent again.

Her chemise was nearly dry by the time she finished bathing. She put her clothes back on, dreading facing Pagan again. But there was no help for it; short of running off into the wilderness, she was stuck.

"Rianne!" Alastair called. "Come up while the food is hot!"

With a sigh, she trudged back to the campsite, stopping only long enough to pull a clean blouse on over her chemise. Pagan and her father were standing at the edge of the ledge, looking out over the tiny valley. Pagan leaned down to pull her up the last few feet, smiling at her like a fond big brother before returning his attention to Alastair.

"How far down have you gotten?" he asked the older man.

"Oh, seven, eight feet," Alastair said. "We'll be hitting bedrock at fifteen feet or so. That's when we'll find out if we've hit paydirt."

"And if we haven't?" Rianne asked.

Alastair shrugged. "Then we cross out the 'Songbird' on that timber and write 'Skunked' instead. Come on, sweetheart. I'm so hungry I could eat a bear."

"That's big talk from a man who was very nearly eaten *by* a bear," she said, linking arms with him and letting him draw her toward the fire.

Pagan's eyebrows went up. "I think a story is waiting to be told."

"Ahh, it's a veritable heroic saga, my friend," Alastair said. "I was in those trees over there, ah, tending to personal business, when this enormous bear—"

"It was a plain old bear," Rianne corrected. "And it looked quite elderly, if you ask me."

The old man snorted. "What do you know about bears? Now, where was I . . . Oh, yes. This terrible, savage bear leaped out of the bushes at me, all gleaming fangs and dripping claws. I called for help—"

"Bleated like a sheep," Rianne interrupted again.

"—And Rianne came charging to my rescue, beating two cookpots together and screaming like a banshee. The bear took off in one direction, and I in another."

Pagan nearly sputtered in surprise at the thought of Rianne charging a bear armed with a couple of cookpots. And he'd called her soft! "You were lucky that time," he said. "I wouldn't try that again, if I were you."

As regally as though they were coming to eat in the

finest restaurant in the world, Alastair escorted Rianne to the flat rock that served as her chair. Pagan, as chef, served the food. Rianne ate in silence, listening to her father chatter away about gold — what it looked like, how it smelled, how badly he wanted it. She wanted to find it too, but not because of the gold itself. She wanted what it would buy her: freedom from Pagan Roark.

Finally, even Alastair fell silent. The sky gradually darkened to indigo, but there was an insistent glow remaining on the eastern horizon.

"The days are very long here," Rianne said.

Her father chuckled. "We're far enough north to get a taste of the midnight sun, sweetheart. And during the deepest part of winter, we have only a few hours of light. No visitors, except those already in the area. Once the river freezes in October, we're cut off from the outside."

"But . . . what about the mines? Can they be worked only in the spring and summer?"

"Ah, now, that's an entirely different matter. Gold beckons in all seasons," her father said. "You dig in the winter so you're ready to put the sluices to work as soon as the streams thaw in spring."

Rianne stared at him in mingled surprise and concern. "So we won't see a . . . large return until next spring?"

"Well, sweetheart, there's always the possibility that this hill is solid gold. Stranger things have happened."

"But—" she prompted.

He scuffed his toe in the dirt. "But chances are we'll have to dig in a couple of different places before we know whether there's gold in this hill or not."

"I see." Discouragement rode her heavily. She hadn't expected this. Foolishly, she had hung her hopes on the gold buying her way out of her dilemma and hadn't considered the fact that they might find only a *little* gold. For a moment she was tempted to give up. Then she squared her shoulders; the game wasn't lost until it was over. She'd just have to pray for a miracle—and work very, very hard.

As though Pagan had read her thoughts, he asked, "Why don't you come back to town with me in the morning?"

"No, thank you," she said stiffly.

"This is no place for you." He raked his hand through his hair. "You've made your point, Rianne. I concede that you have more grit than many men I've seen up here, and I admire you for it. But it's time to stop now."

"No!" She would *not* go crawling back to the Golden Bear. "It takes more than a little dirt to make me quit."

Alastair glanced up at the hill ruefully. "That's more than a little dirt. There's no shame in going back, love."

Yes, there is! she thought, feeling suddenly weary, as though all the energy had drained out of her. Aloud, she said, "I'm doing exactly what I want, and I'm enjoying myself. Now, if you gentlemen are finished, I'll just clean these dishes and head for bed. Morning seems to come all too early out here."

Once she was wrapped snugly in her blankets, however, she couldn't sleep. She lay still, looking up at the tent's canvas ceiling and listening to the sound of Pagan's boots crunching on the gravel outside. He was pacing, making regular trips back and forth across the level ground on which the camp stood. He walked for a long time, his footsteps a counterpoint to the gentle night sounds of the forest. She finally fell asleep. But even her dreams echoed the sound of footsteps, and the feel of her own pain.

Pagan was gone when she emerged from her tent the next morning. Her father had evidently gone up to the mine to work, for she could hear faint noises coming from the shaft. He had already built a fire and put the coffeepot on to boil. Yawning, she poured herself a cup of the thick, strong brew and sat down beside the fire.

"Look out below!" Alastair shouted as he hurried out of the mine.

She smiled. Setting off the carefully placed charges of dynamite was her father's favorite job. He never failed to caper about like some small boy pleased at his own destructiveness.

There was a loud rumble in the depths of the mine, then a cloud of dirt and rock chips belched out of the opening. A flock of birds, startled by the noise, clattered into the sky on frantic wings.

"As soon as the dust settles, we go back to hauling dirt," Alastair said, getting a cup of coffee for himself and sitting down beside her.

Rianne stretched her arms overhead, then winced. Every muscle in her body was sore. Well, she thought, I'll either fall apart completely, or I'll get used to it. "Do you want me to dig this time?" she asked.

"Heaven forbid! I've let you do many jobs that were too hard for a woman, but that's too much." He sighed. "I wish I were a rich man so that you could have fine silks and laces and sit around all day driving your many suitors insane."

She shook her head, thinking that the one suitor she would have accepted wasn't interested. "You're daft, Father. If I sat around all day pandering to men's admiration, *I'd* be the one driven insane."

They finished their coffee, then walked arm and arm up to the mine to begin the day's labor. They worked well into the afternoon, Alastair shoveling gravel into a rude wood wheelbarrow and wheeling it to the surface, where Rianne took it from him and dumped it into a steadily growing pile of detritus from the mine.

The sun grew hotter and hotter. Her hands blistered even inside her gloves, but she merely wrapped a piece of cloth around them, put her gloves back on and kept working. There were many times when she had almost begged to go back to Henderson City. But every shovelful brought her father closer to realizing his dream. *And yours, don't forget,* a small, cynical part of her mind reminded her. *Gold means money, which in turn spells freedom. Freedom from Pagan Roark.* She wouldn't have to see him ever again.

That prospect should make her happy, but it didn't. She realized she would yearn for him for a long, long time. Perhaps forever. But she had fallen in love with a myth, not a man, she told herself harshly. He'd made it clear that he no longer wanted her, anyway. It was her voice he wanted. Not Rianne, but the Songbird.

"Just one more," she said, leaning forward to shove the heavy wheelbarrow a few feet farther.

Then she went back for another load. "Just one more," she said again. And again she went back, and again, each time telling herself that it was the last load. But somehow, it never was.

The pile of dirt and gravel grew. Perhaps someday it would be as big as her dreams.

Chapter Fifteen

When Rianne and Alastair rode into Henderson City Saturday afternoon, they found the town crowded with men.

Alastair stopped his horse and waved to a man who was walking on the boardwalk nearby. "What's going on?" he asked. "What are all these men doing in town?"

"Everybody came to hear the Songbird," the man said.

Rianne groaned under her breath. At another time, she might have been flattered, but now she felt only consternation. The more men came to hear her sing, the more valuable she was to Pagan Roark.

"We'd better go in the back door," Alastair said, nodding a thank you to the man before continuing on.

"Oh, Father, this is terrible!"

"God gave you an angel's voice, sweetheart," he said. "You can't blame lonely men for appreciating it."

No, she thought grimly, but I can blame Pagan Roark for taking advantage of it. She followed her father to the narrow alleyway behind the Golden Bear.

He held out his hands for her reins. "Go on up and get yourself a bath. I'll take the horses down to the stable."

"You'll be back here afterward?" she asked.

"Of course, sweetheart. Tell them to bring up a tub for me, too."

Chewing her lip in worry, she watched him ride away.

His promise only encompassed Monday through Friday; he had every right to drink tonight. But she'd hoped that a few days of sobriety would make him want to give up whiskey altogether. If only they didn't live here in a saloon! There were stronger men than Alastair who would succumb to that kind of temptation.

The back door opened directly into the kitchen, which, fortunately, was unoccupied. Good. Perhaps she'd get upstairs without having to see Pagan. Certainly no one would be able to hear her; the din coming from the saloon was terrific, even at this early hour.

"You certainly are making money for *him*," she muttered to herself. Instead of agreeing to stay for a certain length of time, she should have insisted on a percentage of the saloon's profits. If nothing else came from this awful venture into commerce, she would emerge a much better businesswoman.

She went upstairs, hurrying past the doorway to the saloon in the hope no one would see her. To her surprise, she succeeded. Opening the door to her room, she slipped inside.

"Dear God in Heaven!" she cried, staring wide-eyed at her surroundings.

Her room was completely changed. An armoire and a dressing table had been brought in, as well as two upholstered chairs. A large, flower-patterned rug almost hid the rough board floor. A pale blue comforter replaced the blanket that had covered her bed, and matching velvet draperies adorned the window. The color was disturbingly like that of Pagan's eyes, and she knew he'd chosen it deliberately.

With a knot growing in the center of her stomach, she went to the armoire and flung the doors open. There was nothing inside she recognized as hers. Oh, there were gowns, more than she'd ever owned at one time in her life. The armoire was full of colors and fabrics, a staggering array of silks and satins, beautiful French laces, ribbons and flounces and soft, plush velvet. On the shelf above were hats, confections of veiling and feathers, and below, slippers to match the gowns.

She ran to the bureau, jerking drawers open at random. Her plain cotton underclothes were gone, replaced by sheer, silken garments and provocative nightwear. Pagan had done this, taking everything she owned—including her suitcase—and replacing it with what he wanted her to have. Oh, the gall of the man! It was even more infuriating to note that he'd chosen the correct sizes, down to the shoes and gloves.

In another man, she would have interpreted this as a declaration of his desire for her. But in Pagan, it was something entirely different. This was his way of controlling her, of forcing her to don the Songbird's plumage.

Her temper snapped. Possessed by sheer, reckless anger, she whirled and strode out into the hallway. "Pagan Roark!" she shouted, uncaring who heard her or what they thought. She took a deep breath, intending to shriek loud enough to be heard downstairs, or in the next Territory, if necessary.

"I'm right here," he said, appearing at the end of the hallway. "There's no need to shatter my eardrums."

"I want to talk to you this instant!"

"I see you found the improvements I made in your room," he said, smiling.

Turning on her heel, she marched back into her room. He followed, closing the door behind him. She jerked it open with all her strength, then stood in front of it, arms akimbo, daring him to close it again.

Still smiling, he folded his arms over his chest and looked down at her with an infuriatingly innocent expression on his face.

"Where are my things?" she demanded.

"These are your things," he said.

"I want my old clothes back."

"Sorry, but they've been burned."

She gasped. "What gave you the right to burn my property?"

"Aesthetics, love." His smile broadened. "It was a crime to see such a lovely woman wearing those appalling clothes. And especially not the famous Songbird."

"The moment my back was turned . . . !" She clenched her arms at her sides, her chest rising and falling with her rapid breathing. "How dare you! Well, you're not going to have your way this time! I'm not wearing those clothes or sleeping in that bed. And I'll just go downstairs in what I'm wearing now."

Pagan struggled to control his temper. She was doing it again! Damn it to hell, did she have to fight him on everything? He strode to the armoire and pulled out an evening gown of amber satin trimmed with narrow bands of lace. "Why don't you try this one? I bought it because I knew it would bring out the color of your hair and eyes."

He was right. She couldn't have picked out a lovelier dress herself, and that fact only infuriated her more. "How generous of you," she snapped. "But I would have preferred that you apply that money to my debt."

"Ah, no, sweet. I want *you* to pay that debt." Although Pagan had come in here intending to be reasonable, she was proving to be too much for him. He'd turned the entire territory upside down finding these things for her so quickly, and all she could do was turn her nose up at them. Tossing the amber gown onto the bed, he growled, "And I want you to wear that tonight."

"No."

"No?"

She crossed her arms over her chest. "No."

He smiled, but there was no humor in it. It was the smile of a man who had been pushed too far, and was ready to do something about it. "We'll see about that."

Rianne's eyes widened as he walked toward her. Whirling, she ran to the door. But he reached it first, slamming it closed and turning the key in the lock. She backed away hastily.

"What do you think you're doing?" she demanded. Despite the brave question, there was a hint of a quiver in her voice. And more than a hint in her mind.

"I'm going to see that you wear that dress," he said softly. "Even if I have to put it on you myself."

"Get away from me!"

He took a step forward. With a flurry of skirts, she darted toward the adjoining room, intending to lock herself inside. But Pagan moved much too quickly for her. He shut that door, locked it, and turned to face her again.

"Say you'll wear the dress, and I'll give you this." He dangled the key between his thumb and forefinger.

Rianne felt like the mouse being played with by a cat, darting here and there but never getting away, waiting every moment for the feel of that claw-studded paw to come down on her neck. *No mouse, but a flesh-and-blood woman,* a small corner of her mind whispered. *And he has no right!*

Putting her hands on her hips, she met his gaze squarely. "You can go to the devil," she hissed.

"I probably will," he replied in a quiet, calm voice that sent chills down her spine. "But before I do, you will wear that dress."

Before she could react, he lunged forward, one strong arm going around her waist. He tossed her onto the bed. She rolled toward the opposite side, but his long, hard body came down on hers, pinning her to the mattress.

"Now," he said, grasping her wrists to keep her from clawing him, "Let's talk."

"I have nothing to say to you!"

"Then you can listen to what *I* have to say," he growled. "I spent a small fortune getting these things here so quickly. You can be as ungrateful as you want, but I intend to see that you use them."

She tried to wriggle out from under him, but she might as well have tried to move the building for all the good it did. So, held immobile by his greater weight and strength, she used the only weapon she had, her words. "Money is everything to you, isn't it? Your friend, your lover, your God! No wonder they call you Pagan!"

He stared down at her with narrowed eyes. Who was she to judge him? Her family had been well-to-do. She hadn't had to grow up wondering where the next meal came from, or living in an orphanage where the bigger boys took the smaller ones' food. Well, *he* had. To protect his younger brothers, he had learned to fight. And he'd fought so hard, so savagely, than even the worst bullies had learned to leave the Roark brothers alone.

That orphanage had forged him, molded him steel-hard and razor-sharp. He had worked all his life, schemed and saved and sweated to make his way in the world. By some miracle, he'd managed to keep his dreams and his principles. Telling Rianne would be a waste of time, however; child of privilege that she was, she would never understand. Her principles were different, her whole world softer and kinder than his.

If he had a shred of sense, he'd let her leave. But as soon as that thought entered his mind, his heart rejected it. He couldn't let her go. He had to hold her, make her his again. Obsession though it be, it was stronger than common sense, stronger even than the will he'd once thought to be adamantine.

Angry as he was, his body was reacting to her closeness. Her soft curves molded to his, the faint scent of violet and woman, served to make his senses reel. He wanted her too badly. A moment more of this, and he'd lose what little self-control he still possessed. With a harsh sigh of frustration, he rolled away from her and sat up.

Rianne squeezed her eyes closed. Pagan's withdrawal had been so sudden that it was almost as though she revolted him. She'd demanded to be left alone. Well, she'd gotten her wish. But it had turned out to be a very bitter triumph. And it wasn't until this moment, when he had rejected her utterly, that she realized how very much she still wanted him. Oh, to have been given a glimpse of true love, and then to discover it only an illusion! Her anger

207

evaporated, leaving only sadness. Her mother's reserve, hurtful as it was, had at least been consistent.

"Will you leave now?" She averted her gaze, unable to look at the man who had claimed her body and thrown away her heart.

"As soon as you say you'll wear the dress."

She closed her eyes against the sudden sting of tears. "What does it matter what I look like?"

Because you're beautiful, and I want you to wear beautiful things, he thought. Aloud, however, he said, "They've come to see the famous Songbird, not some prim schoolgirl in a dress a grandmother would wear."

"Perhaps I should show my bosom and kick my legs like Felice Cardonne," she said. "Then I can make even more money for you."

A gambling man, Pagan recognized a bluff when he saw one. "Perhaps," he agreed. But he was ready to tie her to the bed to stop her from engaging in any such nonsense. She could bare whatever she wanted, but by God, he was going to be the only man to see it.

He truly doesn't care! Rianne thought. There was a stabbing ache in her heart. If he did care, he would never allow her to display herself before strangers. He'd never loved her, never intended to love her. That love that had been the fulfillment of her dreams and the banishing of the aching loneliness that had haunted her life, but to him, it had been merely a pleasant tumble in bed. And now it was over.

Pagan had a sudden urge to smooth his hands down her gold-touched hair, but managed to resist it. Barely. "If you're worried about that amber gown showing too many of your charms to the men downstairs, don't. It's modest enough that even your mother would approve."

Rianne's heart contracted with pain at the mention of her mother. Perhaps if Mother had given her a bit of human warmth and kindness, she wouldn't have mistaken lust for love. No, there was no one else to blame for what had happened. She'd been a fool, plain and simple, and it was her own fault. Tears, unrestrained now, slid from the corners of her eyes to wet the hair at her temples.

The sight of her misery made Pagan angry at himself, and angry at her for having the power to affect him so deeply. "I'm going to warn you once, and then it will be up to you," he said, his voice harsh with restrained emotion. "If you come downstairs wearing anything but that gown, I'm going to bring you right back up here, strip you naked, then dress you myself. Is that clear?"

His arrogance dried Rianne's tears in a hurry. "All right," she hissed. "I'll wear the dratted gown! Does that make you happy?"

"Yes, it does." It took every bit of self-control he possessed to move away from her. But he managed it; either he left this room, or he made love to her. And as much as he might desire her just now, bedding her would push her even farther away. Taking his watch from his pocket, he opened it and said, "You'd better get started. You're expected downstairs in less than an hour. I'll have a bath sent up for you."

Rianne was suddenly very tired. Tired of fighting him, tired of crying, of losing every battle. But she had enough spirit left to ask, "Do you have any other orders, *sir?*"

"Yes. I left some perfume on the dressing table. Wear it."

He was conscious of her gaze on him as he strode to the door, and it was a powerful magnet, urging him to go back. Damn! She'd taken his world and turned it topsy-turvy and inside-out. It was almost as if she had become part of his flesh and his spirit. He doubted he'd ever find peace again if not in her arms.

Rianne watched him leave, buffeted by the pain that tore through her chest. This was the end. Pagan had lost interest in her as a lover and a woman. All she was now was the Songbird. He'd dress her in fancy feathers, shut her up in this soft, luxurious cage, and take her out to show her off to his customers. Then he'd put her back again, not caring that her heart was dying inside her.

With a sigh, she got up from the bed. Taking the amber gown with her, she went to stand in front of the cheval mirror. *Fancy feathers, indeed,* she thought, holding the silk up in front of her. Pagan had been right about the color. It *did* bring out the highlights in her hair, and made the brown of her eyes look as rich and soft as velvet. It was almost as though another person looked back at her from the mirror. No, a different Rianne—no girl now, but a woman. A woman scorned, with trembling lips and eyes reddened from weeping.

"Well, why are you crying about it? You said you didn't want him," she told her reflection. "Are you one of those women who like to be pursued even though they have no intention of giving a man what he wants?"

Neither she nor her reflection knew the answer to that question. The ending of their physical relationship ought to make everything much more simple. But it didn't. Did he lose interest this quickly with others, or only with her? What was it that she lacked that his wife had had?

Perhaps if she could leave, she might be able to find the answers to those questions. Certainly it was the only way to heal her heartbreak, for every time she saw Pagan it only deepened the wound.

"Some day," she said, turning away from the mirror. "I hope the Songbird Mine is luckier than the woman herself."

Pagan sat alone at the table nearest the piano. His whiskey sitting untouched beside him, he looked out over the crowded saloon. There were men four deep at the bar, every available seat was taken, and even the spaces between the tables were crammed with the miners who had come to hear the Songbird. He caught sight of Manfred Locke, who worked a claim on Black Bear Creek nearly twenty miles away. At the end of the bar was Gunn Toomey, who had ridden more than thirty miles from his stake.

Sacks of gold dust, panned laboriously from cold river water, were slapped down on the bar. John Ferguson kept a tally in his head somehow, weighing out the proper amount of gold from each. He never cheated anyone, and to Pagan's knowledge he never made a mistake.

Marie, Alva, and the other girls went from table to table, smiling, listening patiently to improbable tall tales, bringing a bit of feminine softness and warmth to the lives of these lonely men.

The air fairly crackled with anticipation. Every man in the room was waiting impatiently for the Songbird to sing for him. Rianne Kierney, who had sung here quite by accident, had become a phenomenon in this wild corner of the Yukon.

And then Rianne herself appeared in the doorway. She was wearing the amber gown, and looked as regal as the Queen herself. The lustrous silk framed her neck, shoulders and graceful arms, the perfect foil for her pale skin. Pagan had chosen a modest gown; only the uppermost slopes of her breasts were exposed. But the hint of cleavage was more alluring than if her breasts had been half-exposed, and jealousy spiraled through him like a knife.

His gaze left the creamy skin of her chest to take in the rest of her. Her hair was drawn back into a simple chignon, but it was right for her, framing her face so that she looked both innocent and sensual.

A sigh went through the watching men. Pagan saw Rianne clasp her gloved hands together nervously. Before he could get up to escort her, however, Alastair hurried forward and took her hand. Pagan ground his teeth together, jealous, for God's sake, of the woman's father!

Rianne took her place beside the piano, more nervous than she'd ever been in her life. So many men! Then she caught sight of Pagan's face. He was looking at her, a half-smile on his lips that might have been approval, might have been challenge. She straightened her shoulders. If this was the only value she had to him, well, he was going to get his money's worth. For whatever reason, she'd make sure he was sorry to

211

see her go when the time came.

Alastair came to stand beside her, and there was no mistaking the pride on his face. After patting her hand in reassurance, he turned to the noisily milling crowd and shouted, "Gentlemen, I give you Miss Rianne Kierney, our Songbird."

There was an answering cacophony of hoots, yells and pistol shots. Rianne was learning to accept this very unusual audience. They might be a bit too loud, a bit crude, but surely no singer had ever been greeted so enthusiastically in the opera houses of Europe!

They made her proud. No longer nervous, she scanned the sea of faces for Francois Gruillot's broad, bearded countenance. She found him sitting at one of the tables near the center of the room, his smile stretching from ear to ear. Rianne raised her hand for quiet and said, "The 'Marseillaise', Father. For my friend Mr. Gruillot."

During the next two hours, Pagan watched her work her magic over the men. It wasn't just her voice, although that was indeed a marvel. It was the woman herself. With a sudden, sharp dart of surprise, he realized that everything she was, everything she felt was poured into her music. And came out again in a flood of emotion that went straight to the heart. That was what made her special. Rianne Kierney—sensual yet innocent, tempestuous yet kind, distilled down into pure, soul-stealing sound.

When she stopped to take a short rest, he felt bereft, as though something warm and very precious had been taken from him. That low, sultry voice had somehow become part of him, as though it had become imprinted in his bones and blood, his mind and heart and spirit.

"Siren," he muttered, watching her from beneath his eyelids as she left the room.

He didn't look away until she was gone. To be honest, he *couldn't* have looked away if he'd tried. Then someone tapped him on the shoulder, and he swiveled to see Lowell Mason, owner of the Nugget Saloon.

"Evening, Mason," he said.

"Evening. Can I sit down?"

Pagan nodded, studying the other man with cool speculation. He'd never liked Lowell, and Lowell returned his dislike intensely. The man was in his early forties but his stooped shoulders and grey hair made him look much older. Spectacles and a broad, bulging forehead made him seem scholarly, but Pagan knew him for a brute. He used his girls hard, and beat them regularly.

"What can I do for you?" Pagan asked.

"I just wanted to take a look at this Songbird everyone is talking about." Mason took his spectacles off and polished them with his handkerchief. "She's brought you a lot of business."

"Yes, she has."

"She's Kierney's daughter, right? I heard the old drunk is back to working his claim."

"He hasn't been drinking," Pagan said.

Mason's thin, flesh-colored lips stretched in a smile. "He hasn't been finding gold, either."

"Where did you hear that?"

"I hear a lot of things from a lot of different places."

Pagan held his whiskey glass up to the light, admiring the play of light in the dark amber depths. If it were a shade darker, it would be just the color of Rianne's eyes.

Mason hitched his chair closer. He opened his mouth to say something, then closed it again as Rianne came into the room. Pagan watched the man's expression carefully, but Mason had always been a good poker player; there was nothing on his face but polite interest.

Then Rianne began to sing. As her rich voice flowed through the room like sweet, dark velvet, Mason's face showed surprise, consternation, then avarice before he got his features under control again.

"A real singer, isn't she?" Mason said at last. "I wouldn't have expected to see her like in this tail-end of civilization. Quite an improvement over Felice, eh?"

Pagan was not interested in discussing anything about Rianne with Lowell Mason. Just the fact that the man was looking at her made his hackles rise.

"Can I buy you a whiskey?" Mason asked.

"No, thanks." Pagan indicated the drink he hadn't touched. "As you can see, I'm not much of a drinker."

"That's why I was so surprised that you kept this place after you won it off old Sam."

"A man doesn't have to drink to own a saloon."

"I suppose not." Mason chuckled, but his dark eyes were as flat and humorless as lumps of coal.

Pagan, impatient with this verbal sparring, asked, "You hate my guts, Mason. You wouldn't have come in here unless you had a very good reason. Now, why don't you just state your business and move on?"

"All right." Putting his spectacles back on, Mason said, "I want to buy the Golden Bear. Ten thousand dollars in gold, lock, stock and barrel."

Ah, so that's his game, Pagan thought, knowing that to Mason, the saloon's employees came under the heading of 'lock, stock and barrel'. "I'm not interested."

"You'll never get a better offer."

Pagan laughed outright. "Surely you must be joking."

"Twenty thousand."

"No."

"All right!" Mason snapped. "Keep the damned saloon. I'll give you twenty thousand for the girl."

"Indeed?" Pagan raised his eyebrows in mock query, hiding the rage that was building in him like a geyser. *Sell* Rianne? "I thought slavery had been abolished years ago."

Mason snorted. "Then you're too innocent to be in this business."

"I prefer to be called scrupulous," Pagan said in a dangerously soft voice.

The older man chuckled, but it was a dry and humorless substitute for laughter. "You've got about as many scruples as I do."

"There's no need to be insulting," Pagan said.

He watched Mason's face, waiting to see how long it

would take the man to get the message. It took longer than he expected; evidently Mason was stupid as well as a brute.

Finally, the older man seemed to realize that *he'd* been insulted. His face worked spasmodically for a moment. Then, with a visible effort, he smoothed his features. "Does that mean you won't be taking my offer?"

Pagan smiled, the tenseness of his muscles belying his relaxed pose. "Get out."

"Give the lady my regards," Mason said, pushing his chair back.

"When hell freezes over," Pagan growled.

"Stranger things have happened." Turning on his heel, Mason left the Golden Bear.

Pagan slowly relaxed. He'd been expecting something like this from Lowell Mason, but it still made him mad clear through. The gall of the man to offer to *buy* Rianne as though she were some kind of trinket! He was going to have to watch Mason carefully. The draw of Rianne's singing was hurting the Nugget's business badly, and Mason wasn't the sort of man to just let it happen.

"Ah, Rianne," Pagan murmured. "Every day you make my life a little more complicated. Well . . ." Catching her gaze, he raised his whiskey glass in a toast. "Here's to chaos."

Rianne frowned in confusion. She had watched the exchange between Pagan and the other man, and although she couldn't hear what was being said, she knew by the set of Pagan's shoulders that there was tenseness between them.

"Hey, Songbird!" a man shouted from the back of the room, distracting her. "Do you know 'Drink To Me Only With Thine Eyes?' "

She hesitated. That was the song she'd sung to Pagan her first night. She had sung it to him, and for him, and because of that it had become special. If she sang it now, it would bring up memories she wanted to avoid.

She glanced at Pagan, but his face was shuttered, unreadable. If the song had significance to him, she couldn't tell from looking at him. *You're a fool even now!* she told herself harshly. He probably hadn't seen anything special about the song the first time, and wouldn't remember it now.

But she did, and it hurt too much.

"I . . . I'm sorry," she said. "May I sing 'Beautiful Dreamer' instead?"

The crowd assented enthusiastically, and she congratulated herself on her successful diversion. Pagan's expression didn't change in the least; his face might have been carved from marble.

She sang for another hour. Just as she was beginning to tire, Pagan rose to his feet and came to stand beside her.

"That's all for tonight, gentlemen," he said.

There was a roar of protest. Pagan raised his hands in a demand for quiet. When the noise had abated somewhat, he said, "Just come back again next week. Miss Kierney will be singing for us every Saturday night."

Alastair left his seat in front of the piano and kissed Rianne on the cheek. "You go upstairs now, sweetheart. I'll be up in a couple of hours or so."

"Father—"

"Now, darling, don't start sermonizing. I kept my promise. I've spent five long days without a drink, and now I think I'm entitled to a bit of fun."

He patted her shoulder, then turned and began making his way through the throng at the bar. Rianne sighed heavily.

"Let him be, Rianne," Pagan said. "He's not a child. He's a grown man, and you can't do a thing if he wants to drink himself into a stupor. Every man in this room will likely be in the same condition in a few hours."

"But I had hoped five days of going without a drink might change things," she said.

"You can't change the world overnight, Rianne. Or a man. Give him time." Gently, Pagan grasped her shoulders and turned her toward the stairway. "You're exhausted. Go upstairs and get some rest. I'll make sure he doesn't hurt himself."

Feeling a sudden surge of tears, Rianne bit her lip to keep them from overflowing. Now Pagan was being kind, and that hurt almost as badly as his indifference. Kind! He was kind to her father, to his employees and his horses. She wanted to be more to him than an employee or à possession. She wanted to be loved.

But she wasn't going to get what she wanted, and wishing for it would be like wishing to pluck the moon from the sky. With a sigh, she nodded and turned toward the stairway.

Chapter Sixteen

Rianne walked slowly down the hall to her room. She felt empty, as hollow as a lightning-struck tree. Certainly Pagan Roark had come into her life as swiftly and as devastatingly as any storm, and had left it a shambles.

"I wish I'd never laid eyes on him," she muttered under her breath. "Arrogant, unfeeling, selfish—"

"You must be talking about Pagan Roark," a man said from behind her.

With a startled gasp, she whirled to face the man who had been sitting with Pagan earlier in the evening. "Who are you? What are you doing here?"

"Now don't be startled," he said. "I'm a neighbor. Lowell Mason, owner of the Nugget Saloon."

He smiled, but there was something about him she didn't like. For all his outward friendliness, his dark gaze moved over her greedily, as though he were stripping her naked in his mind. A surge of revulsion rippled through her.

"How nice to meet you, Mr. Mason," she said, forcing herself to be polite when she wanted nothing more than to turn her back and escape the man's unwanted presence. "But I'm very tired just now—"

"I just wanted to tell you how much I like your singing," he continued, as though she hadn't spoken at all.

"Thank you very much." Suddenly she remembered why his name had seemed so familiar; he was the saloon owner who had thrown that poor, pregnant girl out into the street because she couldn't work for him any longer. A brutal man, she thought, studying his flat black eyes. Brutal by nature, brutal in deed.

She was suddenly conscious of the empty hallway and the noise downstairs that would cover any cry she might make. No matter how many people there might be in the saloon, she was very much alone with Lowell Mason.

With outward casualness, she started to move away from him. "Good night, Mr. Mason."

"Just a minute." He grasped her wrist. His grip was uncomfortably tight, just beneath the threshold of pain, and his hand was hot even through the fabric of her glove.

Rianne, sensing that this man liked the sight of fear, lifted her chin and met his gaze with cool dignity. "You're hurting my wrist, Mr. Mason."

He relaxed his hold slightly, but didn't let her go. "I came up here to ask you to come to work for me."

"I don't think I'd be interested."

"I'll pay you more than you're making here."

Rianne wasn't the least bit tempted. As badly as she wanted to get away from Pagan, no amount of money could induce her to put herself in this man's power. "No, thank you," she said, trying once more to free her wrist.

"I'll double what Roark is paying you. No one's going to make a better offer than that."

"No, thank you." Failing to break his hold, she stood stiffly, wondering whether she ought to try screaming for help. But with the din downstairs, no one would hear her, and it might only incite this odious man to further action.

"Now, be reasonable, pretty Songbird," Mason said. "I'm a determined man, and I want you to sing in my place real bad. You'll find I'm much more generous than Roark."

He licked his thin lips, a quick darting of his tongue. The motion was so eerily like that of a snake that Rianne shivered. She didn't want any part of his brand of generosity.

"I believe Mr. Roark is an equally determined man, Mr. Mason."

"If you want to change employers, he won't have a thing to say about it."

Rianne's eyes narrowed. "If you're so certain of that, why did you come sneaking up here instead of approaching me openly?"

"Because Roark is so damned protective of you that I'll never get the chance."

"I'd say that he has good reason not to trust you," she retorted. Inwardly, however, she was surprised by the man's statement. Pagan Roark had seemed anything but protective!

Mason's expression shifted with startling suddenness, and his face became mottled with dark blood. "I'm tired of talking," he said, tightening his hold on her. "Just come with me and we'll work out the details later."

"What details?" she demanded breathlessly.

"Your duties," he said. "That is, the ones besides singing."

Defiance washed through her, submerging her fear in a sweeping tide. "Get your hands off me!" she snapped.

"Don't get uppity with me, girl!" Showing the edges of his teeth in a grimace that was more snarl than smile, he pulled her closer. "That's no way to treat the man you're going to be working for."

"Let me go!" Rianne twisted her arm hard, but only managed to hurt herself. "Pagan will make you pay for this!"

"Roark will never find us. I'm taking you out of his hellhole, sweet. We'll start over somewhere new. A nice new saloon in a nice warm place. Mexico, maybe."

Truly astonished, she stared at him wide-eyed. "You must be mad. You can't expect to get away with that!"

He smiled again. "Sure I can. We've got a lot of work to do, you and me. And when I'm done with you, you'll do anything I want you to, and beg for the privilege." Cruelly tightening his grip on her arm, he dragged her toward the stairs. "We'll go out the back way, and by the time Roark figures things out, we'll be miles away."

Rianne took a deep breath, ready to scream, but Mason clamped his hand over her mouth and pulled her up against him. He cursed savagely as one of her flailing feet thudded into his shin.

"You little bitch," he gasped. "You're going to pay for that."

She only struggled harder. As Mason lifted her off her feet, she kicked out against the wall, sending him staggering off balance. He crashed into the opposite wall and dropped her. Rianne scrambled to her feet and dashed for the stairs. Her only thought was to get to Pagan. Pagan would protect her.

Just as she reached the top of the stairs, however, she felt Mason's hand on her shoulder, felt his hot breath on her neck as he dragged her back.

"Pagan!" she shrieked. "Pagan, help!"

Mason slapped her, hard enough to make her head spin. She fell to her knees, too dazed to fight as the man tied a gag over her mouth. And then a dark, swooping shape seemed to appear out of thin air. Strong hands grasped her, tearing her away from her attacker. She caught sight of her savior's face. Pagan!

Gently, he removed her gag. His fingertips trailed across her cheek, tracing the imprint of Mason's hand. "Go downstairs," he said. His voice was calm, but his eyes were pools of fury. It was a cold rage, much more deadly than if he had shouted. Rianne trembled, not in fear for him, but in fear of what he might do.

"Pagan—" she began in a desperate bid to blunt that anger somehow.

Mason turned and ran. Pagan was after him instantly, the predator running his quarry down. The two men grappled, crashing back and forth between the walls of the hallway. They fell to the floor, rolling over and over. It was the most brutal fight Rianne had ever seen; this was no gentlemanly fisticuff, but an enraged struggle between two bitter enemies. Rianne gasped as Mason lowered his head and charged Pagan like a bull, hitting him in the solar plexus and driving him against the wall with enough force to knock the breath from him. Taking swift advantage, Mason clamped his hands on his opponent's throat.

"No!" Rianne cried, flinging herself towards the struggling men. She had no idea what she was going to do, but she had to do *something!*

But Pagan didn't need her help. With a heave of his powerful shoulders, he broke his attacker's hold. Then he wrapped his hands around Mason's throat and began to squeeze.

Mason's face turned purplish-red, and his eyes bulged alarmingly. A new fear gripped Rianne, fear that she was about to watch a man killed. For her.

"Pagan!" she cried. "Stop! You're killing him!"

But Pagan's expression didn't change, nor did he loosen his grip. Her heart slamming against her ribs with fear, she ran to him and threw her arms around his shoulders. When she spoke, however, her voice was steady and calm. "Let him go, Pagan. He isn't worth being hung for murder."

Pagan's chest rose and fell with his ragged breathing. For a moment she was afraid he hadn't even heard her. Then he let out his breath in a long sigh and released his grip on the other man's throat. Mason fell to his knees, pulling air into his lungs with great, sobbing gasps.

"You're right," Pagan said, controlling himself with an effort. "You're right. He isn't worth it." Reaching down, he grasped Mason by the collar and heaved him to his feet.

"You bastard!" Mason croaked.

Pagan shook him. "You ought to consider yourself lucky. If Rianne wasn't so civilized, you'd be in hell now. For her sake, I'm going to act civilized, too. But I'm giving you fair warning, Mason. If you ever put your hands on her again, you're a dead man. If you even *speak* to her, you're a dead man."

"I'm going to put you out of business," Mason raged. "I'm going to drive you into the ground and then I'm going to dance on your grave."

"You're welcome to try," Pagan said.

"I'm going to do more than try, Roark."

With a shrug of disdain, Pagan turned his back on the man. Mason, his face twisted with rage, leaped upon his enemy. Pagan was taken completely by surprise. With the other man clinging to his back, gouging for his eyes, he staggered forward.

"Watch out for the stairs!" Rianne shrieked.

But it was too late. The two men teetered on the top step for a long, heart-clenching moment, then over-balanced and went down. A series of thumps followed. Rianne felt every thump like a physical blow.

"Pagan!" she gasped almost soundlessly. "Oh, dear God, please let him be all right. Please!"

She rushed down the stairs just as Pagan, apparently uninjured, sat up. Her heart began beating again. She ran to him, clutching his shoulders as if to never let go.

"You bastard!" Mason moaned. "My arms are broken! Both my goddamn arms are broken!"

Rianne bent over him. She had to force herself to touch him, for at this moment she would rather have put her hands on a rattlesnake. But she simply couldn't turn away from another human being in pain, even this one. Gently, she examined his arms and found that they were indeed broken.

"You bitch," Mason hissed. "This is your fault."

She took her hands from him. "Mr. Mason, I rather think it was your own fault. Attacking a man from behind, a man who had just spared your life—" She broke off as François Gruillot came through the doorway.

"What is this?" the huge Frenchman demanded. "Did I hear a fight?"

Rianne trembled; if François knew what Mason had tried to do to her, he would probably break the man's legs as well. Judging from the look of alarm on Mason's face, he thought so, too. "Mr. Mason had an accident," she said. "He fell downstairs."

"Do me a favor, Francois, and take him home." Pagan

levered himself to his feet. "And get Drew to set those arms for him."

Francois nodded, then bent and heaved Mason up onto his shoulder. Rianne could hear Mason howling and cursing long after the pair had disappeared.

She knew she ought to feel sympathy for him. After all, it was the proper thing to do. But perhaps she wasn't quite as civilized as Pagan had said, for all she felt now was satisfaction that Mason had gotten exactly what he had deserved.

Turning, she looked at Pagan. His jacket was torn, as were the knees of his crisp, dark trousers. The light of battle still smoldered in his eyes and he again seemed the primitive warrior, defending his territory against all comers. "I should have killed him for touching you," he growled.

Rianne drew her breath in sharply, taken aback by the sheer intensity of his tone. She moved a step closer to study his face.

His expression was one of mingled fury and frustration—and desire. There was a molten heat bubbling in the pale depths of his eyes that made her heartbeat accelerate wildly. There was no logic in her thoughts, no memory of betrayal, no shame, only one pure, simple fact: he wanted her. *He wanted her!*

"Why do you care if he touches me?" she asked softly. She could see the answer there in his eyes, but she needed the words. She needed to know that she could make him say the words.

"Because you belong to me," he said.

"As someone who can make you money?"

"In every way."

It was a blunt admission. Too blunt. This wasn't what Rianne had wanted to hear from him. Love was what she wanted, the words and the reality. And still it was an illusion, born of her need. Her disappointment was swift and sharp, and she turned away from him.

"Where are you going?" he asked, grasping her wrist.

It was the same wrist Mason had gripped so brutally, and she gasped with pain. With a muttered curse, Pagan pulled the lantern closer, then stripped her glove off. Large bruises marred her pale skin, seeming to grow darker and more painful-looking by the moment.

"God damn him to hell!" he raged, lunging toward the door.

"Pagan, don't!" Rianne grabbed his coat and hung on with all her strength. "Please."

He turned to her, and Rianne was appalled at the sheer violence on his face. She knew that another man might have hit her for trying to hold him back. But Pagan merely looked at her with those pale azure eyes that glittered with fathomless anger.

And then he reached out to stroke her cheek with a gentleness that brought the sting of tears to her eyes. She felt as though she'd been caught up in a vortex, spun so that she didn't know which was up or down, right or wrong. All she knew was that even with savage anger boiling inside him, he touched her like *that*. In that moment she wanted him, needed him with a force so powerful that it swept everything else away.

"Pagan," she said, unable to articulate her need.

He gathered her into his arms, feeling as though he'd come home. "Ahh, Rianne," he muttered hoarsely. "I missed you."

Her eyes drifted close as his mouth neared hers. The first contact was butterfly-soft, yet full of promise. She rose up onto her tiptoes, wanting more.

With a groan of long-withheld need, he deepened the kiss. His tongue slid into the sweet warmth of her mouth, exploring the edges of her teeth, the sensitive inside of her lips, then delving deep to savor her depths. He groaned again when her tongue darted forward boldly to mate with his in the age-old dance of passion.

Then he broke the kiss, slowly and languorously, reveling in her small, murmured protest. Raising his head just far enough to look at her, he ran his thumb over the pouting

225

curve of her lower lip. She sighed, and he felt the small sound like a caress.

Bending, he lifted her into his arms and carried her upstairs to her room. Closing the door behind him with his foot, he took her to the bed and laid her down on the soft blue cover. She lay in a welter of lustrous amber silk, but her white flesh was more sumptuous than mere fabric could ever be.

As he came down beside her, Rianne opened her arms to welcome him. He fitted his lips to hers slowly and deliberately, and she reveled in the feel of him, the weight of his hard chest upon her breasts, the slow, luxurious caresses of his hands.

She slid her hands beneath his jacket to stroke the length of his back, moving sensually across the long, flexing muscles. He raised himself up enough to pull his shirt out of his pants, allowing her access to his skin.

"Touch me," he rasped, holding himself above her with braced arms. "Please, touch me."

Made bold by his need, and hers, she explored the hard male body beneath her hands. She traced the long, strong line of his spine, moved slowly upward along his ribs to caress the iron swell of his pectorals, dipped lower to tease the pointed nubs of his nipples. Holding her breath with anticipation, she slid her palms lower, feeling the ridged muscles of his abdomen, then moved lower until stopped by the buckle of his belt.

"God, Rianne!" he gasped, coming down upon her to claim her mouth again.

She gave herself up to the spiraling delight of his hard mouth, his probing tongue, the urgency she sensed within him. It was sharp and sweet and so close to love that she had no choice but to believe in it for this brief, glorious interlude. Desire moved through her in a coursing wave, raising her need to fever pitch. She felt her bodice loosen, and a moment later he lifted her to slide the gown down and away. Now she wore only the undergarments he had bought for her, semi-transparent froths of silk and lace. Her skin was so sensitive now that even they were too much.

But Pagan was in no rush to take them from her. He stroked the fine fabric, smoothing it over the overheated skin of her thighs and hips while his mouth explored the skin of her throat. She writhed uncontrollably when his tongue delved into the small hollow at the base of her neck, then slid into the scented crevice between her breasts. Hot liquid passion settled in her core.

Pagan closed his eyes, fighting for control. Beneath his palms he felt skin and lace, skin and silk, then skin again. He was drowning in the feel of her, the heady woman-and-lilac scent of her. She was hot to the touch, as responsive and passionate as he remembered. As high as his desire burned, so did his emotions, fired to white heat by this woman. No one else had ever made him feel like this; no one else had even come close.

He claimed her lips again, taking her hands and placing them around his neck. Rianne clung to him, lost in the sweet, heady magic of desire.

"Pagan," she whispered against his mouth.

She arched her back in mindless passion as she felt his hand slide beneath her petticoat, along her stockinged leg to her garter and beyond. And then he claimed the feminine core of her, parting her flesh and seeking out all her moist secrets. He slid two fingers into her wet depths. Rianne shuddered with reaction, opening her legs wider to accommodate his exploration. His thumb found the small nub that was the center of her desire and stroked it rhythmically. She cried out, burying her face against the hot flesh of his chest.

"I love you," she moaned. "I love you."

"I thought I'd go mad without you," he rasped. "I need you so badly."

Reality burned through the haze of sensuality that had held Rianne in its grip. *I need you, I want you,* he'd said. Nothing about love. He would never, never understand the heart-soreness of missing someone he loved. It was *physical* need he was talking about, not love.

227

With a cry of despair, she scrambled away from him. Huddling against the cold metal of the headboard, she clutched the blanket to her and began to cry.

Pagan stared at her in surprise and frustration. For a moment he thought he'd die from not having her. She'd been wanton in his arms, gasping, her woman's flesh contracting around his fingers in near climax. And then the next moment, she was sobbing as though something awful had been done to her.

"What the hell is wrong with you?" he growled.

"What do you feel for me?"

With a muttered curse, he raked his hand through his hair. "I want you more than any woman I've ever known."

"Such ardor!" she said bitterly. "And when it cools, as lust always does?"

"I told you I'd take care of you. For God's sake, woman, how can you expect me to predict the future? All I know is that I want you in my bed and in my life. Can't that be enough?"

Rianne pulled the cover up higher. God, he was tempting, handsome enough to make her heart beat erratically even now. But her instinct for self-preservation made her strong enough to deny her desire for him. "No, it can't. The price is too high for what you're asking in return."

"So this is a business arrangement?" he asked in that soft, silky voice that revealed his annoyance.

Her eyes narrowed. "Hasn't that always been the basis of our 'relationship'?"

"If so, I've gotten damned little for my investment."

Furious, she crushed the fabric of the coverlet between her hands. "Between the two of us, I'd say *I* was the one who got the poorer bargain."

"Indeed? What made you decide that?"

"How much money did you take in last night?" she demanded.

His jaw thrust forward belligerently. "Why?"

"I think you plan to make considerably more than thirty thousand dollars from me during the next year. If I'd been smart, I would have demanded a portion of the proceeds."

"But you didn't," he growled. "And now you owe me a year."

"If I sing two nights a week, will you let me go in half a year?"

"No." Pagan was unwilling to even consider letting her go. Against all odds, he would hold her.

"It's virtual slavery."

He shook his head. "Had Mason taken you, *that* would have been slavery. What do you think would have happened if you had done to him what you did to me tonight?"

Shame heated her cheeks. "That was . . . I don't know why I let you touch me. But don't worry. I know better now. It will never happen again."

"Damn you!" With a movement so sudden she didn't even have a chance to gasp, he pulled her over to him. Cradling her in his lap, he cupped the back of her head in his large hand and forced her to look at him. "It *will* happen again. You can't deny me any more than I can stay away from you."

"That's not true!" she cried furiously.

Crushing her against his chest, he claimed her lips. It was not a tender kiss, or a gentle one, but it was a thorough one. Rianne struggled not to respond, for she knew it for what it was: his attempt to dominate her in the most primal of ways. But her own body betrayed her. Of their own volition, her lips softened beneath his, her fists uncurled and spread out over his chest.

When Pagan felt that response, he broke the kiss. She lay in his arms, eyes closed, and the sight of her made his heart turn over in his chest. "Do you see what I mean?"

Yes, she saw. But she saw the dangers as well, the sure heartbreak looming in the future. He would pet her, whisper pretty things in her ear, make her his mistress, and then, when he was ready, he'd move on to someone else.

But what if she were wrong? What if he cared more than he'd even admit to himself, and she didn't take the risk of letting him come near her again? Then she would lose him, and never know what she had given away. *Oh, but the risk!* She'd be wagering her heart, her reputation and her future on the hope of breaking through his barriers. But if he learned to love her, wouldn't that be worth the risk? Love, as strong and real as she'd dreamed about, over and over through those lonely years in Wickersham—wasn't that worth some risk?

Ahh, sweet delusion! Pander to it at your own peril, a small, sane corner of her mind jeered. Her shoulders drooped as she acknowledged the wisdom of that cynical thought. Once before she had misjudged Pagan's motives, gauging him according to *her* feelings, not his. And she'd paid the price. The man was as shuttered, unreadable, as elusive as quicksilver. If she made the same mistake all over again, she'd have only herself to blame.

Her heart contracted into a tight knot of misery. To be so close! To glimpse what could be, but be forced to settle for less—no, she couldn't accept it. And yet, if he continued kissing her, she knew she would give in. Tears burned her eyes at the knowledge that he held such power over her.

"Please, just leave me alone," she whispered, her voice breaking.

Pagan nearly groaned, shaken by the sight of tears leaking out from beneath her closed eyelids. Her lips, reddened from his kisses, trembled. She looked completely defenseless, totally vulnerable. He could take her now. He could kiss away her objections, make her forget everything but being in his arms.

And he couldn't do it. Damn him for a fool, but he couldn't. In keeping her here against her will, he had lost her trust. For the first time he realized how precious that trust was. He wanted it back. He didn't want to steal her surrender; he wanted her to come to him in the same joyous, honest passion as the first time.

With a sigh he felt all the way down to his toes, he set her on the bed beside him. He raked his hand through his hair, taking deep, calming breaths in an attempt to cool his churning emotions.

Rianne opened her eyes. Tears, unrestrained now, slid from the corners of her eyes to wet the hair at her temples. "Must you use even your kisses to punish me?" she asked.

"That was passion, not punishment." With an effort, he kept his voice calm. "Never make the mistake of thinking otherwise."

She let her breath out in a long sigh. "Last week you made a bargain with me, do you remember?"

"We agreed to keep our dealings strictly business," he said softly. "Will you hold me to it?"

"Yes." If she had no strength of her own, she must find it elsewhere.

"It's a bad bargain, Rianne. We belong together."

"For how long?"

"For as long as we want to be."

Rianne shook her head. Yes, she wanted him with an intensity that made her limbs weak even now. But she wanted him forever. She wanted marriage, children — *his* children — and respectability. That unknown woman who had been his first wife had been able to claim his name and his future, and Rianne was not about to settle for less. "Can you make me a better offer?" she asked.

He didn't reply, and his very silence was her answer. With all the dignity she could muster, she rose from the bed and donned her dressing gown over her undergarments.

"I think we've said all there is to say." She tied the sash with a finality that echoed her words. "I expect you to honor our agreement. If you do, then perhaps we can get through this ordeal in a civilized manner."

Pagan was not feeling very civilized at the moment. He had the feeling that he ought to toss her back onto that bed and kiss her until everything was right again between them. *No,* a sane corner of his mind urged. *This isn't the right time.* "I'll honor our agreement," he said. "Until you tell me otherwise."

"That won't happen."

He smiled with sudden tenderness, then strode toward her. Stopping in front of her, he reached out to stroke the

231

satin curve of her cheek with the back of his hand. Her eyes darkened in response. "I think it will," he said.

Rianne opened her mouth to protest, but he turned on his heel and walked out. Her bravado leaked out like water from a sieve. She caught sight of her reflection in the mirror. Her hair tumbled around her shoulders in a shining brown mass, her eyes huge in her pale face. She looked wanton and frightened and confused all at once. A woman in love. No wonder Pagan was so sure he could play her emotions against her!

"If you let him get away with it, you're a bigger fool than he thinks you are," she said to the woman in the mirror.

Chapter Seventeen

"Ah, Rianne, that stew smells wonderful!" Alastair sighed, plopping wearily on a nearby rock.

She laid a handful of sticks on the fire, arranging them so that the heat would be evenly distributed beneath the cookpot. "I only wish we had more of a variety. Fish, rabbit and squirrel get tiresome after a while."

He chuckled. "Well, it's that or graze the grass like our horses."

"That's beginning to look rather attractive, Father." Suddenly she began to laugh. "I wonder what my friends in Wickersham would think if they could see me crouched over an open fire in front of a gold mine that has yielded only dirt."

"So far, sweetheart. So far," he corrected. "We'll be hitting bedrock here in a few days. Maybe we'll even have good news to tell Pagan when we go back to town this Saturday."

The mention of Pagan's name brought heat sweeping into Rianne's cheeks, and she bent over the pot of stew to hide her face. Three weeks had passed since the night she had insisted that Pagan promise to treat her only as a business associate. True to his word, he hadn't tried to seduce her. But whenever she stayed at the Golden Bear, he seemed always to be watching her, waiting with the patience of a hunting wolf for her to change her mind about becoming his mistress.

So far, she had resisted. But it wasn't easy, not when he was always there. Thank God she could escape to the mine during the week. Truly, it was a terrible thing to want a man so badly. And even when she was here, he haunted her, turning up in her thoughts whenever she let her guard down. Sometimes the memory of his fiercely handsome face was more real to her than her surroundings.

To exorcise him, she worked herself into exhaustion and beyond. Even then she couldn't sleep easily, for it was at night that Pagan tormented her most. It was loneliness of the worst kind, a heart aching for the warmth of his love, her body aching with the hot urgings of a desire she knew only Pagan could slake.

As her body twisted and turned beneath the blankets, her mind twisted and turned with jealous imaginings. Was she the only one suffering these torments of frustration? Had he forgotten her in the arms of another woman? Was he comparing her to his memory of his former wife, the blonde beauty? It was then, thinking about the phantom Mrs. Roark that Rianne's jealousy fanned white-hot. His wife. Perhaps he still loved her. What quality did she have that he fell in love with her and married her? *And what do I lack that he cannot commit his heart to me?* Rianne asked herself harshly.

"Better throw another potato in the pot, sweetheart," Alastair said, breaking into her somber thoughts. "We've got company."

Rianne glanced up at the ridge to the south and saw the figure of a horse and rider silhouetted against the sky. Her heartbeat accelerated. Pagan. Even at this distance, she knew him. The set of his shoulders, the way he held his head—she'd never mistake him for another man.

"It's Pagan. I wonder why he's here," she said. Then she saw another rider come out of the trees behind him. "Look—he's brought someone with him."

Alastair shrugged. "Better add two potatoes, then. I'm going to wash."

Rianne smoothed the front of her skirt, wishing for a moment she had something more to wear than these patched and faded things. Then she lifted her chin. Patched they may be, but at least these clothes were hers. At the Golden Bear, Pagan could force her to wear the expensive clothes he'd bought. But this was her territory, and here she was going to wear what she pleased.

A short time later, she heard the sound of horses splashing through the stream below, then Pagan calling a greeting to Alastair. In a moment he'd come up to the fire. Her heart began to pound. What did he want? Surely he hadn't come all the way out here to make a social call. Hearing the sound of boots crunching along the trail to the camp, she bent over the stew, stirring for all she was worth.

"Hello, Rianne."

Pagan's deep voice flowed over her like dark velvet, bringing every nerve in her body to quivering attention. Taking a deep breath to calm herself, she laid the spoon aside and turned to look at him. He was alone, as she'd known he'd be.

His raven-dark hair was tousled by the wind, and his eyes were the pure, clear blue of a mountain stream. He was smiling, and looked very glad to see her. The sight of him hit her like a physical blow, making her very bones feel molten. Why, out of all the men in the world, did she love this one?

"Hello," she said.

"I see we're just in time for supper."

"I . . . yes." She clasped her hands, feeling horribly awkward. "It's only squirrel stew and biscuits."

He smiled. "Squirrel! Your father's aim must have improved since the last time I saw him shoot."

"I shot the squirrel."

"You?" Pagan demanded.

"Father taught me," she said, made defensive by his obvious incredulity. "Although I never touched a firearm before coming here, I seem to have some aptitude for it."

Pagan ran his hand over his jaw. He ought to be used to Rianne's surprises by now, but this was most unusual, even for her. The thought of soft, gentle, city-bred Rianne stalking and shooting a squirrel was truly astonishing.

Reaching out, he tilted her face up so he could see her expression better. Judging from the violet shadows beneath her

235

eyes, she hadn't been sleeping much. Neither had he. His nights had been full of her, the memory of the way her skin felt beneath his hands and the fire of her passion. It only made him more determined to do what he'd come out here to do.

"I've missed you," he said softly.

She turned her face away. "Don't. Remember our bargain."

"I told you it was a damned bad bargain, and it's getting worse all the time. One word from you will release us both."

And then I will truly be lost, she thought. "As far as I'm concerned, it's a very good bargain."

Hearing the sound of footsteps coming up the trail, Rianne stepped back, putting several feet between herself and Pagan. She wished he hadn't come, for his presence stirred things in her she didn't want to feel, didn't even want to admit existed.

Alastair came into view, followed by the fellow Pagan had brought. The stranger was a huge man, thick with muscle. He had white-blond hair and the brightest blue eyes Rianne had ever seen. He moved slowly and deliberately, as though planning each step beforehand.

"Hello, sweetheart," Alastair said. "Meet Manfred Locke."

Rianne smiled and held out her hand. "Welcome to the Songbird Mine, Mr. Locke."

"Thank you very much," he replied in a thick German accent. Her hand almost disappeared in his huge paw.

"Manfred is going to be working with me," Alastair said, slapping the huge man on the shoulder.

All surrounding sights and sounds faded as Rianne's attention focused on her father's face. "What did you say?"

"Pagan hired him to work with me," Alastair said, a happy smile creasing his seamed face. "You won't have to come out here any longer."

Rianne's heartbeat thundered in her ears. She knew Pagan had planned this whole thing. It was just one more move in the game he was playing with her life. Oh, he'd played it well,

236

too. All these weeks he'd been letting her get away with avoiding him, watching, waiting like a predator about to snatch its prey. Anger went through her in a red tide.

Slowly, she turned her head to look at him. "I want to talk to you. Privately."

He nodded. "I'm yours to command."

Then I should command you straight to the devil! she thought savagely. Head high, she whirled and marched down toward the stream. Pagan followed behind her silently, but she could feel his gaze on her back.

When she was sure they couldn't be overheard by Alastair and Manfred Locke, she whirled and put her hands on her hips. "How dare you do this to me?"

"It's the only sensible thing to do," he said.

"Sensible!" She laughed, but it was a bitter sound. "It's only the means by which you intend to get your way!"

"Did you think I was going to let you keep coming out here?" Grasping her by the wrists, he turned her hands palm upward. A muscle jumped in his cheek when he saw the raw, red blisters that dotted her skin. Damn it to hell, she'd rather work herself to death than spend time with him! The thought made him angry, with her and with himself. "Look at these," he growled, freeing her with a suddenness that made her gasp.

"It's my choice," she said defiantly. But she hid her hands in the folds of her skirt, ashamed at their ugliness. He had cast her hands aside as though they disgusted him. Perhaps they did. *Flawed goods,* the cynical part of her mind jeered. *Surely he's never had to settle for less than perfect.* The image of a lovely blonde woman rose in her mind.

"Don't be an idiot," he growled. "You can't continue like this, working like a mule all week and then expecting to sing on the weekend."

"Are you saying I might ruin my voice? That would indeed be a tragedy — for your ledger-book."

With an effort, he controlled his temper. "How can one woman sing like an angel one moment, and then be so viciously insulting the next?"

237

"It must be the company," she said with false sweetness.

He raked his hand through his hair, frustration turning his heart into a tight, burning knot. He'd had his fill of rags and worn-out hands in the orphanage, and seeing Rianne like this was like a red-hot needle in his heart. No matter what the consequences, he wasn't going to allow this to go on another day.

"Get your things," he said, completely out of patience. "You're coming back with me."

"No."

His jaw tightened. "Yes, you are."

It was pure arrogance, the smug assumption that he could arrange her life to suit himself. Rianne stood staring at him for a long, tense moment, debating what to say. But she simply couldn't think of anything bad enough. Finally, she whirled and stalked back to the camp.

She could hear Pagan's footsteps behind her, but she wasn't going to give him the satisfaction of looking back at him. By the time she reached the camp, she was seething with rage, her temper bubbling hotter than the stew. It took an act of will for her to resist the urge to whack him with the frying pan.

"So. You've had your talk. I hope you settled your differences," Alastair said, looking from her to Pagan and back again. When no one answered, the old man sighed. "How are those biscuits coming along, Rianne?"

"I'll see." She raised the lid of the big iron Dutch oven and peered inside. "They're ready. Fetch your plates and I'll serve."

After they had eaten, Rianne got up to collect the plates. "I'll just get these washed up—"

"Let Manfred take care of that," Pagan said. "It's time we headed out."

Rianne barely managed to keep her mouth from dropping open in astonishment. The sheer gall of the man! Here he was, giving orders as coolly as you please, and only moments after she'd told him she had no intention of going.

"As I told you earlier, I'd prefer to stay here," she said through clenched teeth.

"Now, Rianne!" Alastair protested. "Pagan's right. This is man's work, and you just aren't strong enough for it. And there's even heavier work coming soon: building sluices, shoveling gravel—"

"So?" She swung around and pointed her finger at her father. "Have I complained? Have I failed to do a full day's work, heavy or not?"

"No." Alastair's voice was sad. "And that's the problem. You're too stubborn for your own good, sweetheart. Now Pagan is doing what's best for you, and I agree with him completely."

"I. Am. Not. Going!" Rianne spoke each word slowly and deliberately, as though they were both hard of hearing. "It's almost the twentieth century, and it's time you two . . . barbarians realized that I am a free woman. *I* will decide where and when I go."

Pagan turned to Alastair. "I told you she'd say that."

"So you did." With a sigh, Alastair threw his hands up in the air. "You know how stubborn she is, Pagan. There's nothing I can do to change her mind—"

"You're right about that!" Rianne retorted.

"—so I leave her to you," her father finished.

"Why, thank you," Pagan said.

Rianne sat frozen with horror as he set his plate to one side and rose to his feet. Then reason swept back into her numbed brain. Whirling, she bolted for the forest.

Before she got a dozen paces away, however, Pagan caught her. Ignoring her struggles completely, he tossed her over his shoulder and walked down the hill toward the horses as calmly as though he were on a Sunday stroll down Main Street.

"Put me down!" she hissed.

He didn't reply. Deciding that to struggle would only increase the ignominy of her position, she held herself stiffly. As Pagan carried her past the campfire, she stared straight ahead, ignoring her father's wave of farewell.

A few moments later they reached the horses, and Pagan let her slide down his body until her feet touched the ground.

She tried to pull away, but he put his arm around her waist, keeping her pressed against him.

She stood still, afraid to make any movement at all lest she stir him to an even more intimate embrace. As it was, the long, strong length of his thighs were molded to hers, bringing back memories of their lovemaking with visceral power. His ice-blue gaze held hers, daring her to defy him.

"Now, I want your word that you won't try to run away," he said with infuriating calmness.

"I'll give you nothing."

He smiled, and with heart-clenching dread she realized she'd fallen into a trap.

"Then I'll have to carry you in front of me," he said.

She shook her head frantically, frightened by the prospect of being held so closely. "NO!"

"Up you go," he said, grasping her waist with both hands and swinging her up into his saddle.

His hands lingered longer than was necessary. Even through the fabric of her blouse, his palms were hot upon her skin. She had the strangest feeling that she had just been branded. Marked as his. His possession. His Songbird.

Her heart yearned to accept that proprietory touch, as did her flesh. Only her mind held itself apart, cautioning 'Beware!' If she had any instinct at all for self-preservation, she had to heed that warning.

Then she noticed that his was the only horse that was wearing a saddle. "You meant to do this all along," she accused.

"Absolutely." With a single, lithe movement, he swung up behind her, sitting just behind the saddle. He reached around her to grasp the reins, very much enjoying having her between his arms like this. Having her close, even unwillingly, was better than not having her at all.

As they rode away from camp, Rianne sat stiffly in an attempt to minimize the contact of their bodies. The motion of the horse thrust Pagan's chest against her back almost constantly, however, and there was no escape. Worse, she found his closeness disturbingly welcome. It was as though she were

240

MORE PASSION AND ADVENTURE AWAIT... YOUR TRIP TO A BIG ADVENTUROUS WORLD BEGINS WHEN YOU ACCEPT YOUR FIRST 4 NOVELS ABSOLUTELY *FREE*
(AN $18.00 VALUE)

Accept your Free gift and start to experience more of the passion and adventure you like in a historical romance novel. Each Zebra novel is filled with proud men, spirited women and tempestuous love that you'll remember long after you turn the last page.

Zebra Historical Romances are the finest novels of their kind. They are written by authors who really know how to weave tales of romance and adventure in the historical settings you love. You'll feel like you've actually gone back in time with the thrilling stories that each Zebra novel offers.

GET YOUR FREE GIFT WITH THE START OF YOUR HOME SUBSCRIPTION

Our readers tell us that these books sell out very fast in book stores and often they miss the newest titles. So Zebra has made arrangements for you to receive the four newest novels published each month.

You'll be guaranteed that you'll never miss a title, and home delivery is so convenient. And to show you just how easy it is to get Zebra Historical Romances, we'll send you your first 4 books absolutely FREE! Our gift to you just for trying our home subscription service.

BIG SAVINGS AND FREE HOME DELIVERY

Each month, you'll receive the four newest titles as soon as they are published. You'll probably receive them even before the bookstores do. What's more, you may preview these exciting novels free for 10 days. If you like them as much as we think you will, just pay the low preferred subscriber's price of just $3.75 each. *You'll save $3.00 each month off the publisher's price.* AND, your savings are even greater because there are never any shipping, handling or other hidden charges—FREE Home Delivery. Of course you can return any shipment within 10 days for full credit, no questions asked. There is no minimum number of books you must buy.

4 FREE BOOKS

TO GET YOUR 4 FREE BOOKS WORTH $18.00 — MAIL IN THE FREE BOOK CERTIFICATE T O D A Y

Fill in the Free Book Certificate below, and we'll send your FREE BOOKS to you as soon as we receive it.

If the certificate is missing below, write to: Zebra Home Subscription Service, inc., P.O. Box 5214, 120 Brighton Road, Clifton, New Jersey 07015-5214.

FREE BOOK CERTIFICATE

4 FREE BOOKS

ZEBRA HOME SUBSCRIPTION SERVICE, INC.

YES! Please start my subscription to Zebra Historical Romances and send me my first 4 books absolutely FREE. I understand that each month I may preview four new Zebra Historical Romances free for 10 days. If I'm not satisfied with them, I may return the four books within 10 days and owe nothing. Otherwise, I will pay the low preferred subscriber's price of just $3.75 each; a total of $15.00, *a savings off the publisher's price of $3.00.* I may return any shipment and I may cancel this subscription at any time. There is no obligation to buy any shipment and there are no shipping, handling or other hidden charges. Regardless of what I decide, the four free books are mine to keep.

NAME

ADDRESS   APT

CITY   STATE   ZIP

(   )
TELEPHONE

SIGNATURE   (if under 18, parent or guardian must sign)

ZB0593

two separate people, the sensible Rianne trying desperately to protect her bruised heart from further damage, and the reckless Rianne, who yearned to taste again the exquisite pleasure of loving him.

More to deny herself than him, she said, "I expect you to respect our agreement, Mr. Roark."

"Your virtue is safe with me." His breath stirred the hair over her ear. "At least for now."

She stiffened again, this time in outrage. But after a while the hot afternoon sun and her own exhaustion took their toll, and she began to doze.

Pagan felt her relax. Realizing that she'd fallen asleep, he gently eased her back so that she was leaning against him. God, this was what he'd been wanting! He studied her face, enjoying the sweet curve of her cheek, the thick sweep of gold-tipped lashes, the slightly sun-burned tip of her ear. He'd known many women, but none could compare to this stubborn Englishwoman. Ragged clothes, work-worn hands and all, she was the most beautiful sight he'd ever seen, and he wanted her back in his bed and in his life so badly he could taste it.

The thought of making love to her again sent a jolt of desire through him. It wasn't only physical desire, although that was there aplenty. He ached to hold her, just hold her. Without his realizing it was happening, she had seeped into his very being, capturing his mind and his senses, filling all those places in his heart he hadn't known were empty until now.

Damn her for extracting that promise from him! Here she was, so close that he could smell the faintly floral scent of her skin, and he was bound by his word not to touch her. The Devil himself couldn't have devised a more painful torment.

"I gave my word," he muttered under his breath.

He squeezed his eyes shut, willing his raging need to cool. But it only grew worse, for with his eyes closed, the scent of her swirled through his head, as haunting and compelling as the woman herself. With a sigh, he resigned himself to spending the rest of the journey in torment.

"It's a hell of the world when a man's honor comes 'round to bite him," he said.

Rianne woke to a cessation of movement, and saw in surprise that they had reached the Golden Bear. Realizing that she was leaning heavily against Pagan, she straightened hastily. Her whole back was warm where it had been in contact with him, and there was a vast, molten warmth coursing through her core. *Fool! Even in your sleep you can't stop wanting him!*

She didn't have the courage to look at him. "I-I seem to have fallen asleep," she said, then blushed at the inanity of her statement.

Pagan merely grunted. The past hour had been one of unholy torture, but her sudden, complete withdrawal was the worst of all. A moment ago she had been so tranquil, her face serene as she slept against his chest. Now that was gone, replaced by a woman who shied away from him as though he were some terrible beast that might rend her here in the street.

He silently cursed himself for throwing her trust away, and even more for not having the strength to let her go when she so obviously wanted to. Truly, Lady Luck had turned from him, for he was doomed to have Rianne hate him for forcing her to stay, and doomed to lose her forever if he let her leave.

"Go inside," he said curtly, swinging her down to the boardwalk. "I'll take the horses down to the stable."

Without a backward glance, he rode away leading her horse by the reins. Rianne stared after him in bewilderment. For a man who had all but tied her hand and foot to get her back here, he had certainly lost interest in a hurry.

Hastily, she ran into the saloon, leaving the door open behind her. Marie, Alva, and the rest of the saloon-girls were sitting at a table near the bar. Rianne saw them look up in surprise as she came pelting into the room, but she was too upset even to call out a greeting.

She ran upstairs to her room and, throwing herself face-down across the bed, she cried her misery into the coverlet in great, gasping sobs. It felt as though her heart were being torn out of her in tiny, jagged pieces. Her awareness of time faded in the torment of her emotions. There was only confusion, hurt, and a well of sadness so deep she didn't think she would ever make her way back to the light.

Just as she reached the darkest recesses of the pit, a gentle hand stroked the back of her hair. Alarmed, she raised her head. "Who—?"

"It's Marie Bell, honey."

Rianne struggled to a sitting position. "Oh, I . . . I . . ."

"You just touched bottom there, didn't you?" There was no judgement on Marie's face, only understanding. "You take it from Marie, honey. There ain't nothin' that bad."

"I'm sorry." Rianne took a deep, shuddering breath. "It's just that—"

"You love him, don't you?"

Avoiding the other woman's eyes, Rianne nodded. "But he doesn't love me."

With a sigh, Marie got up from the bed and walked to the window. "Honey, I been around here a long time, and I ain't never seen him act with a woman like he does with you. Every day you're gone, he gets quieter and quieter, and that scowl of his gets blacker and blacker. Saturdays, when you're here, he seems a different man. If that ain't love, then I'm a nun."

Rianne's heart thudded against her ribs. Oh, God, this was the worst sort of temptation! She wanted to believe Marie so badly, truly wanted Pagan to love her. But she didn't dare believe. For her own self-preservation, she *couldn't* dare let herself believe.

She shook her head, denying Marie's statement, denying her own heart. "Marie, I don't think Pagan knows how to love. Me or anyone else."

"You're dead wrong," the other woman said.

"But—"

"But nothin'. You listen to Marie, hear? Pagan and me was raised to the same kind of life, and that were a hard one. Me, I grew up on a hardscrabble farm, workin' like a plow mule. My daddy sold me off to Madame Vougeot for fifty dollars

243

when I was fifteen. But at least I had enough to eat. Now Pagan, he grew up in an orphanage, taking care of three little brothers, and they didn't have even that."

Rianne felt her mouth drop open with astonishment. "An orphanage? Did he tell you that?"

"No'm. His brother Conor came to visit a couple years back. A right fine man, Conor Roark. He and me got cozy-like, and he told me somethin' about those times. Seems four Roark boys went into that orphanage, but only two came out. But that wasn't from lack of tryin'; Conor told me that Pagan scrapped like a wildcat to take care of them all. I don't know that whole story, fer Conor didn't like to think much about that place."

Only then did Rianne realize that tears were running down her face. Not for herself this time, but for the frightened, hungry little boys Pagan and his brother had been. How terrible it must have been, how heartbreaking to be a child and have to fight so hard to live.

"What I'm tryin' to say, honey," Marie continued. "Is that times like those make a boy hard. An' he grows into an even harder man. Man like that don't talk his feelin's out the way we women do. No, he keeps them all inside, puttin' them where no one kin stomp on it. Maybe you got to look at how he *acts*, instead of waitin' for what he says."

"But the risk!"

Marie nodded. "There is that. Things don't always work out no matter how much two people care about one another. I cain't tell you otherwise. But honey, when I was fourteen I had a fella who was plumb crazy about me. He begged me to run away with him to Chicago. I purely loved that boy, but I was scared he'd leave me out there in the big city."

"So you didn't go," Rianne whispered. "And the next year your father sold you to the . . . the . . ."

"Whorehouse. You kin say it, I know you don't look down on me for what I am. But you listen to me, honey. That boy *might* have left me, just like I feared. But he might not. I'll never know, 'cause I never took the chance. And all these years I been regretting that. If I'd married a decent man and lived my life a decent woman, I'd still regret it."

"Is love so scarce that you couldn't find it again?"

Marie laughed, her gold tooth catching the light. "In my line of work, love is all too easy to find." Then she sobered. Reaching out, she took Rianne's hands in hers. "But I ain't talkin' about *that* kind of love. I'm talking about the kind that makes you hot and cold and hot again, that makes your insides squinch up and your bones turn to jelly. And that's rarer than a five-legged hound dog, Rianne Kierney. Only a damned fool would throw it away."

"I-I just don't know," Rianne said.

"It's your decision. But I got one more thing to say to you: Pagan Roark is one hell of a man. Oh, he's difficult at times, an' sometime's he kin be the very devil. Lovin' such a man ain't ever goin' to be easy. But you got to take some things on faith. If you want him, you're going to have to take him as he is and let the good Lord take care of the rest."

Such courage she has, Rianne thought. *As much as she's suffered, there is still room in her heart to help another person.* Impulsively, she put her arms around the other woman and held her close. "Thank you for telling me," she said. "You're a true friend."

"Aw, I jest hate to see two people I like make each other so miserable." Marie pulled away. "Now don't start dripping tears on me, I got work to do." Her tone was stern, but Rianne noticed suspicious moisture in her eyes when she pulled away.

Holding her head at a jaunty angle, Marie left the room. Rianne sat down on the edge of the bed. 'Take Pagan on faith' Marie had said. Faith. Once, Rianne would have called that God's domain. Faith seemed safe when given to God, but all too frightening when given to a human being.

But if she didn't, would she spend her life wishing she had? Would she look back like Marie, and wonder what she might have had if she had dared take the chance? Perhaps Pagan just couldn't say the words she wanted to hear so badly.

Could she, in her need for convention, have failed to see his true feelings?

She could get hurt, very hurt by becoming his mistress. She would be turning her back on everything society considered right and moral, and there would be a price to pay. But wouldn't there be an equal price to pay by *not* taking the risk? For the first time, she realized that love was not simple or easy or even sensible. It required patience and sacrifice — and faith. A blind leap, trusting in something she didn't understand.

With a hiss of frustration, she got up to look at herself in the mirror. "Dare I?" she murmured, as though her reflection might have more answers than she did. "Dare I?"

Chapter Eighteen

Rianne tilted the mirror so that she could see herself better. She looked so different now. The girl who had fretted beneath her mother's smothering protectiveness, the girl who had craved adventure and new experiences was gone. Hers was the face of a woman who had tasted both joy and pain, and who had learned the price of recklessness all too well.

Something in her reflection's eyes caught her attention and she leaned closer. "What is it?" she asked. "What are you trying to tell me?"

And then it burst upon her, as powerful and stunning as lightning: her heart was reflected there in her eyes. It begged her for understanding, for courage. For trust. *Trust me, not your mind,* it said. *If you love him, you must take the risk. If you love him, you must make the jump, blindly, relying on things your mind cannot see.*

She sighed. "I love him."

Good or bad, the decision had been made. She would listen to her heart. She would take her love, her life and her future, and put them in Pagan's hands. She would take him on faith, the greatest adventure of all.

She washed the evidence of tears from her cheeks and ran the brush through her tangled hair before winding it into a single thick braid at the back of her head. She didn't dare look in the mirror again lest she see something different in her eyes.

"Marie, I hope you're right," she murmured as she left her room.

She hurried down the hall to Pagan's room and knocked on the door, feeling as though her heart was going to beat its way right out of her chest. Surely Pagan must be able to hear it, she thought as she waited.

But there was no answer. He wasn't in. Rianne nearly sagged against the door in reaction. Would nothing go right for her? She'd come here, her heart in her throat, ready to throw herself at his feet. And he wasn't in!

Leaning her forehead against the door, she murmured, "Oh, Pagan!"

Again she was faced with a choice: go downstairs to look for him, or go back into her room and forget the whole idea. *Courage!* she thought, rejecting the second choice. Yes, she was afraid. But for the first time in weeks she had hope that things might work out between her and Pagan. It felt so *right*. She'd made the commitment to herself already, and just couldn't give up without trying.

"So, idiot, go downstairs," she muttered.

When she got to the bottom of the stairs, she heard a buzz of conversation in the saloon. Hesitantly, she went to the door and looked in. There were a dozen men at the bar even on this weekday afternoon. Judging from the glum looks on their faces, they had come from unproductive claim sites to drown their sorrows in liquor. She could only hope that her quest for love would be more successful than theirs for gold.

She scanned the room, finally spotting Pagan at one of the tables near the bar. He didn't look up; his attention was bent on the game of solitaire he was playing. Although he was slouched low in his chair, his long legs stretched out before him, he looked anything but relaxed. There was a brooding air about him, which was enhanced by his black jacket and trousers. He looked dark and handsome and just a bit dangerous, and her heart leaped at the sight of him.

"Pagan," she whispered.

It was the barest breath of sound, much too soft for anyone else to hear. But at that instant Pagan looked up, his ice-blue gaze focusing directly on her face. He didn't look either happy or unhappy to see her; his expression was completely neutral.

She faltered for a moment. That bland look would have made a much bolder woman hesitate. But then she remembered the young boy who had grown up in terrible poverty, who had fought and suffered and learned to hide his emotions from others. She had to believe her heart, for it could see what her eyes could not. She *must* believe. The only alternative was to turn away from him forever. After seeing him here like this, after feeling the irresistible need she felt to hold him, she couldn't abide that alternative. For better or for worse, she was committed.

Smoothing the front of her skirt nervously, she walked across the room to Pagan's table. He watched her come, not the barest flicker of change in his impassive expression.

"Hello, Pagan," she said.

His eyes were fathomless, as unreadable as fog. "Hello, Rianne."

What do I say now? she wondered frantically. *Do I burst out with 'I love you and I want to make love to you? He'll think I've gone insane!* Still, she couldn't stand here staring at him like a ninny. She looked away, her gaze skittering here and there, focusing anywhere but directly at him. Finally, she registered the cards on the table in front of him. "The red six goes on the black seven," she said.

Pagan blinked in astonishment, then glanced down at the card that lay forgotten in his hand. It was the six of hearts. "So it does," he replied, expertly flipping it onto the seven. Then he leaned back in his chair and waited for her to say something else.

"I came to . . . ah," Rianne let the rest of the sentence go unsaid. In her worst imaginings of this scene, she hadn't anticipated having to lay her heart at his feet in front of a

249

dozen half-drunk men. Worse, Pagan wasn't making it any easier for her, not with his cool, composed stare and relaxed pose. She simply could not say the words. But there was another way of giving him her message.

Turning away, she went to the piano and sat down. She wasn't the musician her father was, but she could present a tune passably enough. And the one she wanted to play was etched upon her mind and heart as though it had been written especially for her. She would be eternally grateful to the composer. Perhaps he had been just like her, a lover with something important to say but not the courage to speak the words except in a song.

She played the opening chords of "Drink To Me Only With Thine Eyes", watching Pagan carefully. Still there was no emotion on that sharp-planed face of his. Despair clenched her chest; could she had misjudged everything completely? Was she wrong to think that this song held any significance to him? *Oh, please,* she prayed silently. *Don't let it be that way! It's so terribly important!*

But this was her only chance, and she had to take it. Closing her eyes, she began to sing the melody, pouring her love, her hope and boundless need for him into the lovely old song. Heart calling to heart, love to love—through the medium of her voice. The words didn't matter, although they were perfect, too.

> *"Drink to me only, with thine eyes,*
> *And I will pledge with mine.*
> *Or leave a kiss within the cup,*
> *And I'll not ask for wine . . ."*

It took an effort of will for Pagan to maintain his casual pose as Rianne's voice soared through the room on velvet wings. She was singing for him, and for him alone. That smoky, sensuous voice was filled with her fire, her passion for love and for life. It flowed over and around and through him, insinuating its way through every fibre of his being.

250

The song was special, one he would always associate with her. Siren song.

He was shaken by the power of that call, and the strength of his own towering need for her. His hands curled into fists. He didn't want to be enthralled by her or by any woman. He hated not having complete control over his emotions, and fretted beneath the bonds of his obsession to possess her. But to have her in his arms again, he would walk through solid rock, through the flames of Hell itself.

"Now I know why men take to drink," he muttered under his breath.

Rianne let the last, haunting note fade into silence, hoping she had sung it well enough. *Please, God, make him understand. All I want to do is love him!* When she opened her eyes, she saw Pagan standing before her. Her awareness of the room around her faded; there were no miners, no clinking of glasses, no muted rumble of conversation. Only Pagan.

His hands were clenched into fists at his side, and his eyes blazed like twin blue flames, a fiery outpouring of raw emotion that was stunning in its intensity. Rianne had never seen him so open, so vulnerable. Her heart swelled with a joy so great that for a moment she feared it would tear her asunder. He loved her. He might not be willing to admit it to himself—perhaps he didn't even recognize it for what it was. But the love was there, in his eyes, in the taut, sharp-cut planes of his face. No matter what the future might bring, she would remember this moment as long as she lived.

Without a word, he held out his hand. This is it, she thought, staring at his outstretched palm. The final, irrevocable decision. After this, there will be no turning back. A last, lingering bit of fear made her hesitate. Then she lifted her gaze to his face, and the last bit of caution fled. He loved her. She would hold that to her heart, love him for all she was worth, and hope that she would be able to hold him.

251

She placed her hand in his, trembling as his fingers curled around hers possessively. Still gazing into his eyes, she rose from the piano stool and followed him. He led her up the stairs, but instead of going to her room, he took her to his.

It was a very masculine room, furnished with massive mahogany pieces. Velvet draperies, the same green as the sun-dappled leaves of the forest, matched the coverlet on the bed. There was a shelf of books, a treasure in a land where even a newspaper was a rarity worth its weight in gold. On the opposite wall hung the skin of an enormous bear, its curving claws stark against the rough board walls. The room was a contradiction, just like the man who lived here—on one hand the earthy, primitive note of the bear-skin, on the other, the sense of culture evinced by the collection of books.

Rianne turned to look at Pagan. Her man, the one who had stolen her heart forever. He stood a scant foot away, staring at her as though to consume her utterly. With a sigh, she held her arms out to him.

Pagan wanted to crush her to him, but restrained himself savagely. Until a few moments ago, he'd thought she hated him. He'd been willing to accept even that to have her here with him. Love, after all, was the other side of that coin. But then she had sung that song to him, completely turning his world upside down. He had to know what had prompted that sudden, devastating switch.

So instead of taking her in his arms as she wished and he wished, he took her hands and raised them to his lips. "Why, Rianne?" he asked softly.

"Because I love you," she said. "Because I can't seem to stay away any longer."

"You know I can't—"

"Shh." she murmured, putting her hand over his mouth. "Right now, I'll take what you can give."

Her generosity stunned him. Without asking for a single thing in return, she was offering him everything—her heart, her love, her future. With a groan, Pagan gathered her into his arms and brought her against his chest. It had been so long, so very long since he'd held her like this. All these weeks he'd been forced to watch her from afar, to listen to the velvety caress of her voice, to want her with soul-searing intensity and not be able to touch her. It had been utter torment.

With hands that shook from the force of his feelings, Pagan freed her hair from the braid, letting the smooth, silken weight of it flow through his hands. Then he framed her face between his palms. "I don't know what miracle brought you to me tonight, but I won't question it. I've been half crazy with wanting you, Rianne."

"Kiss me," she begged.

Slowly, he lowered his lips to hers. Rianne wound her arms around his neck and pulled him closer. The kiss began gently, but in moments they were straining against each other, their heads tilting as they sought deeper contact. As she clung to him, begging for yet more, he bit gently at her lower lip until she moaned with almost unbearable arousal. Then his tongue delved into her mouth again. Mindlessly, she sucked it deeper, and was rewarded by his gasp of reaction.

All thought was gone, replaced by a firestorm of sensuality that threatened to consume her. Frantic to touch him, to feel his skin against hers, to revel in the sheer hard masculinity of his body, she pulled his jacket off his shoulders and down his arms, then cast it aside. Unbuttoning his shirt, she slipped her hand into the opening and spread her fingers out over the muscles of his chest. His heart fluttered rapidly against her palm, and the heat of his skin was as intense as that of the summer sun. Slowly, she caressed the ridged muscles, tracing the line of his ribs upward to finally rasp her thumbs over his taut nipples.

"God, Rianne!" he gasped, pulling her hands from his chest. "You don't know what you're doing to me!"

His breath came raggedly now, and she triumphed in the

power she had over him. Yes, she belonged to him, heart and soul and body. But so did he belong to her. Deeply, irrevocably, whether he knew it yet or not. She wanted to drive him beyond restraint, beyond reticence. She wanted to burn herself indelibly upon his very being.

"Pagan," she breathed, pressing herself closer. "Let me touch you."

"Later," he said thickly, running his hands down her sides from breasts to hips, an incredibly possessive gesture. His desire for her raged white-hot. After weeks of separation, he was frantic to claim her, body, heart, and soul. Cupping her buttocks in his hands, he lifted her against his lower body.

Rianne cried out at the delicious contact and lifted one knee high on his hip so as to feel him more intimately. With a groan, he grasped her thigh to lift her leg even higher, then rubbed himself against her heat and softness.

Raising her skirt and petticoat up to her waist, he eased his hand beneath her drawers. She writhed as his fingertips moved along the cleft of her buttocks to the heated secrets below. He slid two long fingers into her wet, welcoming warmth, delving deep into her pulsing heat, withdrawing, then sliding back in. Rianne gasped in response, then gasped again as he claimed her mouth again, savagely, his tongue driving deep in imitation of what his fingers were doing.

The first tremors of a sudden, unexpected climax caught her. She clung to him, swept along by a tremendous surge of sensation. Afterward, she leaned against him, too spent even to support her own weight. She didn't have to. Sweeping her into his arms, he carried her to the bed.

"I-I wanted to wait for you," she whispered, hiding her face against the hard swell of his chest.

"There will be other times."

He laid her down. For all his consideration and gentleness, his eyes looked like pools of blue flame. Rianne wanted to fan that heat higher, and higher still, until they were both consumed by it.

Pagan couldn't wait another moment to see her, to be able to touch all of her. Swiftly, with hands that trembled, he began unfastening her blouse. When the buttons resisted his efforts, he grasped the well-worn fabric between his hands and tore it asunder. He dealt with her chemise the same way.

"These are the last of my old clothes," she said, but without a hint of protest in her voice.

"Were," he corrected, feasting his gaze on her high, full breasts. Her nipples were erect and beckoning, and it was with an effort of will that he held himself back long enough to strip the rest of her garments from her.

Then he stood over her, his gaze raking every delicious inch of her body. He didn't think he'd ever grow tired of looking at her. She was incredibly graceful, her slim, long-legged beauty enough to take his breath away. Her skin seemed to glow like moonlight against the green coverlet, and her long, unbound hair coiled around her as though it were floating on the rich velvet. Siren, he thought. If loving her tonight would mean being drawn down into the depths to oblivion, still he would do it.

"You're beautiful," he said hoarsely, ripping his shirt down his arms and casting it away.

"So are you," she said. As he reached for the buttons on his pants, she struggled to a sitting position and took his hands in hers. "No, let me," she murmured. "Please."

He let his hands drop to his sides. Praying for control, he closed his eyes as she unfastened his trousers and opened them. Her palms were cool against the hot skin of his belly, soft against the rigid flesh of his arousal.

Drawing her breath in sharply, Rianne explored the length and thickness of him. Sweet, liquid desire settled in her core. She wanted to possess, and be possessed, to feel all that heat and strength deep within her. Rising up on her

255

knees, she pressed herself against him. His hands settled on her back, stroked slowly along her spine to her buttocks.

She arched into him, trapping the blatant shaft between their bodies. Skin against skin, softness against hardness, and it was wonderful!

"Pagan," she murmured. "I want—"

"I know," he said. "I want you, too."

With a heave of his powerful shoulders, he swung her up and over onto her back. She welcomed him as he lay full length upon her, spreading her legs to accommodate him. His rigid manhood pressed enticingly against her swollen, eager woman's flesh, and she shifted, trying to urge him inside.

"Not yet," he muttered, kissing her brows, her cheek, the corner of her mouth. "I want to touch you all over. I want to taste every inch of you." He was drowning in her, sight, scent and feel. In all his life, he had never experienced anything to compare to making love to this woman. His Rianne.

With his tongue, he traced the curve of her jaw, the delicate line of her collarbone, then moved downward over the swell of her breast. He made decreasing circles around her nipple, then sucked the rosy nub into his mouth, reveling when she gasped and surged up against him. He moved to her other nipple, suckled her, then nibbled his way down the underside of her breast to her navel.

Awash in a sea of sensation, Rianne sank her hands into the dark thickness of his hair as he kissed his way lower still. Then she gasped, partly in shock and partly in tumultuous passion when he spread her legs wide apart with his hands and settled between them.

"What are you . . . Oh!" she cried softly as his tongue darted out to taste the hot, moist silk of her secret flesh. It was the most incredible sensation she'd ever felt, the most intimate of pleasures, the most exquisite torture. She wanted to stop him, and yet she wanted it to go on forever. "Oh, *Pagan!*"

256

The tremor in her voice nearly sent Pagan over the edge of control. But he forced himself to concentrate on her; he wanted to give her pleasure, to etch this night indelibly in her memory—no, in her very being—as deeply as it would be in his. After tonight, she would never again doubt that she belonged to him.

Rianne thought she'd surely flown the heights of passion, but he showed her there were pinnacles of which she'd never dreamed. A time came when she begged him to take her, but he merely cupped her hips in his large, strong hands and lifted her closer while his tongue drove her to new levels of pleasure.

"Please," she moaned. "I want you!"

As she shuddered with yet another climax, he moved up her body, claiming her eager mouth at the same time that his manhood slid into her hot, velvet depths. She enclosed him fully, contracting around him with the last ripples of her pleasure, and he felt as though he'd come home.

"I missed you," he groaned.

Frantic with need, Rianne arched her back as he withdrew slowly, almost completely, then thrust deeply again. She sobbed as he withdrew again, poising just at her entrance for a seemingly endless moment.

"You belong to me," he said hoarsely. "Admit it."

"Yes," she whimpered. "I belong to you."

He thrust home, and she eagerly accepted the throbbing length of him. Wrapping her legs around his hips, she held him tightly lest he try to stray too far from where she wanted him. He growled something low in his throat, then slid his hands beneath her, supporting her as he increased the pace.

Rianne met him stroke for stroke, gasp for gasp as they strove for the beckoning fulfillment. Then the first tiny ripples began deep in her body, growing and spreading until they became a rushing tide that swept her, and then Pagan over the edge. She clung to him with all her strength, for he was her only anchor in a reeling universe. He poured himself into her, his body shuddering, and called her name over and over.

When reality returned a short time later, she found him propped on one elbow beside her, studying her face. His pale eyes were full of tenderness, yet brimming also with primitive male satisfaction. And there was absolutely no point in trying to puncture his daydream; *he* knew he'd driven her mad with pleasure.

"You look insufferably pleased with yourself," she said.

"I am."

"Pagan." Reaching up, she pushed a lock of raven-dark hair back from his forehead. "Tell me about the orphanage."

He caught her hand and held it still, and there was a hint of ice in his pale eyes. "Who's been gossiping?"

"I'll tell you only that the information was given to me in the spirit of helping us both."

"It must have been Marie, courtesy of my brother Conor's flapping mouth."

"Are you afraid to talk about it?" she asked softly.

"Not afraid." With a sigh, he shifted position so that he was lying on his back. "But it's an ugly story and an even uglier memory. Times like that are best forgotten."

Rianne leaned upon his broad chest, refusing to give up so easily. "No, not forgotten, but let go. And I think that's something you never learned to do."

"Is it so important for you to know?" he asked.

"Yes," she said simply.

He let out his breath in a long sigh. "I've never told anyone before."

"Not even your wife?" she asked.

Especially not her, he thought grimly. Aloud, however, he only said, "No."

"Please, Pagan."

He closed his eyes, wanting to refuse. She had grown up so differently than he, and she'd never understand what his childhood had been like. But she had given him so much

258

and asked for so little in return, that he couldn't refuse her this small, tormented part of himself if she wanted it.

And so he told her the things he'd never before spoken of to anyone but the brother who had lived through it with him: his mother's death from overwork in Chicago, the squalid orphanage where boys were swilled like pigs, where they were beaten and misused and where they learned to fight like wild animals simply to survive. He told her about watching his two youngest brothers, Davey and Ben, die from the dreaded typhoid. He and Conor buried them, small graves since they were only four and six years old.

He didn't tell her how he'd felt as he shoveled the dirt onto those tiny, blanket-wrapped forms or how he'd railed against his own helplessness to save them, how he had damned the sadists who ran the orphanage and cursed the God who had let this happen. Those things could not be expressed in words; they only came out in his dreams. His private Hell. His punishment for not finding a way to save his brothers.

But he did tell her how he and his only remaining brother survived four more years in that hellhole. They'd run away several times during those years, but were always found and brought back. The beatings were bad then. But finally the time came when they were old enough and shrewd enough not to get caught. He'd been twelve years old, Conor ten when they found their freedom in the underbelly of Chicago. It was a maze of slums where the price of life was low and the stakes of living high, but the Roark boys survived and even prospered enough to get out.

The two of them grew up as they roamed America. They became gamblers, soldiers for hire, treasure hunters—risktakers, hard men whom others learned to respect.

As he told his story, his voice calm but his eyes stark, tears began to run down Rianne's face. She wanted so much to be able to take those memories from him, to erase the scars of pain from him with her love. For the first time, she understood why he wrapped his heart away, keeping it inviolate, keeping it safe.

His voice trailed off. His eyes closed, his eyelashes a dark sweep against his high cheekbones. He lay unmoving, long and bronze and seemingly invulnerable, but she knew now the depth of his pain.

"Damn them," she said. "Damn their dirty souls to hell!"

He opened his eyes, surprised and not a little amused by her profanity. "Such language!"

"I am not cursing, at least in the profane sense," she said. "But those people who ran that orphanage certainly deserve to spend Eternity with the Devil." Tears welled up again, but it was obvious that he wasn't comfortable with sympathy, and he certainly wouldn't want pity. So she cleared her throat, repressing the tears sternly, and asked, "Why isn't Conor treading the gold fields with you now?"

"He found his Nirvana," Pagan said, a faraway look coming into his eyes. "The sea. He's a ship's captain now, working to buy his own vessel."

"And you're still looking for your Nirvana, aren't you?"

A slightly crooked smile quirked his lips. "I'll leave that to the dreamers. For myself, I'll settle for Eldorado."

"Is that all you want?" Rianne asked.

"Not all." With a lithe heave of his powerful shoulders, he tumbled her up and over so that she was on her back and he was leaning over her. "There is something else I want."

"A temporary reprieve because you can't find gold?"

"No. There are many kinds of treasure." He moved closer, close enough to see the amber flecks in her eyes, close enough for her to feel how badly he wanted her again. "And some are more precious than others."

She wound her fingers into the thick, dark hair at the nape of his neck. "Truly?" she whispered.

"Truly.

Smiling, she pulled him down.

Chapter Nineteen

Rianne woke to find Pagan curled around her, as possessive in sleep as he'd been awake. It was still night — or rather, the lavender-tinted dimness that passed for night so near the summer solstice. Three days had passed since she and Pagan had been reunited, three days of heaven beneath the midnight sun.

Pagan rolled over onto his back, kicking off the covers so that every inch of his taut masculine body was exposed to her view. Emboldened by the fact that he was asleep, she propped herself up on one elbow to study him.

Truly, he was a beautiful man, with a powerfully muscled chest and shoulders, narrow hips, long, strong legs, and a belly that was as lean and ridged as a washboard. He looked like a great, sleeping panther, graceful and hard, utterly relaxed but ready to spring into motion at any moment. Her gaze settled on the portion of him that had given her such pleasure. As Marie had so colorfully put it, Pagan Roark was one hell of a man. Rianne blushed at the memory of what they had shared, the heated whispers, the even more heated caresses — possessing and being possessed on every level. It was love as hot and wild as passion, passion so searing it had to be love.

She couldn't stop herself from touching him. Lightly running her hand down his torso, she reveled in the varying textures of skin and hair and muscle that was Pagan Roark. Then, almost of its own volition, her hand moved lower. His manhood stirred at her touch, thickening and lengthening until fully roused. She drew in her breath with a sharp sigh, inordinately pleased at the effect she had on him. Passion swept through her in a sweet, liquid rush.

Softly, she traced the well-cut outline of his firm mouth. There were so many unanswered questions between them, so many issues left unresolved. And yet none of those things mattered just now. When they touched, the rest of the world fell away, leaving them in a universe all their own. Even with her inexperience, she knew how rare that was, and how precious. He was her love, her lover.

For now, that would be enough.

Smiling, she reached out again. She wanted to be the aggressor this time, to wake him to love, for she knew it would please him immeasurably. But a shout in the distance stayed her.

"Gold!"

The cry was faint, and yet it echoed through Henderson City like thunder. Others took up the call, a chorus of voices crying the word over and over. "Gold. Gold. GOLD!"

Pagan sat up with a jolt. "What was that?"

"Gold!" Rianne scrambled from the bed and rushed to the window. She could feel Pagan's naked chest against her back as he peered out over her head.

A horse and rider came hurtling down the street toward the saloon. Rianne's eyes widened in astonishment when she saw that the rider was her father, his white hair streaming behind him.

"Rianne! Pagan!" he bellowed. "We've done it! Gold!"

It had happened. Rianne stood motionless, frozen in place by astonishment. It had really happened. She had prayed for this, worked and slaved to make it happen, and now she didn't quite believe it.

Pagan moved away from her, leaving her feeling cold and bereft. Quickly pulling on his shirt and trousers, he rushed from the room. She heard his footsteps retreat swiftly down the hall, then the sound of voices as Marie and the others woke.

Hastily, wanting to leave before the others saw her come out of Pagan's bedroom, Rianne donned her dressing gown and ran downstairs. She found the front door blocked by Pagan's tall, broad-shouldered form.

"Let me see!" she cried, pushing at his back.

Pagan turned, drawing her out and in front of him just as Alastair pulled his horse to a skidding, mud-spattering halt in front of the Golden Bear. The old man leaped down from the saddle almost before the animal had stopped. He stepped up onto the boardwalk, stumbling a little in his haste.

It seemed as though the entire population of Henderson City was running toward them. Everyone was in various stages of dress, or undress, as the case might be, but no one cared. There was only one focus here, and that was Alastair and his cry of gold.

Alastair was breathing so hard, his chest going up and down like a bellows. A strong aroma of whiskey hovered in the air around him.

"Father, you've been drinking!" Rianne said, shocked by the enormity of what he'd done. He had given his word, pledged his Kierney honor not to drink while working the mine.

"Hssh, sweetheart, don't get all upset," he said. "I've kept my word. But today is a holiday, and I'm entitled."

"What holiday?" she demanded.

He laughed. "Hold out your hands."

She obeyed. With a theatrical flourish, he pulled a skin pouch from his pocket and loosened the drawstring, then upended it over her hand. A cascade of nuggets fell into her cupped palms. Some were small, about the size of a

263

pea, but most were as large as a man's knuckle. Gold. It lay heavy in her hands, reflecting the sunlight in a rich, aureate glow.

The crowd sighed, a collective suspiration of awe and envy and acquisitiveness.

"We hit white gravel yesterday," Alastair said, a singsong quality to his voice. "The prettiest white gravel you ever did see. And gold running all through it, thick as the butter in your grandma's biscuits."

"Goddamn," one man breathed. "Goddamn."

Rianne couldn't speak, couldn't do anything but stare down at nuggets she held. Gold. They had actually found gold. Enough to make a new start anywhere in the world. Strangely, that thought didn't make her heart leap the way she'd expected.

"The Songbird is in business!" Alastair cried. Scooping the gold from her hands, he slid it back into the pouch. As though released by his action, the crowd evaporated like fog on a hot morning, each man running for his horse. In just a few minutes, the street was empty.

Empty, that is, except for Lowell Mason. With both arms in slings, he could neither ride nor stake a claim. Looking into his glittering black eyes, Rianne knew he blamed her for it. She had never seen such hatred before, and it sent a shiver of dread rushing along her spine. He held her gaze for a long, terrifying instant, as if to make sure she saw that hatred. Then he turned and walked away.

Still shivering from the effects of that encounter, Rianne turned to look at Pagan. His eyes sparkled with excitement, and his body—no, his whole being—was intensely focused. She'd seen that look during their lovemaking last night, when he had put everything aside, even his own needs, to concentrate totally on giving her pleasure. This time, however, he wasn't thinking about her at all. Her heart contracted with pain; today, the object of his affection was gold, and that was something with which she would never be able to compete.

"Don't worry about anyone jumping our claim," Alastair said. "Mad Francois happened to visit just when Manfred and I were whooping like wild Indians. Ahhhh, you should have seen his face when he saw what we'd found. Took him about five minutes to stake the claim just downstream from the Songbird. He's sitting on both claims, shotgun in hand."

Pagan nodded. "We can trust Francois. What about Manfred?"

"He staked the claim just below Francois'. He took his wages in gold, and said to tell you he quit." Taking a deep breath, the old man added, "There's plenty to go around. You can't believe this strike, not without seeing it with your own eyes." He tossed the sack of gold to Pagan. "How much do you think is in there?"

Pagan hefted the pouch. "Fourteen, fifteen hundred dollars."

"About that." With a smile, the old man patted the sack. "I panned it out of that gravel in less than half an hour."

"WHAT?" Pagan shouted.

"This is it," Alastair said. "The big one. We're going to be kings, my friend. Kings!"

"As soon as word of this gets out, we're going to be up to our necks in gold-seekers. People who are going to want to take what we have. Come on inside, Alastair. We've got plans to make."

Rianne looked from one man to the other and saw identical expressions of triumph on their faces. Hard faces—those of men who had gotten what they wanted and intended to keep it. A shiver went through her despite the warmth of the sun.

"Come, Rianne." Pagan held out his arm to escort her into the Golden Bear, but it was obviously an absent courtesy. His attention was all for Alastair and the gold just now.

The interior of the saloon seemed dark after the bright sunlight. John Ferguson wasn't at his place in the bar; presumably, he'd ridden north with everyone else.

Alastair, arms crossed over his chest, surveyed the room like a general scouting the battlefield. "I always wanted to do this," he said. Marching up to the bar, he slapped the pouch of gold down onto the top.

Grinning, Pagan went behind the bar. "What will it be?"

"Whiskey," Alastair said, his smile matching Pagan's. "And not that rotgut you serve your regular customers. A bottle of your best for Alastair Kierney!"

"Nothing but the best," Pagan agreed, pulling a bottle out from beneath the bar. "My personal stock."

"Ahhhh. I hope you have several of those. I've got a rich man's thirst."

"There's plenty." Pagan poured a glass of whiskey for the old man, then another for himself.

"To plenty," Alastair said, raising his glass high.

"To plenty."

The two men clinked glasses, then Pagan poured another round. Rianne stared at them, bewildered by this strange male rite she could neither understand nor appreciate. She had to get away. Quietly, she slipped out of the room and went upstairs. She might have saved herself the trouble of being quiet; they didn't even notice her leaving. Truly, they seemed to have forgotten she existed.

Once upstairs, she dressed and busied herself in the familiar routine of dusting. But for once the familiar chore did not give her release from her thoughts; this was too important, too close to her heart.

"You're an idiot, Rianne Kierney," she told herself with all the severity of a schoolmistress. "Anyone else would be happy to be rich."

266

But she was no schoolmistress. She was Pagan Roark's mistress. By loving him, she had accepted his world. Even though she had given herself to him, risked everything just to hold him in her arms, she had known her value in that world.

But the gold had changed everything. Pagan didn't need her. If she refused to sing, he could buy another singer. If she refused to be his mistress, he could buy one of those, too. And no matter how much gold her father possessed, she could never buy what she really wanted from Pagan: his love, his name and his children.

All her doubts and insecurities came back in a rush. He had never actually told her he loved her. He had said *want* and *need* and *desire*. But never love. She had assumed it, right or wrong, because she had needed to.

Abruptly, she noticed she'd been cleaning the same spot over and over on a table that had long since been free of dust. With a hiss of indrawn breath, she threw the rag down. Suddenly the room seemed too warm, too confining, or perhaps it was her thoughts that bore her down. She opened the window to let some fresh air into the room. As she did, she heard the front door of the saloon open and close, and then Pagan's deep voice.

"Alastair, I'm going out to the mine to look things over," he said. "Tomorrow I'll make the trip to Fortymile to hire some men. We've got two months before winter sets in; with help, we can get those sluices up and moving before the end of July."

"We're rich," Alastair said, his voice slightly uneven from the whiskey he'd drunk. "Maybe I'll buy that Texas ranch I lost all those years ago. Damn, I'll be so rish . . . rich that I won't even have to run cattle on it!"

"Take it easy, Alastair," Pagan said with a chuckle. "You'd better mine the gold before spending it."

Feeling like an eavesdropper, Rianne reached out to close the window. But then her hand stopped in mid-air when she heard her father ask, "What are you going to do with your half of the money, Pagan?"

Pagan laughed. "Anything I please, my friend. I've always wanted to see Paris and Vienna and ride a gondola in Venice. Maybe I'll buy a ship to match my brother's and try my luck with the sea."

Rianne took a step back from the window, then another. Paris. Vienna. A sailing ship. She simply was not a part of his plans for the future. Perhaps she was merely a goal he'd already attained. Thoroughly miserable now, she listened in silence as the sound of his swift footsteps faded away.

"Stop feeling sorry for yourself, you idiot," she muttered. "Now get downstairs and let your father know you're happy about his success!"

Squaring her shoulders, she went downstairs to the saloon. Alastair was sitting at one of the small, round tables in front of the bar, already halfway through one bottle. Another sat beside him, untouched as yet, but it was obvious he intended to open it. Rianne sighed; always his drinking came between them, the one shadow on their closeness.

"Father—" she began.

"Now, darling, don't begrudge this," he said. "I've worked hard, and I deserve it."

Contrition speared through her. Surely she couldn't be so selfish as to blunt his pleasure in attaining his life's goal, no matter how much she disliked his drinking. This was his moment, his golden moment, and she intended to let him have it.

She went to him, putting her hands on his shoulders. "I'm sorry, Father. You're right. I just want to tell you how happy I am for you."

"Ahh, sweetheart, thank you." He put one arm around her waist and hugged her close. "I'm glad you came down. There's something very important I need to talk to you about. Sit down over there, where I can see your face."

Rianne obeyed, taking the seat across from him. *Has he decided he doesn't need me? Is he going to send me away now?* Alarm shafted through her. "What is it, Father?"

"I know I'm not a . . . disciplined man," he said, eyeing his empty glass. "Gambling and drink are my vices, made even worse because I do them together. I've always managed to lose anything I ever had. It hasn't mattered until now, because I never had much."

"What are you trying to tell me?" she asked, genuinely bewildered.

"I'm going to sign my half of the mine over to you."

"What? Father, you can't be serious."

He reached across the table and took her hand. "I've never been more serious about anything in my life. Are you going to run off with my gold?"

"Of course not!" she said, outraged at the very idea.

"I know myself, Rianne. I can't be trusted with anything valuable. If I sign the mine over to you, I won't have to worry about messing things up again."

Rianne's instincts screamed for her to refuse, for hers and Pagan's relationship was already more complex than she would like. If she became his partner in business, the possible consequences were great. But wasn't something she could tell her father without revealing that she and Pagan were lovers. Alastair might hear it from rumors, he might see it with his own eyes, but she was simply not capable of saying in bold, blunt words, 'Father, I am Pagan Roark's mistress'. "Have you discussed this with Pagan?" she asked.

"No. This is just between you and me, sweetheart." He smiled a bit crookedly. "If for no other reason than an old man's pride. I don't mind admitting my weaknesses to you, but I'd like to *be* someone in this town."

"But you *are* someone, Father. You're a fine man, and you don't have to account to anyone else for your actions."

"Now listen to me, Rianne Kierney." He took a piece of folded paper out of his pocket and pushed it across the table to her. "This is for your own protection. My agreement with Pagan states that if either of us dies, the partner inherits everything. I know Pagan would give you what's yours, but what if something happens to him *and* me? Why, as valuable as the Songbird is, you'd have varmints crawling all over this town trying to get a piece of it. But this way, I can make sure you get your legacy. It's a damn sight more than I ever expected to give you, and I'm glad for it."

Although the only legacy Rianne wanted was her father's love, she unfolded the paper. It was a bill of sale, drawn up in impressively legal-sounding terms. She looked up at her father quizzically.

"I found a fellow who used to be a lawyer," Alastair said in answer to her silent question. "He prospects for gold now."

She looked down at the paper again, trying to gain time to think. "Don't you like the gold, Father?"

"I love the gold. I'm just terrified of the responsibility of holding onto it." He grinned, looking like a wizened, mischievous boy. "Besides, it's much more fun to spend someone else's money."

Rianne was uncertain whether to laugh or cry. "Very well," she said after a moment. A great weight seemed to settle on her shoulders. As heavy as gold.

"That's my girl." Alastair went around to the other side of the bar and rummaged around beneath it. Coming up at last with a pen and ink, he brought them over to the table and watched while Rianne signed the document.

Rianne blew on the ink to dry it, then started to fold the paper up again. "Well, that's that. Now we can—"

"Not yet." Alastair put his hand over hers, stopping her from putting the paper away. "You owe me a dollar."

"A dollar?" she asked blankly.

"That paper reads that I sold you the Songbird for a dollar. It's not legal until you give me my money."

"Father, you're daft."

He held out his hand expectantly. With a sigh, Rianne felt in her skirt pockets for the handful of coins she'd put there earlier. She counted out a dollar's worth, solemnly placing each coin on his outstretched palm.

"Thank you," he said, closing his fingers around the coins.

Thus Rianne became half-owner of the Songbird mine for a dollar. And, she suspected, the price of her piece of mind, as well.

A week passed without word from Pagan. Rianne's despair grew with each passing day. Late on the eighth day, she sat in front of her window watching the afternoon turn into violet-tinged evening. The sun sank to just over the western horizon, where it hung, a blood-red ball that would not set further.

Such a strange land, she thought. Wild and eerily beautiful, vibrant with summer's life, yet even now aware of the hovering threat of winter. What would it be like with everything frozen, and the wind whipping across the dormant land? So cold, so cruel. A shiver went through her.

"I hope you're pining for me." Pagan's deep voice came from behind her, nearly startling her out of her skin.

She turned hastily. He was only a tall, broad shape in the dimness of the room, only his pale shirt clearly visible. "You've been gone a long time," she said.

"Things became very complicated." He didn't want to tell her everything that had happened, the confusion, the jumped claims and hot disputes, the two men who were

271

shot. He wanted to leave it behind, to bury his face against her scented softness and know he was loved.

"Did you miss me?" he asked, a poignant note of hope in his voice.

Rianne couldn't resist that unspoken plea. "More than you will ever know," she said.

A seemingly endless moment passed. Then he came forward to kneel in front of her. The faint, ruddy light of the sun cast odd, shifting shadows across his sharp-cut features. Her heart turned over with love for him, with the need to have him, to hold him.

Of its own volition, her hand went up to stroke the smooth, clean line of his jaw. "What's going to happen to us now, Pagan?" she whispered.

He nodded, understanding what had prompted this somber mood in her. "Because of the gold."

"Yes," she said, grateful that she didn't have to explain what she barely understood herself.

"Why must you make everything so difficult for yourself?" he asked. "Did you think I was going to send you away?"

"Well, I thought —"

"You thought wrong." His heart contracted with tenderness for her. But that warm, gentle feeling was tempered by annoyance that she knew him so little to think that mere gold would sever the ties that bound them. "You still owe me thirty thousand dollars, and I expect you to honor our agreement."

Her head came up in surprise. "But the gold —"

"The gold is still in the ground."

Hope blossomed in her, but she couldn't keep from testing him. She wanted to hear the words. "You didn't keep *your* part of the bargain," she said.

"You released me from it," he countered, a smile playing about his well-cut mouth.

"Will you release me? After all, the collateral is good."

"No."

He wouldn't let her go. Once, that thought would have been anathema to her. Now it was proof that he cared for her. She ran her finger over the firm curves of his lips, shivering as he nipped gently at the tip. Desire flowed through her veins like hot wine. "Once we begin mining in earnest—"

"It will be winter, and you won't be able to leave even if you wanted to."

"Which I don't?"

"Which you don't." Although he continued to play the game, his whole being rebelled at the thought of her leaving. He was rocked with the need to bind her to him body and soul, so deeply that she would never again doubt his claim. "Even if you paid me back a hundred times over, I wouldn't let you go. You're mine, Rianne."

"What a primitive notion!" she said.

"I never pretended to be civilized," he growled softly, grasping her shoulders in a most possessive manner.

Rianne gazed at him from beneath her lashes, unbearably stirred by his blatant claim. Desire moved through her veins like sweet, hot wine. There was an answering flare of heat in his crystalline eyes, a smoldering fire of passion and the promise of pleasure. Tonight would be her past, her present and her future all rolled into one, and she was going to live it to the fullest.

Reading the invitation in her eyes, Pagan drew in his breath sharply. With fingers that trembled with need, he took the pins out of her hair, letting the silken mass cascade down over his hands.

"Beautiful," he murmured.

She slid her hands along the breadth of his shoulders restlessly, wishing to be rid of the interfering fabric. "Why don't you kiss me?"

He grinned. "I'm being civilized."

"I don't want you civilized." She leaned forward, poising her mouth near his. "I want you to kiss me."

She sighed as his fingers sank into her hair, anchoring her for his kiss. It was a kiss fraught with tenderness and passion and inescapable possession, and it was exactly what she'd been craving. She melted into him, lost in a maze of voluptuous sensation.

He raised his head just enough to look into her passion-glazed eyes. "Is that what you wanted?"

"Not quite."

Quirking his eyebrows upward, he asked, "How else may I serve you?"

"Take your shirt off," she said.

"At your command." Rising to his feet, he swiftly dealt with his buttons. Tossing the shirt away, he waited for her next order.

"The rest, too." She could hardly breathe, and it was with an effort of will that she kept from squirming on the smooth upholstery of the chair.

Smiling, he removed his boots, then unbuttoned his trousers and slid them down. He was wearing nothing beneath them, and the sight of his aroused male body jolted her to her toes. He was superb—long-limbed and powerful, his sharp-planed face made even sharper by desire. Her ideal man. Her gaze drifted down to his uncompromisingly rampant manhood, and a rush of liquid heat pooled in her core.

"Now you," he rasped, kneeling in front of her again.

Feeling recklessly wanton, she unbuttoned her blouse and slipped it off, then handed it to him. He tossed it over his shoulder without taking his gaze from her.

"I'll need some help with the corset," she said.

"Damn things," he growled, turning her around so he could reach the laces. "Always getting in the way. I may burn them all."

"Will you have me jiggle for all the other men, then?"

"Jiggle!" His brows contracted in a scowl as the corset

274

laces resisted his efforts. "Just try it. If you think I'm un-civilized now . . . Damn it to hell!" Completely out of patience, he broke the laces and pulled the garment from her. "There."

His hands gentle now, he turned her to face him again. "Ahh, Rianne!" he hissed through clenched teeth. Her breasts were beautiful, high and full, the nipples swollen and eager. He took one into his mouth, rolling his tongue around it.

Boldly, Rianne moved him to the other nipple, her legs moving restlessly as she was caught in a midsummer-hot drift of pleasure. When he began suckling her, she cried out, stunned by the intensity of what he was making her feel.

With an effort of will, Pagan pulled away from her, bracing his hands on the chair arms with white-knuckled force. "Take the rest off," he murmured. "I want to see you."

She unfastened her skirt and slipped it down, then her petticoat. Her drawers were of fine-spun silk, so sheer that the triangle of hair at the junction of her thighs showed through. She was beset with brief embarrassment at her display, but then Pagan reached out and smoothed the semi-transparent fabric against her skin with hands that seemed almost reverent. In that moment, she knew he found her beautiful. Because of that she *felt* beautiful, and all sense of shame was drowned in a tidal wave of sheer, uninhibited sensuality.

"The stockings first," he said, his voice hoarse with desire.

Slowly, she slid her garters off, then rolled the pale silk down her legs. Pagan helped her slide them over her feet, his hands caressing her ankles and graceful calves, straying upward to the sensitive spot just behind her knees.

"Oh!" she breathed, sinking still further into voluptuousness.

His gaze moved over her like a physical touch, and there was a blazing sensuality in his eyes that made her yet bolder. He was teetering at the edge of control, and it wouldn't take much to push him over. She wanted to do that, to plumb the depths of her power. With provocative leisure, she untied the bow at her waist and pushed her drawers down over her hips. Teasing. Inviting. Daring. Pagan watched every movement, his chest heaving, the muscles in his biceps standing out tautly.

"Do you know what you're doing to me?" he asked, staring at her from passion-slitted eyes. "Two can play that game, you know."

Leaning forward, she ran her fingertips along the length of his erect manhood. "Game? It seems to me that you're very serious about what we're doing."

He made a noise deep in his throat, a primal growl of long-withheld passion, and slipped his hand around the back of her neck to pull her closer for a kiss. He delved into the sweet honey of her mouth, claiming, tantalizing, gently nibbling at her soft, passion-swollen lips. She sighed into his mouth, and he groaned with the effort of holding himself back.

Rianne leaned closer, wanting to feel his skin against hers, needing to be touched. As though he'd read her thoughts, he slipped his hands between their bodies, cupping her breasts, his thumbs rasping gently over her nipples. She writhed on the smooth upholstered seat, caught by a jolt of almost unbearable desire.

"Pagan!" she gasped.

He kissed her again. She was hot beneath his hands, sweet, consuming fire, and he wanted to touch her, taste her, and possess her all at the same time. No, first he wanted to look at her, just look. Taking her by the shoulders, he set her back in the chair. She smiled at him, leaning against the upholstery with all the unconscious sensuality of an houri displayed for her master's pleasure. Her breasts peeked at him from the

276

silken waves of her hair, and her flushed skin glowed like mother-of-pearl against the blue cushion. Siren, he thought, come from the depths of the sea to steal his soul. And he would give it.

"You belong to me," he said, possessed by the need to claim her again.

She couldn't have denied it had she wished to. But so did he belong to her, and every time they made love only deepened the bond for them both. "Yes," she murmured. "I belong to you."

She saw his jaw tighten, and knew she had moved him unbearably. Slowly, he slid his hands up her legs to her knees. With gentle pressure, he spread her legs apart. Rianne let her head fall back against the chair as his hands caressed her hips, her thighs, then moved to the slick, swollen flesh between. He stroked her with finesse and devastating intent, sliding deep, moving up to tease the tiny nub that was the center of her desire.

Awash in a sea of sensation, Rianne knew then that he was not about to lose control alone; they would plunge into the fire together, and together they would be consumed. Anticipation and spiraling passion made her squirm on the seat.

Pagan caught that revealing little movement, and triumph surged through him. She was ready, more than ready. The awareness shot through him, fire in his blood. If he didn't have her now, this instant, he would surely die of it. He gathered her against him, entering her with a deep thrust. She was tight, so wet and welcoming, that he had to close his eyes to retain control of his senses. It had been so long since he had held her, felt the wonder and uniqueness of his Rianne.

"God, oh, God, Pagan!" Riánne wound her arms around his neck and slid forward a fraction more, wanting all of him, needing to be possessed completely and irrevocably.

He groaned. "Come here, my wanton Siren." Cupping her buttocks in his hands to keep her against him, he lifted her up and out of the chair with a heave of his powerful body. He lay on his back on the soft rug, covering himself with her scented, silken softness. He put his hands on her hips, lifting her, then sliding her downward again until he filled her utterly.

"Oh!" she gasped, realizing the possibilities of this new position. She could set the pace, go fast or slow as she wished. She could drive him crazy. Excitement coiled within her, sharp and heady, the awareness of a woman's ultimate power over a man.

Bracing herself with her arms, she began to move, riding him to a rhythm that soon had them both gasping. All thought of driving him out of control was gone; the whole concept of control had no meaning in the cocoon of sensuality that wrapped her in its hot, sumptuous arms. There was only Pagan, and pleasure, and the beckoning fulfillment that awaited her.

He arched beneath her, his hands hard and insistent on her hips. Then he slid his thumb between their joined bodies, delving into the heated folds of her flesh to drive her over the edge.

"Pagan!" she moaned, her nails sinking into his shoulders as her climax rocked her.

Buried in her hot, shuddering depths, Pagan was caught in the swirling fulfillment. His hoarse cry of pleasure mingled with her breathy moan, merging even as their bodies did. Pulling her down, he kissed her deeply as the last shudders ended, leaving them both drained and content.

"My," she said when she was capable of speech again. "That was . . . nice."

He smiled, too sated to respond to her teasing with the proper outrage. "Nice is for tea parties," he murmured. "Why not say wonderful, incredible—"

"And elevate your already overblown sense of male self-satisfaction? Never." Propping herself on her elbows, she kissed the curve of his flaring black brows, his straight nose, the bold thrust of his jaw. "But if this is how you act after a weeks' separation, I may have to send you away on a regular basis."

With a lithe heave of his body, he flipped them both over so that he was the one looking down at her. "I was *very* happy to see you."

"So I noticed." Her eyes widened as she felt him move, felt the pulsing hardness of his manhood inside her. She drew in her breath sharply, once again awash in sensation. "I . . . get the distinct impression that you're still rather happy to see me," she murmured.

"I expect to be so for some time to come," he said.

"All night, perhaps?"

He smiled. "Indubitably."

"Oh, good."

Chapter Twenty

"I can't believe it's September already," Rianne said as she slid a batch of biscuits into the oven.

Marie laughed. "Bein' in love sure makes the time go by, don't it?"

"Yes." Rianne glanced down at her hands, wanting to hide the sudden flush of emotion that heated her cheeks. Six weeks had passed since she and Pagan had reunited. And although a great deal of his time had been taken up with the Songbird Mine, he had still managed to make her feel cherished, desired, and very beautiful. Their times together had been fleeting but oh, so precious, brief, glowing idylls amid the chaos that was the Klondike just now.

I never thought to have a mine as a rival, she thought wryly. And the confusion was going to get worse, much worse. Rumors about the gold flew as fast as leaves in the autumn wind, but no matter how wild they seemed, none approached the truth of the richness of this strike. Men were coming from all over the Yukon, and it seemed that every one of them stopped in Henderson City on their way to the stream called Barren. There was an urgency to the pace of things now; the days were growing shorter, the nights colder. Frost, gentle precursor of the savage freeze to come, rimed the ground each morning.

"You goin' to sing tonight?" Marie asked.

Rianne nodded. "It seems to be expected, doesn't it?"

"Expected!" Marie snorted loudly. "They'll tear the place down if you don't. Some of these fellers ain't got much to cheer them up but your singin'."

Rianne blushed. "Good heavens, Marie! They're pulling gold out of the ground like . . . like weeds. That hardly warrants consolation. I think more gold than whiskey crosses that bar at night."

"That ain't no exaggeration," Marie said. "Did you know that Stu Colher took to panning the sweepin's from the floor? Takes in near thirty dollars a night from it."

Rianne laughed incredulously. "From sawdust?"

"Yep. You know, we ought to be grateful for bein' in this place at this time. Where else could we have this much fun?"

"I wouldn't trade it for the world," Rianne said. These were the times people told their children and grandchildren about on cold winter nights, and she thanked God every day for being lucky enough to live them.

She was doubly blessed, for she had Pagan as well. When she began to take more and more responsibility for the Golden Bear, he handed her a sack of gold nuggets, trusting her judgement so completely that he never asked for an accounting. On the nights he was able to come into town, the only thing he asked for was her love and to spend the night wrapped in her arms. Those nights were more than exhilarating. They were pure magic.

Marie propped her elbows on the table, causing her bountiful bosom to almost overflow her chemise. "You got stardust in your eyes agin," she said.

"Sorry. I just can't seem to help myself."

"Did you take that powder I gave you?" Marie asked.

Rianne flushed again at the memory of the day Marie

281

had handed her a jar containing a white, powdery substance. In her inimitable way, Marie had claimed that it would 'keep you from gettin' caught no matter how many times you bed a man. I been whoring near ten years with nary a problem'.

"Well, did you?" Marie prompted.

"No." Rianne's voice was scarcely audible.

Shaking her head, Marie asked, "And why not?"

"I . . . just haven't gotten used to the idea of . . . of . . ." Rianne gulped, then finished in a rush, ". . . of worrying about things like that."

"Think on it," Marie advised. "I ain't trying to tell you what to do, but sometimes it pays to keep things from gettin' too complicated. And gettin' with child when you ain't married is complicated."

"Goodness, those biscuits smell done!" Rianne bent over the oven to hide her expression from Marie's too-knowing gaze. Truly, Marie only had her welfare at heart. But whenever Rianne thought about taking the powder, the picture of a child rose in her mind, a beautiful child with black hair and ice blue eyes. Pagan's child. Pagan's and hers. Rianne wanted that baby with a fierce longing, wanted it and yet feared the price of such recklessness. And yet, despite the fear, despite the possible consequences, the contraceptive remained untouched.

Would it always be like this? she wondered. Would love ever be pure and untrammeled, or would she forever swing between joy and despair, and want what could not be possessed?

John Ferguson, apparently drawn by the smell of fresh-baked biscuits, poked his head into the kitchen. "I'm almost finished putting those supplies away," he said.

"Come in, John," Rianne invited, relieved to have a reason to change the subject. "Have some breakfast with us."

He sat down eagerly. "Thanks." As he buttered the steaming biscuit, he asked, "What d'you want all those supplies for, anyway?"

"Some are for us," Rianne said. "But most are for Julia Nathan. She wants to expand her business, and I'm staking her."

"Women in business." John shook his head. "What's the world coming to these days?"

Rianne smiled. "It's coming to women being fully as capable as men. Something, mind you, we women always knew. Julia is an excellent businesswoman. To quote her, 'Let the men dig their gold; we can get rich serving them eggs at fifty cents apiece.' "

"I'll be damned," John said through a mouthful of biscuit. "Are eggs that dear?"

"Yes, and they're going to get much dearer," Rianne said. "What I wouldn't give to have a shipload of supplies here for the winter."

Marie's eyes widened. "But we jest bought all those things from Ogilvie. I thought we had plenty. And Julia—"

"Julia wasn't counting on feeding the entire Klondike," Rianne said. "Those supplies John put away include the last tinned fruit in the Yukon Valley. By the time she came to us for help, it was too late to send Outside for what we need."

Rianne let her breath out in a long sigh. Even now it was hard to imagine being so isolated from the rest of the world. England had been so small, its landscape gentle and long-tamed. But the Klondike was set like a jewel amid great, jagged mountains. The easiest way in or out was by the Yukon River, which was frozen from mid-October until late in May. It was possible to come in over the Chilkoot Pass or the White Pass, but that was a journey only the very experienced or very foolish would choose to make.

Absently, she tore a biscuit in half and spread molasses on it. "Perhaps we should still try to send someone to Seattle to order supplies, even if they don't get here until next spring. Once word of this strike gets Outside, we're going to have half the world trying to get into the Klondike."

"And ever' one of them is going to want to be fed," Marie said. "Maybe I'll learn to cook."

"They're going to want . . . ah," John glanced at Rianne, then cleared his throat before continuing, ". . . comforting jest as much as food."

Marie laughed, flashing her gold tooth. "Now that's the truth if'n I ever heard it. Best I stick to what I do good, eh?"

"I'd love to teach you how to cook," Rianne said. Despite her embarrassment at the subject of this conversation, she wanted to help Marie. Somehow, she couldn't quite believe that Marie was as happy with her profession as she seemed to be.

"What's this about cooking?"

Pagan's voice came from the doorway, and Rianne looked up in surprise to see him framed in the opening. As always, the sight of him, so dark and lean and poised, took her breath away.

"I thought you left for the mine," she said.

"I forgot something." His ice-blue gaze moved from her to Marie and John and back again. "What scheme are you three working on now?"

"We're trying to find a way to obtain enough food to last through the winter," Rianne said, taking a bite of biscuit. "And next summer, you know the galloping horde will be descending on us."

Pagan was momentarily distracted by the sight of her soft lips glistening with molasses. *Sweet,* he thought. *As seductive as an embrace. I wish I could taste them.* With an effort, he drove his thoughts back to the conversation. "Next winter will be the most difficult one. The

284

cheechakos[1] will be coming in by the hundreds, and most of them won't have sense enough to bring a grub-stake with them. They'll wander in here like wide-eyed sheep, planning to scoop gold nuggets from the ground."

"Well, even sheep need to be fed," Rianne said. "I suggest we send for supplies now, even if they don't get here until spring."

Pagan thrust his hands deep into the pockets of his coat, his brows contracting into a brooding scowl. "I'm afraid Lowell Mason beat you to it. Word has it that he hove into Fortymile late yesterday on the steamer *Beauregard* with half a ton of food. Brought it all the way from Seattle."

"Of all the luck!" Rianne cried.

"Don't worry," Pagan said. "There's plenty to go around."

"Food?"

"Gold," he said gravely.

"You can't eat gold," Rianne retorted.

"True." Suddenly he smiled, and it was like sunshine breaking through the clouds. "Julia had better start thinking of ways to cook moose."

"Moose!" Marie snorted. "Fetch what you came back for and go away, Pagan Roark."

"Very well," he said, his grin widening. "Come, Rianne."

She gaped at him in surprise. "What?"

"It's a beautiful day, and we won't have many more like this before winter comes. I thought you might like to come out to see the mine."

"I'd love to!" Pushing her chair back hastily, she got to her feet.

"The valley has changed since you saw it last," he warned.

1. Greenhorns

"I don't care." Her heart sang; to spend the entire day with him, she'd accept an invitation to watch grass grow.

He held out his arm. "You'd better bring something warm to wear later, for we may be late getting in."

His crystalline eyes were full of sudden, smouldering heat, and she knew that he planned to be late, and why. Feeling as gay and giddy as a young girl going out to her first ball, she ran upstairs to fetch her woolen traveling cloak. As she passed the mirror, she caught sight of her face and stopped. She looked like a woman in love, her skin slightly flushed, her lips parted, her eyes knowing and sensuous. For all the world to see.

"You ought to be ashamed of yourself, Rianne Kierney," she said.

But she wasn't. In Wickersham, life was lived according to a well-defined set of rules. Whether a person liked it or not, the boundaries were set and easily understood. Here, there were no such rules. Life was raw and primitive, unfettered by convention. A man—or a woman, for that matter—could take what pleased him and leave the rest.

And yet, faintly from the shadows of her memory, she heard her mother. *Talk about freedom all you like,* whispered that dry, accusing voice. *But you still want to be his wife. You've settled for being his mistress because you can have nothing else from him.*

It was an ugly, disquieting thought, and she pushed it away fiercely. Mother had been severe and cold, and Rianne wanted only warmth in her life now, the warmth of love and laughter and Pagan.

He was waiting for her at the bottom of the stairs, and the eagerness in his eyes banished the last traces of disquietude. Her pulse tripped and stuttered at the sight of him. His was not the sort of reassuringly mundane handsomeness she'd seen in some young men in Wickersham. No, his stunning good looks came from the

286

man himself, born of the immense vitality within him. It was far more compelling than mere physical beauty.

And how do you expect to hold such a man? The thought rose unbidden, but was instantly forgotten as he came up the stairs toward her.

"You look like a doe about to flee," he said, stopping on the step below her. "Do you want to run from me, Rianne?"

Never. Oh, never! "No," she whispered.

He held out his hand. "Then come with me."

The gesture was so like the one he'd made the night she'd put her doubts aside to become his mistress that her throat ached with repressed emotion. Just as she'd done that night, she reached out and placed her hand—and heart—in his. And just as he'd done that night, he took possession of both.

He led her outside, where two horses were tethered, already saddled and ready. Pagan lifted Rianne into her saddle, then mounted his own horse and led the way toward the outskirts of town.

"You're going east," Rianne said. "The mine is, I remember, almost due north."

He turned to grin at her, a heart-stopping flash of white teeth that made her internal temperature go up several degrees. "I thought I'd try a new route. There are too damn many travelers on that other trail."

They laughed softly, then urged their mounts into a canter, amorous co-conspirators in search of privacy. Pagan led her to a glen tucked between two hills, a dim, shadow-dappled hideaway beneath the branches of towering spruce trees. The air seemed hushed, as though even the wind didn't dare break the magical quiet.

"It's lovely," Rianne said.

"I found it the day before yesterday." Swinging down from his mount, Pagan reached up to lift Rianne down beside him. "I couldn't stop thinking about bringing you here. Our own private Eden. Look around you, Rianne. Have you ever seen a lovelier spot?"

"Never." She sighed in contentment as he drew her into his embrace. Reveling in his strength, his caring, she leaned her cheek against his chest to hear the steady, swift beat of his heart.

"I missed you," he murmured. "It seems like years since I held you in my arms."

"It's been all of six hours," she said, striving for sternness but failing completely.

Pagan heard the tremor in her voice, felt the faint quiver in her body, and felt his pulse leap in response. She always had this effect on him, like heat lightning in a summer sky. It never failed to surprise him that his desire for her still ran fever high. Time had not purged the obsession from his blood; if anything, his need for her seemed to increase every day.

"What are you thinking about?" she asked, lifting her head to look into his eyes.

"I was thinking about how glad I am you decided to find your father. And," he gave her another of those heart-jolting smiles, "how much I want you."

"You're insatiable."

"When it comes to you, yes. You're much too enticing for your own good, Rianne. Or mine."

For all the lightness of his tone, he was utterly serious. Rianne had wrapped him up ten different ways, until he hardly knew up from down, inside from out. In his absorption with her, he found that even the gold did not glitter nearly as brightly as he'd expected. A damned strange reaction from a man who had spent most of his life searching for just such a strike.

Sensing his sudden disquietude, Rianne reached up to smooth his black hair away from his forehead. "Is something wrong?"

"Not as long as I can hold you," he said, knowing it

was true, and yet wishing it were not. But desire had risen in him like a sweet, hot tide, and he intended to drown himself in it until thought ceased, and there would be only sensation.

Sweeping her up into his arms, he carried her to a patch of green-dappled sunlight at the far end of the glen. There, he laid her down on the moss, Nature's soft bed. Her hair had come down, spreading out around her like a golden-brown waterfall, and her eyes looked like warm, dark topaz.

Slowly, almost reverently, he slid her clothes from her. Her white skin gleamed like moonlight, but it was a warm radiance, fueled by the fire within. She was his Siren, his sea-goddess come to land to wrap him in her lovely, sensuous spell. With his mouth and hands and body, he worshipped her.

Rianne looked up into his passion-tautened face, realizing that the beauty of this joining would stay with her forever. He was part of her now, running through her veins with her lifeblood, his heart beating in time with hers, his passion burning, burning until there could be no forgetting the joy of his touch.

"I want you," she whispered, fierce with her need. "I want you *now.*"

Pagan's control vanished. Unfastening his trousers with hands that shook with frustrated desire, he freed his throbbing manhood. He was raging with the need to have her, to possess her completely, to forget everything in the voluptuous sensuality of her passion.

"I love you!" she murmured, pulling him into her, enclosing him in sweet, sumptuous flesh, so deep, so hot that his mind reeled from the intensity of it.

Boldly, he claimed her in the most primal and timeless of ways, mastering her body's most powerful responses. She gave him everything he asked for, and more. And yet her yielding was no passive thing, but a whirlpool of smoldering desire that drew him in with irresistible power. That desire beckoned him, made him reckless, urged him to forget everything in its searing depths.

He went willingly, eager sacrifice on the flaming altar of passion.

Later, Rianne lay cradled in his arms, the sun slanting warm and golden across her naked skin. She felt as though she'd been new-made, forged into another person in love's fiery furnace.

Playfully, she traced the straight line of Pagan's nose. "You promised to show me the mine."

"To hell with the mine," he murmured. "I'm not moving from this spot."

"Don't you have work to do?"

"Yes. But to hell with that, too." He ran his fingers through her hair, thinking that it was like sifting through fine silk. "Will you deny me one day spent with my woman?"

"No." She would deny him nothing on this earth, for he had brought light and joy into her life, and banished the darkness.

It was nearly dusk when they left for Henderson City. Rianne didn't want to leave. During the time they had spent in that peaceful little glade, she had been completely happy. The world had ceased to exist; there was only Pagan and the love they shared. But reality had crept in with the setting of the sun—and so did the cold. There was a bite to the twilight wind, a wintery touch that made their breaths hover in the air like wraiths.

"Well," Rianne said as they made their way toward town, "so much for nighttime trysts in the forest."

"I wish I'd found that spot a bit earlier in the season," Pagan said wistfully. How he'd like to see her naked in the moonlight! But firelight had its attraction as well, he reflected philosophically.

As soon as they neared town, they encountered a steady stream of men. Some were afoot, some astride; all looked weary and travel-stained.

"Still more hopefuls come to curry Fortune's favor," Rianne noted.

Pagan grunted. "And more to come."

When they reached the Golden Bear, they found the front door open, allowing a flood of light and music to pour out into the street. Pagan leaped lightly down from the saddle, then lifted Rianne down from hers. Playfully, he let her slide down along his body until just her toes reached the ground.

Rianne raised her brows, feeling the iron-hard line of his manhood against her body. "Haven't you had enough?" she asked.

"Apparently not," he said.

A woman's high-pitched laugh behind them brought them both around with a start. Rianne saw a tall woman silhouetted in the doorway of the saloon. Although her face was not visible against the light, her hair was a brilliant gold coronet around her head.

Pagan let go of Rianne abruptly, and she drew her breath in with a sharp gasp. She didn't need an introduction to know who the newcomer was; Pagan's reaction told her more clearly than words. His former wife. The only woman he had ever loved.

The woman stepped forward. "Hello, Pagan," she said.

"Sylvia."

"It's been a long time."

"Five years."

His voice was bland, revealing nothing. The woman tilted her head to one side, showing the long, graceful line of her neck. Then she took another step toward him, allowing the light to hit her face. She was the most beautiful woman Rianne had ever seen, with classical yet

291

sensuous features and a red, pouting mouth that seemed to beg for a man's kiss. Her eyes were as deep and rich a green as the finest jade, her hair spun gold.

Misery was a hard knot in the center of Rianne's chest. No wonder he's never forgotten Sylvia, she thought. No wonder every other woman falls short; he's already met his ideal, and lost her. Then, noticing the heated interest in Sylvia's eyes, Rianne thought that perhaps he hadn't lost her after all.

The woman gazed up at Pagan, her lips curved in an alluring smile. There was blatant invitation in her expression, as well as the calm assurance borne of great beauty. In contrast to that worldly poise, Rianne felt ugly and awkward.

Rianne wished desperately that Pagan would touch her, put his arm around her, anything to show that he had claimed her. But his attention was focused on the blonde woman, unwavering and intent. It was as though Rianne Kierney had ceased to exist. Despair, sick and biting, lanced through her chest.

"Why don't you introduce me to your friend, Pagan?" Sylvia asked without glancing in Rianne's direction.

A muscle jumped in his jaw. "Rianne Kierney, meet Sylvia Martel. She and I were married once."

Each word hit Rianne like a blow. Harsh words, spoken in a flat, emotionless voice. Reality, in the shape of a lovely blonde woman whose smile was sharp enough to cut flesh.

Sylvia's small, even teeth flashed in the light. "Oh, Pagan, you *are* a tease. I haven't been Sylvia Martel for a very long time."

"So, what are you calling yourself these days?" he asked.

"Why, darling! Just what I ought to be calling myself: Sylvia Roark." Studying him from beneath thick, dark-

292

gold lashes, she added, "I'm terribly hurt that you've forgotten that we're married."

"You seem to have forgotten that you divorced me."

"Oh, that!" Sylvia waved her hand negligently.

Pagan's eyebrows went up. "Most people would hardly describe a divorce as 'oh, that'. As though it hardly mattered."

"But it doesn't matter, darling Pagan." Sylvia laughed, a high-pitched trill that scraped over Rianne's nerves like sharp iron filings. "You see, I never went through with the divorce. And now your loving wife has come back to you!"

Chapter Twenty-one

"You're lying," Pagan growled.

Sylvia flowed towards him, deftly managing to insinuate herself between him and Rianne. Rianne caught the overwhelming fragrance of perfume. It reminded her of the flowers at her mother's funeral, sweetly sickening.

"Would I lie about a thing like that?" Sylvia purred.

Rianne believed her. One thought played over and over like a refrain, an endless loop of agony. *Pagan is still married. I've become a married man's mistress.*

Pagan was tensely alert, as taut as a strung bow. "How did you know I was here, Sylvia? I moved around for two years after you left, and I don't imagine you tried very hard to keep track of me."

"Oh, darling, still so cynical! If you must know, I happened to run into Mr. Lowell Mason in Seattle a few weeks ago. We got to chatting, and he told me all about Henderson City and its inhabitants. You can imagine my surprise when I discovered that you and he lived in the same town!"

Pagan's teeth flashed in a smile that had nothing of humor in it. "What a coincidence. And why did you decide to come?"

"Because I wanted us to be together again. There was never anyone better for me than you, or you for me."

"Really?" Letting his breath out in a long sigh, Pagan

crossed his arms over his chest. "Not even that gambler you ran away with?"

Running one pointed fingernail down the row of buttons on the front of his shirt, she added, "I was young and terribly foolish, Pagan. I was carried away by the flash and dash, and blinded to what was really important."

"I see. But then, we were both young and foolish."

His voice and expression were still controlled, but Rianne sensed a raging current of emotion coiling just beneath the surface. Her chest was a solid knot of pain. He still cared for this woman. After everything she had done to him, after all the hurt, he still cared. *Leave!* a small, sane corner of her mind screamed. *Run away, anywhere, just get away from this!*

But her legs refused to obey. Some force rooted her in this spot, trapping her. Like the fly in the spider's web, mesmerized by the baleful grace of its own approaching doom, she had to watch Pagan reconcile with his wife. The woman's perfume coiled around her like a sticky net, filling her nostrils, her throat, a too-sweet taste of darkness.

She swayed, reaching toward the post for support. Pagan was there in an instant, his warm, strong arm going about her waist to steady her. As much as she'd craved his touch a moment ago, now she couldn't bear it. Pain and despair rang along her nerves until she felt like crystal about to shatter.

She tried to push him away. "Please," she whispered, a hairbreadth from tears. "Please, Pagan. Let me go."

"Yes, Pagan. Let her go," Sylvia purred. "This should be a private discussion between husband and wife, after all."

Pagan swung around to face his wife, and there was such a look of savage anger on his face that Rianne clutched his sleeve, afraid that he might strike the woman. "Damn you, Sylvia! Damn you to hell for showing your face here!"

"Now, darling, don't be like that," she said. "I'll make everything up to you. I'll—"

"First thing in the morning, I'm putting you on a boat to Seattle," he growled. "I don't want anything to do with you."

Rianne stared at him as hope, fragile and tentative, began to bloom in her. There was still a chance for them; as long as he didn't love Sylvia, there was a chance.

Then Sylvia laughed, and there was such malicious triumph in her voice that Rianne's new-found confidence shriveled. "I'm afraid it isn't quite so simple as that, Pagan darling," the blonde woman said. "You've got responsibilities, and I intend to see that you meet them."

"What the devil are you talking about?" he demanded.

"I have *such* a wonderful surprise for you." Sylvia glanced over her shoulder. "Tessa!"

A small shape entered the doorway, hesitating with obvious shyness. Rianne gasped. It was a child, a little girl perhaps four years old.

"Come here, girl," Sylvia said impatiently.

Slowly, the child walked toward the group of adults. Rianne took one look at her face and knew there was no doubt as to her paternity. This was Pagan's child. He was there in those pale blue eyes, her straight black brows and thick, curling eyelashes, the wealth of hair that possessed the midnight iridescence of a raven's wing. Pagan's child. Turning to look at him, Rianne saw his eyes narrow as the realization hit him, too.

Rianne's throat was tight with restrained tears. Tessa was the embodiment of the child that had haunted her dreams these past weeks. But this was cold, hard reality, not a woman's fancies, and the child had been born to another woman.

Placing her hands on the girl's fragile shoulders, Sylvia turned her toward Pagan. "Meet your papa, Tessa."

"Hello, Papa," she said, gravely, her brows low over her eyes.

Pagan knelt so that his face was on a level with hers. She looked so much like his youngest brother, the one who had died of fever in the orphanage. Emotion bloomed within him, as new and precious as the first flower of spring. He was rocked by the instant, powerful caring he felt for this small human being who was part of his flesh. His daughter. "Hello, sweetheart."

"She was born October twentieth," Sylvia said. "Exactly eight months after I left you."

Pagan looked up at her, his eyes glittering with sudden, smoldering anger. All this time, he'd had a daughter. Years had been lost between him and Tessa, precious years that could never be regained. "You never told me," he said.

"True," Sylvia murmured. "I'll make it up to you somehow."

Pagan had never laid violent hands on a woman, but he was sorely tempted right now. But he restrained that urge, for there was something much more important to tend to just now: his daughter. Dealing with Sylvia could wait. Slowly, he extended his hand toward Tessa.

"Come with me, Tessa. It's time we got to know each other, don't you think?"

"Yes, Papa."

Rianne watched as he took her tiny hand in his and led her inside, and knew he loved the child. Instantly, completely, he loved her. Tessa was his flesh and blood, and now that he'd found her, he'd never let her go.

With a sinking feeling in the pit of her stomach, Rianne glanced at Sylvia to gauge her reaction. The

297

blonde woman was watching Pagan and Tessa, too, and there was such a look of triumph on her face that Rianne's heart began to race with dread. She had planned this, counted on just this reaction from Pagan.

Slowly, Sylvia turned to look at Rianne. "He seems to have forgotten you," she said.

The sneering tone of her voice stiffened Rianne's spine. "He is only getting to know his daughter, as is only right."

Sylvia smiled. "Yes, his daughter. And I am that child's mother. As that, and as his wife, I have first claim on him."

"Claim?" Rianne repeated, raising her eyebrows. "What an odd way of putting it. You of all people should know that no one owns Pagan Roark."

"Least of all his mistress."

Yes, least of all his mistress. But the agreement was internal, the pain self-inflicted. It was certainly not for this woman's viewing. Aloud, Rianne said, "What really brought you here, Miss . . . Mrs . . . ?" She couldn't say it. She simply couldn't call this woman 'Mrs. Roark'.

"Why, just as I told Pagan, I want all of us to be re-united," Sylvia said. "I always regretted leaving Pagan. He's quite a man."

"I know." Rianne was proud that her voice didn't waver.

Sylvia's green eyes narrowed, and her beautiful face twisted with sudden hatred. "You might as well forget any notions of him keeping you as his mistress, Miss Kierney. I am his wife, legally and morally, and I plan to fight for what is mine. I am not about to let some half-grown English baggage steal my husband."

'My husband'. Those two words burned into Rianne's heart like red-hot coals. She hadn't known Pagan was married when she had fallen in love with him. She had

298

become his mistress, willingly accepting all the risks, but never, never in her wildest dreams could she have anticipated this.

She could hear her mother's voice echoing in the recesses of her mind. 'Who so diggeth a pit shall fall there'in', said the cold, intolerant voice that Rianne had tried to leave behind. But this time she couldn't ignore it, for this time Leonora was right. Rianne knew she'd dug her own pit. Begun by desire, deepened by love, it had become a chasm with no bottom.

"You look a trifle ill, Miss Kierney. Has the great revelation burst upon you at last?" Sylvia leaned close, trapping Rianne in the sweet, sickening tentacles of her perfume. "You saw his face when he looked at Tessa. He loves her already. You know as well as I that he is not about to send her away. And I am that child's mother. Where Tessa goes, I go. We are his world, and you have no place in it."

It was the truth, horrible and hurtful, but the truth. This was Sylvia's game, and she held all the cards. *I wouldn't play, even if I could win, for I will not gamble with a child's welfare for my own happiness.*

Pagan's wife stood smiling her lovely, cruel smile, as though reading Rianne's thoughts and rejoicing in them. And then she laughed, a spiteful sound that sent Rianne stumbling away, rushing blindly through the doorway into the saloon.

"It's the Songbird!" Francois Gruillot boomed.

Rianne faltered to a halt. Her gaze skittered around the room, finding the big Frenchman at the far end of the bar. She liked Francois, truly she did, and looked forward to seeing him at every performance. But just now she could have throttled him for calling attention to her.

"Sing! Sing!"

The voices rose in a deep male chorus, punctuated by

299

the heavy stamp of feet on the dusty boards of the floor.

Rianne closed her eyes, trying to resist the pull of those voices. There was no joy in her now, no music.

"Sing! Sing!" The mingled voices speared through her, demanding that she respond. She felt devoid of will, a ship adrift in dark seas of emotion, moving with whatever current was nearest. And the demand of the voices was a powerful one. It was easier to meet that demand than it was to go up to her room, where there was only the prospect of her own bleak thoughts to keep her company.

So she let the voices pull her forward, towards the piano where her father waited, smiling, his hand extended to welcome her. His smile faded when she drew closer.

"Are you feeling all right, darling?" he asked.

"I'm . . . fine," she said.

She swallowed convulsively, afraid that she might faint right here in front of everyone. But then Alastair took her hand in his, and the warm human touch steadied her.

"Stage fright?" he asked.

"Yes," she lied. "That's it."

' "Marseillaise!" ' Francois roared.

Alastair grimaced. "Shall we humor the monster? He's very rich now, you know." He said the same thing every time. It was part of their ritual before every performance.

Taking a deep, calming breath, Rianne squared her shoulders and answered as she always did. "Anything for my friend Mr. Gruillot."

She began haltingly, one small step from tears. But then the music seeped into her. Her voice rose, sure and true, fulfilling the demand of her audience. When the "Marseillaise" was over, she began another lively song, hoping to drown her depression in the spirited music.

But her soul needed something very different, and finally its demand became too strong to resist. She swung into the opening bars of an old ballad whose quiet melody stirred a measure of peace into her tumbling emotions. Alastair followed on the piano, his eyes sparkling, his fingers dancing over the keys. Rianne closed her eyes, pouring all her pain, her despair and her impossible love into the melody. She was only vaguely aware that the saloon had gone completely silent, as though every man there was holding his breath.

When the last plaintive note faded away, the crowd sighed. Then the applause began. She stood unmoved amid the thunderous clapping and raucous shouts of her audience. She didn't deserve it; for once, she hadn't sung for them. That song, with all its soaring emotion, had been for her.

She opened her eyes again. Pagan stood before her, incredibly handsome in black evening clothes. Instantly, her whole being focused on this man she loved so desperately and could never have. They stared at one another, a small island of silent longing in a sea of noise.

"That was beautiful," he said when the applause died down a bit.

Rianne inclined her head, accepting the compliment. "Where is Tessa?"

"She's sleeping."

"Ah. It was a long journey for a child." Rianne felt terribly exposed and vulnerable; her emotions were so intense that she was sure they were written on her face for all to see. If she could look away from Pagan, she might be able to regain a measure of control. But his fathomless ice-crystal eyes held her gaze too powerfully to resist.

"Will you sing my favorite song for me?" he asked. "I think you know which one."

Yes, she knew which one. And singing it now, when

she knew there was no hope for them, would be like tearing her heart into pieces. "I can't," she whispered.

"Yes, you can." He was possessed by the desire to hear her sing that song, for it would be the affirmation of her love for him. He wanted it, craved it, needed it like he needed air to breathe.

She clasped her hands to still their trembling. She knew what he was asking of her; even now, he wanted her love, her loyalty, her soul. She was weak, so terribly weak. Every fibre in her body wanted to answer that demand, to put off the inevitable just a few moments more. To love him a little longer, if only for the space of a song—was that too much to ask? But then she saw Sylvia standing a few yards away, her beautiful green eyes as hard and cold as granite. Pagan's wife.

And then Rianne knew that it *was* too much to ask. It was not because of Sylvia. It was Tessa, the beautiful child who looked so much like Pagan, who mattered. Of them all, only Tessa was innocent. A man's mistress had no right to make demands on him at the cost of his family. "I can't," Rianne pleaded. "Please don't ask."

His face hardened. "Sing it," he growled.

Rianne panicked. She would have torn her heart out to give to him, but she couldn't sing that song. Not in front of his wife. Whirling, she ran from him. His footsteps were loud on the stairs behind her, inexorably closing the gap between them.

She reached her room a scant foot ahead of him. Breathing in great, sobbing gasps, she tried to close the door against him. But he pushed it open easily, striding into the room before slamming it closed behind him.

For a moment he stood, legs wide-planted, fists jammed into his narrow hips. He was breathing as hard as she, but she knew it was from anger, not exertion.

When he spoke at last, his voice was harsh with suppressed emotion. "Why did you run from me?"

"I had to." *Because I love you too much, because I can't have you.* She hadn't the courage to say it aloud.

"Sylvia means nothing to me."

"She's your wife."

"Not by choice!" Striding forward, he grasped Rianne by the shoulders. "Not by choice," he said, punctuating each word with a gentle shake as though to impress understanding upon her with his hands.

Rianne stood motionless between his hands, offering him no fight. She closed her eyes to shut out the sight of his starkly handsome face and the raw need in his eyes. "She's your wife," she said again.

"Wife!" He flung himself away from her and began to pace the room in long, angry strides. "I met Sylvia in San Francisco nearly six years ago. Like every man in town, I was captivated by that damned beautiful face of hers. And she was attracted to the ten thousand dollars I'd won in a poker game." He burned to touch Rianne. But if he did, he'd never be able to finish this story. So he thrust his fists deep into his pockets and kept pacing. "Sylvia was charming and lovely, and I was . . . stupid. Before I quite knew what was happening, I was married to her. It didn't take long to find out that the face masked a greedy, lying soul."

"But by then it was too late."

"She fooled me, plain and simple. But I soon realized that she was running through my money faster than water, and that she'd leave as soon as it was gone. I was right. It took her less than three months to spend that ten thousand dollars, and then she ran off with the next likely prospect."

"Didn't you try to find her?"

"No." He laughed, a harsh bitter sound. "I found that what I thought was love had evaporated faster than my money."

Rianne clasped her hands together to keep them from

303

trembling. So that was why his heart was walled up inside him, impervious to a woman's touch. Sylvia had hurt him, but *she* had paid the price. "And when she wrote telling you she'd divorced you?"

"I didn't give a damn."

"I'm sorry," Rianne whispered. "Sorry for everything."

"You make it sound so final." He moved to a spot in front of her, so close that she took a step backward to create some space between them. Grasping her clasped hands, he raised them to his lips. "There's no reason why we still can't—"

"No!" Pulling her hands away, she took a step backward. "You're a married man."

"Not for long. All I need is a little time to work this thing out."

Tilting her head back to look at him, she asked, "And if you do succeed in divorcing Sylvia, then what?"

"Then we put our lives in order again."

And I will still be only your mistress. "What of Tessa?"

His jaw tautened. "Tessa is mine."

Rianne had heard that note of absolute possession in his voice before. She should know better than anyone that Pagan Roark did not let go of something he wanted. "Oh, Pagan!" She laughed, but there were salt tears on her lips. "How can Tessa be yours if you divorce Sylvia? What law will allow you to take a child from her mother?"

"I'll find a way."

"That's horrible! I can't believe you would do such a thing!"

"Do you think Sylvia came here for *Tessa's* sake?" Pagan demanded. "I doubt it very much. That woman has the maternal instincts of a rattlesnake."

"Perhaps she's changed since you knew her last," Rianne said, wanting so badly to believe him, yet not

304

daring to. It would be so easy to hate Sylvia, so easy to be blinded to the real truth of the situation. "Having a child can change the most selfish of women into a good, caring mother."

"Not Sylvia." Sighing, Pagan shook his head. "Can a scorpion change its nature? No, Rianne. Sylvia plans to use the child to pry a piece of the Songbird Mine away from me. Money is what drives Sylvia. Not me, not Tessa, but money."

For money, Rianne thought. But she doubted it was true. Pagen was too vital and compelling a man to be entirely eclipsed by the glitter of gold. Surely Sylvia must see the advantages of having both.

Suddenly Rianne hated the mine, hated the gold for doing this to them. She wished her father had never found it. "Will Sylvia be staying here at the Golden Bear?"

"What choice do I have?"

"No more than I," Rianne said. "I'll be leaving first thing in the morning."

He grew very still, the predator about to pounce. "If you do, I'll only bring you back. I'm not letting you go, Rianne."

"You can't expect me to remain your mistress with your wife and child living under the same roof!" she cried passionately. "Don't you understand that I cannot do that; don't you care whether you hurt me?"

"I understand," he said, deep lines bracketing the sides of his mouth, "and I care."

"But not enough!" She closed her eyes, took several deep breaths, then dared to look at him when she had regained a measure of control. "I asked you once before, Pagan, and now I ask it again. Let me go."

"And again I refuse."

"Why? Why must you hold me when it can bring nothing but disaster?"

He turned away, raking his hand through his hair. "I hold you because I can't let you go. You belong to me, and I'd fight the Devil himself to keep you."

It was the final blow to Rianne's already overwrought emotions. She began to cry, silently and painfully, holding it in so he wouldn't know.

But he swung around suddenly, his eyes widening when he saw her tears. He came back to her, gently folding her in his arms. "Shhh. Don't worry, love. It will work out. I'll *make* it work. Just promise me one thing."

"W-what?"

He framed her face between his hands, tilting it up so he could see her expression better. His Rianne. She was so sad, her beautiful honey-brown eyes flooded with tears. The sight of her pain wrenched at his heart. Damn Sylvia, damn her greed, her nasty machinations, damn everything!

Rianne waited breathlessly for him to speak again. For a long moment he held her, gazing into her eyes. When he finally spoke, his voice was as smooth and soft as velvet. "Promise me that you'll give me some time. As much as I'd like to send Sylvia packing, I can't let Tessa walk out of my life now that I've found her. But I'll work this thing out as fairly and peaceably as possible. Trust me."

"I trust you," she said softly. "But I will not be your mistress."

Pagan wanted to change her mind—*burned* to change her mind and force her to admit his claim. But this was not the time. He might push her into leaving, and that he couldn't abide. For now, he would be content to secure her presence in Henderson City. "I only ask that you stay," he said. "Trust me to put this mess right. I've got a hell of a fight ahead of me, Rianne, and I need you."

She gazed into his clear blue eyes, knowing that she ought to refuse. To stay here in this saloon, trapped by winter for eight long months, forced to watch Sylvia ply her wiles on him . . . Rianne pushed the thought away hurriedly. She intended to refuse. She even opened her mouth to tell him no, she wouldn't stay.

But the words wouldn't come. Pagan needed her. For the first time, he truly needed her. He was such a strong, determined man that until now, he had never seemed to want or ask for help. That he did now was an irresistible lure. His eyes were tender, his hands oh, so gentle, and she loved him so very much. Trust, comfort, time—none of those things seemed as difficult as leaving him forever. Feeling like she was about to take a plunge into the vast, treacherous currents of some unknown river, she whispered, "Yes, I'll stay."

He bent toward her, and she watched helplessly as his mouth came closer and closer. Their lips met and clung with almost savage desperation, a violent grasping for warmth and security in a world that had turned to chaos. Rianne wrapped her arms around him and held him close, wishing she could hold him like this forever.

But she couldn't. Feeling as though she were leaving her soul behind, she pulled away. She had to be strong enough for them both. "Don't," she said. "You know what will happen."

"Let it happen," he said, clenching his fists at his sides to keep himself from drawing her back. "There is no shame in what we share, no wrong."

"You have a wife and a daughter. I'm afraid there's a great deal of wrong in it," she said. But her heart did not accept the words. It yearned for Pagan, for his touch, for his love. Fighting her own weakness, she took a step backward, then another. "Good night, Pagan. It's better if you go."

"Are you sure?" he asked softly.

No. "Yes," she said.

His face tautened with the effort it took not to take her in his arms again. But there was such pleading in her eyes that he curbed his need. She had been hurt by circumstances that were completely out of his control; at least he could give her this small measure of peace. "Good night," he said.

Rianne waited until the door closed behind him, then went and turned the key in the lock. Locking him away. She leaned her cheek against the cool wood, remembering the warmth of his flesh, the solid beat of his heart.

Slowly, she slid downward until she was huddled upon the floor. There were no tears; this hurt was too deep, too intense for any such release. She pressed her face against her sleeve, welcoming the texture and warmth of the wool.

"I'll get over it," she whispered against the uncaring fabric. "Somehow, some day, I will get over it."

The echo of Sylvia's laughter seemed to hang in the room, mocking her brave words.

Chapter Twenty-two

Rianne fell asleep there on the floor, her cheek against the cold oak boards. Pagan walked through her dreams, laughing, his hair blowing like a black fan upon the wind. She tried to touch him, but he disappeared just before she reached him. And although she cried his name into the wind, there was no answer.

A roar of voices from the saloon woke her with a jolt. The Saturday night revelries were in full swing, and there were sure to be dozens of men lying about in the morning, sleeping off their drunkenness.

"There will be a number of pounding heads tomorrow," Rianne muttered. "The streets will be full of men too sore to do more than feel sorry for themselves. Somehow, I don't think that is quite what the Lord meant when he set Sunday aside as a day of rest."

With a groan, she sat up and stretched to relieve the stiffness caused by sleeping in such an unnatural position. After a moment, she rose and began her nightly ritual.

As she stood in front of the mirror, braiding her freshly-brushed hair, she leaned close to her reflection and said, "You look like you've seen a ghost. Well, one thing is certain, Rianne Kierney. You don't need a fortune-teller to reveal the meaning of that dream you had."

Sighing, she turned down the bedclothes and put another log on the fire. She wished she could hibernate like the bears, to sleep and sleep until the hurt dulled. If only it were possible!

Just as she climbed into bed, she heard a strange snuffling noise out in the hallway. "What on earth . . . ?" she muttered, slipping her arms back into her dressing gown and padding to the door.

When she opened the door, she saw Tessa standing outside, looking tiny and fragile in her voluminous cotton nightgown. Her bare toes curled up from the cold floor.

"Why, what's the matter, dear?" Rianne asked.

"My fire went out, and I was cold and I had a bad dream," the child quavered. "Papa wasn't in his room, and then I couldn't find my way back to mine."

"Everything is all right now," Rianne soothed, putting her arm around the girl's shoulders. "Your Papa hasn't gone. Do you hear those voices downstairs?"

"Y-yes."

"Well, those men are your Papa's guests. He must stay downstairs until very late to make sure . . . that everything goes well." Actually, she reflected, he stayed to keep the miners from tearing the place down in their Saturday night revelry. "You're shivering, Tessa. Why don't you come in and warm yourself in front of my fire, and then I'll take you back to your room."

Tessa moved forward, as warily as a fawn slipping through the forest.

Rianne pulled the coverlet off the bed and wrapped it around the child's shaking body. "There," she said, "in a moment you'll be all warm and cozy. Doesn't that feel good?" Tessa didn't answer, but Rianne wasn't bothered by the lack of response, having been a shy child herself. "It's scary to wake up all alone in a strange place, isn't it? I used to visit my grandfather sometimes, and he would put me in a great, dark room

310

where the corners were all shadowy. I used to stay awake for hours, too frightened to close my eyes. Do you know what that's like?"

Tessa nodded.

"I used to beg to sleep with my mother," Rianne continued. "She told me I was too old for such nonsense. But I was only eight, and eight isn't too old to be frightened, is it?"

Still mute, Tessa shook her head.

"Shall we go find your mother?" Rianne asked. "Would that make you feel better?"

Tessa's eyes turned wary. She put her thumb in her mouth, obviously avoiding the question. Rianne didn't push; she didn't think Sylvia was any more likely to sympathize with a child's night-terrors than her own mother had been. Kneeling so that she was on a level with Tessa, she gently stroked the child's sleep-tousled hair. "You've got lovely hair, sweetheart. Just like your Papa's."

"Mama says it's ugly, straight, and black like a Chinaman's."

Rianne took a deep breath, appalled by the thoughtless cruelty of the remark. She still remembered the pain she'd felt when her own mother had said, 'You should be grateful you have a good nature instead of beauty, Rianne. Looks are nothing but trouble.' If people would only understand how deeply such things hurt a child, surely they would never say them!

She felt a powerful sweep of kinship with Tessa. Gently, she stroked the child's hair again. "Of course it's black. Just like a raven's feathers. Have you ever seen a raven's feathers in the sunlight?"

Tessa shook her head.

"You can see every color shining from them, a whole rainbow—iridescent, like dark pearls. Now, how could anyone think pearls aren't beautiful?"

Tessa sucked her thumb rhythmically, obviously considering that. Rianne smiled. "You've gotten some tangles in your hair. Would you like me to brush them out for you?"

For a moment the wariness returned to the child's face. Then, removing her thumb from her mouth with an audible pop, she said, "Can you braid it just like yours?"

"Of course."

"You can brush it, then."

Rianne went to get her brush and comb from the bureau, hiding her smile of amusement at Tessa's suddenly peremptory manner. There was more of Pagan in her than mere looks.

Rianne sat on the edge of the bed, patting the spot beside her. "Come, Tessa, sit beside me."

The child obeyed, still clutching the coverlet around her. Yards of excess material slithered after her, pale blue like her eyes. Like her father's eyes.

Once Tessa was settled beside her, Rianne tucked the coverlet around her and began working the knots out of her thick, lustrous hair. There were a great many tangles, more than should come from a single night's sleep. Rianne wondered at that, and at the child's wary, timid manner. The one flash of spirit a moment ago told her that Tessa had the potential to be a much more outgoing child. Could Pagan have been right about Sylvia not caring about her daughter except as a way to obtain money?

If so, it was a disturbing thought. If Tessa were being neglected, then it was necessary that she stay here, where her father could help her.

"Ouch!" Tessa cried when Rianne hit a particularly bad tangle.

"I'm sorry," Rianne said, "but some of these knots are very tight. Would you rather I stop?"

312

Tessa shook her head emphatically.

Rianne resumed brushing. "Does your mother fix your hair like this sometimes?"

"Sometimes." It was a noncommittal answer, spoken in an exceedingly noncommittal voice.

It was yet another trait of Pagan's, Rianne noted. No one got information out of these Roarks unless they wanted to give it. With a rueful smile, she decided to drop the subject. There was plenty of time to find out. As gently as possible, Rianne worked at the knots until the child's hair flowed down her back in a smooth, silken sheet.

"Oh, that's pretty!" Rianne said. "Just like a dark waterfall."

Tessa twisted and turned in an attempt to see. Rianne brought her over to the cheval mirror and showed her how to use the hand mirror to see her back.

"It *is* pretty," Tessa said.

Deftly, Rianne plaited the child's fine, black hair into a braid, then stepped back to admire her handiwork. "There, that's done. And now it's time that I took you back to your room—"

"I don't want to go!"

"But sweetheart, your mother will be worried if she can't find you in the morning. Are you frightened to be alone? Shall I wake her for you?"

Tessa shook her head. Her thumb went into her mouth, and there were the beginnings of tears in her eyes. Rianne saw depths of emotions in them, uncertainty, pleading, a need to be held and reassured. A child's fear of the unknown. How terrible that she felt that only a stranger could help her.

Rianne could no more turn from Tessa's need than she could Pagan's. "Would you like to stay with me?" she asked.

"Oh, yes, please."

313

The soft plea went straight to Rianne's heart. *I wish she were mine.* With sudden self-disgust, she pushed the thought away. First she coveted Sylvia's husband, now her child. Was there no end to her envy?

"You get into bed here, and I'll tuck you in," she said, and soon had Tessa secure and comfortable. "Now I'll just throw another log on the fire to keep us until morning and blow out the lamp, and then we'll be all ready."

Just before extinguishing the light, she turned to look at her young guest. Tessa looked impossibly tiny in the bed, such a small, fragile being. For some reason, Rianne mused, she's put her trust in me. Strange. With a sigh, she blew out the lamp and climbed into bed.

"You know, we haven't been properly introduced," Rianne said. "I'm Rianne Kierney."

"Mama says you're Papa's in . . . inamorata. What exactly is that?"

"It's a . . . sort of friend, dear." Rianne was glad the darkness hid her burning face. What a horrible thing for Sylvia to say to a child!

There was a pause, then Tessa said, "May I call you Rianne?"

"Of course. I hope, Tessa, that we can be friends, too."

For a moment, Rianne thought the child had fallen asleep. Then Tessa murmured, "I'd like to have a friend."

The wistfulness of her voice touched Rianne deeply. Hadn't the child had friends before? Just exactly what was wrong between mother and daughter? Perhaps it was nothing; perhaps she was seeing problems where there were none because she *wanted* Sylvia to be a bad mother and a terrible person.

Rianne gave up. She could lie here, her thoughts going 'round and 'round like a top, and never know the answer. "Good night, Tessa," she said.

"Good night, Rianne."

Closing her eyes, Rianne forced herself to relax into the soft warmth of the bed. Just as she began to drift off into slumber, she felt Tessa's small hand creep into hers, a trusting little gesture that brought tears to sting the back of her eyelids.

No wonder Pagan loves her already. I do, too.

It was nearly three o'clock in the morning when the crowd in the saloon thinned enough for Pagan to go upstairs. He had broken up three fights and prevented at least a dozen others tonight, and he'd had more than his fill of drunken, brawling men. Damn, but he wished he could slip into Rianne's room and find comfort in her arms.

Just before retiring, he went to look in on Tessa. His heart pounded with alarm when he saw she was gone. His mind conjured up a wealth of frightening images: she could easily have gotten lost in the unfamiliar house, fallen over something and hurt herself; she might even have wandered outside into the cold night. He began searching the upstairs room by room. But there was no Tessa. He was frantic with worry by the time he got to Rianne's room. And there Tessa was, snuggled in bed beside Rianne as though they'd been friends forever. They were both asleep, looking peaceful and cozy. His breath went out in a long sigh of relief.

His lips curved upward in a tender smile as he opened the door wider. Light from the hallway spilled across the bed, sparking a wealth of highlights in the depths of the light-brown and midnight black braids upon the pillows. Quite a pair, those two, and both infinitely precious to him.

He moved silently to the bed. In repose, Tessa's face had a serenity that was lacking when she was awake. He studied his daughter's delicate, elfin features. He'd found her a nervous, wary child, eager to know him, yet a bit suspicious of his attention as if she were afraid it would soon be taken away. He hadn't quite known how to reassure her, or what to do to win her trust.

But here she was, curled up in Rianne's bed, her small form snuggled comfortably into the curve of her companion's body. Somehow, Rianne had managed to break through the child's reserve, to gain her trust and affection.

The simple generosity of Rianne's nature staggered him. Another woman would have resented the child. If Sylvia had been in the same situation, she would have scorned the child as yet another rival. But not Rianne. She was a gambler, just like he was, but it was herself she risked. It was a kind of courage he hadn't realized existed; he found it easier to risk a fortune than to risk his own heart.

Drawn to her like a moth to a flame, he moved closer to the bed. Suddenly Rianne opened her eyes and looked straight at him. Her expression was so vulnerable and tender that he had no choice but to lean down and kiss her. Just before their lips met, however, she put her hands on his chest, holding him away.

"Don't," she whispered. "You'll wake Tessa."

Pagan glanced at his daughter, finding her sleeping deeply and peacefully. "I'm not going to wake her. I just want a kiss, love. One kiss to keep me warm until morning."

Rianne sighed. *Love,* he'd said. Perhaps it was just a casual endearment to him, but it sharpened the deep loneliness within her. Her dreams had been full of him, aching, desperate dreams. And now he was here beside her, and she wanted to feel his touch, to wrap herself in his warmth just for a moment. She slid her hands up from his chest to his neck, feeling the deep, rapid hammering of his pulse.

Pagan claimed her lips with a conqueror's boldness, his tongue seeking entrance and gaining it. She was so sweet, honey sweet, and warm as golden sunshine. Desire speared through him like a bolt of lightning—hot, compelling, and almost irresistible. *You can't have her, not now, with Tessa here,* a small, sane corner of his mind chided. Reluctantly, he broke the kiss, resting his forehead against Rianne's as he fought to get his breathing under control.

"I ought to snatch you away, take you to my room and never let you out again," he muttered.

His breath blew across her lips, a warm caress. A shiver of desire went through her. "How primitive."

"Would you like me to steal you away?"

More than anything in this world. "No," she whispered. "Now go away before you wake the child."

"I intend to have you both," he said. "You and Tessa."

"Don't say that." Rianne shook her head. "You have no right."

He straightened abruptly. "Then I'll *take* the right."

She stared up at him. Every line of his body was sharp-cut and taut, and his pale eyes glittered with violent emotion. She realized she was looking at the Pagan Roark who had been forged in the hell of that orphanage. A hard man, one who knew exactly what he wanted and went after it with single-minded determination.

He was like a strung bow, arrow notched and ready to shoot. In that moment, she knew that with a word of invitation, a kiss, she could set that arrow into flight. But doing so would tear his family apart, and

317

the one who would be hurt most would be the innocent little girl lying so trustingly beside her.

With a sigh, Rianne knew she couldn't do it. "All you will do is hurt me, and hurt your daughter."

"Damn it, Rianne! I—" He broke off, ramming his right fist into the palm of his other hand. "Look at me. Look at me, and tell me you truly want me to stay away from you."

She met his gaze unflinchingly. "I truly want you to stay away." Every word felt as though it were taking a piece of her heart with it.

"I don't believe you." Every instinct he possessed screamed at him to claim her again, to love her and pleasure her until she admitted the lie. But he couldn't. When he had asked her to give him time, she had given in as generously as she had accepted his daughter. He could do no less. For as long as he was able, he would give her time.

Rianne saw the tension drain out of him, and realized that for the moment, she had won herself some peace. The victory did not make her happy. "Good night, Pagan."

"Good night." Leaning over, he kissed Tessa lightly on the cheek. "She's every inch my daughter, isn't she?" he whispered, straightening.

"Yes." Rianne closed her eyes, resisting the urge to reach out for him.

"Look at me," he commanded.

She obeyed, half wishing and half afraid that he was about to kiss her again. *It isn't fair to be so weak!*

But he didn't touch her. He only gazed into her eyes for a long moment, then he left, closing the door behind him. It seemed such a final gesture, and Rianne felt as though a door had closed in her heart.

"Oh, my love!" she whispered.

Tessa stirred beside her, but still didn't awaken.

Rianne tucked the covers more securely around the child, then lay back on her own pillow to stare up at the shadowy ceiling.

Pagan seemed so certain of what he wanted. But Rianne was not so sure, for she did not for a moment underestimate Sylvia's attractions. She was lovely, sensual, and worldly, a woman who could take a man's heart without half trying. Once, she had taken Pagan's. No matter what he might say now, he had once loved her. Now she was obviously determined to do whatever was necessary to win her husband back, and Rianne doubted many men could resist that sort of campaign.

Truly, Pagan had more reason to reconcile with Sylvia than not. Just now he was surprised and off balance. But as time passed, he might begin to appreciate his wife's attributes, not the least of which was the fact that she was the mother of his child.

"And I have nothing to offer him," Rianne whispered into the darkness. "Nothing at all."

Sylvia lay in Lowell Mason's arms, her body automatically performing passion's movements while her mind dwelled on other things. She knew he was making love to her out of a desire to strike a blow at Pagan. So be it; he had told her about the Songbird Mine for the same reason, but that didn't mean she hadn't used it to advantage.

"Ah, Sylvia," he moaned into her ear.

"You feel so good," she murmured into his, smiling as she thought how very easy it was to fool a man. A few judicious flutters of one's eyelashes, a bit of pandering to the man's ego was all it took.

She wished Pagan were making love to her. Truly, she had forgotten how devastatingly attractive he was. There had been men since him, many men, but once she saw Pagan again, she realized that none of the

319

others compared with him. She had come to this godforsaken place, intending to trade Tessa for a small fortune, but now her plans had changed. Now she wanted the man *and* the fortune.

She looked up at the man who was making love to her, but it was not Lowell Mason's face she saw. It was Pagan's. Now *that* was a man who knew how to take his time with a woman. She imagined him above her now, his hard arms holding her, his even harder manhood stroking her to a climax that would not have to be feigned.

"Is it good for you?" Mason asked.

Sylvia's attention focused on him reluctantly. At this moment, she would rather shove him away. But she might need his help, so she played the game she had learned so well with so many men. "Give it all to me, lover," she whispered. "You feel so good!"

He lunged into her, grunting. As soon as he was finished, he rolled off her and lay on his back at the other side of the bed. His eyes were closed, so Sylvia allowed herself a small smile of disdain. The moment she had arrived in his room, he had leapt at her like a starving man. Fifteen minutes later, he was finished. She recalled whole nights of passion during the short time she and Pagan had lived together as man and wife, nights where he had brought her to ecstasy time after time. Then Mason turned on his side to look at her, and she put a look of sated pleasure on her face.

"Did you like that?" Mason asked.

"It was the best."

He grinned. "I bet Roark never made you feel like that."

"Never," she breathed with mock enthusiasm, staring at the slack folds of skin on his belly. *What a jackass! But a useful one; I'll keep him for a while.* "Tell me, Lowell. What do you know about this Kierney girl?"

He grunted. "She's his mistress. Must be a hot one, too, for him to be so damned possessive of her."

"Possessive?"

"Yeah. No one touches her but him. Strange, isn't it, when he's got a whole houseful of whores *anyone* can have?"

Sylvia sat up, frowning. There was nothing about the girl that seemed special in any way. She wasn't even very pretty. Oh, there was that beautiful young skin, which only a woman of Sylvia's thirty-three years could truly appreciate.

"Why, I wonder?" she mused aloud. "There's nothing about her to attract a man like Pagan."

"Have you heard her sing?"

Sylvia shrugged, unwilling to admit she'd been consumed with jealousy over that beautiful voice. Who would have thought such a plain exterior could harbor such talent? "Actually, I found her voice rather low and throaty to be pretty."

Mason grinned. "Honey, it's different for a man. Hearing that voice of hers is like being wrapped in a woman's arms, petted and stroked and loved all at once. Hooked like a fish, caught—"

"I get the idea," Sylvia gritted through clenched teeth.

"Don't like the competition, huh? Do you know what they call her?" His smile broadened. "They call her the Songbird."

"Pagan named his mine after her?" For the first time, Sylvia felt a twinge of alarm.

Mason began to laugh. "You should see the look on your face, Sylvia. Bad news, isn't it? But like it or not, Rianne is young and willing, and Roark wants her. Not only that, her father owns half the Songbird Mine. Roark is in deep with those two, and you're not going to get him back just by wiggling your hips."

"Why, Lowell," she purred, running her fingers up his

arm. "You don't sound jealous at all. I would have thought you'd want to keep me and Pagan apart."

"What for?" he demanded. "I don't give a damn who you sleep with."

"How charming," she murmured.

"Go to Roark if you want charming. You want a piece of that mine, you come to me."

Sylvia inclined her head, accepting the distinction. "Why do you want Rianne Kierney so badly?"

"Because she's Roark's."

"So am I."

He grinned. "But I've already had *you*."

"How dare—"

"Don't give me that holier-than-thou crap, Sylvia. I've met your kind a hundred times, and your song never changes. I don't give a tinker's damn whether you want Roark or the gold or both. I just want the Kierney girl and a share of whatever money you get from Roark."

"Why? What is it you men see in that scrawny slut?"

"That voice of hers is pure gold. The man who owns her has it made for the rest of his life." His dark eyes turned cold and hard. Absently, he rubbed his arms. "Besides, I've got a debt to collect from that haughty little Songbird."

Sylvia smiled, remembering the slings he had worn during his stay in Seattle. Evidently he had tried to seduce plain Miss Kierney, and had suffered at Pagan's hands. "I see. What exactly did you have in mind, lover?"

"Roark has a soft spot for kids. Doesn't like to see them mistreated in any way."

"What has that to do with anything? You could say the same thing about most men."

"But it's something more with him. Once I saw him pull his pistol on a man who was hitting a kid, swore to shoot the fellow if he even *heard* a rumor of another

322

beating. The look on Roark's face was something fierce, like a wild animal's when it's about to jump for your throat. That other man backed up fast. I didn't understand it until I heard that Roark grew up in an orphanage where he was beaten and starved, and that two of his younger brothers died there."

Completely astounded, Sylvia tried to assess the implications of this news. Why hadn't Pagan said anything about it to his own wife? "But . . . how . . . I don't understand."

"You mean he didn't tell you?" Mason laughed. "Then again, if I were him, I wouldn't tell you, either. But his brother wasn't so close-mouthed about it. He told one of Roark's whores, who told his bartender, who sold the information to me for fifty dollars."

"But I don't see how it helps me."

Mason smiled derisively. "Then maybe you're not as smart as you think you are. Come now, Sylvia. Knowing what you now know about him, what will be your greatest hold on him? Who will he protect at all costs, even if it means giving up his prize singer?"

Sylvia's numbed brain was beginning to work again. She'd come here intending to use her daughter as an excuse to see Pagan again, but expecting her own beauty and wit to pave the way into his life. Now she realized that Tessa was her lever, her ace-in-the-hole, her trump card. If she used the child properly, she could bind Pagan so tight he'd never get away.

"So," she said. "I use Tessa to manipulate Pagan into sending the Kierney girl away."

"Yeah. And I'll be waiting for her. Roark won't even know what happened, and you'll never see the woman again. What do you say, Sylvia? Is it a deal?"

"Absolutely," she said, smiling at the prospect of knowing Rianne would be in this man's hands forever. Oh, sweet revenge!

"Good. But first . . ." Mason pushed Sylvia onto her back, prodding her legs apart ungently. Without further ado, he thrust into her.

Sylvia endured his touch, his selfishness, knowing all the while that the moment he'd gotten what he wanted, he'd cheat her.

But she had learned to bide her time, to play men's games until she could get what *she* wanted. And she wanted Pagan. She wanted him as a man, and as the owner of the Songbird Mine. The whole mine. There were but two obstacles in her way: an old man and a chit of a girl, both named Kierney.

Sylvia smiled. One day soon she'd show Mason whose game it really was. She'd show them all.

Chapter Twenty-three

When Rianne woke the next morning, she found Tessa's small body tucked against hers, creating a warm nest beneath the blankets. She propped herself on her elbow to look down at the sleeping child's peaceful face. With her thumb in her mouth and her eyelashes lying on her cheeks in a dark fan, Tessa looked much younger than her nearly five years.

Again, Rianne was beset by the wish that Tessa was hers. Hers and Pagan's. Gently, she brushed a stray wisp of hair back from the child's face. She hoped Sylvia appreciated the precious gift she'd been given. Somehow, however, she doubted it; Sylvia seemed the sort who did not appreciate what she had, only what she hadn't. With a sigh, Rianne slid from beneath the covers, carefully so as to not awaken Tessa.

The fire had burned itself out during the night, and the room was very cold. Shivering, Rianne slipped her dressing gown on, making a mental note to bring more wood up for tonight. It was going to be a brutal winter, she thought a bit grimly, and in more ways than one.

"Rianne?" Tessa's voice was thick with sleep, and just a bit alarmed.

"I'm right here," Rianne said, moving so that the

child could see her. "I was just going downstairs to light the stove and get some biscuits started. Or would you prefer hotcakes and sausage? We got some lovely sausage from Ogilvie the other day. I'm not sure exactly what *kind* of sausage, but I suspect it's venison."

"I like any kind of sausage," Tessa said.

Without warning, the door swung inward so hard that it hit the wall behind with a crack. Sylvia strode into the room, the skirts of her sheer silk nightgown kicking out with every step. "Pagan, if you've dared bed her right under . . . Tessa! What are you doing here?"

"The child had a bad dream," Rianne said. "She only — "

Sylvia's green eyes snapped with anger. "I was speaking to Tessa."

Rianne started to reply, but one look at Tessa dried the words in her throat. The child had sunk beneath the covers until only her eyes were showing. The palpable fear in those eyes made the hairs rise on the back of Rianne's neck; as stern as her own mother had been, she had never been *afraid* of her.

"Come here, child!" Sylvia snapped.

Tessa just stared, obviously too frightened to obey. Sylvia's face twisted. "Come. Here. This. Instant."

The tone of Sylvia's voice and the child's fear set Rianne's own temper flaring. Although she might not have challenged Sylvia for her own sake, she did not hesitate to do so for Tessa's.

"What are you doing here?" she demanded. "How dare you come into my room without asking?"

"You know very well how I dare, you conniving. . . ." Sylvia took a deep breath, obviously struggling with her temper. Rianne knew the only reason the woman was not shrieking insults at this moment was the fear that Pagan would hear.

Rianne waited with outward patience, glad that the

326

woman's anger was now directed at her instead of Tessa. The child, after all, had only been the hapless recipient of Sylvia's rage at her husband's mistress.

Finally, Sylvia seemed to gain a measure of control. But her face was pinched and drawn with anger, her lips bloodless, and a small, leaping flame of hate burned in her green eyes. "Why is my daughter here?" she hissed between clenched teeth.

Rianne met that furious green gaze calmly. "As I tried to tell you before, Tessa had a bad dream. She was alone in a strange place, and when she couldn't find you or Pagan, she came to me. I didn't think there would be any harm in letting her stay here."

"No harm!" Sylvia stepped forward, her hands clenched into fists, and for a moment Rianne thought the woman was going to strike her. "I very much doubt that any mother would allow her daughter to seek the company of a woman of questionable morals—"

"There is nothing wrong with my morals!" Rianne snapped, both distressed and humiliated that this conversation was taking place in front of Tessa. And this was the protector of the child's innocence? "See here, Miss . . . Mrs . . ." She floundered, still unable to call the woman by her proper name. By Pagan's name.

"Mrs. Roark," Sylvia supplied for her. "Try to remember that in the future. And now stand aside and let me punish my daughter as I see fit."

"I will not let you strike that child." Rianne clenched her hands into fists, ready to fight if necessary to protect Tessa.

Sylvia laughed derisively. "Oh, heavens! I never strike my child." Slowly, she turned her head to look directly at Tessa. "Do I, Tessa?"

"No, Mama."

Rianne shivered to hear the child speak in a colorless voice that revealed no emotion at all; she might have

327

been a pretty little doll. No, not a doll—a marionette, jumping to Sylvia's hands on her strings.

"Very good," Sylvia purred. "Now get out. If I ever find out that you've come here again, you'll be sorry."

Tessa scrambled out of bed, but Rianne put out her hand to stop the girl from leaving. "That's no way to talk to the child. She did nothing wrong."

"I'll talk to her any way I please. And you can stay out of my business!"

Calling up every bit of cool dignity she possessed, Rianne turned her back on the woman and went to kneel in front of Tessa. Taking the child's hands in hers, she asked, "Do you want to go, Tessa?"

Tessa never even looked at her. "Yes, Miss Kierney."

Rianne sighed. Reluctantly, she let go of the child's hands. Tessa ran from the room, her white nightgown billowing out behind her.

Smiling triumphantly, Sylvia turned to Rianne. "I'll thank you to stay away from my daughter. It's my duty as a mother to keep her from being corrupted."

Rianne's eyes narrowed. "If you're such a wonderful mother, then why are you punishing her when *I'm* the one who made you angry?"

"You—"

"I thought I heard voices," Pagan said, appearing in the doorway. His ice-blue gaze raked over Rianne's face, gauging her emotions, then moved to Sylvia. "Is there a problem here?"

He was barechested and barefooted, his only garment the same dark trousers he had worn the night before. He folded his arms and leaned one shoulder against the doorjamb. There was a night's growth of whiskers shadowing his lean jaw. That, coupled with the lean, hard-muscled grace of his body, made him seem even more the untamed male.

Sylvia turned, as gracefully as a dancer. "Nothing is

wrong, darling," she said. "I was just telling Miss Kierney how nice it was for her to let Tessa spend the night in her room."

The lie was so blatant that Rianne's mouth dropped open in astonishment. What on earth could she say to counter that bald-faced fabrication?

"I'm glad to hear that you two are getting along so well," Pagan said. "For Tessa's sake."

"Darling," Sylvia breathed, "You know I'd do anything for Tessa. Or for you."

She put her hands on her hips, pulling the sheer silk of her nightgown taut across her heavy breasts. She might as well have been naked, Rianne thought. 'Here I am, Pagan, come take me', her body seemed to be saying. Rianne drew her dressing gown tight around her neck, misery stabbing through her with the knowledge that she could never compete with this woman.

Feeling as dull and plain as an old kitchen table, she said, "I-I was planning to get some breakfast started. If you don't mind, I'd like to get dressed."

"Come, darling," Sylvia said, moving forward, breasts outthrust. "We have a great many things to discuss."

Pagan fended her off absently, staring over her shoulder at Rianne. "What about you, Rianne? Do you have anything you'd like to discuss with me?"

"No."

He looked at her from beneath half-closed lids. Although she was trying to conceal it, he knew she was furious; evidently her conversation with Sylvia had been more acrimonious than either woman had let on.

"Are you all right?" he asked.

Rianne knew that if she said no, he would stay here to find out why. It would be the perfect revenge for the humiliating comments she had endured from his wife. But it would only make Sylvia even angrier than she already was. Rianne didn't care for her own sake, but the woman had a perfect target upon whom to vent her anger. A target who couldn't fight back: Tessa.

Rianne saw the ugly emotions that clouded Sylvia's beautiful green eyes, and knew she couldn't take the risk. So she thrust her own feelings aside and shrugged Pagan's concern away.

"I'm fine," she said. "Why wouldn't I be?"

"You see, darling?" Sylvia purred, taking possession of his arm. "You were worried about nothing. Miss Kierney and I understand one another perfectly. Don't we, Miss Kierney?"

"We do indeed."

Sylvia laughed, that same high-pitched trill that Rianne was fast coming to hate. Yes, she thought, it was indeed going to be a brutal winter.

"Come, darling," Sylvia said, looking up at Pagan from beneath her lashes. "There's something I simply must show you."

Pagan was still looking at Rianne, and hardly noticed that Sylvia was pressing his arm to her breasts, or that her silk-clad leg was brushing against his. "I'll see you downstairs, Rianne," he said.

"Yes." Rianne held herself stiffly, fearing she might crumple if she allowed herself to relax.

She watched as Pagan and his wife moved down the hall. She had to admit that they made an impressively handsome couple. The thought sat in her heart like a smouldering coal, a slow, devastating burn. She closed her door softly, wishing she might tear it from its hinges. This was jealousy at its worst, and it was a green-eyed, razor-clawed demon, indeed.

Rianne sat with Marie in the kitchen, drinking tea while waiting for the day's bread to finish baking. The wind rattled the windowpanes, whistling like a hungry beast wanting to get in.

330

"This keeps up, we're goin' to git snow," Marie said.

Rianne glanced outside. It was nearly dusk, and the sky was slate grey, pregnant with heavy, swollen clouds. "I think you're right."

"It's goin' to be a long winter." With a sigh, Marie added. "Especially with that uppity bitch here. I cain't believe she's only been here a week. It feels like a month."

It feels like a year, Rianne thought. "But Tessa is a love, isn't she?"

"Yeah, you're right about that. But that Sylvia . . . The way she acts around Pagan is plumb disgustin'. Cooin' and squeezin' and rubbin' herself agin him whenever she gets the chance . . . And she's got the gall to call *me* a whore!"

Rianne ducked her head. During the past week, Sylvia had managed to make herself very unpopular with the other inhabitants of the Golden Bear. Everyone except Pagan. Sylvia was sweetness itself around *him.* Worse, he seemed to be enjoying it. He and Tessa and Sylvia had been inseparable. The reunited family.

Rianne's lashes were suddenly wet with tears. Although she tried to wipe them away surreptitiously, Marie noticed.

"She gettin' to you, honey?" the older woman asked.

"That's an understatement, Marie." Rianne pressed the heels of her hands against her eyes. "I'm discovering things about myself I don't like very much. I should be noble about this, and not burn inside every time I see him with that woman."

"Noble!" Marie snorted. "There ain't no sech thing as noble when another woman is huntin' your man. If I was you, I would've snatched her bald by now."

Rianne shook her head. "There's nothing I can do to hold him if he wants to go." She paused for a moment, trying to still a treacherous quiver in her bottom lip. "It

331

isn't as though he wanted to marry me even before she came."

"Darlin', you cain't . . . Hey, if it ain't Mad Francois, and all clean and tidy!"

Turning hastily, Rianne saw Francois Gruillot standing in the doorway. He was wearing a suit, and looked much less comfortable than in his furs. His face was clean-shaven except for a neat moustache. To Rianne's surprise, it was a very nice face, with a strong, square jaw and, most astonishing of all, deep dimples in both cheeks. "Why, Mr. Gruillot!" she said. "You look wonderful!"

"I am a man of means now," he said, rolling his hat brim around in his huge hands. "I must keep up appearances."

"Would you like a cup of tea?" Rianne asked.

"*Oui*. But also, Mademoiselle Rianne, I would like to speak to you privately, if I may."

Marie rose, a grin tugging at the corners of her mouth. "I'll jest run upstairs and change. The crowd's goin' to be here before we know it. Are you goin' to sing tonight, Rianne?"

"I doubt it, Marie. I don't feel much like singing."

Francois sat in Marie's chair, his broad frame overfilling it. Rianne clasped her hands in her lap and waited for him to begin.

"Mademoiselle Rianne," he said, "I have come to ask you to marry me."

Rianne stared at him, unable to comprehend for a moment. "Mr. Gruillot—"

"Please, Mademoiselle, let me finish. This is difficult for me, for I am not a man for the words." He cleared his throat and continued, "I know you are in love with Pagan. But there are the beautiful wife and daughter who have come back into his life. This is very bad for you, no?"

332

"Yes," Rianne murmured. "Very bad."

"I know you do not love me. Perhaps you never will, for I am a rough and uneducated man and you are . . . well, you are the Songbird. But I would be honored to have you as my wife, to share my life and home and fortune. And if you carry Pagan's babe, I will be honored to give my name to the child and raise it as my own."

Rianne was stunned. Not by his assumption that she was carrying Pagan's child, but by his generosity. No one had ever offered her so much and expected so little in return. And for what? For singing his favorite song.

Overcome with emotion, she looked away, blinking back a sudden rush of tears. And they called him Mad Francois! Well, if madness meant having a loving and unselfish heart, then his was a wonderful sort of madness, indeed. She wished she could accept. But she couldn't. Even if Pagan didn't want her, she still belonged to him, body and soul. There was nothing but a shell of a woman to give any other man, and Francois deserved better. Fool she might be, but she was no cheat.

Francois heaved a gusty sigh. "I can see your answer in your eyes," he said.

He started to rise, but Rianne put her hand on his arm to stop him. "No, Francois. Please, stay." She knew she could no more have held him there than she could have held the wind, but he sank back down into the chair and let her continue. She smiled at him shakily. "I can't marry you, but it isn't because you aren't worthy of me or any other woman. Under other circumstances, I would be proud to be your wife. But you deserve more than I can give you. You deserve a woman who can give you her heart without reservation, and that isn't in my power to give."

"You could learn to love me," he said.

Tenderness swept through her for this man whose rough-hewn exterior hid such a gentle soul. She clasped his huge hand in both of hers. "I already do. But as a friend, Francois. I'm sorry. I wish it could be more."

"That is a great deal," he said. "I will accept it if you promise to come to Francois if you are in need of a friend."

"I promise."

"Good." He stood up, seeming to fill the whole room. "There is one thing you English ladies can learn from our Frenchwomen."

Rianne's brows went up. "What is that, Francois?"

"If you think a man is about to leave you, you should make yourself as beautiful and desirable as possible."

"To get him back?" Rianne asked, perplexed.

"*Non.* To make him regret. To make him wonder if he didn't let the best of all slip through his hands. So tonight you dress up, smile, laugh, and most of all, sing. You are the Songbird. You are unique. No other woman can compare."

"Oh, Francois!" Rianne laughed, but it was a bitter sound. "Have you seen his wife?"

He nodded. "She is very beautiful, very chic. But she is not the Songbird. Promise that you will sing tonight. If not for Pagan, for Francois."

Rianne sighed. If he had asked her any other way, she could have refused. But this man had offered her his name, his fortune, and his love, and she'd had no choice but to refuse. Now he was asking only for a song. "For you, Francois, I will sing." It was the only thing she could give him.

"Thank you, Mademoiselle." With immense dignity, he put his hat on and turned to go.

"Wait." Rianne raised up on tiptoes and kissed him on the cheek. "Thank you for believing in me," she said softly. "Perhaps I can learn to believe in myself. *"Au revoir,* Francois Gruillot."

He flushed with obvious pleasure, and his dimples reappeared. *Au revoir,* lovely Songbird."

John Ferguson busied himself by polishing the bar as Francois Gruillot left the kitchen and headed for the front door. Once the huge Frenchman was gone, John let out a long, low whistle of surprise.

"Francois Gruillot and the Songbird!" he muttered under his breath. "Who would have thought it?"

Oh, Rianne had refused Gruillot's proposal. But just the fact that Mad Francois had shaved, let alone asked a woman to marry him, was astonishing.

Lowell Mason would pay well for the information. And so would Sylvia Roark. It would be interesting to discover which would pay more.

John smiled, blessing his own good luck. How many times did a man stumble across information that could be sold twice in one day? A small twinge of conscience nagged him, but he pushed it aside. Rianne was nice enough, but he needed the money.

"Besides, what harm can it do?" he said to himself, throwing his rag down on the bar and reaching for his coat. "There's no crime in a lady receiving a proposal, even from Mad Francois."

Chapter Twenty-four

The sound of voices was deafening as Rianne came downstairs. She stopped just outside the door, where she could look out over the saloon without being seen. It was a very large crowd tonight, all miners who had come either to drink to their success or drown their sorrows. She saw Francois Gruillot standing at the far end of the room, bulking head and shoulders above most of the other men. Her father's white head was barely visible among the miners who crowded the bar. There was no sign of Pagan.

Nervously, she smoothed the front of her silk gown. It was one she hadn't worn before, a slim evening dress that depended more on cut and richness of fabric than on decoration. The color was most unusual, a pure, pale shade of topaz that seemed to change and shimmer as she moved. Although the sleeves were mere puffs, white silk evening gloves covered her arms from her fingertips to above her elbows. To complement the simplicity of the gown, she had swept her thick, glossy hair into a loose knot at the top of her head. The result was pleasing, she thought, if woefully unfashionable. But since she couldn't hope to match either Sylvia's opulence or style, she knew she must compete on a different level altogether.

For tonight, she was leaving plain, brown-haired Rianne Kierney behind. She would be the Songbird. She would be unique.

"Francois, my friend," she murmured. "I hope you're right."

She scanned the crowd again, but Pagan was nowhere to be seen. Three miners were playing cards at the table he usually occupied on Saturday nights. Rianne's heart sank; had she donned her finery for nothing? Was he off somewhere with Sylvia?

"Hello, Rianne."

Pagan's deep, rich voice came from behind her. Rianne closed her eyes, praying for courage, then opened them again. Slowly, she turned to face him.

He was dressed all in black, with only a white wedge of shirtfront to relieve the somber hue. His expression was brooding, and the straight, dark slash of brows only made the paleness of his eyes more arresting. Sylvia stood beside him, her gloved hand on his arm. She was wearing a crimson velvet dress, trimmed with a froth of ribbon and fine French lace. It was daringly fashionable, even more daringly low cut over her abundant breasts.

"That's a most unusual gown you're wearing, Miss Kierney," she said. "So very . . . simple and girlish."

Rianne knew that those seemingly innocent words had been calculated to shatter her confidence. And the ploy worked; faced with Sylvia's opulent display of flesh, the gown that depended on cut and color seemed terribly inadequate.

Then she looked up at Pagan. Her gaze was caught and held, trapped by the desire that showed in every taut line of his face. In that moment, she knew he found her beautiful. And because he did, she *felt* beautiful. Triumph, sweet and heady, swept through her.

"You're lovely," Pagan said softly. His voice was intimate, caressing.

"Thank you." She tried to look away from that compelling gaze, and failed. Irresistibly, she sank into the crystalline depths of his eyes, wanting nothing more than to immerse herself in the flame of passion that burned within.

"Were you planning to sing tonight, Miss Kierney?" Sylvia asked.

Her high-pitched voice shattered the lovely spell. Rianne felt the heat of a blush on her cheeks, and wished she dared cover them with her hands. Mustering every bit of dignity she could, she met the blonde woman's gaze. "Yes, I'm planning to sing."

Sylvia giggled. "Well, you'd better change your plan, then. It seems your accompanist has become incapacitated."

Rianne turned to see two men coming toward her, carrying her father's limp form between them. Alastair was not unconscious, but he was very, very drunk.

"Father—" she began.

" 'S my daughter," he slurred, peering at her from bleary eyes. "Take me to t'piano, boys!"

"Take him upstairs," Pagan said.

As Alastair was carried up the stairs, he sang "The Blue Bells of Scotland" in a very loud and very off-key voice. Rianne started to follow, but Pagan caught her by the arm and held her still.

"Let them take care of him," he said. "He'll be asleep as soon as he hits the bed."

With a sigh, Rianne acquiesced. She'd seen her father in this condition enough times now to realize that Pagan was right. It saddened her. She had hoped that her love would cure Alastair of his need of the bottle, but it hadn't. And why should it? she reflected with more

338

than a tinge of bitterness. Love was not a solution to problems. In her naivete, she had thought that if one loved enough and believed enough, everything would turn out right. Well, she'd learned otherwise.

"It's such a shame, isn't it?" Sylvia asked. "However are you going to explain him to polite society when you leave here?"

Pagan's eyes narrowed. "Just a damned—"

"No, Pagan," Rianne said, putting her hand on his arm for emphasis. "He's my father, and I want to answer." She met Sylvia's derisive green gaze squarely. "I don't have to explain my father to anyone. He's got more vision and courage than most men could ever hope to have."

A spot of red appeared high on each of Sylvia's cheeks. "I only meant—"

"I know what you meant," Rianne said. Too furious to trust herself to speak civilly to the woman any longer, she turned on her heel and marched out into the saloon.

The crowd roared a welcome. The noise was like a vast sea, swelling and ebbing, then growing again into a crashing wave. She faltered, intimidated by the sheer volume of sound. Then she heard a familiar voice booming above the rest.

" 'Marseillaise!' " Francois Gruillot roared.

You are the Songbird. You are unique, he had told her this afternoon. Her chin came up in sheer Kierney stubbornness. Pagan was watching. Sylvia was watching. And by all that was holy, Rianne was not about to fail.

Squaring her shoulders, she went to the piano and sat down. When the noise gradually abated, she looked over the heads of the crowd straight at Francois Gruillot. "This first song is for my friend, Francois," she said. She played the opening chords of the "Marseillaise", then began to sing.

Pagan sighed as that sultry, marvelous voice swept him up in its enchantment. He'd heard that particular song a hundred times, but he never tired of hearing her sing it. And with the dress of shimmering topaz silk, and her hair casting the lamplight back in a swirl of golden sparks, Rianne seemed mysterious, ethereal, a sprite born of music and man's fantasy. *His* fantasy.

Sylvia's shrill, biting tones broke into his musings. "Did you happen to notice how Monsieur Gruillot has suddenly become Francois? And look at the man, shaved and pomaded and dressed in a suit! One might almost think he's come courting."

Pagan had been too absorbed in Rianne to notice anyone else. Now, however, his startled gaze focused on the big Frenchman. He *had* shaved, by God. It was the first time Pagan had ever seen what was below those whiskers.

"He's handsome in a brutish sort of way," Sylvia said. "And those dimples are rather appealing. And don't forget, he's very wealthy now, and that has its own sort of attractiveness. And he does seem rather interested in your little Songbird."

Pagan scowled. Francois was indeed interested in Rianne; the man never took his gaze from her. With jealousy and pure male possessiveness singing through his veins like wildfire, Pagan folded his arms over his chest and watched Francois watch Rianne. Then Sylvia tapped him on the arm, and he reluctantly turned to look at her.

"Would you like to come have a drink with me?" she purred.

"No. *Has* he come courting?"

With a laugh, Sylvia trailed her fingertips down his

340

arm as she swayed past him into the saloon. "Goodness, Pagan, how would *I* know?"

Pagan's attention returned to Francois Gruillot. The man was still staring at Rianne, and admiration was plain on his face. The hot tide of Pagan's jealousy surged higher. Just the possibility of another man pursuing Rianne made his blood burn. It didn't matter that Francois was his friend, a man he knew to be honest and honorable.

"Rianne is mine!" he muttered in a savage undertone. "Mine!"

For her sake, he'd spent the past week in Hell. To remain here with her and Tessa, he'd had to endure Sylvia's presence almost constantly. He had rejected her almost every way a man can reject a woman, but Sylvia had a habit of not seeing anything that didn't suit her. There were days when it had taken every bit of his willpower not to throw the damned woman out the window.

He'd stayed, not because he liked living in torment, but because he thought Rianne needed time to adjust to this bizarre situation, and to see Sylvia for what she was. *He* knew he had to find a way to break Sylvia's hold on his daughter; just the thought of the woman having control of the child for all these years made his blood run cold. It was a matter of finding the right price, or the right lever. But he wanted Rianne to understand that he was not doing it for revenge, but to protect his daughter.

Well, he'd given her time. And now the time had run out.

Rianne sang for another hour, then rose from the piano and called a farewell to her audience. A shower of nuggets fell at her feet. She smiled, thinking that at the Metropolitan Opera, the diva received flowers. Only

341

here in the madness that was the Klondike could a singer from a church choir become a chanteuse in a bawdy house, and receive her ovation in gold.

She glanced over her shoulder at Pagan, but found him gone from his table. No matter, she thought as she made her way upstairs. Her point had been made. She had been the Songbird. For one magical evening, she'd had the power to make her audience laugh and cry and yearn. She even sung some hymns, and had moved those hard-bitten men, some of whom hadn't seen a church in years.

And Pagan had watched her the entire time, his eyes burning and intense. He might choose another woman some day, but he'd never forget the night Rianne Kierney sang hymns in his saloon. Of that she was very sure.

She made her way to her room, unpinning her hair as she went. Then, absently humming under her breath, she unlocked her door and pushed it open, revealing Pagan lying upon her bed like a great jungle cat. He looked dark and dangerous, and there was a hot glint to his eyes that sent alarm shooting through her veins.

"How did you get in?" she asked breathlessly.

"I have a key to every room. It's my hotel, you know."

She wished she hadn't taken her hair down. It fell around her shoulders in wanton disarray, and she could see that he liked it very much. Too much.

"Come here, Rianne," he said.

"I don't think that would be a very good idea."

He came up from the bed in a single lithe movement. Rianne's breath caught in her throat, but all he did was strike a match and light the lantern that sat upon the bureau.

"Now," he said, reaching to close the outer door, "I think it's time we talked."

"Nothing has changed since the last time we talked," she said.

Smiling, he strode toward her. There was an edge to that smile, a determined sort of aggressiveness that made Rianne edge backward in an attempt to keep some distance between them. She'd seen that look before. But he kept coming closer and closer, his eyes gleaming like pools of crystal fire, his height and wide shoulders blocking out the rest of the room. Finally, her back came up against the wall, and there was nowhere to go.

He braced his palms on the door on either side of her head, trapping her between his arms. Rianne couldn't have run if she'd been free. He was too close now, and her whole being was filled with the sight and scent of him, the awareness of his arousal. Her love for him was an irresistible force, keeping her here when reason screamed for her to go.

"Don't," she pleaded.

"I've stayed away from you for as long as I intend to," he said, lowering one hand to her hair. Fascinated by the silken weight of it, he sifted his fingers through it. "Why did you wear this gown, if not to bring me here? Why did you sing, wrapping me up in your Siren's spell, if you didn't want this?"

"I . . . I . . ." The protest died in her throat, for there was no possible answer to his questions but the ones he already knew. She *had* dressed for him, sung for him, poured everything of herself into her music, hoping to touch him unbearably because she couldn't bear to be nothing to him. Weak, weak, bound by her desire, trapped by her love, she had brought this to pass.

Pagan saw the love in her eyes, and the surrender. "You take my breath away," he murmured. Leaning forward, he kissed one corner of her mouth, then the other, then traced the soft curve of her lower lip with his tongue. Her mouth blossomed beneath his, and he allowed himself a brief, delicious foray into the sweet depths.

Rianne sighed when his mouth left hers, wanting him back. He smiled, taking one of her gloved hands and raising it to his lips. Then, slowly and sensually, he slid the glove down her arm, his mouth following the retreating fabric.

She shivered, overwhelmed by the warring sensations of the cool air and his hot mouth. When he reached her wrist, he lingered for a moment at the wildly hammering pulsepoint, then pulled the glove off completely and tossed it away. He kissed her palm, the length of her fingers, and, one by one, her sensitive fingertips.

She closed her eyes, afraid that she was going to sink to the floor at his feet, so powerfully did he arouse her. Of their own volition, her fingers curved so that her hand cupped his mouth. His tongue darted out to taste her palm, lightly caressing the pads of flesh at the base of her fingers, then teasing the tender flesh at the center.

"Tell me you don't want this," he said, his voice hoarse with restrained passion. "Tell me, and I'll stop."

Rianne knew she should send him away. She even opened her mouth to say the words, but only a sigh emerged. And although she tried to fight the sensuality that was coursing through her in a hot, voluptuous tide, she failed. Her love was too strong, and her desire.

"I missed you," he whispered. Impatient now, he stripped her other glove off, then took her hands and drew them up and around his neck.

"Look at me," he said.

She opened her eyes to see his face poised above hers. The lamp's illumination highlighted the sharp planes of his face, the high cheekbones, the strong, straight nose, the well-cut mouth that was curved with passion now. He framed her face with his hands, his gaze burning her with its heat. Then he kissed her. She opened her mouth to welcome him, helpless to do anything else.

His tongue toyed with hers, playing a sensual game of touch and taste and withdrawal until she moaned and drew his head down. With a soft laugh of sheer male triumph, he pulled her into the hard heat of his body, enclosing her, surrounding her, putting his claim on her all over again.

Rianne gave a moan deep in her throat as he kissed his way along her jaw to her ear, working his magic there, then made tiny, nibbling kisses down her throat. He pulled her sleeve away from her shoulder and pressed his open mouth against her skin, heat against heat. Mindlessly, she slid her hands beneath his jacket, wanting still more.

"Yes," he muttered in a husky whisper. "Touch me, Rianne. I'm dying to feel your hands on me."

Unbearably stirred by his fierce demand, she drew her breath in sharply and pushed his jacket off his shoulders and down his arms. She spread her hands out across his chest, reveling in the taut, muscular feel of his flesh. The beat of his heart, swift and powerful, pounded against her palm and transmitted itself into her blood, her bones until her whole body felt as though it were pulsing in time with his.

"Is it like this for everyone?" she whispered, her pelvis moving in a slow, rhythmic motion against his.

He groaned, surging closer, his hands tightening upon her hips. "No. This is special, it's pure magic, yours

345

and mine."

"Then—" she broke off abruptly, hearing a faint snuffling noise out in the corridor. "Pagan, do you hear that?"

"Yes." He groaned, his frustration was so great that it was actually painful. God damn it to hell, would there never be a chance for them? Cursing under his breath, he strode toward the door.

"Pagan, wait!" Rianne whispered frantically. What if it was his wife, come to find out what her husband was doing in another woman's room?

The alarm in her voice halted him where nothing else might have. "What's the matter?"

"Let me answer my own door . . . What if it's Sylvia?"

His brows went even lower. "If she's come creeping around listening at keyholes, I'll—"

"Please."

He raked his hand through his hair in vexation, then nodded. Rianne dashed past him and opened the door.

Tessa stood in the hallway, dressed in the same cotton nightgown she'd worn during her last visit. Her thumb was in her mouth, but even so, she was sobbing quietly. Rianne didn't hesitate. Flinging the door open wider, she scooped the child into her arms and carried her into the room.

"Pagan, stir up the fire," Rianne ordered, settling on the bed with Tessa in her lap. "Her feet are like ice."

He did so, then went to stand beside the bed. Tessa's thin arms were around Rianne's neck, and the child was crying steadily now. His hands clenched into fists. Rianne seemed to know exactly what to do, what to say. Why couldn't he?

"I was so scared," Tessa sobbed. "I had the dream, and the room was dark and then I couldn't find Papa

346

and—"

"Shhh," Rianne murmured, rocking back and forth. "I'm here, and so is your papa. Nothing can hurt you here, sweetheart."

"Papa!" Tessa scrambled from Rianne's lap and launched herself at Pagan.

And there it was, the answer he'd been searching for. It was so easy, so terribly easy; all she wanted was for him to be her father and to hold her. He drew her close, letting his presence and his love comfort her. Such a small, frightened little being, he thought, and so infinitely precious. Still holding her, he sat down on the bed beside Rianne.

"Why don't you tell me about this dream that frightened you so?" he asked, gently stroking Tessa's hair.

The child buried her face against his shirt. "I tried to run, but my legs wouldn't go fast . . . Oh, Papa! Please don't leave me! I don't want to be alone, please!"

Her terror made alarm pound through his veins. This was no mere fancy, but real, gut-wrenching fear. His brow furrowed in concern as he glanced up at Rianne. He could see that she, too, recognized the unusual depth of Tessa's fear. "I won't leave you," he said. "I'll sit in a chair beside your bed tonight and keep the bad dream away."

She looked up, her eyes brimming with tears. She looked so much like his brother, Davey, dead these many years, that his heart swelled with love and concern and the determination to protect her. He'd failed to protect his brother, but he wouldn't fail Tessa.

Rianne saw the gentleness in his hands, the tenderness in his eyes. Rianne's throat ached with a sudden surge of emotion. She loved Pagan more than ever. And more than ever, she realized she could not be his mis-

347

tress any longer. Silently, she thanked God for sending Tessa here just in time.

"Pagan," Rianne murmured. "The child is exhausted. You should take her back to her room."

Tessa clutched his collar so tightly that the knuckles on her tiny hands were white. "You won't leave me?"

"No, sweetheart, I won't leave you," Pagan said. "You don't have to be afraid ever again. I won't let anything hurt you, I promise."

"I love you, Papa." She gave a shuddering sigh and closed her eyes.

"I love you, too, Tessa." Gathering her up against his chest, he rose from the bed and strode out of the room.

Those words, Rianne thought, closing her eyes against the sting of tears. Three little words that were so precious, so beautiful, spoken as they were in that deep, velvet voice of his.

But they were not for her.

Chapter Twenty-five

When Rianne woke the next morning, she discovered that the air of the room had a definite nip to it, even though the fire was still crackling gently in the fireplace. Sliding out from beneath the covers, she padded to the window and looked out. It had snowed during the night. The world was transformed into a white fairyland, pristine and beautiful. Even the mud of the street was hidden beneath the snow.

Wrapping a woolen shawl around her shoulders, she slid the window open. The air was cold, stabbing her face with needles of frost. She ignored the discomfort, wanting to be a part of a world born anew. Henderson City was utterly still, sleeping soundly in its cloak of white. Winter had stolen in with the darkness.

Suddenly, a fast-moving shape came into view, skimming along the street towards her. It was a dog sled, that strange vehicle peculiar to the frozen North. She'd seen several of them stored in the stable and had thought them ungainly things. But in motion it was beautiful to see, especially the furry, powerful-looking dogs moving together with marvelous efficiency.

The sled came nearer, the dogs loping along in a fog-cloud made by their own breathing. Their tails curled up over their backs like defiant banners, and their tongues lolled from the sides of their mouths as if they were laughing with the sheer joy of running. The driver poised on the back runners gracefully, looking like an animal himself in his fur-trimmed clothing.

"Oh, isn't it *marvelous!*" Rianne whispered, hugging herself in delight.

The dog sled slowed, then stopped just beneath her window. The driver hopped down from the runners. With a swift gesture, he pushed his hood back from his face.

Rianne gasped in astonishment. "Pagan!"

He chuckled. "In the flesh."

There were snowflakes in his eyes and hair, matching the flash of his even white teeth. Rianne's breath quickened. Just the sight of him made her feel hot and cold, joyous and despairing all at once. Would it ever change? Would she ever be able to look at him and not feel this way?

"What are you doing?" she demanded.

"I'm going out to the mine." The corners of his mouth went up. "And you're coming with me."

She shook her head. "I couldn't possibly."

"Of course you can."

He leaned over the sled and lifted something out. Rianne's mouth dropped open in astonishment when she saw that the 'something' was Tessa, bundled in fur clothes like her father. Pagan set the child on her feet, then handed her a cloth-wrapped bundle. "Go take these clothes up to Miss Kierney, sweetheart. We don't want her to get cold."

"You can call her Rianne, Papa," Tessa said. "She said it was all right."

"Thank you for telling me," he said, grinning up at Rianne like a small boy caught robbing the cookie-jar.

Rianne heard the front door open and close. Taking advantage of the momentary privacy, she leaned out the window and hissed, "You ought to be ashamed of yourself, using a child to get your own way."

"A man does only what he has to," he said. He didn't look a bit contrite.

"Pagan, I can't go. You know it's only going to start trouble. Sylvia is bound to think—"

"I don't give a damn what Sylvia thinks." He crossed his arms over his chest, still smiling, still determined to spend the day with her. "I'm taking you and my daughter out for a ride, and that's that."

Hearing a timid knock at the door, Rianne called, "I'll be there in a moment, Tessa," then turned back to Pagan. "You're an arrogant man. You're far too used to giving orders."

"True. Now put those clothes on, or I'm coming up there and dress you myself."

Rianne sighed in exasperation. She really ought to refuse, but the part of her that always seemed to get her in trouble whispered, *Why not? You want to ride that marvelous sled, and more than anything else, you want to be with him.* If she were a stronger person, if she didn't want to go so very badly, she would surely have thought of a way to convince him. But, instead of arguing further, she closed the window and went to let Tessa in.

"Good morning, sweetheart," Rianne said. "I'm sorry I made you wait."

"Papa said you'd want to argue."

Rianne couldn't help but laugh. "Truly, Tessa, wouldn't you rather have him to yourself today?"

The child smiled at her, shyly, but there was a definite echo of her father in that grin. "I like you," she said. "And so does Papa. I expect we'll have fun."

Rianne sighed. "That Roark charm," she muttered under her breath. "It's just too much for flesh and blood to resist."

She accepted the bundle from Tessa and unwrapped it, gasping in awed delight when she saw the clothing within. No fabric had been used in the long tunic and wide, comfortable-looking trousers, only animal pelts with the hide outside, the fur inside for warmth. The boots were made of sealskin, as were the gloves. The tunic's hood was trimmed with the fur of the blue fox, whisper-soft and beautiful.

Rianne couldn't wait to put them on. She dressed quickly, fumbling with the unfamiliar lacings on the trousers, then took Tessa by the hand and drew her to the cheval mirror. "Let's see what we look like, shall we?"

With her gleaming black hair and delicate features, Tessa looked as exotic as an elfin princess. Rianne searched her own reflection for some equally exceptional quality, but found only Rianne Kierney, whose rather unremarkable looks were far outshone by the beautiful furs.

"It's just not fair," Rianne said, pursing her lips in a mock pout. "You look like you were born wearing furs, while I look like a scrawny bear."

"*I* think you're beautiful," Tessa said with fierce loyalty.

Absurdly, Rianne found herself blushing. Both father and daughter had said the same thing; both must have woefully bad eyesight. She met Tessa's gaze in the mirror, and they both broke into giggles at the same instant.

"Oh!" Rianne gasped. "Oh, Tessa, we're a fine sight, aren't we?" She tried vainly to fan her hot face with her hand. "One thing I can say about these clothes is that they certainly keep a person warm. Shall we go test them outside?"

Tessa nodded, her sharp little face glowing with joy. She would be a beauty one day, Rianne thought. Pagan was going to have a terrible time chasing away all the young men who'd be swarming around her. The notion was an amusing one; fathers always seemed to pay for their wild youth by worrying about their own daughters.

Taking Tessa by the hand, Rianne tiptoed downstairs. Pagan came forward to meet them when they stepped outside. He bent to kiss Tessa on the cheek, then gazed down at Rianne with laughter sparking in his eyes.

He fought the urge to touch her. She looked slim and elegant, her pale skin glowing like porcelain against the fur. Although the bulky clothing masked her body, his mind knew every graceful inch of her. "You look lovely," he said.

"I look ridiculous," she retorted, but she absently reached up to stroke the beautiful fur of her hood.

Pagan wished he could kiss her but, hearing the snap of harness behind him, realized he'd better get moving. If a fight broke out among the restless malamutes, he'd be an hour separating them and untangling the harness. And nothing, but nothing was going to spoil this day for him.

"May I pet the dogs?" Tessa asked.

Pagan shook his head. "These aren't lap dogs, and they won't let you touch them while they're in harness. Later, when they've finished working, you can pet them all you like." There was pride in his face when he looked at the malamutes, and Rianne knew there was real affection between him and the dogs.

He directed Tessa and Rianne to sit side by side upon the hides that lined the bottom of the sled, then piled several layers of fur on them. Taking a thick leather thong, he tied the whole lot down to keep it from blowing off in the wind.

"I must admit, this is the first time I've ever been wrapped like a parcel for the post," Rianne said.

"You're both too precious to lose," he replied.

The dogs stood alertly, waiting for his command.

Rianne asked, "Did you train them yourself?"

"Yes. But you can't train a dog to pull unless he's got the heart for it. These do. They're one of the finest teams in the Klondike. Only Francois Gruillot's team has beaten them, and believe me, they didn't like that at all." At the mention of Francois' name, he glanced at Rianne to gauge her reaction. But she was watching the dogs, and hadn't seemed to have heard.

"Do you go very fast?" Tessa asked.

"Sometimes," he said. "If we find that you and Rianne aren't afraid of riding in the sled, then perhaps I'll let the dogs go fast. Now hold on to your hats, ladies, the wind's going to be brisk." He checked the lashings one last time, then hopped onto his perch on the runners and shouted, "Pull!"

The dogs leaped into motion, their muscles rolling powerfully beneath their thick coats. Rianne gasped in delight as the sled began to move swiftly down the snow-covered street. In what seemed like moments, they passed through the outskirts of town and entered the forest beyond.

"Are you frightened?" Pagan shouted.

"No!" Rianne cried.

"Faster, Papa, faster!" Tessa squealed.

He called a command to the dogs. Smoothly, effortlessly, they increased the pace until it felt to Rianne that the sled must surely be flying. A laugh bubbled up, pure exhilaration, and she was unable to keep it from bursting forth. She heard Tessa giggling beside her.

Hearing them, Pagan grinned. He remembered his first ride on a dog sled. It had been a wild ride, that one, hanging on for dear life to a sled driven by a man who had drunk far too much. But Pagan had never felt so alive, so completely in tune with the stark white world that was the Klondike in winter. Hanging on to the wildly swinging sled, he had laughed with a joy too deep to be held inside.

He maintained the swift pace for a few minutes, then slowed the dogs to their distance-eating lope. Rianne turned to look at him, and his heart turned over at the sight of her face. Her cheeks were flushed, her lips parted, and there was a dusting of snow on her eyelashes and brows. Her hair had come free of the braid and lay in wind-tossed disarray upon her shoulders. He wanted her so badly that he found himself leaning forward, disturbing the balance of the sled. He straightened, gritting his teeth against his own need.

Rianne settled into the rhythm of the ride. The malamutes ran tirelessly, their plumed tails bobbing above their furry backs. Once a rabbit, which hadn't yet gotten its white winter coat, burst almost from beneath their feet. Expecting disaster, Rianne put her arm around Tessa and braced herself against the frame of the sled. The team did break stride and one dog gave tongue, a ululating howl that made the hair rise up on the back of Rianne's neck. Then Pagan whistled sharply, and the team obediently settled back to work.

Rianne sighed with relief. "I'm impressed," she said.

Pagan chuckled. "That's one of the hardest things to teach a dog. But if you once see a team running pell-mell in pursuit of an animal, howling like wolves and trailing a broken-up sled behind them, you don't shirk that lesson."

The miles passed like a dream, the sled skimming along like a ghost through the white-shrouded forest. The only sound was the jingle of harness and the thump of snow dropping from overloaded branches. There were no tracks on the surface save those of small animals. It was as though time stood still here, trapping this corner of the earth in primeval winter forever.

Once they neared the valley where the mine was,

however, everything changed. A pall of smoke hung low over the trees, and the air was full of the sound of hammers and the dull rumble of dynamite exploding far underground.

Even though Rianne thought she was prepared, her first sight of the valley hit her like a blow to the stomach. Here, most of the snow has been churned to dark slush by the steady tramp of feet as men swarmed the valley, all occupied with the task of wrenching gold from the unwilling earth. Every slope had been stripped of trees. Oak, aspen, birch, spruce — all had gone to make the sluices that used gravity and water to separate gold from gravel.

"And so Man came to Eden," Rianne murmured. "To make it over in his image."

"I told you the valley had changed," Pagan said.

"Yes, you did, but I didn't imagine . . . Oh, this is terrible!" She closed her eyes, imagining the valley as it had been, green and lush. "It used to be so beautiful. And now it's brown and dead and—"

"And gold," Pagan said.

"Is that all you think about?"

"No."

There was a note in his voice that made Rianne open her eyes and look at him. He stared out over the valley, the bold lines of his profile sharply outlined against the pale blue sky. The wind lifted his hair, letting the sun gild the dark strands. Seeing the fierce regret on his face, she realized that he hated this desecration as much as she did.

"It's a high price to pay, isn't it?" she asked.

"Yes. But the trees will grow back. Ten years after we're gone, there will be little trace of us." His eyes were bleak and cold, and she knew that time couldn't come too soon for him. With a word of command, he headed the dogs toward the Songbird Mine.

The original campsite had changed with the valley; the tent Rianne and her father had used was gone, replaced by a crude log hut. Squat and ugly, it sat upon the ledge like a dark fungus. Pagan stopped the team and jumped down to unlash his passengers. Rianne eased her cramped limbs out of the enveloping furs, feeling rather like an insect coming out of its cocoon. Tessa, with the resilience of a child, bounced out without apparent discomfort.

"Do you live in that house, Papa?" Tessa asked.

"I do when I'm here," he said, moving to unharness the dogs. "But so do the four men who work for us. You see, Mr. Kierney and I share the responsibility of making sure things go well here."

Tessa cocked her head to one side. "Mama says you're very rich."

From the mouths of babes, he thought. "Well, sweetheart, I'm not quite rich yet. We know the gold is there, but it's still in the ground. And until we take it out of the ground, it belongs to the earth."

"Oh." With her foot, Tessa made patterns in a nearby patch of snow. "May I go pat the dogs now?"

"Of course," he said. "Don't stray too far." He watched his daughter disappear around the corner of the house. "Riches cannot compare with dogs, it seems."

"Be glad of it," Rianne said. "Perhaps she'll treasure your love more than your pocketbook." A sharp, tantalizing image focused in her mind. It was of her and Pagan and Tessa as a family. Without conflict, without doubt. She wanted it to be true, so badly that she had to close her eyes against it.

"Rianne."

She felt Pagan's arm come around her waist, and opened her eyes. His gaze caught hers, and it was as though it tugged at her very soul. Slowly, yet irresistibly, he drew her close. Her hood fell back, exposing her face and neck to the cold. But even the winter wind could not cool the passion that coursed through her body. She loved him—beyond reason, beyond honor, beyond conscience. It was weak, reckless, foolish, and incredibly dangerous . . . but it was true.

And he knew. There was a flame of passion in his eyes, a vortex of heat that swept her up into a whirlwind of need. His. Hers. Theirs. His arm was tight around her, hard and possessive.

"Pagan—" she began, truly not knowing if she were about to protest or to plead for his kiss. But he put one finger across her lips, stopping her.

"Don't say anything," he murmured. "Words just seem to get in the way."

His hand slid into the hair at the back of her head, holding her still for his kiss. All thought of protest fled. She parted her lips in invitation, and sighed as he possessively fitted his mouth to hers.

"Papa, there's a man coming down the hill," Tessa called.

That sweet, childish voice brought Rianne jolting back to reality. Frantically, she pushed against his chest. He kept her for a moment, his hands holding her shoulders with a grip she felt even through the heavy clothing, his eyes blazing with fierce need and savage frustration. "Please, let me go," she said.

He obeyed, slowly and reluctantly, his hands sliding down her arms as if to prolong the contact just a few moments more. Tears stung Rianne's eyes; for one brief, compelling instant, she had believed that she might truly have him. If only she could hold the fantasy just a little longer!

But this was reality. Pagan belonged, not to her, but to that beautiful little girl. With a sigh that seemed to come from her toes, Rianne stepped away from him to watch the man striding down the hill toward them.

"That's Nathan Shore," Pagan said. "He's one of the men I hired to work the mine.

Nathan Shore was short and stocky, with curly brown hair and grey eyes. He was in the process of growing a very scraggly beard, which would have looked villainous if his face weren't so ruddy and good-natured.

Tessa came running around the corner of the house, hiding her face shyly against her father as the stranger approached. Pagan made the introductions, his hand stroking the child's hair reassuringly.

"Pleased to meet you," Nathán said, tipping his hat to Rianne and nodding to Tessa. His voice was cultured, with a lilt to it Rianne couldn't quite place. "I've got some tea made, if you'd like to have some."

"We'd love some," Rianne said.

Nathan led the way to the cabin, his heavy boots squelching in the thick mud. "You've come at a good time, Mr. Roark," he said. "We've got a great deal of gold to go back to the Golden Bear for safekeeping. Some is ours, some belongs to Mr. Gruillot, some to Elias McManus and Joshua Byrne. I've got it tallied and marked."

Pagan nodded. "I'll take it back with me."

"Watch the step, now," Nathan warned, moving through the doorway of the cabin.

Rianne followed him, blinking in the sudden dimness after the sunlight outside. The cabin was lit only by a single window high up on the southern wall, and with its rough log walls and dirt floor, it seemed a cold, dank den. Nathan left the door open, which let in more light and unfortunately, more cold. Four low cots were the only furnishings, and nearly filled the tiny hut.

"Sit down, ladies, and let me serve," Nathan said. "I'm afraid these cots serve as living, dining, and sleeping quarters."

Pagan shook his head, declining a seat. Rianne sat

359

down on the nearest cot. Tessa joined her. Rianne put her arm around the girl, shielding her from the breeze as best she could.

As graciously as if the hut were the finest of hotels, Nathan served them lukewarm tea and tinned crackers. "I'm afraid there's only molasses for sweetening," he said.

"None for me, thank you," Rianne said. Molasses! she thought with a mental shudder. In tea! Her English soul rebelled at the very idea. "Where are you from, Mr. Shore?"

"Virginia, ma'am."

Rianne was aware of Pagan leaning against the far wall, his arms folded over his chest. He hadn't stopped staring at her since they came in here. With an effort, she returned her straying attention to the conversation. "Virginia, you said? You're a very long way from home."

Nathan nodded. "Yes, ma'am, but I intend to go back some day. There is . . ." He broke off abruptly as a vast shape blocked the light from the door. "Oh, hello, Mr. Gruillot."

Pagan was coldly alert as he regarded the big Frenchman. Francois was his friend, a man he liked and respected. But he was also interested in Rianne. Pagan straightened, ready to answer whatever challenge might be issued. "Have you come to join us, Francois?"

"As much as I would like to visit with the lovely Songbird, I cannot," Francois said. "Elias is very ill. I do not know what to do for him. I thought perhaps Mademoiselle Rianne has had some experience with nursing—"

"I have, a little," Rianne said. "Of course I'll be glad to help any way I can."

"We'll come with you," Pagan said, holding his hand out to Tessa.

360

Francois led them to a tent a few hundred yards upstream from the Songbird Mine. Pagan sat Tessa upon a crate in a spot that was protected by the wind. "Stay here, sweetheart. Rianne and I will only be a few minutes." Taking Rianne by the arm, he steered her past Francois and into the tent.

Rianne gasped as a horrible stench enveloped her. The patient was huddled beneath several soiled, reeking blankets, and even from a distance she could see that he was shivering uncontrollably. Sympathy for the poor man filled her, and she no longer noticed the smell.

She moved toward the cot, but Pagan held his arm out to stop her. "Let me," he said. His voice was grim and taut, and she didn't dare protest.

He felt the man's forehead with the back of his hand. "Elias," he said. "Can you hear me? It's Pagan."

Elias opened his eyes, but they were glassy with fever, and it was obvious that he wasn't seeing anything. A muscle jumped in Pagan's cheek as he gently grasped the man's chin and opened his mouth. Elias' tongue and teeth were covered with a thick, white film.

"What is it?" Rianne asked.

Pagan was utterly still. Only his eyes moved, and they were as bleak as a winter storm. For a moment she thought he hadn't heard her at all.

Alarm shot through her. "Pagan, what's wrong?" she asked, laying her hand on his arm.

Her touch seemed to release him from the unnatural tension. He raked his hand through his hair, awareness of his surroundings coming back into his eyes.

"It's typhoid fever," he said.

Typhoid.

The word seemed to hang in the air above them. Rianne swallowed convulsively. Typhoid—the same disease that had killed Pagan's two brothers in the orphan-

361

age. No wonder he looked like he'd seen a ghost; perhaps he had.

For a moment she saw his past in his eyes, raw and painful. Then his expression became hooded, closing the rest of the world away. Closing *her* away.

When he spoke, his voice was completely without emotion. "Francois, you'd better tell the others what's happened. Make sure they understand that typhoid comes from contaminated water, and they'd better start boiling their drinking water."

"Oui." Francois moved more swiftly than Rianne would have believed possible. A moment later she heard his bull voice echoing through the valley.

Rianne reached up to wipe her mouth, remembering the lukewarm tea Nathan Shore had served them just a few minutes ago. Everyone in the valley used the water from the stream for cooking, drinking, and bathing. And the Songbird Mine was downstream from this camp.

She gave herself a mental shake. Worrying about it wasn't going to change anything. First things first, and there was a very sick man who needed help. But when she moved toward the bed, Pagan stopped her.

"I'll get him settled," he said.

"Shouldn't we take him back to town where he can be nursed properly?"

A muscle jumped in Pagan's cheek. "Look at him, Rianne. He'll be dead by morning."

Rianne knew he was right; her mother had had that gaunt, grey look to her face just before she died. Her heart ached for the unfortunate man before her. He was so far from home, with no loved ones to ease him through his suffering. "Is there nothing we can do for him?"

"Only clean him up and make him comfortable so he can die with a measure of dignity."

With a sigh, Rianne bent her head. "The others, though, will have to be brought into town for nursing," she said. "We must be prepared."

Pagan turned to look at her. 'The others', she'd said, knowing as well as he that there would be more cases of typhoid. Another woman would have been daunted, perhaps hysterical, when faced with such a prospect. But he'd learned that Rianne was not like other women. Her courage was a flame, burning away the icy coldness that had numbed his chest. With such a woman at his side, he thought, a man could face the Devil himself.

He wanted to take her in his arms, to forget the past and the future in her warmth, her caring, and her courage. But before he could, there was the present to be dealt with.

"You're right," he said. "There's no way of knowing just how many people are going to get sick, so we'd better plan for the worst. Get someone to take you and Tessa back to town. Go through our supplies and see what we have in the way of disinfectant—carbolic acid, lye soap, anything."

"I will. One thing we *do* have in quantity, and that's whiskey. If," she added, forcing a smile, "we can keep them from drinking it instead of washing in it."

Taking her by the shoulders, he kissed her hard, wishing he had given her more, done more to show her how precious she was to him. "I should send you away. You and Tessa."

"No," she said.

"I could make you." His fingers tightened.

Rianne met his gaze squarely, willing him to see her determination. Her father was here, and so was the man she loved. No power on this earth was going to make her leave—not Pagan, not Sylvia, not even typhoid fever. "No, you cannot make me. You aren't my husband, Pagan. I go or stay as *I* please."

"Damn it, Rianne . . ." He let out his breath with a hiss of exasperation. "You don't know what this is going to be like. There's still a ship at Ogilvie, but it's going to be steaming out of there within a week. Once the river freezes, there will be no more ships. If you would take Tessa and—"

"If Tessa leaves the Klondike, it will be with her own mother," Rianne said. "Do you want Sylvia taking her away? And we might already have the illness—all of us."

Pagan gritted his teeth, hating all his choices. He could keep them here, exposing them to the dangers of typhoid, or he could send them away, perhaps leaving them to fall ill among strangers. He'd known of ships' crews who, afraid of disease, had abandoned sick passengers on the shore. He'd seen the remains of those unfortunate souls, frozen solid in their blankets. No, he couldn't risk that fate. It was far better that they stay here, where he could watch over them.

He moved away from her, slamming his right fist into the palm of his other hand. "There has to be a way to keep you safe!"

"Pagan." Softly, she put her hand on his shoulder. "There is nothing you can do. Our fate is in God's hands now." With a sigh, she added, "And there is no safety for any of us."

Chapter Twenty-six

"Mr. Harelson, finish this broth for me, won't you?" Rianne asked.

"Too tired," the sick man mumbled, falling back to his pillow.

Setting the bowl aside, she sat on the edge of the cot and put her arm behind his shoulders to lever him up again. Patiently, she spooned the rest of the broth into his mouth.

"It's very important for you to have liquids, Mr. Harelson," she said as she worked. "And this broth is very good; Julia Nathan brought it over just for you."

Her gaze moved across the room, checking the ranks of cots. The saloon had been turned into a makeshift hospital; the table and chairs had been taken away and replaced with hastily-built beds. As more people had fallen ill, more beds had been built, until there were two dozen in the room. Some cots, she reflected sadly, were bearing their second occupant. Too many had died. Every one of the women who lived at the Golden Bear had worked hard to save as many as they could. Perhaps, if there had been better medicines and more nurses, they could have saved more. As it was, Willa and Jewell had fallen ill themselves, while the rest moved like automatons through endless rounds of tending, scrubbing, and feeding the sick.

Setting the empty bowl aside, Rianne let the man lie down again and pulled the covers up around his shoulders. He was one of the lucky ones; he would live. Repressing a groan, she pushed herself up from the cot and went to scrub her hands in the basin of carbolic acid solution she always kept nearby.

"Water," a patient croaked. "Please, water."

She made her way through the ranks of beds to the man who had spoken. Laying her hand on his forehead, she found that his fever was raging high. "Of course you can have some water," she murmured soothingly. "I'll be back in a moment."

He closed his eyes, his head moving fretfully from side to side. Rianne brushed his perspiration-soaked hair back, then turned and trudged toward the kitchen. It was nearly dusk, time to wake Alva and Kate, time to take her own six hours of rest before beginning the rounds again. Thank God the outbreak seemed to have reached its peak, and fewer cases were coming in.

She was too tired to feel glad about that. In the month that had passed since they'd found the first case of typhoid, poor Elias . . . Elias . . . Dear Lord, she was too weary even to remember the man's last name. Such a shame, since he had died among strangers, and someone really ought to remember his name . . .

With a sigh, she pushed the kitchen door open and went in. The room had become a veritable witches' den, filled with bubbling cauldrons that reeked of lye soap and carbolic acid. This was Marie's territory, where soiled clothing and bed linens were boiled and purified.

Marie looked up from stirring one of the largest cookpots. Her hair hung in wet strands along her cheeks, and her chemise was soaked with sweat. Brandishing her ladle, she asked, "Now you tell me, Rianne Kierney, if there ain't worse things'n whoring. I think I'll be seein' dirty sheets in my nightmares for as long as I live."

Rianne smiled; no matter how tired she was, she always found relief in Marie's tart humor. "It wouldn't be so bad if we didn't have things hanging all over the house to dry," she said. "If we could only hang them outside—"

"You tried that last week, remember? It took all of fifteen minutes for everythin' to freeze solid."

"I remember." Rianne's grin widened as she remembered John Ferguson carrying the blankets in and stacking them like boards beside the stove. They had laughed like complete fools over that, tears running down their faces, holding their sides against the uncontrollable mirth. Strangely, it had given them just a little more strength to keep going.

"The lye soap is gettin' low," Marie said. "And I got to have it for the laundry. Better start scrubbin' that floor with Pagan's whiskey, honey."

Rianne sighed. Their supply of carbolic was almost gone; for the past week, they had been using it only to wash their hands. "We'd better pray the worst of the outbreak is over, then, and not just a lull before things get bad again."

"Yeah. Pagan might jest have to boil them malamutes of his down fer grease to make more soap," Marie said, swiping at the sweat-soaked hair upon her forehead.

"I think he'd boil *me* down before he'd touch those dogs. And as far as usefulness goes, they're probably worth more than you and I put together," Rianne said, managing a ghost of a smile.

"Useful!" Marie pointed her ladle like a sword. "They been bringin' more people in for us to nurse. Now tell me, is that useful?"

If Rianne hadn't been so tired, she would have laughed. Still, she had energy enough to thank God for giving her such friends with whom to share the burdens of such a terrible time. "Has the water in the kettle been boiled?"

367

"Yep. And *Miz* Sylvia was down tryin' to git it for her evenin' abo-lutions." Marie scowled. "*I* offered to give her a bath, all right. I offered to scrub her damned lazy hide with lye soap and a bristle brush. She lit out of here like a big, fat pigeon with a hawk on its tail."

Rianne's mouth twitched with amusement. Taking a mug down from the cupboard, she filled it with water from the kettle, then winked at Marie and headed toward the saloon.

Sylvia's shrill, demanding tones shattered her fragile good humor.

"What a stink!" the blonde woman said loudly. "Are we *ever* going to get back to normal?"

Rianne sighed as she turned toward the stairs. Sylvia was wearing a gown of green plaid taffeta that wrapped sleekly around her generous curves and turned her eyes emerald and her hair pure gold. At another time, Rianne would have been ashamed of her own stained and wrinkled dress, plain brown hair and reddened hands. But now, after seeing that Sylvia's perfect, powdered nose was wrinkled in disdain and those lovely green eyes were hot with intolerance, she was glad she was different.

"What does one have to do to get a cup of tea around here?" Sylvia demanded.

"One has to have typhoid fever," Rianne said.

"How uncharitable of you, Miss Kierney."

Rianne's temper flared, lit by annoyance and exhaustion. "Look around, Sylvia. Everyone but you is working, either nursing the sick, boiling dirty laundry, or scrubbing floors with disinfectant."

"Oh, dear." Sylvia put her hand over her heart with a theatrical flourish. "I've been *so* thoughtless! But then you and the other . . . ladies are used to labor. Albeit on your backs."

Rianne's eyes narrowed. She was sorely tempted to, as Marie so colorfully said, 'snatch the woman bald'. But a very sick man was waiting for the mug of water she was holding, and he was more important than Sylvia. Swallowing a retort, Rianne turned on her heel and strode into the saloon.

She knew Sylvia wouldn't follow her into the sickroom, for the woman had been vocal about hating the stench of typhoid. So did Rianne. For the rest of her life, she would remember the smell of sickness, the eyewatering stink of carbolic, the fear and pain, and the unmistakable look of approaching death. She had held the hands of men while they died, men whose names she didn't even know. She had fought for them, unsuccessfully, but hard, and she had cried for the loss of every one. Yes, she hated typhoid.

She went to the man who had asked for water and sat on the edge of his cot. Slipping her arm beneath his shoulders, she tried vainly to lift him. She adjusted her position, tried again, nearly sobbing in frustration as she failed again.

Then a strong, fur-clad arm slid beneath hers, taking the weight from her. She knew without looking that it was Pagan, knew by scent, touch, and the wild beating of her heart. The mug shook in her hand.

Pagan knelt on the floor beside the bed, his chest pressed tightly against her side. "Come on, now," he said to the sick man. "You've got to drink this."

Rianne swallowed against a sudden tightness in her throat as Pagan's warmth and strength seeped into her, buttressing her faltering courage. Her hands steadied. She held the mug to the sick man's mouth, letting him have the water in small sips. When he finished, Pagan gently laid him back down onto the pillow.

"He's asleep," Rianne whispered.

Pagan lifted her to her feet. "You look tired," he said.

"So do you. So do we all." Her hands were on his chest, feeling the softness of the fur he wore. Beneath it, she could feel the slow, steady beating of his heart. "Is my father well?"

"He's fine. I brought him back with me, by the way. He asked me to tell you that he had a few errands to run, but will see you as soon as he's finished. How is Tessa today?"

"She's been waiting impatiently for you to come." And so have I, Rianne thought. So have I. "It's hard for her, being the only child in town and forced to stay in a house full of sick people."

He sighed. "There's a full moon tonight. I'll take her for a ride on the sled." Cocking his head to one side, he added, "Why don't you come with us? Just for a few hours, we can forget this hell we've been living."

"I can't." Rianne shook her head, wishing things could be different. "I have six hours' sleep coming to me, and even a ride on a dog sled isn't going to make me miss them."

Pagan took her hands in his, his thumb caressing the skin of her palms. Rianne tried to pull away, suddenly, acutely aware of her many imperfections. She didn't want him to see her like this. Her hands were no longer soft, but work-worn and reddened from harsh disinfectants. Her hair was lank, her clothes bedraggled, and she knew there were huge, dark circles beneath her eyes. And although Pagan had been working as hard as she, tending a number of men at the valley and also burying the dead, he only looked leaner, harder, and even more devastating.

"Let me go," she said. "I'm a mess."

"You're beautiful." Tenderly, he raised her abused hands to his mouth and kissed them, one at a time.

They were precious to him, these small, capable hands that had tended the sick and soothed the dying. And so was the woman. During the past month, he had watched her give of herself, give and give and then give some more, until he'd been afraid there might be nothing left. But there was some vast reserve of strength in her that never seemed to run out. When things had been bleakest, he'd seen her reach within, tapping that reserve to give yet a little more to those who needed it.

And as he stood there, looking down into those warm-honey eyes that were so shadowed with sorrow, he knew he loved her. He had thought himself safe from love, his heart protected behind walls of cynicism and mistrust. Women came, women went without ever truly reaching him. Even Sylvia. Especially Sylvia.

Then Rianne had come into his life, changing everything with her sweet Siren's voice, her passion, her courage, and generosity. She had stolen his heart and touched his soul, and in doing so had taught him what was real and fine between a man and a woman. He *would* have her. He *would* claim her, now and forever. Slowly, inexorably, he slipped his arm around her waist and pulled her close.

Rianne knew he was going to kiss her. More than anything else in the world, she wanted it. Of their own volition, her hands slid upward to delve into his thick black hair. She didn't care that they were standing in full view of everyone in the room. She'd had so much of death and illness, sadness and loss. Pagan was life and love, and holding him right now was more important than having air to breathe.

Then a high-pitched, mocking laugh intruded, and she sprang away from Pagan. The overpoweringly sweet smell of Sylvia's perfume cut through even the sickroom odors. A hothouse orchid, Rianne thought, swallowing hard against the lump of disgust that rose in her throat. Sweet, lovely poison, just like Sylvia.

"Pagan, darling!" the blonde woman said, gliding forward to take his arm. "I thought I heard your voice. Did you know that Tessa is simply dying to see you?"

Pagan didn't look away from Rianne. "I'll be up in a few minutes."

Rianne shook her head, denying him, denying herself, and took a step backward. She couldn't deal with this just now. "I've got to get some sleep," she said. "I'm on my way upstairs to wake Alva and Kate; I'll send Tessa down to you."

Pagan's lips curved in a smile of self-deprecation. Here he was, finally ready to declare his feelings to the woman he loved, and she was too damned tired to hear it. Reaching out, he took Rianne's hands and raised them to his lips again.

"Good night," he said. "If you need me for anything, just call."

Her blush pleased him. He watched her walk away, wishing there were something he could do to take the burden from her. He'd tried, several times. She had rounded on him like a wildcat, telling him in no uncertain terms to mind his own business, reminding him—and this had become a most irritating point—that he was not her husband and had no right to give her orders. Well, he thought, things were about to change.

"Darling." Sylvia touched his arm, bringing him back to reality with a jolt.

An unpleasant jolt. "How much do you want?" he growled.

"I beg your pardon?"

"I want out of the marriage, and I want Tessa. How much will that cost me?"

"Truly, I'm hurt. As I've told you before, I came here to reconcile, not to arrange another separation."

He sighed, beyond anger with this woman. All he

wanted was to be rid of her, completely and finally, so that he, Rianne and Tessa could be a family. Only the risk that Sylvia would strike at him through Tessa kept him from heaving her straight out the door into the snow.

Instead, he turned on his heel and walked away. Let Sylvia come to him; let *her* make the next move in this sordid little game she was playing. He took the stairs two at a time. As he strode down the hall toward his room, he heard Sylvia coming after him, the heels of her fancy shoes clicking on the wooden floor.

"Pagan, wait!" she called.

He stopped, turning to watch her come. She came to a halt before him, her cheeks flushed from running, her generous bosom heaving so deeply that it strained the bodice of her dress. Once, he would have thought her beautiful. But no more.

"Darling," she said breathlessly, pressing close. "You can't mean those terrible things. You know you still care for me. And I love you so much I can hardly keep it all inside." Boldly, she ran her hands along his sides to his hips, then moved to stroke his manhood. "Remember how good we were? It can be that way again. I can make you happy, so happy you'll never think about another woman."

Despite her caresses, Pagan didn't feel the slightest urgings of lust. He'd seen men fight to possess this woman, to love her. But to Sylvia, love was something to be used but never returned; likewise, generosity, courtesy and gratitude were all gifts, homage to her beauty. Inside, she was empty, as cold and hard as glacier ice. It chilled him to think that he'd given her his name and his child. It was a miracle that Tessa had come through the past years unwarped and still able to love.

Taking her by the shoulders, he held her away from him. "I don't want you."

"I don't believe you," she said, straining toward him. "I'm your wife. I intend to remain your wife, and no amount of money is going to change that. Neither is that mouse of an English girl you seem to want."

"Rianne is warm and genuine and truly beautiful, and I'm in love with her."

That hit the mark, he noted with satisfaction. Sylvia's face congealed into a mask of bitter rage. This was the real Sylvia. Not the lovely, perfumed woman she presented to the world of men, but the greedy, grasping, selfish creature he knew her to be.

"Love her all you want," she spat. "I'll never give you a divorce. Bed her, have a dozen brats by her, but by God, she'll never have your name."

He let her go, repressing the urge to thrust her from him, and folded his arms over his chest. "You mean I haven't found your price yet. But I will, Sylvia, for one thing I know about you is that there is always a price."

"You arrogant bastard," she hissed. "You're not going to get away with this! I beat you at your own game before, and I can do it again."

Pagan met her gaze squarely, letting her see his contempt. "Don't you know why I never bothered to come after you all those years ago, Sylvia?" He smiled, a slash of a grin that held true humor. "It was because I just didn't give a damn. But now you're playing with Tessa and Rianne, and I *do* care about them. So I warn you; name a price I'm willing to pay and get away clean, or take the risk I'll strip you of everything."

For a moment she looked daunted, but only for a moment. Then she laughed throatily, and smoothed the bodice of her gown so that her thrusting breasts were clearly outlined. "Go ahead, lover. Strip me. I'll make your blood sing, I'll love you until you beg for mercy."

"You're fooling yourself, Sylvia," he said in genuine pity. "Now, if you'll excuse me, my daughter is waiting."

"Our daughter," she murmured. "Yours and mine. A matched set, both with the last name of Roark. Remember that."

For the second time in just a few minutes, Pagan turned his back on her and walked away.

The Nugget Saloon was bright and noisy, just the sort of place Sylvia was craving just now. She pushed the door open and went in, unbuttoning her coat and hanging it on the brass rack beside the door. This saloon was smaller than Pagan's, with only this one room downstairs. Upstairs were two more rooms, but they were accessible only by an outside staircase. One room was Mason's, the other served as living and working quarters for the five prostitutes he maintained.

Everything, upstairs and down, was covered with many years' accumulation of filth. No wonder the miners preferred the Golden Bear, Sylvia thought. It was a clean saloon with clean girls and unwatered whiskey, and gave a man his money's worth. But since Pagan had allowed his place to be turned into a hospital, the Nugget was the only game in town.

A man staggered up to her and put his arm around her waist. "Now, ain't this a fine piece," he slurred, his breath, whiskey-thick and foul, settling over her in a cloud. "How 'bout you an' me havin' a good time?"

"I'd rather bed a bull moose," she said. Putting her hand on his face, she shoved him away. He sprawled against a nearby table, whose occupants pushed him in another direction. He reeled away, bellowing for another drink.

Standing on tiptoe to survey the room, she spotted Lowell Mason sitting at a table near the back. One of his whores was perched on his knee, her blouse pulled down to her waist. Mason was squeezing her breasts,

375

tugging at the nipples while having a conversation with another man.

Sylvia repressed a shudder, thinking that such a fate might be in store for her one day. An all-too-familiar desperation laid its cold hand on the back of her neck. Once, she'd had her pick of men. Rich men. But rich men liked their mistresses young and fresh, and she was no longer that. When she'd met Mason in Seattle, she'd been all but destitute. She had pinned all her hopes on coming here.

She'd like to win Pagan back; his good looks were as attractive as his money, and marriage would give her security. But failing that, she had to get enough money from him to keep her for the rest of her life. And that didn't mean a few paltry thousand, either. She'd learned to like a certain style of living, and she intended to keep it. No, she needed a great deal of money, surely more than Pagan would be willing to pay.

"What are you doing here, Sylvia?"

The voice came from behind her, and she turned to see Alastair Kierney standing a few feet away. "Why, Mr. Kierney, I just needed to hear some laughter and music after slaving away in that sickroom over there. You?"

He shrugged. "The same. I went to visit Rianne, but they said she was sleeping. So I went for a walk, heard the music, and here I am."

Smelled the whiskey, more likely, Sylvia thought. "A man after my own heart! Wouldn't you like to come have a drink with me?" She didn't want his company; she just wanted to hurt Rianne by making him break his promise not to drink.

"I can't." He rubbed his hand over his lips, his gaze fixed on the bar. "I . . . you see, it's Tuesday. I, ah, don't drink during the week."

"Then will you just come and keep me company?

376

These men are so rough-looking, and I'm afraid of staying here alone." She looked at him pleadingly, knowing he would do it. She knew drunks. He didn't want to break his word, so he'd let her take the responsibility for it. "Besides, you owe yourself a chance to relax a bit. Surely your daughter won't begrudge you a few moments of play after all your hard work."

"Well—"

Sylvia slipped her arm through his. "Come, Mr. Kierney. Enjoy the music. Laugh. It will make tomorrow just a little bit easier to bear."

"All right." He grinned at her, smoothing his white hair back with his free hand as he led her to the bar. Slapping a doeskin bag on the top, he told the bartender, "Give the lady whatever she wants."

Sylvia laughed, her gaze on the bag. "Why, Mr. Kierney, how kind of you! I'll have a glass of your finest champagne."

"Champagne!" The bartender stared at her. "We got whiskey. Take it or leave it."

"Oh, very well, I'll take it." Sylvia smiled seductively at Alastair. "And one for Mr. Kierney."

He held up his hand. "Not for me. And call me Alastair."

"I'm sorry, I forgot . . . Alastair." Sylvia noticed that his gaze was following the bottle as the bartender poured drinks. Her smile widened. "I'm sorry we haven't had much time to get to know one another, especially as you and my husband are such good friends. Or partners, rather."

"Pagan's a good man."

She took a sip of her whiskey, then set it on the bar near the old man's hand. "Dreadful stuff," she said with a delicate shudder. "I don't think I can finish it."

He stared at the glass, obviously yearning for a taste of the liquor. His hand twitched.

377

Pretending not to notice, Sylvia said, "You weren't at the Golden Bear this Saturday night past. But then, Saturday nights aren't quite as they were."

"Pagan and I were hauling corpses," the old man said.

"I do miss the music." She put her hand on his arm, gazing earnestly into his eyes. Inwardly, however, she was quivering with malicious laughter at the thought of him staggering back to the Golden Bear drunk as a lord. Wouldn't that spike that Kierney woman's tail? "Alastair, I think I know your daughter well enough to know that if she were here, she would give her blessing for one small drink after what you've been through."

"Well . . ." he rubbed his chin thoughtfully, still staring at the whiskey. "It's true I haven't had a drink in over two weeks. They've been scrubbing floors with good liquor down at the mine. It's hard on a man."

"Of course it is." She pushed the glass a fraction of an inch closer to him.

A hand fell on her shoulder, and she turned to see Lowell Mason standing behind her. "Go ahead, Alastair," he said. "When that's gone, have another. On the house."

The old man sighed. "I can't. Kierney honor, you know."

Sylvia shrugged. She didn't really care that much; she'd just wanted to start trouble. She started to turn away, but Mason's hand tightened, holding her in place.

"I got a couple of cheechakos just itching for a friendly game of poker. High stakes. You got any Kierney rules against that?" Mason asked.

With a grin, Alastair picked his gold pouch up from the bar. "Not a one, Lowell. Not a one."

Chapter Twenty-seven

"What are you up to?" Sylvia whispered in Mason's ear when Alastair turned away.

"Just getting myself a bit of Songbird gold," he hissed back. Taking her by the arm in a grip that hurt, he urged her after the old man. "You see if you can stand behind him. If he's bluffing, rub your nose. If he's got winning cards, scratch your cheek."

"I get half of anything you win."

"Done." He walked away, following Alastair. Sylvia followed, her curiosity running high. Mason's whore was gone from the table, replaced by two hard-eyed men. They might be greenhorns here in the Yukon, but Sylvia was sure they could take care of themselves. She knew the type well: adventurers, will-o-the-wisps, seekers of whatever they didn't have. A bottle of whiskey sat on the table between them, and a deck of cards.

"You want a game, old man?" one asked, shuffling the deck in his reddened, chapped hands.

"Deal me in," Alastair said. "Wish me luck, pretty Sylvia."

"Luck," she said, putting one hand upon the back of his chair. Alastair didn't complain about having her at his back, so she stayed. A trusting man, she thought. A lamb for the slaughter.

Although she gave Mason signals whenever necessary, the old man would have lost on his own. Truly, she had

379

never seen a worse poker player, drunk or sober, than Alastair Kierney; in less than three hours, he lost more than five thousand dollars. She had watched him take heavy little pouches out of his pockets one by one and toss them on the table, and she watched him lose them one by one, until his pockets were empty.

One of the strangers raked in his winnings and got to his feet. "That's enough fer me," he said. "Thank-ee kindly, Mr. Kierney."

"Wait!" Alastair shuffled the cards. "How about one more hand, double or nothing? My luck has changed, I can feel it."

"Hell, man, ain't you got no sense?" the man asked, sliding back into his seat.

Alastair smiled. "No, but I've got a gold mine. How about it, boys? Five cards, no draw, and the best hand wins it all?"

He can't stop at cards any more than he can stop at gambling, Sylvia thought, looking across the table at Lowell Mason. The saloon owner pressed his steepled hands against his lips and stared back at her, his eyes triumphant.

"I'm in," he said, shoving his winnings into the center of the table.

The other men followed suit. Alastair shuffled, slapped the cards down on the table for Mason to cut, then dealt the last hand.

"A pair of tens," one of the strangers said, tossing his cards on the table in disgust.

"Not a goddamned thing," his companion growled. "I should've stopped while I was ahead."

"I'll buy you a drink," Alastair said.

"Better find out if you've got anything to buy *with*," Mason countered, laying three queens on the table.

With a sigh, Alastair flipped his cards over. "Two pair, kings and eights. Looks like I'm skunked tonight."

The two other men left the table, leaving Mason, Alastair and Sylvia alone.

"You owe me twelve thousand dollars, Alastair," Mason said, showing the edges of his teeth in a smile better suited to a fox than a man. "I hope you can pay up."

"Of course I can. I'll give you an IOU. Tomorrow—"

"Not tomorrow. Tonight."

Alastair leaned back in his chair. "My gold is locked up in Pagan's safe, along with a lot of other people's. Even if I knew the combination, I wouldn't be able to go in there and just take what I want. But first thing in the morning, I'll see that you get your money."

"Some men might take offense at that."

"Some might," Alastair agreed. "I suppose you could shoot me." The old man was smiling, but there was a flinty look in his eyes that showed his rising temper. "But then my half of everything would go to Pagan, and then you'd be going to *him* for your money. I doubt he'd believe an IOU written the same night of my killing."

A vein throbbed in Mason's forehead, but all he did was nod. "First thing in the morning, old man."

"You have my word." Alastair inclined his head regally. "Kierney honor." Rising to his feet, he turned to Sylvia. "I think I'll take a walk down by the river. Right now, just before it freezes, the water seems as thick and smooth as velvet. Gives a man peace to see the stars swimming in it."

She smiled a little shakily, stunned by the night's events. And revelations. Oh, yes indeed, revelations. The beginnings of a plan burst in her mind, half-formed, but very, very promising. "So you're a poet, too. A man of many talents."

He chuckled. "Poker, however, isn't one of them. Would you like to come walk with me?"

"Perhaps another time," she said. "I fear I'm not quite acclimated to the weather here. The cold—"

"This isn't cold," Alastair said. "This is bracing. There will be days when the air will feel like red-hot coals in your lungs, and when your eyelashes freeze closed when you blink."

"Please, no more," she said, shuddering at the very thought.

"Are you sure you won't come?"

"Quite. Good night, Alastair, and thank you for keeping me company."

When he was gone, Sylvia let a man buy her a drink. She counted the minutes while flirting with him *and* his companion, and skillfully brought the two drunken, amorous men to blows just at the right time. She slipped away while a third man struggled to separate them. Good, she thought. They would all remember that she'd been here after Alastair left.

Taking her coat from the hook beside the door, she hurried outside. The wind whipped her skirts about her legs and drove frost-needles into her unprotected face. Her teeth chattered uncontrollably. She leaned forward into the wind, determined not to let this opportunity pass.

She left the street behind and trudged through the snow toward the river. Spying a distant figure standing on the riverbank, she quickened her steps. Soon she could see Alastair's white hair gleaming beneath his hat. She labored through the snow toward him, her breath blowing out in a great steam cloud upon the night air.

"Alastair!" she called when she was near enough.

He turned. "Ah, so you changed your mind!"

"I couldn't resist your poetry," she said. The crunch of her feet in the snow was loud. Everything seemed sharper, clearer, more in focus.

"It's going to freeze over in a day or so," he said.

"How do you know?"

He grinned, tapping his nose. "I can smell it. In spring, men bet on when the ice is going to break up. I win more often than not."

Sylvia moved closer. Her pulse hammered in her ears, growing louder and louder until it grew to a roar. Faintly, through the noise, she heard Alastair's voice.

"Be careful here," he warned, steadying her with a hand on her arm. "It's very slippery."

He was between her and the water. This was the time! With an indrawn gasp, she pushed him with all her strength. He fell backward, his feet going out from under him, and she knew that the look of complete astonishment on his face would stay with her forever. Everything seemed to be moving in slow motion. First, his arms flailing as he tried to regain his balance, the wide-open 'O' of his mouth, his hat falling off, spinning over and over before landing in the water behind him.

Then his head landed with horrible force upon an ice-glazed slab of rock. For a moment she thought he was dead, but then she saw his chest rise and fall with his breathing.

Pressing her knuckles against her teeth so hard they drew blood, she stared at the unconscious man. Twice she reached out to him, twice she pulled back, aghast at what she had done, what she was going to do. But she had to. Hadn't she come out here precisely for this? Hadn't she decided to do it because his half of the mine would go to Pagan? And the more money Pagan had, the more generous he would be. If she worked things right, he might even give her Alastair's half of the Songbird so that he could have his child and his damned mistress. That was worth any risk, any price.

Sylvia took a deep breath, then another. She had no

choice. "I'm sorry, Alastair," she murmured. "I truly did like you."

Bending, she rolled the inert form into the cold, dark water. He floated for a moment, his white hair spreading out upon the surface like wisps of fog, then sank quietly out of sight.

By the time dawn came, Rianne had been working for hours. She set her washrag aside for a moment and went to the window to watch the sun come up. Truly, she thought, the Klondike had the most stunning sunrises and sunsets in all the world. Even the pall of smoke that constantly hung over the town couldn't dim the glory of the turquoise and lemon-yellow sky, the long, stark shadows of the trees against the snow and the humped ranks of mountains that glittered like quicksilver in the new-born light.

The sight warmed her to her soul. Typhoid, cold, and isolation notwithstanding, the Yukon had been especially blessed by the hand of God. Its grandeur, its stillness, yes, even the unconscious savagery of the untamed Nature that was the only ruler here—all seemed to twine a spell about a person's soul, making the rest of the world seem too small, too tame, too . . . used.

"Rianne," Marie called from the kitchen, "The soup is done. You ready fer it?"

"Yes." With a sigh, Rianne turned from the window to face her duties again.

Just as she started towards the kitchen, however, the front door swung open with a crash. A blast of frigid air blew into the room, sending a glistening shower of powdery snow across the ranks of beds.

"Close that . . ." She broke off, seeing Pagan's broadshouldered form silhouetted in the doorway. He came forward, closing the door behind him. His eyes were as bleak as the snow outside, shot through with grief and pain and rage.

"What is it?" she whispered, knowing it was bad. "What's happened?"

A muscle twitched in his jaw. Striding forward, he put his hands on her shoulders. She could feel the cold of them even through the wool of her dress.

"It's your father," he said. "There's been an accident."

"He's hurt?" she gasped.

"He's dead, Rianne." Harsh words, he thought, short and hard and ugly. He didn't want to say them. But there were no others. No pretty phrases, no clever euphemisms could soften this blow. So he gave it to her straight, and hoped that he could somehow find a way to comfort her.

Rianne shook her head. It was too horrible to be believed. This couldn't be happening, not now, oh, not now! "No. It can't be true. I won't let it be true!"

"I'm sorry, love." He drew her into his arms, offering her the only comfort he could.

But there was no comfort for Rianne. She felt dead inside, as though her feelings had run out of her like water. Vaguely, she felt the soft fur of his parka against her cheek, smelled the faint pine scent of it, but everything seemed very far away.

"What happened?" she asked.

"It looks like he was walking by the river, slipped on a patch of ice or something and hit his head. From what I can tell, he was unconscious before he went into the water."

"He never had a chance, then?"

"No."

She closed her eyes, wishing she could shut out the pain as easily. Her father loved the river, loved walking there late at night. And now he was dead, drowned in those cold, clear waters he had thought his friend. "Take me to him."

"Rianne, it isn't . . . Don't do this to yourself."

Gently but firmly, she pushed free of Pagan. "Take me to him."

Pagan opened his mouth to protest, then closed it again. After all, who was he to question her decision? She had proved her courage over and over again, and he could only assume she would face Alastair's death with the same grace and strength with which she had faced everything else.

"Go get something warm on," he said, his voice rough with suppressed emotion. "It's damned cold out there."

Rianne took a blanket from a stack of newly-washed laundry and wrapped it around her shoulders.

"You'll freeze like that," Pagan growled. "Here." Stripping his parka off, he put it on her, lacing her up like a child. "And don't argue. I'm more used to this climate than you are."

He clenched his hands into fists as he watched her walk outside, her head held high, her shoulders squared. She was unique, a woman of strength and gentleness—steel sheathed in velvet. But even the finest steel could break, he thought grimly, if given the proper blow.

He caught up with her, taking her cold, bare hand in his as he led her toward the river. The cold was fierce, but he hardly noticed it. He was warmed by the coals of helpless anger for the waste of his good friend's life, anger that Rianne was in torment. If he could bring Alastair back to life, he would; if he could take Rianne's pain, he would do that, too. But no one could fight Death. Strength did not suffice against it, nor did courage. One merely grieved, then went on. So would Rianne. And he would be there beside her.

Rianne felt Pagan's touch, and some deep-buried part of her mind knew he wanted desperately to comfort her. But her whole being was focused toward the river and what waited for her there. She could hear the squeak of snow beneath her boots, smell the wood-and-pine tang of the air, hear the soft bellows of her breath, but all were muted by the sound of water lapping the shore.

Now she could see a cluster of men standing beside the river. The water behind them was slate-grey and sluggish beneath a coating of mist. The men, looking larger than normal in their bulky winter clothes, stood in a grim circle around a dark shape that lay upon the ground.

Her father. Stiff and still, as still as ice-covered rocks upon which he lay.

Rianne pushed through the knot of men to kneel in the snow beside her father's body. She dared to touch his cheek, recoiling when she found it hard and cold. This could not be her father, not the laughing, mischievous man she had known, with his huge appetite for life.

She looked up at the watching men wildly, wanting someone to tell her it was a dream, a nightmare, even some cruel hoax—anything but that this pitiful, frozen thing was Alastair Kierney. All that life, all that vitality come to this? In the short time they had been together, he had given her more warmth and joy than she'd had in her entire lifetime. Her chest rose and fell with her suddenly ragged breathing. None of the many deaths she'd seen, not even her mother's, could begin to compare with the loss she felt over this one.

"Oh, Father," she said, a wealth of sorrow in her voice.

Her hand shaking violently, she reached out to smooth his white hair back from his forehead. But it, too, was frozen, and resisted her touch like a mat of stone. It was too much; even the smallest of human comfort was denied her. She rejected it, body, mind, and soul, wanting to scream her outrage to the sky.

But her throat was closed, her words, her breath itself trapped by pain. A strange, roaring darkness swooped down upon her, dimming her vision, roaring in her ears. Her gaze went to Pagan, seeking him automatically. As though from a great distance, she saw him start toward her, tossing men aside like twigs as he came.

She reached out to him, needing him desperately. Only he could help her, only he could protect her from the terrible blackness that pressed on her from every side.

"Rianne!" he shouted. "Rianne!"

His voice released hers. "Pagan!" she shrieked, pouring all her grief, her despair into that frantic cry.

Then the roaring darkness claimed her, and she pitched forward across her father's cold, unyielding body.

Chapter Twenty-eight

"Rianne. Rianne, open your eyes."

She resisted the call. Only reality waited for her if she woke, and it was much safer to stay here, cocooned in the velvet web of unconsciousness.

"Rianne!"

The summons was insistent, demanding. She knew this voice; it drew her as nothing else could. Slowly she drifted upward, toward the light and awareness. Toward Pagan.

The first thing she saw was his eyes. Pale, ice-crystal eyes, full of concern and shared grief. "Where am I?" she asked groggily.

"My room."

She began to orient herself in her surroundings. Pagan was sitting in a chair near the fireplace, cradling her in his lap. How long he'd sat like that, she had no way of knowing; the curtains were closed, the room twilight-dim. She levered herself upright, then slid off his lap.

Pagan didn't try to hold her, as much as he wanted to. She'd have to come to him in her own time, not his. He could wait, for he knew their love was destined to be. He'd been a fool to risk it before, and he was not about to jeopardize the gift again.

For as long as he lived, he would remember the look on her face when she'd reached out to him there by the river. She'd been at the edge of oblivion, ready to fall over. And in her extremity, she had called to him. *To him!* The knowledge was a song in his soul. She was a part of him, irrevocably entwined in his being.

"How long was I unconscious?" she asked.

"Not long," he said. "Too long. You scared me good, Rianne Kierney." He clamped his hands on the armrests, struggling to control the urge to hold her.

Rianne went to stand before the fire, her back to him. His sympathy was too much to bear just now, and she had to turn away from it to keep from breaking down. Although she stood close to the fireplace, she felt as though she would never be warm again. Her father was gone, his laughter and love relegated once again to memory. "My father . . . They'll say he was drunk."

Pagan sighed. 'They' were already saying it. Rumors about the circumstances of Alastair's death were circulating fast. A dozen men swore they'd seen him in the Nugget last night, drinking, and a dozen others swore he'd left the saloon alone and sober.

Wanting to see his reaction, Rianne turned to face him. This was so terribly important to her, both the question of whether her father had broken his promise, and what Pagan believed of him. "Do you think he was drunk?"

For a moment, he weighed what he'd heard against what he knew about Alastair Kierney. Then he shook his head. "If your father gave you his word, I believe he kept it."

She let out her breath in a long, shuddering sigh. "Thank you, Pagan." Absently, she pleated the fabric of her dress between her hands. "How could it happen? He was so happy, and everything was going so well. And now he's dead. So simple, so terribly final."

"Rianne—"

"I had only a few short months with him. Half a lifetime of waiting to be with him, and then he's snatched away . . . Oh, God!" Her voice broke. She was tired of being strong, tired of holding it all in. "Hold me," she cried, reaching out to him. "Hold me, please!"

He was up in an instant. Gathering her into his arms, he drew her against his chest, enclosing her, warming her. Shudders ran through her, not sobs, but regular waves of shivers as though she'd been chilled to her soul. Perhaps she had. With infinite gentleness, he stroked her hair, her heaving back, wishing he could insulate her from her pain.

"Oh, Pagan," she whispered, undone by his tenderness. She drew in her breath, held it until she could hold it no longer, then expelled it in a long sigh. It was then that her tears began, a wild outpouring of fear and loss and anger.

"Why did he have to die?" she raged, beating her fists on his chest. "He had a wonderful future ahead of him. *We* had a future. His dream was reality. And now he's dead. Dead and cold and dreamless. How could it happen? Why did it happen? Why, why, why?"

He put his arms around her again, understanding her anger, absorbing her grief. He knew she didn't expect an answer; there were no answers. "Go ahead," he said, his voice tight with suppressed emotion. "Get it all out, honey."

Rianne didn't know how long she cried there in his arms, only that it seemed like forever. She raged, she sobbed, she railed against God for his indifference. Through it all, Pagan stood, loving her, sorrowing with her. He was her lifeline in the dark abyss of grief, and she clung to him desperately. And when the worst of her anger was spent, she let him pull her back into the light.

When she had no more tears left, when she had drawn a deep, shuddering sigh to calm herself, Pagan tilted her head back so that the was looking at him.

"I love you," he said.

"What?" She stilled, her world reeling, then refocusing around him.

"I love you," he said again, framing her face with his hands. "For what it's worth, I love you."

The words went through her like a fiery whirlwind, burning away the unnatural cold that had gripped her. She had lost so much. And now, just when the world seemed a very dark and cruel place, Pagan had given her gifts of inestimable value. Surcease. Love. Life. She closed her eyes against the flood of bittersweet joy. He loved her. He loved her!

"Oh, God," she murmured brokenly. "Tell me again."

Tenderly, he brushed the tear-dampened hair back from her forehead. "I love you. This is the first time for me, and it's strong and true and fathoms-deep. I want to hold you forever. I *will* hold you forever."

"What are you trying to say?" she whispered, not daring to hope. Not yet.

"I want to marry you," he said. "I want you for my wife."

Rianne shook her head, watching him through the glittering haze of tears upon her lashes. She wanted to believe so very badly. Her father's death had pulled her so deep, so very deep, that for a moment she'd thought never to rise back up. Now Pagan was offering the heights, and she hardly dared believe it could happen.

Sliding his hands down to her shoulders, Pagan said, "We are going to be married, you and I. We'll raise Tessa, and have a dozen other children, too."

Our children. Pagan's children. The thought moved her irresistibly, even though she felt a renewed sense of loss that those children would never know their grandfather. Then she took a deep breath. Loss and gain, pain and hope, the depths and the heights—this was life. Alastair had known that better than anyone. "But . . . Sylvia?" she asked.

"Sylvia wants money." His jaw hardened, and his pale eyes had the temper of cold steel. "I'll give her the whole damned mine if that's what it takes to free myself of her."

"You would give up the mine?" Rianne asked in a small voice. "Pagan, you can't! What about your dreams? What about Eldorado?"

He held up the long braid of her hair, letting the firelight gild each fine, silken strand. "This is all the gold I need. And you are my dream. Eldorado means nothing if I can't have you."

She gazed into his eyes, searching for any hint of doubt, but all she saw was love. For the rest of her life, she would remember how he looked in this moment—tender, loving, passionate, and possessive all at once.

Then something magical happened, bright joy spearing through the darkness of her grief. She hadn't forgotten her father, and she never would. But her grief was now tempered by love and desire, a tempestuous need to affirm everything she and Pagan were together. And yes, a need to affirm life in all its joy and pain and renewal. Tears brimmed in her eyes again, brought by a wild tide of emotion that she was too small to contain. "Oh, Pagan!" she murmured.

Leaning forward, he kissed the curve of her cheek and tasted salt tears. He wanted her so badly he shook with it, but he restrained his need with iron will. This was not the time; she needed gentleness now. He kissed her brow, her temple, then, feeling her shiver, pulled back so that he could look at her. God, she was forlorn and lovely and vulnerable all at once, and he would give his soul to see her happy again.

"This will pass," he murmured, his hands stroking over the slim, straight line of her back. "Time will blunt the worst of the pain."

Laying her palms upon the hard plane of his chest, she tilted her head back to look at him. "I'm not only crying for Father . . . Well, I am, and it hurts terribly, but I'm also crying because . . . because . . ." She broke down completely then, the tears flowing in a hot cascade down her cheeks. Pagan's hands tightened upon her, and she saw concern flaring in his eyes.

She loved him to distraction for it, but just now he was beginning to look as though he were ready to sweep her away to ply her with brandy and smelling-salts. "Don't worry, Pagan. I haven't gone hysterical," she said, laughing through her tears.

"No?" He wasn't sure he believed her; that laugh was decidedly unsteady. In the past month, she'd faced more travail than most people see in their lifetimes. And now, after losing her father so suddenly and tragically, she might very well be treading the edge of hysteria. "Why don't you lie down for a while? You're exhausted—"

"Don't you want to kiss me some more?"

He closed his eyes. "Don't tempt me. I'm being noble."

"I don't want you to be noble," she said, reaching up to twine her hands in his thick, dark hair. "I want to love and be loved. I want to forget all the ugliness and death in your arms. I want to *live!*"

Nobility be damned, Pagan thought, driven beyond restraint by her demand. With a groan, he pulled her close, fitting her to him as though he wanted to pull her right into his heart. Their lips met and clung, sighed and shifted, seeking greater contact, greater warmth.

"Are you sure?" he whispered into her open mouth, driven by one last, chivalric impulse.

"I've never been more sure of anything in my life." A heavy, burning ache settled into the core of her, and she welcomed it, for it was life, sweet and hot and reckless. Her father had known how to embrace life to its fullest, and she was certain to the depths of her soul that he would approve of her actions. She could almost hear his hearty laugh in the recesses of her mind. *He* would not have hesitated. Neither would she.

She unfastened the top few buttons of Pagan's shirt, sliding her hands inside to stroke the hard-muscled expanse of his chest. His heart beat frantically beneath her palm, echoing the thunder of her own pulse. She leaned forward to press her open mouth to his skin, reveling in his taste and scent and heat.

"You're going to drive me crazy," he said hoarsely.

She paused to look up at him. "No, not crazy, Pagan. It's the world that's mad, not this. Never this. Love is the only thing that makes sense."

"Ah, love," he murmured, claiming her lips again. Fiercely, possessively, driving deep into her sweet warmth. She closed her mouth, sucking his tongue deeper, and he felt a jolt of heat down to his toes.

Rianne arched as his hands moved along her spine to her buttocks, cupping them and pulling her into the cradle of his thighs. He was powerfully aroused, his manhood hard between them. She pressed closer, wanting more, wanting to drown herself in the heat of his passion, the glory of his love.

Without breaking the contact of their mouths, he unfastened her blouse and chemise and pulled them open, exposing her breasts to the cool air. She shivered, her nipples tightening in anticipation as he slid to his knees in front of her.

"God, it's been so long," he said, skimming the rosy peaks of her breasts with his fingertips. He did it again, loving the way she trembled and the way her eyes half-closed with reaction.

"It's been too long," she whispered, running her hands through his hair and down the strong column of his throat, sighing as his mouth closed around one achingly eager nipple, then the other.

With exquisite leisure, he tasted her, exploring every inch of her breasts with his mouth and tongue. But Rianne didn't want leisure. She wanted to feel his body against hers, in hers. She wanted to forget the past and present, and cling to the future promised by his kisses. With a single, sharp motion, she pulled his shirt down his arms, sending buttons bouncing across the rug.

"Impatient?" he asked, his eyebrows going up as she tossed the ruined garment away.

"It feels like years since you touched me, since I touched you," she whispered, her voice trembling. "I can't wait, Pagan. Please, don't make me wait."

Still holding his gaze, she slid down so that she was kneeling between his legs, her bare breasts all but brushing his chest. And then she unbuttoned his trousers and spread them open, freeing his straining manhood. She took him in her hands, reveling in his strength, exploring the different textures of his man's body.

"Ah, no!" he rasped, capturing her hands and putting them behind her back. That forced her breasts upward, and he took full advantage.

She cried out in exquisite torment as he suckled her, tugging gently on the taut peaks, then soothing them with his tongue. When he released her hands, she sank them into the dark thickness of his hair, unable to do anything but hold him close.

Suddenly the world tilted as he bore her down to the rug. He came down on top of her, parting her legs with his, and even through the layers of clothing she could feel his heat and urgency. And then he kissed her, his mouth possessive, demanding.

"I wanted this to last," he growled. "But you're just too beautiful, and I love you too much. I'm crazy from wanting you."

In answer, she ran her hands down his back and over the hard swell of his buttocks to his thighs, seeking the source of heat. He surged against her, a groan rumbling deep in his chest. Lifting his hips, he reached between them to unfasten her drawers and slide them down.

Pagan's chest rose and fell with his ragged breathing. She was so sweet, so sumptuously aroused, that it took an effort of will not to bury himself in her. But he wanted to savor this joining to the fullest, for this time it was love for them both. Smiling down at her tenderly, he stroked his fingertips over her swollen woman's flesh. Finding her slick and ready, he slid one finger into her sweet, incredibly hot depths, then two.

"Oh!" Rianne gasped, staring up at him wide-eyed, surprised even now at the depth of the passion she felt.

"Yes," he said. "Open your mouth, love."

She obeyed mindlessly. Then he leaned down to kiss her, his tongue darting against hers to match the sensual rhythm of his fingers. The sensation was utterly voluptuous, almost too delightful to bear.

"Now," she murmured against his mouth.

"Now," he agreed.

They were in complete unison now, two people with one mind, one goal. She cried out as he came into her, all that heat and hardness pressing deep into her softness, and lifted her knees to take him even deeper.

Holding himself over her on braced arms, he watched her face as he began to move. She was close, very close to climax, and he wanted to watch it happen. His eyes narrowed to slits as he ignored the clamoring of his own body to focus totally on her. Rianne—his love, the woman he was going to love for the rest of his life. Then she moaned, tiny, breathless cries that excited him immeasurably. He saw her lips part, her eyelids flutter, felt her hands move frantically on his back.

"Let it come," he commanded.

She cried out. And then he felt her tighten around him, her hot, velvet depths contracting around him in convulsive waves. He savored it, savored her, his body shaking with the reflected echoes of her pleasure.

"Pagan," she whispered. "Pagan."

"I love you," he said. "I will love you forever."

Feeling him begin to leave her, Rianne tried to hold him. "Not yet," she pleaded. "Oh, not yet."

"Shhhh," he soothed, holding her against his chest as he shifted onto his back.

"Oh," she said, understanding. "I was afraid you were going to be noble again."

"I've given up being noble," he said. "Now I'm just a man in love, holding a beautiful, passionate woman in my arms. The woman who will be my wife."

"Your wife," she murmured. "Then I can expect this sort of attention on a regular basis?"

"Every night," he said, shifting her so that she was straddling his lean hips. "All night."

"Mmmm." Rianne was swiftly losing track of the conversation, delightful that it was. But his erection was trapped between their bodies, and she could feel him, hot and hard, against the tender flesh of her core. She was caught by reawakened need, a violent desire to possess and be possessed.

Spreading her hands out over his chest, she sat up and moved her hips, sliding along the length of him. And back again. His face tautened, and tiny beads of sweat popped out upon his brow. She ran her thumbs over his nipples and he gasped, his back arching in response.

"Do you belong to me?" she murmured. It was the question he had asked her so many times before.

"Yes," he rasped. "Sweet siren, from the moment I first saw you, my heart was no longer mine, but yours. Now I offer you the rest; my body, my soul, my name. Do you want them?"

"Oh, yes." Smiling, she moved again, sliding along his throbbing shaft with tantalizing slowness. "I want them."

Her breath went out in a long sigh as he grasped her hips in his hands, lifted her, then lowered her, impaling her gently, completely.

For a moment he held her there, letting her savor the feel of the hardness inside her, and then he began to move. Deeply, strongly, delving that last, delicious inch. He had never felt sensations so intense, so incredibly erotic, than what he was experiencing now. Love lifted sensuality to a higher level, making it sweeter, hotter, more urgent than he would have believed possible. What a fool he had been to think that love was for fools, a weakness he couldn't afford!

Rianne closed her eyes as he caressed her breasts, stroking their fullness, lifting them, tugging gently at the passion-engorged peaks.

"Tell me you love me," he said hoarsely.

She opened her eyes. His face was flushed with long-withheld need, his eyes pools of crystalline flame. It was raw, this need in him, primitive, compelling, powerful enough to bring this strong man to the edge of control. Suddenly she wanted to push him over that edge, to know there were no limits between them, no boundaries she couldn't cross.

"I love you," she said, sliding slowly, exquisitely up the length of his shaft, pausing for a heart-stopping moment, then sliding back down.

With a muttered exclamation, Pagan caught her to him, reversing their positions so that she was beneath him. It was too much; he was burning with desire, shaking with need and long-restrained frustration. When she wrapped her legs around his hips, he lost control completely, burying his face against the fragrant skin of her throat and thrusting into her with scorching abandon. She panted his name and met him thrust for thrust, gasp for gasp. He plunged deeper, harder, driving them both into a frenzy of passion.

They rode the spiral together, bodies straining, hearts beating in unison. Rianne cried out, arching into him as tremendous waves of fulfillment crashed through her. It was incredible, stunning, and she felt as though she were falling off a cliff to oblivion. But Pagan's arms anchored her, holding her safe. He was lifeline, her love, and she clung to him while a firestorm of pleasure shook the foundations of her being.

"Oh, God, Rianne!" Pagan groaned, his hands gripping her hips as he poured himself into her still-quivering depths.

She held him tightly, savoring his weight, the slick heat of his skin, the way his back heaved with his deep, ragged breathing. After a time, he rolled over onto his back, taking her with him. The fire crackled lazily behind her, warming her back and sending shadows dancing across the sharp-cut planes of his face. But even the flames were no hotter than her love for him, and the future was brighter than gold could ever be. Pagan had pulled her from the depths, given her love and joy in the midst of her blackest grief.

"We didn't even take our clothes off," she murmured.

"Good. That leaves us something to do later." Smiling, he took the long braid of her hair and stroked it down his cheek. A faint trace of lilac clung to it. He breathed the delicate perfume, preferring the clean, simple scent to the most expensive of French concoctions, for this was Rianne. "Do you want to move to the bed?" he asked.

She shrugged. "I'm happy wherever you are."

"Let's enjoy the fire, then." Pulling her close, he shifted into a more comfortable position.

Rianne smiled. He looked as sleepy and sated as a well-fed tiger. She watched his eyes drift closed, and the sight of his black eyelashes fanning along his cheekbones made her heart pound against her ribs. He was hers, finally and completely, pledged in the oldest and most binding of ways.

"You rescued me," she murmured, tracing the shape of his mouth with her fingertip. "I was so sure that everything was bleak and cold, and then you came and gave me my hope back. Thank you, Pagan."

Laying her cheek on his chest, she closed her eyes. His heartbeat, slow and strong, lulled her, and a moment later she drifted into the smooth, dark sea of slumber.

It seemed but an instant later when a loud knock awakened her. There was an urgency to the noise that jolted her upright before her sleep-befuddled brain knew what it was.

Instantly alert, Pagan surged to his feet and reached for his trousers. "Who is it?" he called.

"Pagan, it's me, Marie! Come quick!"

"Something's wrong," he said. "Hurry, Rianne."

Hastily, she pulled her clothing to rights and followed him toward the door. A glance in the mirror told her she looked like she'd been . . . doing exactly what she had been doing.

As soon as she was decent, Pagan flung the door open. Marie wasn't alone, however; Kate and Sylvia were with her. Rianne flushed painfully at the sight of

Pagan's wife. Sylvia stared back at her with such burning hatred in her eyes that it was a wonder the woman didn't burst into flames right there.

"What's the matter, Marie?" Pagan asked, ignoring Sylvia completely.

"I . . ." Marie hesitated, fairly wringing her hands in agitation. Then she continued in a rush. "Tessa's sick. Now, don't go gettin' all upset, she's —"

"Is it typhoid?" Pagan asked, his voice deadly quiet, deadly calm.

Marie nodded. "I jest don't know how it happened. We been so careful, keepin' her away from the sickroom and all —"

"No. Oh, no!" Rianne gasped, her heart pounding in terror. "Not Tessa!"

She reached out to comfort Pagan, but he was already gone.

Chapter Twenty-nine

"Pagan!" Rianne cried again.

There was no sign of him, but she knew where he had gone. She brushed past Sylvia and ran down the hall to Tessa's room.

She found Pagan standing beside the child's narrow bed. His back was to her, but she could see Tessa's face. She was asleep, looking as pale and fragile as a porcelain doll. Then Pagan reached out and brushed a lock of hair back from the child's forehead.

"Pagan," Rianne whispered.

He looked over his shoulder at her, his face set in grim, granite lines. His eyes held such terrible pain, such searing, helpless anger that Rianne nearly cried out. But this was his time of need, and she had to be strong for him. Just as he had helped her bear her father's death, so would she help him during Tessa's illness.

With the outward calm she had learned so well in the past few weeks, she went to the bed and laid the back of her hand against Tessa's cheek. The child was in the grip of a raging fever, her small body a furnace that was burning her strength away. Her skin was taut and dry, the fine, blue veins clearly visible in her temples and eyelids. Terror, thick and choking, rose in Rianne's throat.

With an experienced nurse's efficiency, she checked

the supplies Marie had placed on the bedside table. There was a pitcher of water so cold that condensation had pooled upon the table beneath it, a tin cup, a basin of carbolic solution and a stack of clean cloths. Little enough with which to fight for a life. Then she noticed a bowl on the floor beside the bed. As she bent to pick it up, Pagan spoke, his voice so full of pain that it jerked her upright.

"She's so small," he said. "And so sick."

Rianne put her hand on his arm. "She'll fight, Pagan. After all, she has a great deal of her father in her."

He covered her hand with his, drawing comfort from her. Then a high-pitched laugh trilled behind them, bringing them both around to face the doorway. Sylvia stood there, looking lovely and hateful, her green eyes snapping with anger.

"Isn't this a touching little scene?" she cooed, her tone scathing.

"What do you want?" Pagan growled.

"Well, it's obvious what *you* want." Sylvia lifted her lip in a sneer that drained the beauty from her face. "Are you planning to bed your whore right here in the room with your daughter?"

Rianne gasped, astounded that even Sylvia could utter such a crudeness of the remark. She couldn't have replied if she'd known how to. Then Pagan strode toward the blonde woman, rage showing in every taut line of his body. Alarm replaced Rianne's shock, and she ran forward to block his path. He didn't even slow, merely grasped her by the waist and lifted her aside, continuing on his way until he was standing directly in front of Sylvia.

"Get out," he said.

"I have every right to be here," she retorted. "If anyone should leave, it's that woman." Lifting her arm dramatically, she pointed at Rianne. *"She* is the intruder here."

Rianne edged toward the door, desperate to avert trouble. "Perhaps it would be better if I left—"

"No," Pagan growled, glaring at her over his shoulder.

That look froze Rianne in place. She had never seen him so angry, or so determined, and she simply did not have the courage to challenge him. Perhaps courage was not the right word—it would be utter foolishness to defy him now.

Satisfied that Rianne wasn't going anywhere, Pagan returned his attention to Sylvia. Damn her for provoking this scene, he thought. Tessa should be the only thing on anyone's mind.

"Papa!" Tessa's voice was weak, hardly audible, yet it instantly pulled him from his anger.

Completely forgetting Sylvia, he turned and strode to the bed to take the child's tiny hand in his. "Hello, sweetheart," he murmured. "How are you feeling?"

"My head hurts. And I feel so hot . . ." Tessa broke off to lick her lips. "I'm thirsty."

Rianne hurried to the bedside table and poured a few ounces of water into the cup. Pagan lifted Tessa enough so that she could drink. The child was shaking so badly with fever that her teeth chattered loudly on the rim of the cup as she drank. After only a few sips, she closed her eyes and turned her face away.

"She has to drink more," Pagan said, worry etching deep grooves at the sides of his mouth.

Rianne dipped the corner of a cloth into the water and laved the child's parched lips. Poor Tessa. And poor Pagan, forced to watch his child suffer. "Patience," she said. "She'll drink. We'll get it down her a little at a time. Every few minutes, if we have to."

"We?" Sylvia demanded, striding around to the other

side of the bed. Arms akimbo, she faced Pagan and Rianne across the expanse of counterpane. "I don't want that woman anywhere near my daughter."

Gently, Pagan lowered Tessa to the pillow, then straightened slowly. "By God, Sylvia, if you were a man—"

"If I were a man, I wouldn't have been stuck taking care of the kid . . ." She broke off, evidently realizing how that sounded.

"Such a solicitous mother," Pagan said with biting sarcasm. He wanted to say a great deal more, but Tessa was looking from him to Sylvia and back again, her little brow furrowed with concern. Just that one comment of Sylvia's was cruel enough; the child didn't need to observe her parents' bitterness firsthand.

But Sylvia had no such scruples. "Who are you to cast stones?" she demanded. "After all, you were busy enjoying yourself with your—"

"Don't say it, not if you value your hide." Pagan's voice was intense and deadly. If he heard the word 'whore' out of that woman's mouth one more time, he wasn't sure he could control his temper. "Rianne is worth ten of you, and if I hear you call her anything but Miss Kierney, I'll make you regret it."

A flush stained Sylvia's cheeks, and Rianne knew that Pagan had scored. "You're a cocky bastard," the blonde woman hissed. "One day, someone's going to take you down."

Pagan's jaw tightened, but he didn't reply. Rianne was proud of his restraint. This was neither the time nor the place for this discussion, and he knew it as well as she. Just now, only Tessa was important.

Rianne looked down, away from his glittering, angry eyes, and her gaze settled on the bowl she'd noticed earlier. Bending, she picked it up, grimacing at the strong odor of brandy that clung to it.

Sylvia's mouth opened and closed, but Rianne could hear nothing but the sudden thunder of her own pulse. The bowl fell from her suddenly nerveless hands. *Brandy,* she thought. And Tessa being tended by Sylvia, who had taken great pains not to learn anything about nursing typhoid fever.

"Dear God!" Rianne cried. Rushing around the bed, she grabbed Sylvia by the shoulders and spun her around. "What did you give her, Sylvia?"

"It's none of your business!"

"What did you give her?" With a strength she wouldn't have believed possible, Rianne shook the bigger woman hard enough to bring her hair tumbling down.

Sylvia's eyes widened. "Why, ah, some brandy, that's all."

"Not in a bowl," Rianne snapped. "What else?"

"I only gave her some bread soaked in brandy," Sylvia said.

"Bread!" Rianne's gaze went to Pagan, whose eyes mirrored her own stabbing fear.

"Well, so what?" Sylvia retorted. "My mother always used to give us bread and brandy when we were ill."

Rianne let Sylvia go, unable to touch the woman even for a moment. The fool, the utter fool! she thought. And it was Tessa who was going to pay the price for her mother's foolishness. "The greatest risk of typhoid fever is that it creates ulcers in the intestines, Sylvia. Give a patient solid food, and it can perforate the organ itself."

"Surely just a little—"

Tessa moaned sharply. "Papa?"

With a muttered exclamation, Pagan slid his hand beneath her head. "I'm here, sweetheart. Does something hurt?"

Sylvia sat down on the bed beside her, adroitly cutting off Rianne's access to the child. "Come to Mama, baby," she crooned. "Mama will take care of you."

Tessa began to cry. "My stomach. Oh, my stomach!"

Suddenly she lurched up to a sitting position, startling them all, and vomited into Sylvia's silk-clad lap. With a scream that rattled the glass in the window, Sylvia leaped to her feet.

"Oh!" she shrieked, staring down at her dripping gown. "Oh, oh, oh! The disgusting little beast! Somebody do something!"

Pagan looked across the bed at Rianne. She was already busy comforting Tessa, washing the child's face with a wet cloth and urging her to drink just a bit more water. But he could see her hands shaking as she worked, and knew she was as angry as he was.

He strode around the bed toward Sylvia, who was still howling like a banshee. Although he heard Rianne call out, urging restraint, he ignored her. Damn restraint. Damn being civilized, and damn Sylvia for being a selfish, grasping, unpleasant woman!

Sylvia stopped in mid-shriek, her eyes widening as he neared. She started yelling again, however, when he scooped her into his arms and carried her from the room. Resisting the impulse to chuck her straight down the stairs, he dumped her into a pile of dirty laundry that lay in the hallway nearby.

"You bastard!" she screeched. "I'm going right back in there!"

"If I were you," he drawled, "I'd see about washing myself. Typhoid is spread through contaminated . . . discharges."

With a gasp, she scrambled up from the floor. A moment later she disappeared downstairs, and he could hear her shouting for hot water. Pagan smiled grimly. Always thinking of herself, was Sylvia. He ground his teeth together, remembering how she'd called a sick child a 'disgusting little beast'. And she'd called herself Tessa's mother.

Her perfume lingered, an overly sweet smell of corruption. He wiped his hands on his pants, as though touching her had soiled his skin, then went back to Tessa's room. He paused in the doorway, watching Rianne. She was singing softly as she tended Tessa, a sweet lullaby that made his very soul ache. Her voice coiled through the room like smooth, rich velvet, dark as the night, yet warm as the fire of the midnight sun.

His gaze focused on her hands. They were red and chapped, work-worn and blistered—and infinitely gentle as she lifted Tessa and slipped a clean nightgown over her head, then tucked her back beneath the covers. Those hands had comforted many sufferers, tended them, fought for them. And now, he realized with sudden clarity, those small, capable hands held the threads of his daughter's life.

As he saw Rianne bend to press her lips to Tessa's forehead, Pagan was gripped by determination so fierce, so powerful that he trembled with the force of it. These two beings were more precious to him than anything on this earth.

If he had to stare Death in the eye, if he had to wrestle the Devil himself, he would hold them. Both of them.

Sylvia stood in her chemise and petticoat, trying futilely to work lye soap into a lather in her washbasin. As she struggled, she cursed Marie for only allowing her to take a single bucket of hot water, cursing Pagan for humiliating her, and most of all, cursing Rianne Kierney.

"She's ruined everything!" Sylvia muttered. "If she hadn't been here Pagan would never have turned from me!"

409

Shuddering with distaste, she began to scrub her arms with the harsh lye soap. Horrible stuff, horrible. It was sure to dry her skin terribly. When she had mentioned that concern to that odious, ill-bred whore in the kitchen, the woman had suggested she smear herself with lard afterward.

"They're all against me." Sylvia sniffled. Tears began to run down her face, but she didn't dare reach up and wipe them away with her soapy hands. Nothing on this earth was going to get her to put that awful soap upon her face!

There was a knock on the door. It was a soft, stealthy sound, and her heart began to pound. Grabbing a nearby towel, she dried her arms and tiptoed to the door.

"Who is it?"

"Open the damned door before someone sees me," Lowell Mason growled.

"Lowell?" She opened the door a crack. "What are you doing here? Are you mad?"

He pushed the door wider and slipped into the room. She turned the key in the lock, then whirled to face him.

"If Pagan finds you here, he'll kill you," she hissed.

Mason shrugged. "I won't be long. I just came to tell you that I heard the news."

"What news?"

"That Pagan's going to marry the Kierney girl."

Her eyes narrowed. "Where did you hear that?"

"Ah, that's a tender spot, eh?" Chuckling, he moved around the room, lifting her silver-handled brushes from the bureau, fingering the porcelain figurines she'd brought with her, ruffling through the dresses that filled the armoire. "You don't travel light, that's for sure," he said.

"What do you want, Lowell?"

410

"Pagan is storing nearly a hundred thousand dollars in gold somewhere in this house. Some of it is his, some belongs to other mine owners."

"A hundred . . ." She broke off, her mind churning. Perhaps she might not be able to win Pagan back, but a hundred thousand dollars would be great consolation. "Where is it?"

"If I knew that, I wouldn't be here."

"Ah. So you expect me to find it for you." She sauntered to the mirror and began to brush her hair.

"Fifty-fifty split."

"But if I find it," she murmured, moving her head from side to side to admire the way the lamplight was reflected in her hair, "why should I share it with you?"

"Because I know you killed Alastair Kierney."

Shock held her immobile. She felt as though a great, dark chasm had opened up beneath her feet, and she was teetering at the edge, ready to fall in. To hide her panic, she began brushing her hair again. This time, however, she wasn't admiring her own reflection; she was watching Mason's, her gaze flicking from his cold, obsidian eyes to the smile that had more of ownership than humor in it.

A memory swam through her mind unbidden, the vivid picture of Mason's whore sitting on his lap, her naked breasts being fondled in front of a crowded room of men. He'll do that to me one day, she thought . . . if she let him. Inwardly she shook her head. Never. She'd see him in Hell first.

"Why, Lowell," she said, putting as seductive a note into her voice as she could. "Surely you are mistaken. You couldn't possibly have seen me with Mr. Kierney. After leaving the Nugget, I came straight back here."

"I followed you. With my own eyes, I saw you push him in the river." He grinned. "Four Mounties rode into town today, all pretty in their nice red jackets. And

411

now we got law in Henderson City. And I'm a law-abiding fellow. If a Mountie came to me, asking about Kierney's murder, well, I'd just have to tell him what I know."

Sylvia turned, putting her hands behind her for support against the bureau. "Even if your wild story were true, it's your word against mine."

He snorted. "Do you think I was stupid enough to bring you here without finding out about you?" Grinning sardonically, he came to stand behind her, looking over her shoulder at her image in the mirror. "That young man back in Seattle—I'll call him a man, although he wasn't but fifteen—complained to the police about you. Seems you bedded him at his home when the rest of the family was out, got him drunk, and when he woke up, all his Mama's nice, expensive jewelry was gone. You *had* to leave Seattle, and I bet if anyone looked into some of the other places you've been, they might find even more interesting things about you. Somehow, I don't think the Mounties are going to believe the word of a thief."

Whirling, she tried to push him away. "You bastard."

He pinned her against the bureau with his body. "But I'm the bastard who owns you. You do what I tell you, or I'll see that you rot in prison."

With a brutally swift motion, he ripped her chemise down to her waist, baring her breasts. Sylvia looked up at him, knowing the trap had snapped shut around her. She had to do his bidding, at least for now. When his hands grasped her breasts, kneading them painfully, she didn't struggle. Survival, that was the important thing. She had bedded worse men for worse reasons.

But he would be the last. A hundred thousand dollars in gold would ensure that. "You said fifty-fifty on the gold," she said.

His breathing was beginning to quicken. "Sure. Right

down the middle, just like I said. We're partners, aren't we?" With one hand, he pulled up her petticoat and fumbled beneath to unfasten her drawers.

She knew he was lying. The instant he had the gold, he'd turn her in to the Mounties. There's nothing more vulnerable than a man with his pants down, she told herself, locking her hands behind his neck as he unbuttoned his trousers and lifted her legs up around his waist.

A moment later he rammed into her, driving her back painfully against the bureau. "Oh!" she moaned, feigning excitement.

Glancing up at his face, she realized he was watching himself in the mirror. A shudder went through her.

"You like that, eh?" he rasped. "You want it harder, eh?"

"Yes," she whispered. "Harder." *You'll pay. You'll all pay, every one of you.*

Rianne balanced a tray with one arm and opened the door of Tessa's room with the other. She found Pagan where she'd left him the night before, slumped in a chair beside the child's bed. Hoping he was asleep, she tiptoed across the room and started to set the tray down on the bedside table.

"Is it morning?" he asked.

"Yes. I was hoping you were asleep," she said, setting the tray down before turning to the bed.

Tessa's condition had worsened during the night. Her lips were dry and cracked, and there was a raspy note to her breathing that frightened Rianne. Every morning the child looked a bit more gaunt, her eyes a bit more sunken than they had the night before.

Rianne heard Pagan move to the window, and a moment later a shaft of pale morning sunlight poured into the room. Glancing at him over her shoulder, she saw only a dark silhouette against the prismatic sparkle of the icicles that hung from the eaves outside.

When he sat down in the chair again, however, she got a good look at him. Stubble covered the lean planes of his face, and his eyes were shadowed from lack of sleep. Her heart contracted with worry. In the past ten days, he hadn't left Tessa's bedside for more than a few minutes. It was as though he believed his presence would keep Death from claiming his daughter.

She opened her mouth to chide him for not getting any rest, then closed it again. How could she tell him not to worry, not to care, when his child was wasting away before his eyes? Instead, she knelt beside his chair, wordlessly laying her hand upon his shoulder.

He drew in his breath in a sharp sigh. "She's getting worse, Rianne."

"It's only natural," she said, speaking with a confidence she didn't feel. "It takes three weeks for typhoid to run its course."

With a stab of alarm, she saw that although he was looking straight at her, he had gone somewhere within the recesses of his own mind, a place where she couldn't follow. His eyes were bleak, twin crystals of glacier-ice.

"She looks just like Davey," he said.

"Your brother?"

"Yes."

The one who died.

The thought seemed to hang in the air between them, shared and yet too terrible to be spoken aloud. Rianne knew then that Pagan was reliving his own personal Hell. She couldn't reach him there; just now he dwelled in a place where there was no comfort, no surcease for pain. For his sake, she had to find a way to pull him out lest he become lost in it forever.

414

"Pagan—"

"This is my fault."

"What?" she asked, staring at him in astonishment. "Pagan, don't be ridiculous! You can't blame yourself for typhoid fever, for Heaven's sake."

"I *do* blame myself," he said. Rising to his feet, he strode to the window, putting his back to her. When he spoke again, his voice was colder than the ice that coated the inside of the glass, and sent shivers slithering down her spine. "I should have sent her away. I should have sent you both away," he said. "Then this wouldn't have happened."

She went to stand behind him. His shoulders were so wide that they all but blocked her view of the window. As always, he reminded her of a lean, male animal, possessing boundless strength and vitality. But she knew pain was tearing him up inside.

"Your reasons for not sending her away are as valid now as they were then," she said. "And I refused to go."

He nodded, acknowledging her point. But the pain didn't lessen, nor did the burden of his guilt. He gripped the windowsill until his knuckles turned white. "I promised her that I wouldn't let anyone or anything hurt her. I failed, Rianne."

"You couldn't—"

"I failed Tessa, just as I failed Davey and Ben all those years ago."

Desperation rose in her throat, sick and choking. "Pagan, there are fights that simply cannot be won."

"I can't believe that."

"But . . ." Rianne bit her lip as understanding stopped the rest of her protest. He'd been a child when his brothers had died. Thinking it was his own child's helplessness that had failed Davey and Ben, Pagan had relied on his intelligence, his courage, and his strength to keep him from being hurt again. But now it had come around full circle, and he was as powerless to help his daughter as he'd been to help his brothers.

He shuddered, a man in torment. There was the sound of splintering wood, and then the windowsill cracked beneath the pressure of his hands.

Rianne put her arms around his waist and held him, giving him what she could: her love, her caring, her compassion.

"Ah, Rianne!" He turned within the circle of her arms and clasped her to him, holding her against his chest so tightly it hurt her to breathe. But she smiled, glad that he loved her enough to let her share his pain.

Reaching up, she stroked the hard curve of his cheek. "Whatever happens, I'll be with you."

"She's my daughter." Stark frustration was in his voice.

"I love her, too. We'll fight for her together."

Some of the tenseness left his body. But not enough. She knew he had not accepted his own innocence, or his helplessness. Perhaps he never would. After a moment he pulled away and returned to the bed, as though drawn to Tessa by steel-strong springs.

"Do you think she'll make it?" he asked without looking at Rianne.

"If good care, love, and prayers are enough, no power on this earth can take her from us."

She saw his raven hair swing with the shake of his head, and sighed. Twice she reached out to him, twice she dropped her hand to her side. His torment was too great just now. Finally she said, "You'd better give her that broth before it gets cold."

He didn't answer, just stood there as though turned to stone. Tessa coughed weakly, a dry, hacking sound, and Rianne saw his shoulders hunch.

Suddenly she was looking at him through a glittering

haze of tears. He wouldn't want tears. Turning away hastily, she moved toward the door. "I'll . . . I'll go downstairs and see about getting some water to bathe her," she said.

He didn't seem to hear her. By the time she reached the doorway, she was almost running. Closing the door behind her, she dashed the wetness from her eyes with the backs of her hands and made her way down the hall.

She met Sylvia on the stairs. The blonde woman was wearing a scarlet wool dress that made her look even more curved than usual. Her mouth was a lush red curve in her pale face, echoes of the gown she wore. Rianne would rather have met Satan himself at this moment. But there was nothing that could be done but face her or flee, and she'd cut off her arm before turning tail and running from Sylvia. So she merely nodded coldly, and tried to continue on her way.

"How is Tessa?" Sylvia asked.

Rianne paused, her brows lifting in surprise. This was the first time Sylvia had shown any interest in the child. "She's very ill, you know, but she's still fighting. In a few days, the fever will peak."

"And then we'll know if she lives or dies."

It was said in such a flat, emotionless voice that Rianne was chilled. Looking deeply into Sylvia's eyes, she saw that the lack of emotion was echoed there. Pagan had been right about this woman all along. Tessa meant nothing to her mother save as a pawn to use to gain her a better life.

Rianne swallowed convulsively, appalled by the thought of Sylvia raising Tessa for nearly five years. No wonder the child had bad dreams, no wonder her natural high-spiritedness had gone into hiding. Spirit was surely not a quality Sylvia tolerated, at least in others.

With a deep sigh, Rianne took another step down-

417

ward. "I really must go. There are a great many—"

"You'd better hope she dies."

Shock rooted Rianne to the spot. "What did you say?"

"You'd better hope Tessa dies." Sylvia's upper lip lifted in a sneer. "If she lives, you'll never have Pagan."

Rianne stared at her, powerless to speak. Had Sylvia turned into a serpent before her eyes, she wouldn't have been more astonished.

"Oh, yes," Sylvia purred. "If she lives, Pagan will either have to give you up or I'll take that child away where he'll never find her again. And don't think I can't do it. A change of name, a journey by ship or rail, and he'll never see his daughter again."

"You couldn't!" Rianne whispered.

"Couldn't I? It's interesting, isn't it, Miss Kierney, that a strong, canny man like Pagan can be brought to heel by so tiny a being as a child. Now, how do you think he would feel if he learned that his daughter had been placed in an orphanage?"

Horror weakened Rianne's legs, and she put her hand on the wall for support. Somehow, Sylvia had learned about Pagan's past. And unerringly, she had hit on the thing that would tear the very heart from him. Never, never had Rianne ever come across a human being with more cruelty or miserliness of spirit.

Sylvia laughed. "Think about the sort of abuse a *girl* would endure in a place like that. Pagan will. And what do you think your lives will be like after I tell him his daughter was the price he paid for keeping you?"

The words drove Rianne backward, her hand clutching her throat. "Tessa is your own daughter!"

Sylvia followed, her face twisted with hate. "Pagan will hate you. Oh, not right away, but the knowledge of what you cost him will eat at him until he does. He'll look across the dinner table at you and see only that his daughter is suffering because of you."

Unable to bear it a moment longer, Rianne turned and fled down the hall to her room, pursued by the sound of shrill, spiteful laughter. Once inside, she locked the door, then stood with her back against the wood panel.

Slowly, her breathing returned to normal. Pushing herself away from the door, she went to look in the mirror. Her eyes were haunted, shadowed by what she had learned this day.

'You'd better hope Tessa dies', Sylvia had said. The thought was so ugly, so monstrously evil, that Rianne's whole being rejected it. And the worst thing of all was that there was a twisted sort of truth about it; the knowledge that his daughter was suffering in an orphanage, neglected, perhaps even abused, as he had been, would tear Pagan apart.

But Rianne knew he wouldn't blame her, and he wouldn't hate her. He would blame himself. He would hate himself. And he would withdraw into that bleak place deep inside where no one could follow.

One thing was certain: she couldn't — wouldn't — have him at the cost of his child's life. She would fight for Tessa with every bit of skill she possessed, and God willing, that child would live.

"And afterward?" she murmured, leaning forward to peer at her reflection. "Afterward . . . well, you'll just have to let your love for him be your guide."

It was another leap of faith, perhaps the greatest one of all. She had to trust love to conquer hate and greed and the corruption of a woman who would destroy her own daughter to strike a blow at Pagan.

Will it be enough? her reflection seemed to ask.

"It has to be," she said. "It's all I've got."

Chapter Thirty

Rianne stood at the window of Tessa's room, looking down at a landscape that was etched in stark black and white. Mostly white, she reflected. Winter was firmly entrenched now; the air was so cold that smoke hung low over the rooftops, people scurried before the wind like great fallen leaves, and the Yukon River, completely frozen now, was a broad platinum ribbon stretching to the horizon. The sun shone off the snow in a scintillant display of light; glorious, but capable of blinding the unwary. Nature's twin aspects: beauty and cruelty, bounty and privation.

She glanced over her shoulder at Tessa. The child was resting, her hand secure in Pagan's solicitous grasp. He hadn't left her side for more than a few minutes, and had even brought a cot in so that he could sleep in the room. But despite his love, despite all Rianne's hard-won skill at nursing typhoid, the child was growing steadily worse.

Pagan looked up, his eyes bleak, his face grim with worry. "She's burning up."

Rianne turned. With swift steps that didn't reflect her despair, she hurried to him and put her hand on his shoulder. "If my guess is right, the crisis will come tonight."

Tonight, Pagan thought. Tonight he would know if he would keep his daughter, or lose her. He had watched

Tessa slip away, inch by inch, and he had been helpless to stop it. He had used his mind, heart, and soul to try to hold her, as though wishing might work where everything else failed. But she had merely slid a bit further away.

Now she was facing the end—life or death in a few short hours, and he was powerless to affect the outcome. He reached up and covered Rianne's hand with his, drawing comfort and strength from the contact. "What do you think?" he asked.

Will she live or die? Rianne closed her eyes. She really did not know. Tessa had clung to life tenaciously, fighting where many strong men had given up. *Warrior-spirit. Just like her father.* But there were limits as to what the spirit could force the flesh to do.

Pagan shifted his grip to her wrist, willing her answer. "Tell me."

"I don't know," she whispered. "I truly don't know. It's in God's hands now."

With a harsh sigh, he let her go. "Then we are truly on our own."

"You don't believe that any more than I do."

"Then tell me why my brothers died. Tell me why your father died. And tell me why my daughter has been stricken down."

Gently, she stroked the hard, stubbled line of his cheek. "Tell me why the storm wind blows, or the wolf hunts the deer, or why the snow falls."

"You mean there are no answers."

"Yes. There's only faith."

He shook his head, for that was no answer, either. But he knew he wanted the impossible; he wanted to meet Death face-to-face, to fight Him for his daughter's life. Anything but to sit here, helpless, and watch the life ebb from her. "I lost my faith years ago, Rianne. When Davey and Ben died in my arms, I swore I'd have no faith in anything but my own right arm."

Rianne couldn't accept that, not after he had drawn her from the depths of grief. "You said you loved me," she murmured. "Do you?"

"God, yes." His eyes were opalescent with emotion, raw, naked, fierce. "If nothing else makes sense in this damned foul world, *that* does."

"Then you *do* have faith, for love can't exist without it." Although she managed to keep her voice calm, her heart was racing. The declaration hit her like some elemental force, primal and powerful. His love shone like a beacon through the dark mists of worry and despair.

There was a knock at the door, and Rianne was jerked back to reality. But that moment would stay with her for the rest of her life: the look on his face when he'd told her he loved her, the utter surety in his voice and the affirmation in his eyes.

After giving his shoulder a squeeze, she went to answer the door. Marie stood in the hallway outside, flanked by Francois Gruillot and a man Rianne didn't know.

"This is Bert McManus, Elias' brother," Marie said. "They got business with Pagan. And now I got to git back to my work." With that, she turned and strode down the hall toward the stairs.

For a moment, Rianne stared at the two men in bewilderment. And then she remembered poor Elias McManus, who had been the first to be taken by typhoid. It seemed like several lifetimes ago. No, she amended grimly, it had been many *lives* ago.

She glanced at Pagan over her shoulder, but he didn't seem to be aware the rest of them existed. His attention was focused totally on his daughter as though he were willing every breath she took.

"I know you're busy," McManus said. "I wouldn't have bothered you a-tall, but Francois here told me that

Pagan Roark stored some of my brother's gold. I'd like to git it, if you don't mind."

"Oh . . . I . . ."

"We would not have come now," Francois said. "But you see, I am selling my claim to Bert."

"You're selling your claim?" Rianne came further out into the hall. "Whatever for, Francois?"

"This digging in the dirt . . ." With an expansive shrug, the Frenchman spread his hands wide. "It is not for me. I sell my claim to Bert, I have more money than I ever thought to see. And then I will have my freedom back."

"Will you leave?" she asked, dreading the prospect. She had come to value this great, gentle man who had become almost as a brother to her.

"When the stampede begins this summer, perhaps," he said. "But for now, I think I will go into the mountains for a time and hunt the moose. The snow, the clean air—they are good for the soul."

So simple, Rianne thought. So utterly straight and clear and true. *And people call him mad!* She put her hand on his arm. "I think you've made the right decision, Francois. I'll go speak to Pagan about the gold."

Returning to the bed, she explained the situation to Pagan. His expression didn't change, and for a moment she thought he hadn't heard her. Then he pulled a ring of keys from his pocket and handed it to her.

"You know the seaman's trunk in my room?" he asked. When she nodded, he said, "The gold is in there. Each sack has been tallied and marked with each man's initials, and there's a paper on top where Elias signed for the amount. Have Bert sign that he received it."

"Wouldn't you rather go yourself?" she asked.

He shook his head, not letting go of Tessa's hand for a moment. Rianne took the keys from him. She let her fingers linger in his, and he clasped them briefly before returning his attention to his daughter.

Rianne led the two men to Pagan's room, where she unlocked the trunk and lifted the lid. A sigh escaped her at the sight of the neatly stacked doeskin bags that filled it. Gold. A fortune in buttery metal. She looked up at Bert McManus and saw the hunger in his eyes. Gold. Men had killed for it and died for it, had thrown away their homes and families and futures for the hope of finding it. And it was worthless. If it couldn't purchase one small child's life, then what good was it?

"Why don't you count it out, Mr. McManus?" she said. "It's your gold."

"Thankee kindly, ma'am." He and Francois set to work, and in a few minutes had a pile of long, narrow sacks stacked up on the floor beside the trunk. McManus licked the tip of the pencil and laboriously scrawled his name below his brother's on Pagan's tally.

"Thirty thousand dollars," Francois said, hefting one of the sacks in his hand. "Not bad for two months' work."

"Yeah," McManus said. "Jest sign over that claim and it's all yourn."

The claim was duly transferred, with Rianne acting as witness. Then McManus slapped his hat back on, waved a farewell, and strode out of the room, new owner of a gold mine.

"And may it give you all you wish," Rianne said as she shut the trunk.

Francois stood for a moment, turning his cap around and around in his huge hands. "The little girl, she is very bad, no?"

"Yes," Rianne said. Volumes of heartache were contained in that one word. It was as though all the weeks of fear and death and helplessness had all come into focus tonight. All those men who had died had at least

424

lived. Good or bad, they'd had that much. But Tessa's life had barely begun.

"I will stay in town two, three more days. You and Pagan need a friend, you will call Francois?"

His kindness brought the hot sting of tears to her eyes. "Oh, yes," she said. "Thank you."

"Bien." Bending, he put the gold back into the chest.

"You aren't taking it?" Rianne asked.

"Non. I find that the looking for it is much more enjoyable than the having of it. And it is no good for hunting the moose, Songbird. You understand?"

"Yes," she whispered, her throat tight with emotion. "I understand."

She reached out, and he took her hand in his. With a courtly gesture, he raised it to his lips.

"I must grow my beard back," he said. "It is dam' cold in the mountains without the beard. *Adieu,* lovely Rianne." Whistling the "Marseillaise" under his breath, he strode out of the room.

Rianne closed the trunk and locked it, feeling rejuvenated in mind and spirit by her brief encounter with Francois. If lack of gold-hunger made a man mad, then she, too, was mad, and so was Pagan. The three of them seemed to be a half-turn from everyone else in this town; Francois yearned for the clean solitude of the mountains, Pagan wanted his daughter's life, and she . . . She only wanted the impossible. She wanted to marry Pagan, raise Tessa, and have a dozen more children with black hair and ice-crystal eyes.

With a sad shake of her head, she started back to Tessa's room. As she stepped out into the hallway, she saw Sylvia walking rapidly away from her.

"Wait!" she called, hurrying after the blonde woman. "Please, won't you come and see Tessa?"

Sylvia glanced over her shoulder, annoyance brimming in her green eyes. Then she went into her room,

425

closing the door with a finality that took Rianne's breath away.

She wanted to walk away. For her own sake, she would have. But Tessa was terribly ill, perhaps dying, and if having her mother nearby would help, Rianne was willing to swallow her pride and beg this hardhearted woman for mercy.

"Sylvia," she called through the door. "Please. Tessa needs to hear her mother's voice—"

"Go to hell."

Frustrated, Rianne grasped the doorknob and rattled it, wishing she could rattle some compassion into Sylvia so easily. "For Tessa's sake, not for mine!"

"Tessa," said Sylvia, slowly and very distinctly, "can go to hell, too."

Rianne let go of the doorknob as though it had burned her. Sylvia's answer should have angered her, but all she felt was sadness. "I feel sorry for you," she whispered, turning away.

The encounter left her feeling weighted down in mind and body. It was incomprehensible to her how a woman could be so uncaring toward her own child. How horrible it must be to be bound by such a wasteland of a soul!

Pagan appeared in the open doorway of Tessa's room. Every line of his body screamed urgency, and the sight of it got Rianne's feet moving before her mind fully reacted. She started toward him at a walk. He saw her then, and his eyes blazed at her like twin blue coals. *Tessa!* Rianne's feet moved faster and faster, until she was running.

"Hurry!" Pagan called.

When she was near enough, she reached out to him, and he took her hand and pulled her into the room. Tessa was sitting up in bed, her eyes open, but focused on nothing.

"Papa!" she cried, the rasp of her breathing loud in the room. "Don't send me away!"

"I won't," Pagan said, gathering her into his arms with a gentleness that brought a lump into Rianne's throat. "I'll keep you with me forever, sweetheart."

"I didn't mean it!" the child wailed. "Please don't punish me, please!"

"No one's going to punish you, Tessa," he said. "You can—"

"No! It's dark in there. Please, Mama, I'm afraid! Don't put me in there."

"Where did she make you go?" Pagan demanded. "What did she do to you?"

Tessa began to cry, her gaunt little body shaking with the force of her sobs. Pagan looked at Rianne, his eyes hard, as bleak as death.

Rianne trembled, knowing what he was thinking, terrified of what he might do. Putting her hand on his shoulder, she said, "Now is not the time. Tessa needs you."

Letting his breath out in a harsh sigh, he nodded. Gently, he eased Tessa back onto the pillows. "Rest, sweetheart. I won't leave you. Rest, and get better."

But she only slipped further into delirium, and there was nothing Rianne could do but bathe her in lukewarm water to try to control the fever. Over and over again she performed this one small kindness for the child, until she lost all track of time. Finally, Pagan took the cloth from her.

"Go lie down," he said. "You're exhausted."

"You're more exhausted than I am."

"I can't leave her, Rianne. Even for a moment." He brushed the black wing of his hair away from his forehead with the back of his hand. "If I close my eyes, I'm afraid I'll lose her."

427

Rianne shook her head. "Whatever happens, I'll be with you."

As night fell, the shadows lengthened in the room. They looked like long, grasping fingers reaching toward the bed.

"I can't see! Papa, I'm afraid!" Tessa moaned, flailing her arms as though to ward off the encroaching darkness. "Help me, help me!"

Pagan went to his knees beside the bed and slipped his arms around her. "I'm here, sweetheart. You don't have to be afraid."

Although he held her gently, inwardly Pagan was raging. Raging against Fate and against his own helplessness. If he could have cut his right arm off to spare his daughter this, he would have. But nothing he could do or say could change the course of this night.

He felt Rianne kneel beside him, felt her arm go around his shoulders. God, she'd been through so much, and she still had the strength to comfort *him*. He wanted to tell her how much he loved her, how much she meant to him. But everything was tied up inside him in a great, knotted coil of pain and rage, and he was unable to speak those words of gentleness. But he knew that she would understand what was in his heart, for generous Rianne had never denied him anything. And now she was giving him her strength at a time he needed it most.

"I'm not beaten yet," he muttered in a voice taut with fury and determination. "Death, you cold bastard, you're not going to walk in here and claim her. You've got to *take* her from me. Do you hear me?"

Hastily, Rianne got up and went to the window. She was going to cry, and she couldn't burden Pagan with her tears. With the moisture hot upon her cheeks, she stood with her back to the room and watched the stars come out, one by one. They were bright and very clear, like brilliants scattered across indigo velvet.

They're so far away, she thought. Do they look down on us like gods, perhaps, wondering about our swift-paced little lives but not really caring? Pagan thought God was like that. Rianne sighed. Her mother, too, had thought of God as harsh, and every affliction of mankind a punishment for their sins. But what sin did this child have? What stain could be upon her soul that she deserved *this?*

It was clear, so very clear where the fault lay. "*I* am the one who sinned," Rianne whispered, laying her palms against the frost-covered glass of the window. "*I* love another woman's husband. *I* covet that woman's child."

She closed her eyes against the tears, but they flowed anyway, seeping out from beneath her lashes and splashing, hot and stinging, upon the raw skin of her hands. A sob bubbled up inside, but she held it in. For the first time she understood Pagan's withdrawal into a private place of agony. Some pain could not be shared. It must simply be endured.

Tessa was dying. Only a miracle could save her now. Echoes of Sylvia's voice, sharp-clawed and cruel, skittered through Rianne's mind. 'You'd better hope the child dies', it said. 'You'll never have him if she lives'. And if Tessa did die, Rianne didn't doubt that Sylvia would accuse her of being glad.

Glad that the child was gone, glad that she could have the father unencumbered? Every instinct Rianne possessed rebelled against the very idea. Her chin lifted, her shoulders straightened.

Dry-eyed, completely in control now, she whispered. "Show me there is mercy in You. Don't take the life of this innocent to expiate my sins. Give me the life of this child, Lord. Give me that, and I will gladly pay the price."

She stared up into the sky as though giving challenge. Then she turned back to the two people she loved so desperately. Pagan was still kneeling by the bed, Tessa clasped in his arms. He stared at his daughter's face with eyes that rivalled a hawk's for fierceness, and Rianne knew he was still waging his personal battle against Death.

Rianne sat on the bed at Tessa's other side, taking the child's hand in both of hers. "I love you," she murmured. "Fight, Tessa. Fight. For all our sakes."

Her words faded into silence. Tessa's raspy breathing was the only sound in the room, the only movement the slow, inexorable movement of the clock's hands. Eight o'clock, nine o'clock, ten. Rianne bathed the child again, hoping to bring the fever down. But Tessa was so hot that Rianne could feel it through the washrag. She wanted to pray, but the words wouldn't come; she had already made her bargain.

Pagan watched Rianne tend his daughter, hour after hour. He felt her love, and it sustained him. For as long as he lived, he would remember this night, and this woman who had walked through Hell with him. He would love her forever.

Another hour passed, then another. Pagan slipped into a strange, hazy fog, his vision narrowing until his world was encompassed by the white rectangle of pillow and the small, wasted face upon it. His daughter, the precious gift he'd had such a brief time, was dying. Even as he treasured what he'd had, he grieved for what wouldn't be. That fragile beauty of hers would never blossom, and she would never experience the joys and pains of life. She would never love, she would never hold her own child in her arms.

Suddenly her breathing changed, becoming slower, deeper. He gave a strangled groan, sure that the end had come. Still, he gathered her closer, intending to ease her passage if that was all he was allowed to do for her.

Rianne reached over his shoulder to touch Tessa's face. It was cooler, and there was a beginning sheen of perspiration upon her forehead and upper lip.

"Pagan—" she began.

"I know," he rasped. "I'm losing her."

"No, oh, no!" Grasping his shoulders as hard as she could, she said, "The fever's broken."

He stared at her, uncomprehending. He'd been ready for death, for grief. Not this. "She's—"

"She's going to live." The tears were running down Rianne's face again, but these were tears of happiness. Joy flowed through her in a burning torrent, almost too great to contain. "She's beaten it, Pagan, she's beaten it!"

For a moment Pagan looked at her, stunned. He had expected the worst, prepared for it, and now everything was changed. It took a moment for him to absorb it. Then, slowly, he pressed his daughter to his chest. He laid his cheek against hers and rocked her, his raven hair mingling with hers, indistinguishable. He felt as though someone had just handed his own life back to him.

"Tessa," he murmured. "Tessa. So I do get to keep you."

Rianne smiled at him through her tears. Briefly, she rested her hand upon his shoulder, then went to the window to give him a bit of privacy. As she stared out at the night sky, she saw a strange luminescence come into being just over the horizon. It shifted and changed color, sheer beauty hung upon the window of the world. A painting by the hand of God, she thought. Vast and yet ethereal, heartbreakingly lovely beyond anything Man might have created for himself.

"Aurora borealis," she breathed. "The northern lights.

431

I'd heard so much . . . But I never expected them to be so beautiful."

The display was, she knew, affirmation of the bargain she had made with Him earlier. A bargain she intended to keep.

She drank in the sight of the light-born banner that hung like a necklace of precious jewels upon the breast of Heaven.

"Thank you," she whispered.

Rianne returned to Tessa's room to find Pagan sleeping in the chair beside the bed, his hand grasping Tessa's even now. They looked so alike, father and daughter, with their sharp-honed faces and hair like a raven's wing.

Pushing the hood of her fur parka back from her face, she laid the letter she'd written upon the bedside table, putting Pagan's ring of keys upon it so he would be certain to notice it. She had planned to leave them in her room, but he would find them sooner here. It was as though some force was at work for her, smoothing her way out.

"I must do this, my love," she murmured, the barest breath of sound. "It's the only way to make sure Tessa is safe. But I will wait for you to come for me. For as long as it takes, I will wait."

Even now, exhausted as he was, there was such vitality in his features, in the long, lithe lines of his body. It was hard not to cling to him, to hold him just a moment longer. She loved him so terribly much. But she also loved him enough to leave him, enough to spare him from paying the price of keeping her with him. Sylvia's threat hung over Tessa like Damocles' sword. Rianne knew Pagan would never bow to the woman's blackmail, even as she knew that somehow, legally or not, Sylvia would take the child. And she would make Tessa suffer, knowing that Pagan would suffer, too.

But most importantly, Rianne thought, there was the bargain she had made with God. Some people might laugh at the notion, thinking it a hallucination of an over-tired mind and body. But to Rianne, it was proof that there was a merciful God, a God who listened to the beings He had created. Her decision was clear, simple, and inarguable.

She bent to brush her lips over Pagan's in a butterfly-soft caress. "I love you," she murmured. "But I cannot be with you at the expense of your child. And the longer I stay, the angrier your wife will become, and the more risk there will be for Tessa."

Reluctantly, she stepped away from him, taking a moment to lay her fingertips upon Tessa's cheek. The child's skin was cool, her breathing regular and deep. I got my miracle, Rianne thought.

Leaving that room was the hardest thing she had ever done. Everything she loved was behind her, everything she wanted. Tears blurred her vision, and she had to lean against the wall to keep from falling.

"Stand up, Rianne," she muttered from between clenched teeth. "Stand up!"

She found the strength to push away from the wall. Slowly, like a child taking her first, uncertain steps, she moved toward the stairs. Memories flashed through her mind like small, bright stars: Pagan looking at her with love in his crystalline eyes, Pagan's hard body caressing hers, his face taut and tender with passion as he drove her to fulfillment, Pagan holding his daughter against his chest, a world of emotion blazing in his eyes as he realized she was going to live.

Rianne bit her lip to keep from sobbing aloud. She loved him. And because of that, she had to leave him. For his sake, for Tessa's. Those words became a rhythm that got her feet moving, one after the other. Her back straightened, her chin lifted as her love gave her strength she wouldn't have believed possible—the strength to leave.

Quietly, she slipped downstairs to the kitchen. Marie wasn't there; somehow, Rianne knew she wouldn't be. Nothing was going to stop her, for she had Heaven on her side. She paused for a moment, looking around the tiny room with its array of bubbling pots, then walked outside.

Francois Gruillot was waiting there, poised on the runners of his dog sled. The malamutes were eerily silent, their breath-fog coating their fur with ice crystals. Rianne saw by the expression on the Frenchman's face that he was having second thoughts about taking her out of the Yukon.

"You are certain you want to do this?" Francois asked. "The journey, it is not for a lady."

"I must," she said. "Please, Francois, you are the only man I trust."

"Then I will take you." He lifted his shoulders, then dropped them, accepting her decision. "Do you have money?"

"I took enough gold from my father's share to get me back to England. I need no more than that."

Again, that Gallic shrug. *"Bien.* We will take the Chilkoot Pass, it is better in winter than the White. And I am friends with the Chilkoot Indians; they will take us through the pass and on to Dyea in Alaska. From there you will be able to take a ship to England."

"That will be fine," she said. "Thank you, Francois."

"Some day, you may not be so grateful. It is very far from here to England."

An entire continent, she thought. "Yes, a very long way."

The wind gusted, sending a cloud of snow drifting

434

through the alley. Rianne didn't dare cry, knowing the tears would freeze as soon as they began to flow.

Francois settled her in the sled, then hopped up onto the runners. *"Allez!"* he called to the dogs.

The pace was fast, but Rianne felt none of the exhilaration she'd felt when she had ridden Pagan's sled. There was a place in her chest that was achingly empty, and it would stay there until she felt his arms around her again.

"Goodbye, my heart," she whispered.

Chapter Thirty-one

Sylvia parted the curtain that covered the kitchen window and peered outside. "Now, what are you up to?" she muttered as she watched Rianne climb into Francois Gruillot's dog sled.

As the sled moved away down the alley, Sylvia's eyes narrowed. Her inquisitive instincts had been roused when she'd happened to see Rianne, wearing those absurd Indian clothes, slip downstairs.

"Humph, the little whore is probably going to play Florence Nightingale somewhere else," Sylvia said.

Then she smiled. This was her chance to try for the keys to Pagan's treasure-chest. Gold—she hadn't been able to think of anything else since she had seen Rianne open the trunk for the two men who had visited earlier. A whole trunk full of gold. She had to have it, and *damn* anyone who tried to stop her.

She slipped quietly upstairs to Tessa's room. Pushing the door open a crack, she peered into the room. Pagan was sleeping, and so was the child. Good. Now, where would he keep those keys? She moved farther into the room. Pagan looked completely worn out, and so deeply asleep that lightning might strike without waking him. Even if he did wake, she could just play the worried mother, and try again for the keys another time.

As she moved toward the bed, she caught sight of something glittering on the bedside table. The keys!

Quickly, she snatched them. Then she noticed the letter, and, seeing that Pagan's name had been written on the outside in a feminine hand, opened it and began to read.

My dearest love, it said. *By the time you read this, I will have left Henderson City. I had planned this to be a long missive about my feelings, my hopes and dreams, and most of all, my reason for leaving. But I find that three short words say it all: I love you. I love you far too much to see you suffer because of me, and rest assured, you shall. For all our sakes, but especially for Tessa's, I must go. But if and when you and Tessa are free, come to me in Wickersham. I will wait. Forever, if necessary. Yours, R.*

So, Sylvia thought, the interfering little chit is gone at last. 'Come to me', indeed! Swiftly, she thrust the letter into the fire and watched it burn. Soon there was nothing left of it but fine, grey ash.

There. Let Pagan think his precious lover ran away from him. And with another man. Oh, it was too wonderful! Sylvia smiled with smug self-satisfaction. She could even blame the loss of the gold on the fleeing lovers. The only thing that would be more enjoyable would be to know that Rianne Kierney was in Lowell Mason's filthy hands. But then, one couldn't have everything.

Sylvia smirked at the man who was sleeping so peacefully in the chair. Oh, she was going to make him suffer. He had spurned her for that plain, skinny English girl, and now it was time to pay the piper. With a derisive toss of her head, Sylvia slipped out into the hall.

"You can have the kid," she murmured. *"I'll* take the gold, and thank you very much."

She went directly to Pagan's room and unlocked the trunk. Holding her breath in anticipation, she knelt

437

down and lifted the lid. There it was. Gold, bags and bags of it. She hefted one of the long, narrow pouches, her eyes narrowing when she discovered how heavy it was. She had always thought of it in terms of dollars. But she hadn't realized that such an amount of gold would weigh *hundreds* of pounds.

"Well, I'll just have to make more trips," she said.

First things first; she had to get the gold out of here and into her room, and then she could move it again later. She couldn't help but open one of the sacks, however, for the urge to see the gold, to hold it in her hand, was too strong. It lay in her palm, cool and bright and heavy. The stuff of which dreams were made. She rolled the nuggets between her hands, gauging their weight, feeling the richness of them. "I'm rich," she breathed. "Rich, rich, rich!" The open sack fell off her lap, spilling its contents across the floor. Some were stopped by the edge of the rug, but many rolled across the floor, a gleaming, fugitive flood. Sylvia scrambled after them on her hands and knees.

She knew she should have left them, for it was only one sack among many. But those skittering chunks drew her irresistibly, and in her madness she had to retrieve every one. After each nugget she told herself that it would be the last. But the next one always seemed larger and more precious, and she couldn't seem to pass it by.

A slight sound behind her startled her back to reality. She turned to see Lowell Mason and John Ferguson standing in the room. Absurdly, she thrust the sack of nuggets behind her, even though there were fifty other sacks sitting in plain view.

"Well, well, well," Mason drawled. "You've been a busy girl, Sylvia."

She rose to her feet, rage coursing through her veins. She'd been so close! How dare he show up now, right

438

when she had everything in her hands! "How did you know I was here?"

"John here keeps an eye on things for me." Striding to the trunk, Mason picked up two sacks and tossed them to John. "Here's your pay. If I were you, I'd keep my mouth shut."

John nodded, but his gaze was focused on the trunk. "That there's a hell of a lot of gold."

"Yeah. But it's *my* gold," Mason growled. "Any man who says otherwise is going to get a bellyfull of lead. Now lead is almost as heavy as gold, but not nearly as pretty."

"I was jest admiring it," John said.

Mason's flinty gaze didn't waver. "Go admire your own."

John backed away, and a moment later the door closed behind him. Sylvia swung around to Mason, her fists jammed against her hips.

"What do you mean, it's *your* gold?" she demanded.

"Just what I said." Bending, he began taking sacks out of the trunk and stacking them on the floor.

"You're not going to do this to me," she hissed. "Half that gold is mine."

"Sure, just like you were going to share with me." Mason sneered. "If John hadn't spotted you coming in here, I never would have seen this gold."

"I won't let you take it!"

He gave a low bark of laughter that was more menacing than mirthful. "Just exactly how do you plan to stop me?"

With a hiss of anger, she ran at him, fingers outstretched like claws. He held her off easily, smiling at her. Smiling! She kicked out furiously, landing a glancing blow to his groin.

"You bitch!" he rasped, clutching himself. "You bitch!"

Sylvia raked at his eyes with her nails, but he knocked her hands away with his forearm. The next thing she saw was his fist, flying towards her face much too fast for her to dodge. There was a crack, a flash of pain, and then darkness.

When she woke again, Mason was gone. She sat up groggily, pain pounding in her skull. She found a lump the size of an egg at the back of her head, and her lips felt strange, numb and painful all at once. He'd hit her! No man had ever hit her before.

"Ohhh, you bastard!" she moaned, scrambling to the bureau to look at herself in the mirror. Her upper lip was swollen, and cut in the inside from the force of Mason's blow. Gingerly, she touched the tightly-stretched flesh. It was hideous! *She* was hideous!

Then, in the mirrored background, she caught sight of the empty trunk. "No!" she gasped. "Oh, no!"

Her gold was gone. She whirled, putting her own ugly reflection behind her. Although the rest of the room was blurred, she focused clearly on the gaping mouth of the trunk. It leered at her, its emptiness echoing what the rest of her life was going to be like.

"No," she said, her hands closing into fists. "It's not going to be that way."

She pushed away from the bureau. At first she was dizzy, but soon her equilibrium returned and she was able to return to her own room. For once, she was glad of the frigid water in her washbasin. She wet her handkerchief and pressed it to her injured lip, holding it there until the fabric warmed, then repeating the process until her lip began to look almost normal.

Mason had well and truly caught her, damn him. She couldn't very well go to the Mounties and complain that he'd stolen the gold she'd planned to steal from Pagan. Her lip lifted in a snarl, painfully stretching the lacerated inside.

"Damn you," she hissed. "Damn you, damn you, *damn* you!"

The throbbing in her lip eased, but was replaced by a steady pounding in her skull. She felt through her hair for the lump, and found it even larger than before. Pain, waves of it, rushed through her head. She didn't like pain.

She went to her small case and took out the laudanum she always carried with her. Carefully, she measured three drops in a cupful of water and drank it down with a shudder. Now she could sleep. She lay down fully clothed upon the bed. In the morning, she'd think of a way to get her gold back from Lowell Mason.

It seemed like only moments had passed when a knock on the door roused her, but a glance at her window told her that dawn had come. She yawned, wincing when the movement stretched her torn lip. The twinge of pain brought her crashing back to reality; her gold was gone, and right now, she hadn't the slightest idea how to get it back.

The knock sounded again, more imperative this time. She swung her feet over the side of the bed and stood up.

"All right, all right, I'm coming!" she called.

When she opened the door, she saw Pagan standing outside. With him were two Mounties, and her attention instantly focused on the two lawmen. Despite the bright red of their uniform jackets, their manner was decidedly cool. As though they were looking at a criminal. She reached out for the doorknob for support.

"Wh—what do you want?" she asked.

"Are you Sylvia Martel, also known as Sylvia Roark?" the taller of the Mounties asked.

Sylvia tasted bile. She had to swallow several times before answering. "Yes, I'm Sylvia Roark."

"I'm Sergeant Carraway of the Northwest Mounted Police. I'd like to look in the armoire," the lawman said.

The words were spoken politely, but she knew there could be no refusing the request. "Why, ah ... Of course."

Carraway stepped past her and began looking through her clothing. She glanced at Pagan and saw by his expression that he didn't know why the Mounties were here. Perhaps there was a chance she could bluff her way through this.

"What is this about?" she demanded with false bravado.

"We're looking into the murder of Alastair Kierney —"

"I don't know anything about it," she said.

"You were seen with him by the river the night he died," Carraway said.

"It's a lie!" she cried. "Whatever Mason told you, I wasn't near that old man!"

"How do you know it was Mason?" Pagan asked, his eyes narrowing.

"That's a good question, Mr. Roark." Carraway turned, holding one of her gowns. Her heartbeat accelerated when she saw that it was the very one she'd worn the night of Alastair Kierney's murder. Carraway held out the sleeve to show that a piece of lace was missing from the sleeve. Closing her eyes, Sylvia remembered the old man putting his hand on her arm to steady her just before she pushed him. Her shoulders slumped.

"We found the matching piece of lace in Mr. Kierney's hand," the Sergeant said. "Mrs. Roark, we must arrest you for the murder of Alastair Kierney."

"Damn you to hell, Sylvia! " Pagan exploded, pushing past the Mounties. "That old man did nothing to you! And after what Rianne had done, half killing herself nursing the daughter you'd spurned, you should have been grateful."

A red mist of rage shot through her, sweeping caution away, sweeping even her well-honed sense of self-preservation away in its hot tide. Now she wanted only to hurt. Pagan had become all men to her, the men who had ignored her in recent years, the men who had used her then discarded her, the men who had failed to give her what she wanted from life. If she'd had a gun in her hand, she would have killed him where he stood.

But she had a weapon fully as devastating as a gun, a weapon centered directly on his heart. She smiled as she used it, for she knew it would hurt him more than any physical blow.

"Oh, yes, your wonderful Miss Kierney!" she spat. "I wonder if you'll think her so wonderful when you find out what she's done."

"What are you talking about?" Pagan started forward, his fists clenched, then stopped, for he was too angry to trust himself close to her.

She smiled, glad to be able to hurt him, even for a short while. "Why, your little Songbird has flown. She's run off with your friend Francois Gruillot, and taken your gold for good measure."

"That's a damned lie!"

"You're a fool when it comes to women," she said, gazing up at him from beneath her eyelashes. "You always have been. But I'm telling the truth. I *saw* them."

He turned his back on her. "You wouldn't know the truth if you fell over it."

The Mounties moved forward then, flanking Sylvia. "Come with us, please," the taller one said.

Sylvia still didn't move. One of the lawmen put his hand on her shoulder, and something snapped inside her. Shrieking, she tore out of his grasp and ran for the door. She didn't know where she would run, didn't even care. They caught her before she reached the hallway, but still she struggled. Kicking, beating at them with her fists, plunging like a fear-maddened horse beneath their weight, she was finally subdued. They tied her hands and feet, then lifted her between them like a sack of potatoes.

As they carried her out into the hall, she shouted, "You ought to be grateful to me, you bastard! The old man's share of the mine goes to you now! *I* gave you that, not your precious Rianne!"

She drew her breath in harshly, realizing what she'd just said. It was over. Everything was over. Laughter bubbled up in her, and even the revulsion on the men's faces couldn't make her stop laughing.

Pagan sat alone in his room, staring into the fire. A glass of whiskey was in his hand. It was his third, a great deal of whiskey for a man who didn't drink, but he didn't feel it at all. Hell, he hadn't even tasted it. And although he knew the fire was crackling away merrily, the only thing he could hear was Rianne's voice. It coiled along the edges of his mind, as smoky-smooth as fine brandy, as much a part of him as his own heartbeat.

Six days had passed since she had left Henderson City with Francois Gruillot. He didn't have to believe Sylvia; a dozen people had seen the pair head out of town together. The reality of it was only now beginning to seep into his numbed mind. And with it came anger as bright and hot as the leaping flames in front of him.

The trunk was still open; he hadn't touched it since he'd come in to find it empty. It had been opened with a key—the key he had entrusted to Rianne. But he didn't give a damn about the money. The Songbird was producing gold in staggering amounts, and it wouldn't take him long to pay the others back. What hurt was the fact that he had put his faith in Rianne, trusting her as he'd trusted her with his daughter's life. And with his heart.

She had betrayed him. For money, and for another man.

Pagan took a long drink of whiskey. He ought to be drunk by now. He *wished* he were drunk. Then he might have some surcease from the white-hot coal burning in his chest where his heart used to be.

How could he have been so *wrong?* Could her self-lessness, her love, her caring for others been just an elaborate pretense? Had he seen what he'd wanted to see in her, and not what was really there? Or was it Francois she wanted? Had she wanted him so badly that she'd trade everything the owner of the Songbird could give her just to share her life with the Frenchman?

The thought bit through him savagely, and he hurled his glass into the fireplace. The liquor made the flames burst upward with blue incandescence.

The women he'd known before had been like Sylvia, women whose honor and passion had been available to the highest bidder. Then Rianne had swept into his life like a clean spring breeze, bringing grace and light into his cynical existence. It hurt to know it was an illusion. He wished he were the sort of man who could hold an illusion in the face of all reality, but he wasn't. The yawning mouth of the empty chest was solid and damning, and he couldn't ignore it.

There was a knock at the door, but he didn't look up. "Go away," he growled.

"Mr. Roark, it's Sergeant Carraway."

With a sigh, Pagan pushed up from his chair and went to open the door. The stocky Sergeant stood outside, his bright uniform belying the seriousness of his expression. Pagan opened the door wider. "Please come in, Sergeant. Have you any news for me?"

"There's no sign of either the Kierney girl or Mr. Gruillot. Their trail leads toward the coast. I'm afraid, sir, that they plan to take your gold out of the Territory."

Pagan chopped the air with his hand. He didn't give a damn about the gold. He wanted to find Rianne. He wanted to stand before her and her lover, and he wanted to look into her eyes as he did it. "Are you sure this fellow McManus isn't a shill for Gruillot?"

"No, sir, he bought that mine fair and square. He even has a paper to prove it. It seems Mr. Gruillot was in a great hurry to leave without encumbrances."

Except for one, Pagan thought. Although not many men would count the Songbird as an encumbrance. Certainly not Francois; it had been obvious that he worshipped Rianne.

Carraway's expression didn't change, but there was sympathy in his eyes. "Mr. Roark, your wife—"

"Don't call her my wife!"

The sergeant nodded. "Sylvia Martel, then. She's giving us a bit of a problem."

Pagan's shoulders hunched at the thought of dealing with Sylvia again. He'd gone to see her several times, but she had only been interested in taunting him about Rianne's betrayal, and he'd stopped going. "What about her?"

"She's very . . . difficult."

"You have my sympathy, Sergeant. But I've already sent for the best lawyer in the Territory to handle her defense, and beyond that, I don't care to deal with her any longer."

"I understand perfectly, sir." Carraway cleared his throat. "Then you won't mind if we take her to Circle City, where there's a proper jail?"

"Not at all," Pagan said. "I suppose, however, that she doesn't *want* to go?"

"She did resist that suggestion."

"Then I hope you will be firm with her, Sergeant."

Carraway's lips twitched. "Indeed I shall, sir."

Almost, Pagan smiled. He'd seen the good Sergeant's brand of firmness. Sylvia would probably make the trip to Circle City bound and gagged. "I can't say I'm sorry to see her go, Sergeant. She's made my life a hell."

"I expect she has," Carraway said. "What would you like me to do about Miss Kierney and Mr. Gruillot?"

"Nothing." Pagan's brief flash of humor faded, and he returned his gaze to the fire. "Nothing at all."

"Yes, well . . . Good night, sir."

"Good night."

Then Pagan was alone again. He stared into the bright, leaping flames, wondering if a time would come when he *didn't* feel alone. Rianne had given him a glimpse of what could be possible between a man and a woman when their love was strong and true. He'd believed her. He'd believed in her, and he had given her his heart, his love, and an abiding gentleness he hadn't known existed until he met her. When she left, she took it all with her. Only her voice remained, the memory of it imbedded in his very being. Siren song. He couldn't stop hearing it. He'd hear it, no doubt, for the rest of his life. And he'd never be able to forget what might have been if she had loved him.

"God damn you to hell!" he hissed. "Damn you for showing me Heaven, and then for taking it away!"

His chest heaved with a frustration so great he thought it would tear him apart. A long, low groan of inexpressible pain sounded deep in his throat. Then his gaze fell on the open trunk. Heaving it up from the floor, he hurled it against the wall with all his strength.

447

Wood splintered, metal groaned, and burst rivets flew in every direction.

He stood looking down at what he had wrought, wishing he could get some sort of satisfaction from it. But it was only a pale echo of what was going on inside him; if he tore down the house itself, he wouldn't be able to ease his pain.

Years ago, he hadn't gone after Sylvia, but then Sylvia hadn't meant anything to him. Rianne mattered, and her betrayal mattered. He burned to go after her. The Royal Mounted Police could never catch Francois Gruillot, but *he* could. If he were free, he would have harnessed his dogs and pursued the fleeing pair. But there was Tessa to consider, and until the child was well enough to go with him, he had to stay here.

"Papa?" As though thinking of her had summoned her, Tessa called through the door. "Papa, are you all right?"

Sanity returned to him like a dash of icy water. She shouldn't be up and about in that cold hallway! Striding to the door, he flung it open to find the child leaning against the wall for support. With a hiss of indrawn breath, he swept her into his arms and carried her back to her room.

"You shouldn't be up yet," he chided. "Do you want to get sick all over again?"

"I heard a noise, and I thought you fell," she said, wrapping her thin arms around his neck.

"I . . . dropped something." Gently, he tucked her back under her covers. Her sharp little face was even more finely honed from her long illness, but the frightening gauntness was gone. She was healing, slowly but definitely. There *were* compensations in life, he thought. At least he had Tessa.

He started to straighten, but she locked her hands behind his neck. "Papa, there's no more smile in your eyes."

"I'm worried about something, sweetheart."

"Is it because Rianne left?"

Her bluntness staggered him. But then, he'd learned that Tessa was no ordinary child; she'd had to grow up early, and had become very wise because of it. Wiser, in a way, than any adult could hope to be. Although he would have cut off his right arm before confiding in another man, he found he could make no excuses to this lovely child with the too-old eyes.

"Yes, darling, it's Rianne. When she left, she took my smile with her."

She put her small, cool hand on his cheek. "Well, why don't we go get it back from her?"

He took her hand and clasped it in his to warm her. She had hit unerringly on what was bothering him, and on what would cure him, and he thanked God for having her. "You're right, Tessa darling," he said. "This spring, when you're better, we'll do just that."

By God, if he had to follow Rianne to the end of the earth, he'd find her. He was going to face her, and he was going to make her sing for him one last time. And then, knowing she was a liar and a cheat, he'd be able to walk away.

Only then would he be free.

Chapter Thirty-two

Wickersham, England
October, 1897

Rianne adjusted the sleeves of her amber gown as she prepared to sing at Wickersham Church's Evensong service. She yearned to be outside, for the sky was a riot of yellow and red and orange, far lovelier than the church's stained glass windows.

So many months, so many miles of distance, and she hadn't stopped pining for the Yukon. England seemed too gentle now. She wanted the vast Northern forest with its soaring mountains and the wind that blew wild and raw against her face. She wanted to hear the eagle's scream high overhead and the ululating wail of the malamutes as they celebrated the rebirth of the moon.

But most of all, she wanted Pagan. Heart and mind and soul, she wanted him. Many times she'd been tempted to board a ship and return to the Klondike. But even if she'd had the money for it, she couldn't. She had made a bargain with God. If Pagan were free, he would come to her. If not, she must let him go.

But it was hard, so terribly hard. Every morning, she woke to the hope that he would come today, and every night she cried herself to sleep because he hadn't. She prayed to God for the strength to endure, to accept her sacrifice as its own reward, but there was a gaping hole in the fabric of her life, and only Pagan could mend it.

"Why?" she whispered into her prayer book. "Why haven't you come? Even a letter, if that is all you can manage. Just a few words to let me know how you and Tessa are, and that you . . . that you think of me a little."

The organist changed chords, and Rianne forced herself to concentrate on the hymn. It was "Nearer My God To Thee", a lovely song, yet in its way as tame as Wickersham. As she began to sing, she looked out over the placid, comfortable faces she'd known much of her life. Their expressions didn't change with the music, merely became a bit more placid and comfortable. One thing that could be said about the clientele of the Golden Bear: they certainly were lively. She wondered what this lot would do if she suddenly began singing the "Marseillaise" or, or heaven forbid, "Ave Maria", which she had learned for one of the miners.

They'd probably burn me at the stake, she thought wryly. Her gaze was drawn upward by the soaring Gothic arches of the church. Once, they had seemed so huge, as though they reached all the way to Heaven. But she had been to the Yukon.

For the rest of her life, she would remember the day Francois and the Chilkoot Indians had carried her down the last great precipice in the Chilkoot Pass. Afraid of the height, she had fixed her gaze above her, to the mountains. And there, hanging precariously between two granite peaks, was a glacier. It was a mammoth sheet of ice hundreds of feet thick, glittering diamond-white where the sun touched it, shot through with sapphire and turquoise in the lee of the twin peaks that anchored it. She had never seen anything so beautiful or so staggeringly immense. It was God's own church, built by His hand on a scale humans could scarcely comprehend.

That memory triggered others — hauntingly vivid remembrances of the time she had spent with Pagan. His

451

face was as clear today, nearly a year later, as if she had seen him only yesterday. The feel of his arms around her, his lips on hers, hot and demanding, the shatteringly exquisite sensations of making love to him. She had wanted his child desperately, something of him to hold to her heart forever. She had prayed that she had conceived during their last, beautiful night together, but it was not to be.

Battered by her emotions, she closed her eyes and poured them into the music. Everything she'd lost was in her voice, and it filled the staid little church with love and passion and aching loneliness, the raw, naked need of a heart in torment.

As she let the last note trail away, the double doors at the front of the church banged open with a violence that drew all eyes. Silhouetted against the fiery sky outside was a man, broad-shouldered and tall, his open coat swirling around him like the wings of a great, dark bird. The candles guttered in the wind that swept in behind him, sending shadows skittering along the pale marble floor of the church.

Although Rianne couldn't see the newcomer's face, she knew him. With her heart, her soul, and her body, she knew him.

"Pagan!" she cried in a high, breathless voice that was hardly any sound at all.

He had come! Just when she had reached the end of her strength, he had come. Joy surged through her in a hot rush, making her legs weak. Unable to move, she stood waiting for him, her hand clasping her throat.

He closed the door behind him with a crash that echoed through the building. The candlelight steadied. Then he strode down the aisle toward her. Joy turned to bewilderment, and then shock when she saw his expression. Where she had expected to see happiness to match her own, there was hate. It was etched in the grooves bracketing his mouth, in every sharp-honed plane of his face. Hate! Rianne shook her head, denying this reality. After everything she'd been through . . . it just couldn't be happening!

But it was. Pagan kept coming, dark and cold as the Angel of Death himself. A babble of speculation swirled in his wake, but the people before him were silent, apparently not willing to dare that cold, crystalline stare. Rianne's entire being shrank from him, even as her love held her in place.

The priest thrust himself in front of Pagan, demanding an explanation, and was set aside like a piece of furniture, gently but impersonally.

Finally, Pagan stood before Rianne. He crossed his arms over his chest and stared down at her, his eyes hooded by raven's-dark brows and lashes. She let her breath out in a sigh, unaware that she'd been holding it. How many times had she played this scene over in her mind? Dozens, no, hundreds. But never like this. The world had become a mad place, where love became hate, joy became anguish. Her mind reeled as she tried to make sense of it.

Without a word, Pagan reached out, taking hold of her wrist in a grip that brooked no resistance. Then he turned and stalked back down the aisle, pulling her after him. Rianne wouldn't have resisted even if she'd been able; she loved this man more than life itself, and she would have followed him to Hell if he asked it of her. Their love was greater than time and distance, and surely stronger than any misunderstanding.

A closed carriage waited at the bottom of the church steps. The coachman sat in his high seat, holding the reins of a pair of fine, bay horses.

"Pagan, wait . . ." Rianne gasped, out of breath midway down the stairs.

He swept her into his arms and carried her the rest of the way as the coachman scrambled down from his perch to open the door. Before Rianne could say a word, she'd been thrust into the coach. Pagan climbed in after her. Then the door slammed closed, and a moment later the coach lurched into movement.

Rianne braced herself against the seat as the vehicle made the turn from the church drive. She glanced at Pagan, daunted by his silence. He sat beside her, his profile toward her, and his manner was cold and forbidding. Except for his collar and cravat, he was dressed all in black. The starkly elegant clothes matched his hair and brows, and made his eyes look even paler in contrast. And for all the fashionable clothes, he still looked as untamed and untameable as a panther. Her heart beat a staccato pattern against her ribs as a sudden, powerful rush of desire swept through her, as primitive and powerful as the man who had caused it. Nothing, by Heaven, was going to come between them now!

"Pagan . . ." she began, laying her hand on his arm.

He turned to look at her, and there was such cold fury in his eyes that she gasped. "Don't touch me," he said in a voice as hard as steel.

Stunned, she could only obey. What had happened to change the lover she had known into this granite-hard man? Bewildered, she clasped her gloved hands in her lap and fixed her gaze upon them. She didn't know how to deal with this man. *Her* Pagan had been hard-edged and unpredictable, but there had always been passion to temper those aspects.

Pagan kept his face impassive with iron self control, but inside, he was seething with fast-shifting emotions. After months of searching for her in San Francisco and Seattle, Paris and Marseille, Francois' home, he had finally found her. And he discovered that he was as unprepared to deal with her as if he'd left the Yukon yesterday.

Just hours after he'd settled into the house he'd engaged through an agent, he had happened to drive past the church to hear that beautiful Siren's voice of hers. He'd had no more power to resist than he'd ever had, and that sultry, velvet sound had pulled him right into the church to her. The muted light had gilded her hair and softened her ethereal features even more, and she had looked like an angel standing there upon the dais. The sight of her, the well-remembered scent of her delicate perfume, brought a wealth of memories flooding into his mind. He thrust them away savagely. They were all lies; *she* was a lie.

He'd come halfway around the world to tell this woman how much he despised her, and now he found that he didn't. Couldn't. He despised himself, because he couldn't help but love her even after what she'd done. His arms itched to hold her, to fold her close, to sweep away the past and claim her all over again. *Damn her!* Having her beside him now, with her betrayal between them, was a torment worse than anything he'd ever endured.

The thought of her with another man went through his heart like a white-hot spear, and made him savage. He wanted to hurt her as he'd been hurt. She didn't have the grace to try to explain herself. And it was only now that he realized that he'd been hoping she *would* have some plausible reason. Fool that he was, he still wanted to believe in her.

Rianne studied him through her lashes, desperately trying to discover what had turned him against her. Although his manner chilled her to her soul, she had to try to reach him. "How is Tessa?" she asked.

"Fine."

"Is she here in England with you?"

"Yes."

His tone was little more than a growl, and he never turned his head to look at her. Rianne fought the burgeoning tears. She fell into silence, too distraught to speak coherently. And Pagan, sitting there like an iron-forged statue, remained equally silent. The air in the leather-scented interior of the carriage was fraught with tension, vibrating with pain. Rianne knew he still wanted something from her, or she wouldn't be here now. But where was he taking her? If he hated her so, why did he bother?

There were no answers in the grim, brooding figure beside her. It was as though no love had passed between them at all, as though they were enemies and had always been. Could all that joy have come to mean nothing? God, she hoped not. But, looking at the unyielding tautness of his profile, she felt no hope, only a deep, grinding dread. A single tear splashed down upon her clasped hands, making a star-shaped pattern on her glove.

Pagan saw that tear, saw it glitter like a liquid diamond as it fell. His chest heaved as he strove to resist an almost uncontrollable urge to comfort her. Remember what she is, he told himself savagely. And remember what she isn't. His brows lowered even more. Surely the great Lily Langtry herself couldn't have done better. And the tear was the perfect touch. It had almost worked. Almost.

The rest of the ride passed amid the rhythmic squeaking of the springs. Rianne's tension increased until she was almost frantic by the time the carriage pulled to a halt in front of the sprawling Tudor house that had once belonged to Colonel Merton, but which had sat empty since the old man's death. It was blazing with lights now, the windows of every downstairs room bright golden rectangles in the gathering darkness.

In other circumstances, Rianne would have met the sight with anticipation, knowing she would soon see Tessa. But now . . . Would the child wear the same cold expression as did her father? Would she, too, hold hatred in those pale, beautiful Roark eyes? That would be the final blow, the last, crushing defeat. Rianne bit the inside of her lip to keep from crying.

"Why have you brought me here?" she asked.

Pagan didn't answer, but leaped down from the carriage and swung her down beside him. Taking a firm grip on her arm, he led her toward the house. A uniformed butler opened the door as they neared. He was a stranger to Rianne. Not a flicker of surprise crossed his impassive face as Pagan all but dragged her into the house.

"Good evening, Miss. Good evening, sir," he said.

"Evening, Harris," Pagan growled, letting go of Rianne's arm. "But not a good one."

Rianne heard the door close behind her with solid finality. She'd never get away now. Get away! she thought bitterly. And where would she go that her love for him could not follow? No, she was trapped by her heart as surely as if he had shut her into an iron cage. Whatever he had planned for her, she would endure. She'd become very good at enduring.

He's done well for himself, she thought. The foyer was somberly elegant, the walls wrapped in dark wood paneling, the Italian marble floor nearly covered with rugs of a burgundy hue. A chandelier burned overhead, its light a solitary gay note in the room. Standing beneath it, Rianne felt exposed and vulnerable.

The butler expertly divested Pagan of his coat. "Did you have a pleasant drive, sir?"

"A productive one, rather," Pagan said. "My daughter?"

"Sleeping, sir. She did say that it was all right for the lady to come upstairs and give her a kiss."

With a wordless growl, Pagan turned away. Tessa had never stopped believing that Rianne was her friend, and he hadn't had the heart to tell her otherwise. "See that I am not disturbed for the rest of the evening, Harris."

Pagan stalked to the doorway at the far end of the foyer and flung it open. When Rianne didn't follow, he glanced over his shoulder at her. She looked so small and lost standing there in the glow of the chandelier, and so hurt, that he wanted to go to her. With a muttered curse, he steeled himself against it. He'd been gentle with her once, and she had thrown it in his face. Not again—oh, no, not again. But instinct warred with intellect, crying out for him to take her into his arms. Choosing to obey intellect, he jammed his fists against his hips and waited for her to come to him.

With a sigh, Rianne gathered her courage and moved forward. There was nothing else she could do; Pagan was the master here. This was his game, if this terrible ordeal could be called play, and she didn't even understand the rules. Whatever it was, he wanted something from her even in his hate. And her love for him made her take the chance, however slim, that this would prove to be a terrible dream and that she would wake to his arms and the warmth of his love.

Bowing her head, she walked through the doorway. She got a brief impression of a sumptuously furnished room and the bright heat of a well-laid fire before the sharp sound of the door closing brought her around again. Then all her world was encompassed by Pagan, by his size and strength and anger, and by her despairing love for him.

"Couldn't you let me see Tessa, if only for a moment?" she asked.

"Tessa's life has been made a hell by one woman. She's just begun to heal, and I'll be damned if I'm going to let you upset her," he growled.

"But—"

"No!"

"Why have you brought me here, then?" she cried, undone by his harshness. "What do you want from me?"

The words were there on the tip of his tongue. *Truthfulness. Loyalty. Love—all the things you cannot give.* But he couldn't speak them; his anger allowed him only one. "Sing," he growled.

She stared at him, numb with shock. "What?"

"Sing. You know what I want to hear."

With a sinking heart, she studied his eyes. Yes, she knew what he wanted. But she didn't know why, for his were not the eyes of a man who wished to hear a love song. They belonged to a man who wanted revenge.

"What have I done to deserve this?" she whispered.

"You left me."

"There were reasons, good ones," she said. "I couldn't tell you at the time, because it would only cause trouble—"

"Now that, at least, is the truth." His eyes were as hard and flat as steel. "And as for the 'reasons', you can save your breath. There is no excuse for what you did."

It was then that Rianne knew that he had come all this way just to punish her. Without even asking for an explanation, he had tried her, judged her, and sentenced her.

He'd had no faith.

She felt as though a yawning pit had opened up beneath her feet. All the months of weeping, of suffering agonies of loneliness and uncertainty, of living a half-life because she'd left her heart back in the Yukon with him—they had all come to this. She was left with nothing but the dry husks of her dreams and the bitter taste of his hate.

"Call the carriage," she said with all the dignity she could muster. "I'm leaving."

His hands tightened, and he pulled her up onto her tiptoes. His breath, warm and tinged with mint, fanned her lips. Of their own volition, her eyelids drifted closed. She could no more have stopped that automatic reaction than she could have stopped her heart from beating.

Her response rocked Pagan to his toes. It was always like this between them, like holding a flame to gunpowder. His hands shook with the effort it took not to kiss her. He was possessed by a sudden, powerful desire to forget the past, forget everything, and make her his again. Then all the remembered pain came back, and he let go of her with a suddenness that made her stagger.

"I said sing!" he said in a quiet, deadly voice.

She lifted her chin defiantly. He could have his anger,

and he could wallow in it! Although she'd almost rather cut out her tongue than sing a love song to him now, she'd do it to end this torment. "If I sing, will you let me go?"

"Yes." He'd come here just for this, to hear her sing their song one last time, and then to walk away. It was what he needed to purge himself of his damned obsession for her, and afterwards he could forget she existed. *Are you sure?* a cynical part of his mind asked, prodding him like an over-sharp needle.

"Then I will sing." She watched him as he took his jacket off and flung it carelessly across a nearby chair. Then he sat on the sofa, draping his arms across the back with an air of languid ease that didn't fool her a bit. His whole body was taut, the muscles in his arms and powerful chest straining the fabric of his shirt. Surely no singer had ever performed for a more grim and unfriendly audience.

It's only a song, she told herself. But it wasn't. It was the embodiment of the love that had been theirs, however briefly, and every note, every word was precious to her. She closed her eyes, marshalling the dregs of her strength, and began to sing.

> *"Drink to me only with thine eyes*
> *And I will pledge with mine.*
> *Or leave a kiss within the cup*
> *And I'll not ask for wine.*
> *The thirst that from the soul . . . doth . . ."*

She faltered to a halt, silently begging him for mercy. But there was none in him. Hard-eyed, he curtly gestured for her to continue. Taking a deep, shuddering breath, she tried.

> *" . . . The thirst that from the soul doth rise*
> *Doth ask . . ."*

Tears slid down her face in a flood. The room whirled around her in a silver blur, at the center of which was Pagan's iron-hard face. She'd believed that she could endure anything life put before her, but she had been wrong. This was too much. One more note, and she would surely die. "I can't!" she cried. "If there is any compassion left in you, don't ask this of me!"

He might as well have been carved from stone for all the response he gave her. It's over, she thought in despair.

Turning, she stumbled toward the door.

Chapter Thirty-three

"Rianne!"

She ignored him. Pagan's footsteps sounded behind her, sharp and peremptory, and she broke into a run. Before she reached the doorway, however, his hand came down upon her shoulder, pulling her to a halt. His touch burned her through the fabric of her dress. But where once that heat had been from desire, it was now the brand of his hatred.

"Let go of me!" she cried. "You have no right to treat me like this!"

Even as she spoke, she knew her words were futile; Pagan was not a man to be turned from his chosen course. He was like a dark whirlwind, powerful, implacable, an elemental force that could not be swayed. But she still fought, resisting as he slowly turned her to face him.

She struck out at him blindly, but he caught her hand and held it fast. Her glove, too worn to withstand the stress, came apart in his grasp. But it was no more tattered than her heart, no more ruined than her future.

"Why must you do this to me?" she sobbed. "Do you have to tear my very heart out before you're satisfied?"

"You tore *mine* out," he gritted.

Rianne's legs gave way, and she slid down out of his grasp to her knees. "Please," she whispered brokenly. "Please, don't."

Pagan was astonished by her collapse. He'd prepared

himself for lies, pleading and, knowing Rianne's mettle, defiance. But not this. Her pain was too real to be denied, even though caution warned him against believing in it. All these months he'd wanted to hurt her as he'd been hurt, planned for it, worked for it. And now he'd done it. But it was a bitter victory, one that gave him no satisfaction.

Gently now, he tilted her face back so that he could look at her. Her features were as finely drawn as he remembered, perhaps more so, and there was a sadness about her that made his heart contract with an emotion he didn't dare identify. His gaze was caught by the warm-honey eyes that had haunted his sleep all these months. She looked back at him unwaveringly, and he saw something in those liquid brown depths that made him stiffen in shocked surprise.

Her innocence was there before him, as clear and pure as newly fallen snow. There was no art to it, no artifice, and even through his own pain he knew it for what it was. He drew in his breath with a harsh sigh. He'd have to be blind not to see it, stupid not to recognize it, and a fool not to believe in it. He'd been all three more than once in his life, but not now. Hope ran up his spine like a warm touch.

"You didn't run away with Francois Gruillot, did you?" he demanded.

"Run away? You thought I . . . Oh, Pagan!"

"You and he left Henderson City together. And neither of you came back."

She stared at him in bewilderment, trying to piece together what had happened. "Francois escorted me to Dyea. Afterward, he said he was going to hunt the moose. I thought he was going back, but I suppose he just went off into the mountains."

Pagan closed his eyes. 'Hunt *the* moose', she'd said. The phrase was so uniquely Francois' that no one who knew the big Frenchman could doubt that he'd said them. She was telling the truth. Clenching his hands into white-knuckled fists, he asked, "Why did you leave me, then? When I found out you'd gone away with Francois, I damn near went crazy!"

Outrage washed away the fog that had gripped Rianne's mind. "How could you think I'd *ever* let another man touch me?" she demanded, rising to her feet with her own fists clenched.

"What was I supposed to think?" he shouted. "You stole away in the middle of the night with a man who had made no secret of his feelings for you—"

"I left you a letter!" she cried.

His breath went out in a harsh gasp. "What?"

"I left you a letter! I told you where I was going, and that I loved you, and I begged you to come for me if you and Tessa were free! When you didn't . . ." She broke off abruptly, seeing the astonishment in his eyes. "You didn't find it? I put it on the nightstand beside Tessa's bed. Beneath your keys, so that you would be sure to see it."

He shook his head. "It wasn't there."

"But—"

"The keys were gone, too," he said. "And so was the gold I'd been storing."

"I was the last person to touch those keys."

He turned away from her again, striding to the fire to gaze down into the leaping flames. "Yes."

Rianne took a deep breath. This was the decisive moment, the time when Pagan must make his own leap of faith. She had no proof that she'd written the letter, no proof that she hadn't stolen the gold or been Francois Gruillot's lover. There was only her word. Pagan must *believe,* if there was to be a chance for them.

She went to stand behind him. The firelight gilded the broad, straight lines of his shoulders and put dancing sparks in the smooth blackness of his hair. She could see his awareness of her by the way his jaw tightened. At another time, she might have tried to soothe that tautness from him. But in a moment she was going to find out if she was to keep him or not, and her own fear rode her hard.

Taking a deep breath to steady herself, she said, "I have no proof of my innocence."

"Proof? Rianne . . ." So quickly that she gasped in surprise, he whirled to face her. "Your innocence is in your eyes. I need nothing more."

A dizzying tumult of joy and relief poured through her, and for a moment she was afraid she might faint. She had won. He had found his faith, and his love. It was a gift of inestimable value, sweeping aside the past, the doubts, and the suffering in one glorious moment. "You believe me?" she asked wonderingly, reaching up to touch his face.

"I believe you." His eyes were stark with remembered pain. "When you left, seemingly without a word of farewell, it tore me apart. I wondered whether I knew you at all, whether I had fallen in love with a lie."

"And now?" she prompted.

He raked his hand through his hair. "Now I find that I can't believe in anything but that your love was the most precious gift I had ever been given. And that I wronged you by ever thinking otherwise. God, what I put you through because of my damned pride!"

"Ahhh, Pagan." She put her palms flat against the hard plane of his chest, feeling the slow, steady beat of his heart. "A saint might have had doubts, considering the circumstances."

"And I'm no saint."

"I never wanted a saint," she said. "I wanted you, with all your arrogance and pride."

Wanted, not want, he thought. As though wanting him was over, relegated to the past. Every fibre of his body rebelled against that notion. There had to be a way to win her back, to regain the trust he had so foolishly thrown away. "Why did you leave me?" he demanded.

There was a fierce note in his voice that made Rianne's heart pound. She had learned to treasure that brand of gentle savagery, for it was tied irrevocably to the untamed passion that was so much a part of the man. Heat spread through her limbs, finally pooling deep in her core.

"Tell me," he growled.

Rianne sighed. "I left because you and Tessa would have suffered if I had stayed."

"That's ridic—"

She put her hand over his mouth to stop his protest. "Sylvia said that if I didn't leave, she would steal Tessa away from you. And then she vowed to put the child in an orphanage just to punish you."

"What?" he shouted.

"She knew what would hurt you the most," Rianne continued. "And she was right. How could we be happy together, knowing that Tessa was being abused in some terrible place? After seeing how you suffered when she was ill, how could I allow you to choose between your daughter and me?"

Pagan's mind churned with the memories of the foul hole where he had lost two brothers. Tessa, in such a place? His entire being recoiled from the thought. Rage sparked deep in his chest, a hot, abiding anger against Sylvia for even considering such a thing. "I should have strangled that woman the moment she set foot in my saloon."

"Somehow, I don't think strangling women is your cup of tea," Rianne murmured.

"I could learn."

Rianne cocked her head to one side, sensing that he was only half jesting. "Pagan, there is no protection from a person with no scruples. Believe me, the only possible decision for me was to leave Henderson City."

He let out his breath in a long, ragged sigh, staggered by the enormity of her sacrifice. And in return, he had hurt her. Cruelly and callously, without even allowing her to explain. He had let his jealousy take over his thoughts and his life, and it had driven him to hurt the woman he loved. Self-disgust washed through him in a black tide.

Taking her hand, he raised it to his lips. Only then did he become aware how work-worn her hands were. Running his thumb over the callouses on her palm, he asked, "How did you get these?"

She tried to pull away, but he held her fast. "I've been . . . taking in a little washing, things like that."

"You've been working like a drudge," he growled, furious at himself. Was there no end to what he'd done? He'd been so sure she was living high on his gold, and she'd been working as hard as his mother ever had. And through it all, she had loved him.

With a muttered curse, he flung himself away, turning his back so he couldn't see the inevitable recrimination come into her eyes. "You gave me my daughter," he rasped. "And I repaid you poorly. You'd proven your courage and honor a hundred times over, and I still let my damned pride blind me."

Tears beaded Rianne's eyelashes as she went to stand behind him. "So, Pagan Roark. You've discovered you're human, after all."

His shoulders hunched, and she knew his self-recrimination was more savage than anything she could do or say. He had always been larger than life to her, a man of vision and drive and great passion. Now, all that strength and will were turned inward. If she walked out that door forever, he would deem it a fit punishment for doubting her, and then he would tear his own heart to ribbons because of it.

And it was all so completely unnecessary. She had never stopped loving him, and she never would. Yes, he had doubted her. But in the end, when it counted, he had reached within himself and found his faith. Against all evidence, he had chosen to believe in his love, and that was enough for her.

With a sigh, she put her arms around him and laid her cheek upon his back. She felt him stiffen, then relax against her. His hands, those strong hands whose touch she had been craving all these lonely months, closed over her wrists.

"I thought you would hate me for what I did to you," he said in a voice that was almost a groan.

"Hate you?" She rubbed her cheek against the smooth, fine linen of his shirt, reveling in the heat of the hard male flesh beneath. "If I loved you any more, I think I would die of it."

Pagan's breath caught in his throat. Turning within her

467

encircling arms, he pulled her tightly against his chest. "God, Rianne!" He kissed her over and over, murmuring, "I love you, I love you," against her lips.

She clung to him, sobbing, and he kissed the salt tears from her cheeks before claiming her mouth again. All the despair of the past months was gone, burned away by boundless joy. She had her love back.

Endless moments later, Pagan lifted his mouth from hers. She tried to draw him back, but he took her hand and led her to the sofa.

"We have things we must talk about," he said. "I want no questions left unanswered, no shadows to haunt our future." He sat down, pulling her onto his lap. Much as he hated to bring up the memory of her father's death, it was important for her to know how and why Alastair had died.

Rianne noticed the reluctance in his eyes, and her heart gave a leap of alarm. "What's the matter, Pagan? Is something wrong?"

He sighed, wishing he knew the words to soften what he had to say. But there were none. There was only the truth, and she had always shown herself able to bear what life dealt her. "The morning after you left, the Mounties arrested Sylvia for your father's murder."

"Murder? She killed my father?" Rianne closed her eyes against the sudden rush of tears, for the pain of that loss was still deep and new. "Why, Pagan?" she whispered. "What had he ever done to her?"

"Nothing," he said. "But he was half owner of the Songbird Mine. Sylvia knew that his half would come to me if he died, and in her own twisted way, she thought I would be more willing to buy her off handsomely if I had it all."

"She killed my father for *that?*" Rianne cried in horror. "Was she mad?"

"Mad with greed. I've seen it happen a hundred times. Gold fills a man's mind until he can't think of anything else, until he kills for it — or dies for it."

Rianne shook her head, unable to understand how anyone could destroy a human life for money. A piece of cold metal, no matter how bright, could not begin to pay that price.

"I wouldn't be surprised if she had something to do with the disappearance of your letter," Pagan said. "The act would be just malicious enough for her."

"Do you think she took your gold?"

"I don't know." Pagan stroked the smooth curve of Rianne's cheek. "And I don't care. I have you back, and that's all that matters."

Sighing, Rianne turned her face into his hand to kiss his palm. There had been so much ugliness, and all due to one woman's selfish greed. "What's going to happen to Sylvia now?"

"Her trial was a few months ago," Pagan said. "She'll spend the rest of her life in prison."

"She killed my father, nearly tore us apart, and destroyed her own life, and for *money*," Rianne murmured, searching inside herself for the hate that ought to be there. But there was only sadness that she would never see her father again, never hear his laugh, never be able to tell him again how much she loved him.

Drawing in a deep, shuddering breath, she buried her face against the strong column of Pagan's neck. "She killed my father for nothing. He didn't own half the Songbird. I do."

"What?"

"Father didn't want the responsibility. He was afraid of gambling it away, so he sold it to me for a dollar." A shiver rippled down her spine. "If Sylvia had asked it of me, I would have *given* her the dratted thing."

"And so would I," Pagan said. "But Sylvia wouldn't have believed it. In her world, no one gives anything away. One only takes."

"Then I'm glad I don't have to live in her world." Tears threatened for a moment, but then Rianne straightened her spine. The past could not be changed. She would always miss her father, but she had already learned to be grateful for having found him, for having had the chance to love

469

him and to know he loved her, too. Some people were never given so much, and she would treasure it forever.

Now it was the future that beckoned, and by the grace of God, it was a bright one. She had come so very close to not having it that it was doubly precious. Reaching up, she ran her hand through the silky darkness of Pagan's hair.

He took her hand and kissed her palm. "It's a shame to have the Songbird's ownership split. I suggest a merger."

"Are you free?" she murmured.

"My divorce was final before I left the Yukon." He stroked her back slowly, loving the sweet firmness of her flesh, the warmth of her through the amber wool of her gown.

She arched into his hands. "Are you sure Tessa won't mind having me as her stepmother?"

"She never stopped loving you. And neither did I." His voice turned hard and determined. "You're not going to get away from me again. We're getting married tomorrow."

"What about tonight?" she whispered.

He drew in his breath sharply. There was a small, leaping flame in his pale eyes, a fire of the heart, a fire of passion. "Tonight," he said softly, "we'll have our honeymoon."

Rianne's body responded instantly and powerfully. His love was there before her, strong and vital and true. There were no more doubts between them. She, who had yearned all her life for love, had been given more than she'd ever dreamed possible. Passion flowed through her in an all-encompassing wave, pooling within her like fire. She needed to possess him again, completely and forever, and be possessed by him.

Pagan needed no encouragement; body and soul, he was afire to claim her for his own. He captured her lips with his, his tongue delving into the sweet depths of her mouth like a starving man allowed the feast. Slowly, gently, he eased her down upon the cool brocade of the sofa.

He tried to be gentle, but Rianne would have none of it. Wanting to feel him, she pulled him down with all the long-restrained hunger that had tormented her these past months. She tore at his shirt with shaking hands, crying out her need.

Pagan's control vanished beneath the fierceness of her demand. He loved her too much, missed her too desperately to go slowly. "You're all I want," he said. "You're all I ever want."

He unfastened her dress and slid it down, then, too impatient to unlace her corset, he merely broke the ties and flung the offending garment aside. Next were her petticoat and drawers, and she was naked at last.

He stood up to remove his own clothing, then came down upon her again. Rianne sighed, clasping him close. Her love, her lover, the man who had given her the greatest treasure of all. It had been so long, so very long. She looked up into the crystalline eyes so close above her. His love was there, raw and powerful, a bonfire of emotion as fierce and untamed as the man himself. She knew it would warm her for a lifetime.

With a sigh, she spread her legs to urge him in. "Come to me," she said.

Pagan poised himself at her threshold, reveling in the sumptuous heat and moisture that beckoned him. Nothing could compare to this woman, her passion and the power of what she made him feel when he held her in his arms.

"I love you," he rasped, sliding slowly, deliciously into that hot nest. He was home.

Then all thought ceased as they reaffirmed their love in the oldest and most primitive of ways. Skin against skin, touching, tasting, loving—their joining was tender and yet fierce, fraught with the memory of loss and loneliness and long-withheld desire.

Together they strove for love's completion, together they found it. Bodies locked in passion's intimate dance, they soared to the heights. For one brief, glorious moment, the moon and stars were theirs. When they sank slowly back to earth, they found that the glory did not fade, for they were warmed by the glow of a love that rivaled the sun itself.

Later, when Rianne had gotten her breath back, she

reached up to trace the self-satisfied curve of Pagan's mouth with her fingertip.

"Does Tessa still want brothers and sisters?" she asked.

"At least six," he said, propping himself on his elbows so that he could see her face. His Rianne. Forever. "Does six suit you, Siren of my heart?"

"If they have black hair and ice-crystal eyes, then I want a dozen." Although her tone was light, she was wishing for it with all her heart. "We may have already begun, you know."

"Perhaps," he murmured. "But perhaps we'd better try again. Just to be sure."

Smiling, she drew him down. "Perhaps you're right."

Chapter Thirty-four

"I won, I won!" Tessa cried.

Rianne looked up from her embroidery to smile at the child, who was facing Pagan across the draughts-board. Father and daughter were so alike, dark-haired, sharp-featured, and as stubborn as a pair of mules. How she loved them both!

"That's the third time you trounced me," Pagan growled in mock irritation. "It's a hell of a thing when a man loses at draughts to a child."

"Don't curse, Papa," Tessa said in perfect imitation of Rianne's gentle, but oft-repeated warning. "Besides, Rianne helped me, so you can't be but so humil . . . humil . . ."

"Humiliated," Rianne supplied helpfully, shooting a teasing glance at Pagan.

"Let's try some poker," he growled. "I'll bet the little minx can't beat me at that."

"Poker," Rianne said, "is not at all appropriate for a young lady."

He snorted. "Neither is chasing a grizzly off with a frying pan, and yet I remember a certain young lady doing just that."

"That wasn't a lady, that was the Songbird," she murmured.

473

She knew by the light in his eyes that he would like to kiss her. Truly, she reflected, it was wonderful to be loved, and even more wonderful to be loved by Pagan Roark. Smiling, she tucked her feet under her, curling into the big armchair like a contented cat. Tessa abandoned the draughts-board to wriggle her way onto Rianne's lap.

"There," Rianne said, putting her arms around the child and holding her close. Tessa was healing, the wounds left by an unloving mother slowly fading. Although the girl was still afraid of dark, closed places, her nightmares were coming with less frequency now.

Rianne sighed. Sylvia had affected all their lives deeply, and as destructively as she could. Only the miracle of love had enabled them to overcome that ruinous taint. But then Rianne bent to press her lips against the smooth fall of Tessa's straight, black hair. Despite all the pain and loss, life had turned out to be wonderful. She, Pagan, and Tessa were together and happy, and nothing could ever tear them apart again. Truly, she'd been given not one, but *two* miracles. And both of them were named Roark. Joy, never far away these days, bubbled into her heart.

"Thank you," she whispered into the child's hair. "Thank you."

Glancing at Pagan, she saw that he was watching her with an expression she'd come to know very well. She didn't know how other husbands acted, but hers was *very* attentive. And she loved it, loved holding him, possessing him, sharing her life with him.

Pagan was so wrapped up in his wife's warm brown eyes that he almost didn't notice the discreet knock that always heralded the butler's arrival. Reluctantly tearing his gaze away from Rianne, he got up and went to open the door. "Yes, Harris?" he asked.

"A letter has come from town, sir," the butler said.

"Thank you." Pagan examined the worn and much-handled letter. Evidently it had followed him on his travels, for there were many notations upon it from the people who had forwarded it to his next destination. That, however, didn't surprise him as much as did its origin. "Rianne, Tessa," he called. "It's from Marie."

"Well, open it!" Rianne said excitedly.

"It's dated June eleventh," he said, opening it with a flick of his long fingers. "Tessa and I left Henderson City on June second. Strange, that she would write to me so soon after we left."

Completely out of patience, Rianne cried, "Well, read the dratted thing so we can find out!"

With a grin, he unfolded the paper and began to read aloud. *'Dear Pagan. I can't write, so I had someone write this for me. Since I didn't know exactly where you were headed once you left San Francisco, I just sent it along in the hope it will catch up to you somewhere. The Mounties found Lowell Mason buried in an avalanche off Lucan mountain, dogs, sled, and all. When they dug him up, they found the sled packed with gold. The sacks had numbers written on them in your hand, so the Mounties brought them back here. I'm keeping them for you.*

Francois Gruillot came back into town last week, as fit and eager as a hound dog in the spring. When I asked him what the hell he'd been doing, taking Rianne away and then disappearing the way he had, he just looked at me like I was a crazy woman and said he'd gone hunting the moose. I think I'm going to try and marry that man.

By the by, the saloon is doing fine; thank you for giving it to us girls. We're going to retire rich women, and I think I just may buy myself a handsome husband when this is all over. You see Rianne, tell her we love her. Marie.

"You gave them the saloon?" Rianne asked.

He shrugged. "I didn't need it any more."

"I suppose you offered them money and they wouldn't take it," Rianne murmured.

He merely shrugged again, but she knew she'd guessed right. Pagan was not a man to leave the Yukon without seeing to the welfare of those who depended on him. But when she spoke, it wasn't to him, but to his daughter.

"This is your first lesson about men, Tessa darling," she

475

said, combing the child's hair with her fingers. "They are embarrassed by their own kindness, and they only want to seem gentle when no one is looking."

"Hell," he growled. "Why shouldn't I give them the saloon? I don't need it. The mine is putting out more gold than I could use in three lifetimes."

Pagan met Rianne's teasing gaze, and was instantly caught. Her face was soft with love, her eyes lit by the heat of burgeoning desire. If a bit of gentleness had *that* result, he'd just have to get in the habit of it.

"Papa, I don't understand how that man had your gold," Tessa said.

"I don't either, sweetheart. One thing is certain: it didn't do him a bit of good."

"Well, at least you have it back," Tessa said.

"I don't care about the gold, the saloon, *or* Lowell Mason," Pagan replied. "I have everything I want right here in this room."

Rianne held out her hand for the letter, and he strode across the room to give it to her. She smoothed the wrinkled paper with her hands, remembering the brief, precious summer she had spent in the Yukon. She'd made so many friends: Marie, with her tart humor and generous heart, Kate, Alva, and the rest of the girls; Julia Nathan, who could cook a souffle or a moose with equal aplomb.

Smiling, Rianne called up the memory of Saturday nights at the Golden Bear, with François Gruillot's bull voice shouting "Marseillaise!" over the din of a raucous crowd and pistol shots for applause. She held her breath, almost sensing a breath of a mountain breeze with its sharp scent of spruce.

"I miss the Yukon terribly," she said.

"So do I," Pagan murmured.

His eyes had a faraway look, and Rianne knew he was seeing the Yukon. What did England have to offer a man like him, who had become part of a land of tall mountain peaks and wild, pine-scented wind and a sky that went on forever?

"Let's go home," she said.

He looked down at her, fierce tenderness coming into his eyes. "Wherever you are, that is my home."

Rianne knew he was telling the truth, but she also knew that like the wolf and the high-soaring eagle, this man needed space, needed challenge. England was simply too small and too tame. And although no prison could hold this man, her love could. She found that she had no desire to make him pay that price. No, like him, she had learned to take life as it came, to enjoy the savor and ride the swift wings of adventure.

And as long as she had Pagan, she would be content.

"If we leave now, we can reach the Klondike by summer," she said.

"Yes!" Tessa cried, jumping to her feet so she could twirl happily around the room.

"You're both mad," he said. "We've got everything here, all the comforts a person could want."

Rianne shrugged. "So? The Yukon has different things to offer that are just as valuable. It just depends on one's point of view."

"You really mean it, don't you?" he asked.

"With all my heart. Although . . ." Rianne paused for dramatic effect. "We ought to get started as soon as possible."

"There's no need to hurry," he said. "The Yukon will be there, waiting."

"But there are other things that *won't* wait," Rianne said. "As I figure it, we have exactly seven and a half months to get there."

He stared at her, bewildered. "Seven and a . . ." His voice trailed off as he realized what she meant. Then he gave a whoop of joy and scooped her up off the chair and into his arms. "You're going to have my child," he said, feeling as though his heart might burst with the joy of it.

Rianne reached out and gathered Tessa into their embrace. "I can't seem to make up my mind whether I want a second daughter or a son. What do you think, Tessa?"

"A sister would be nice," Tessa said, cocking her head to one side. "But then boys can be rather fun."

With a theatrical sigh, Rianne said, "Well, whatever we get this time will just have to do until the next, won't it?"

Tessa giggled. "You're—"

"Just a moment," Pagan growled. "I think you ladies are losing sight of something here. We can't journey across half the world with Rianne in a delicate condition!"

"Of course we can," Rianne said. "I'm as healthy as a horse, and you know it."

"Oh, please, Papa," Tessa begged.

Pagan was tempted, so very tempted, but Rianne's welfare was more important than anything else. "I'll think about it. You run upstairs and play for a few minutes, sweetheart, and give me and Rianne a chance to discuss it."

"I'm going to start packing now!" Her little face glowing with excitement, Tessa rushed out of the room.

Pagan followed his daughter to the door, although at a more sedate pace. To Rianne's surprise, he closed the door, locked it, and dropped the key into his pocket before turning to face her again. "Somehow I have the feeling I'm being managed, Mrs. Roark, and very expertly."

"Whyever would you think that, Mr. Roark?" Rianne murmured.

He crossed his arms over his chest. "Now, I'd like to discuss this baby business with you."

"Yes?"

"I can't allow you to make that trip."

Rianne looked at him from beneath her lashes. "Will you come with me, or shall I go without you?"

With a few strides, he was before her, his hands coming down upon her shoulders. "Don't even joke about it, Rianne. If you think I'd ever let you leave me again—"

"Shhh," she said, putting her hand over his mouth. "I was only teasing. But I know my own strength, Pagan. And I want my baby to be born beneath the midnight sun. Trust me."

He drew in a sharp breath, deeply moved by what she had said. His wife was unique among women, and by God, he was going to give her the faith she deserved. "When do you want to leave?"

"I'll start packing tomorrow." She wound her arms around his neck, going up on tiptoes to press tiny, biting kisses along his jaw. "Now, tell me why you locked the door."

"You know why," he said, his voice as intimate as a caress.

Secure in his arms, in his love, and the future they shared, she let him lay her down upon the rug before the fire. This was love, more precious than gold, hotter than the bright, leaping flames in the fireplace, wider than the boundless Yukon skies.

And it was forever.

FEEL THE FIRE IN CAROL FINCH'S ROMANCES!

BELOVED BETRAYAL (2346, $3.95)
Sabrina Spencer donned a gray wig and veiled hat before blackmailing rugged Ridge Tanner into guiding her to Fort Canby. But the costume soon became her prison—the beauty had fallen head over heels in love!

LOVE'S HIDDEN TREASURE (2980, $4.50)
Shandra d'Evereux felt her heart throb beneath the stolen map she'd hidden in her bodice when Nolan Elliot swept her out onto the veranda. It was hard to concentrate on her mission with that wily rogue around!

MONTANA MOONFIRE (3263, $4.95)
Just as debutante Victoria Flemming-Cassidy was about to marry an oh-so-suitable mate, the towering preacher, Dru Sullivan flung her over his shoulder and headed West! Suddenly, Tori realized she had been given the best present for a bride: a night of passion with a real man!

THUNDER'S TENDER TOUCH (2809, $4.50)
Refined Piper Malone needed bounty-hunter, Vince Logan to recover her swindled inheritance. She thought she could coolly dismiss him after he did the job, but she never counted on the hot flood of desire she felt whenever he was near!